Richard V Frankland's early career in the construction industry included working abroad in Zambia and Jordan before returning to England to work with a Japanese trading house in London administering civil and industrial engineering projects.

Moving back to near his birthplace along the south coast with his wife and two daughters, he read for a masters' degree in Maritime Studies and now operates a chauffeured tours business under the title of 'The History Teller'.

Apart from writing, his other interests are giving history talks to local societies, sailing and watercolour painting.

A Cast of Hawks

Richard V Frankland

A Cast of Hawks

Vanguard Press

ISBN 978 184386 607 7

Vanguard Press is an imprint of
Pegasus Elliot MacKenzie Publishers Ltd.
www.pegasuspublishers.com

First Published in 2010

Vanguard Press
Sheraton House Castle Park
Cambridge England

Printed & Bound in Great Britain

To Jane and Martin who rekindled the flame of enthusiasm for my writing this story.

ACKNOWLEDGEMENTS

My grateful thanks go to Lee Fisher of HM Coastguard for his assistance and time and Watch Officer Lucy Tanner for her clear and concise explanation of their duties. I could not have completed this book without the wonderful support of Sandra, my wife, and my daughter, Caroline.

Chapter 1

Kiboko dropped off the back of the wave like a stone, one moment the sensation of falling, the next the bone-shattering crash as she hit the trough, sending a huge sheet of spray up into the wind to be driven across the cockpit in a deluge of salty spume that stung the face and chilled to the bone. On his knees, pain lancing through his bruised ribcage, the salt stinging his split lip and cut eyebrows, Ian spun the wheel instinctively to bring the yacht's stern to face the next wave. His eyes, closed in pain, left him defenceless to the woman's boot as it swung, viciously striking him in the solar plexus.

"Get up!" she screamed at him. "You worthless excuse for a man. Get up!" Again the foot crashed into Ian, this time just below the collarbone, sending him crashing against the transom seat moulding. "You will do what we want well or your family will be hurt, do you understand, shitabakaraki? They will be released unharmed only if you co-operate!" The look of fury and hatred on her face was terrifying.

Reeling, he staggered to his feet only to be knocked down again as the boat fell badly off the next wave. This time Ian was on his feet quickly. Glancing to starboard he saw another wave approaching and hauled the boat round just in time. Now erect and alert he cursed himself for the lack of concentration that had caused him to miss the rogue wave which *Kiboko* had taken on the beam, setting in motion the sequence of events that had led to this last beating. Another mistake like that and we will all be dead, he thought, wheeling defensively to face the woman. This time, however, there was no blow, just a satisfied glare as her cruel eyes met his and saw his fear and pain.

Back in control of himself, his eyes swept the yacht, checking her, his senses probing for damage. He moved to the porthand locker quickly, lifted the lid, removed the bilge pump handle from the clips on the underside and closed it again. In these seas, where a wave could swamp the cockpit in an instant, open lockers were a risk. Inserting the handle into the starboardhand bilge pump head he worked it for several seconds. At first there was the resistance of water as it passed through, but after a dozen or so strokes the pressure disappeared and it was obvious that he was only pumping air. His checking the bilges for water was for him instinctive in this rough sea where a yacht could take on quite a weight of water without the crew on deck being aware of any significant leak. Leaving the handle in place, he settled back into the starboard quarter of the cockpit, marvelling again at the strength of the boat. The new Victoria 34 was cutter rigged and was making 9 knots in a force 8, gusting 9, with all three reefs in the mainsail and a storm jib set on the inner forestay. Her generous freeboard and buoyant ends made her a very seakindly yacht, more than capable of taking these steep and confused seas off Ushant.

The course of 235 degrees was taking them out beyond the Bay of Biscay towards the Azores. In spite of the wind screaming in the rigging and the dramatic movement of the yacht in these seas, Ian did not fear the elements; his main threat to survival was the couple on board with him. The man, Arni, six foot six, was about 200lbs with broad shoulders. Thick black hair cut short over a tanned chiselled face placed him as being of Middle Eastern extraction. He was mid to late thirties with a moustache under a hawk-like nose. For his size, he was surprisingly agile and, like the woman, a sadist, but was obviously the second string, his usefulness to the duo being the fact that he could apparently sail and navigate. It was under his instruction that the evil bitch, Hamaura-san, in the opposite corner of the cockpit, was enforcing the course to steer. She was a masochist's dream; lithe like a cat, with a good figure, shapely legs, slightly square shoulders, long jet-black flowing hair surrounding a hard but beautiful face spoilt by a cruel mouth which when open was normally spitting venomous comment and when closed, set in a sneer. It was the eyes that brought a chill to Ian's heart: indescribably cruel and capable of glowing with a cold light at the sight of pain.

A boastful threat they had made earlier had Ian assuming that they were some international criminal gang, but he could not be sure. There was something in the driven way they had about them that appeared more fanatical than just mercenary; they had also mentioned that it would be they who would be remembered, not the scene of their crime. Fully focused now on the ocean, Ian again swung the wheel to counter the threat of another wave, correcting again as *Kiboko* slid down its back to meet the next one. He had been at the wheel for nine hours in this sea and tiredness was adding to his weakened condition, making him feel a little seasick.

The movement of the hatch caught his eye, then the large hand removing the top washboard. Two mugs of soup were handed out; as the woman handed one to Ian she intentionally spilt some of the boiling contents onto his hand.

"Ahhh!" he yelled snatching his hand away and glaring at her.

"That to remind you of pain we can inflict upon your wife and children if you give any trouble," she said.

A cold hatred gripped him and he was close to chancing it all by leaping at her and strangling her, but she had read the look and raised the gun just enough for him to know he could not win. Holding the scalded hand against the cold, wet, spray dodger, Ian knew that his family had little to do with this torture; this was being done purely to satisfy her pleasure in causing pain. After a few minutes he sipped at the liquid, its warmth easing the queasiness in his stomach. He had just finished the soup when Arni climbed up from below; taking the wheel he shoved Ian towards the cabin.

"Get below," he snapped.

Down in the main cabin, Ian struggled out of his wet gear and hung it up to dry in the heads compartment. In the galley he found a stew concoction had been prepared.

"Eat, then sleep," the woman ordered, then climbed down into the cabin herself and slithered like a snake onto the port-side settee.

As Ian moved to serve the food the yacht rolled and crashed, taking his feet from under him. In one bound the woman was across the cabin to the companionway and yelling at Arni to watch what he was doing.

"Hey, if you think you can do any better you come up here, eh," Arni shouted back.

"You here to steer boat, I here for other work, just you do job," she replied, then turned and, pushing Ian out of her way, resumed her seat. "Hakuchi gai-jin," she mumbled.

Ian forced down the meal, which had been getting cold for some time before he had come off watch. Going to the forward cabin, he removed his outer clothing and slipped into his sleeping bag, but sat with his back against the bulkhead as the greasy meal he had just consumed threatened to bounce back.

He was aware all the time of the punishment the yacht was taking from the poor helming of Arni who continued to steer the yacht in a way that had it bouncing and crashing through the waves. If the yacht was dismasted, Ian was sure that he would be executed, as neither of his companions would want him around when they were rescued, but despite his worry he had finally fallen into an exhausted sleep.

It was the pain of her cigarette against his ear lobe that woke him, but as he went to strike out, his arm was pinned painfully back.

"Get up and cook breakfast," she said, releasing his arm as she stepped back into the main cabin.

He glanced at his watch. It was four o'clock, and he'd been asleep for only three and a half hours. By the feel of it the storm was decreasing and the compass proved that they were maintaining the same course. As he made tea he glanced at the chart table. On the chart itself, neat lines marked their course and circles showed the estimated position, which, was now due west of Ushant by some 100 miles. Jamming himself in the corner against the top-load fridge, Ian broke eggs into the pan alongside some bacon. As they sizzled he contemplated whether he could throw the lot in her face before she shot him. No, it wasn't worth the risk.

"Very wise." Her voice came at him from the chart table, where she was holding on to the structural post. He made a mental note to avoid showing any facial expression whenever possible.

"When you've finished cooking get up here and take the wheel," came Arni's voice, reaching him from the cockpit. "You will maintain a course of 240 degrees. You listening to what I am saying?"

"Yes, I heard you," said Ian, craning to look up the companionway at the figure on the wheel. Then he served his breakfast and the woman's.

Back on the wheel, his breakfast congealing on the plate alongside him, Ian noticed that Arni declined any food, throwing his arms up into the air in complaint.

"I am not allowed to eat this filth," he yelled, before going into the forward cabin and slamming the door. The bacon, of course, Ian thought. Arabs, like Jews, don't eat pork.

Consuming his meal, whilst there was still some warmth in it, Ian went through his normal sequence of checks when taking over a watch. He was by most standards a very experienced sailor having been associated with the pastime since the age of seven, when his father had taught him to sail aboard the family's Finesse.

Looking down from the cockpit into the cabin, he watched as the woman finished her breakfast in a leisurely manner unaffected by Arni's ranting, then went across and put her plate and cutlery into the galley sink, no doubt for Ian to wash up later. Surprisingly, instead of coming up into the cockpit to sit watching his every move, she stayed below, apparently reading some instructions she had pulled from what looked like a small sail bag. Was she going to give up the task of guarding him? To test this, Ian bent down and, removing the bilge pump handle, slid across the transom seat, carefully moved forward and reaching down, opened the porthand locker. Having clipped the handle back into its storage point he closed the locker and glanced up to find her standing glaring at him from the bottom of the companionway. He returned her stare, then moving back to behind the wheel made a point of checking the yacht's heading against the compass. Though trivial, the event proved just how vigilant she was and from that point of view had taught him never to assume that she wasn't paying attention.

At the end of her watch the woman had gone forward to wake Arni and then returned to take up her sleeping berth aft of the chart table. Unlike the woman, Arni was not that interested in what Ian was up to on deck provided that the course was being maintained. Approaching noon, Arni came on deck, sextant in hand, hoping to get a noonday sight but soon returned below to put the instrument away again. Coming back on deck he ordered Ian to let out the furled foresail and take in the storm jib. The yacht surged forward under the increased press of sail, her bow driven down on the limit.

Now back in the forward cabin at the end of his watch Ian, not for the first time, considered his situation. In reality there was little he could do without endangering his own life and that of his family. Hi-jacked, his family were being held hostage to his good behaviour; he was seething inside with anger he dare not express for fear of the reprisals. The questions racing through his brain had been why him, why *Kiboko*, and where were they bound?

God, what an awful year it had been, starting with that innocent-looking brown envelope on his desk containing his redundancy notice, resulting from a company takeover. It had been the company accountant who had engineered the whole business, making sure in the process that he would be safe under the new regime. Though Ian had been suspicious of the man's sycophantic attendance to a group of visitors to the firm a few months earlier, he had failed to predict the events that had so rapidly unfolded. The whole business had turned him sour towards being 'an employee' ever again.

He would never forget his arrival home that night, to be met at the front door by Sarah, radiant and bubbling with joy at being told that day she was pregnant again, or the two weeks of hiding the redundancy news before breaking it to her on the day he had completed the sale of their much loved boat in order to reduce their mortgage. There followed more weeks of worry, searching for a business that he could operate and one that would earn sufficient to keep them. It was out of the blue that he was offered this yacht delivery across to France due to the owner, Claude Raymonde, being rushed into hospital and unlikely to be fit enough to sail for some months. Happily, Claude, who knew of the Vaughan's recent change of fortunes, had kindly suggested that they turn it into a short family holiday, probably their last for some time. So it was that Ian and a friend had taken the boat over from the builders in Warsash, sailed her east, past Portsmouth and, on the tide, up into Chichester Harbour and Bosham Creek.

The next morning had seen him rowing his friend ashore to be collected by his wife, who had brought Sarah and the girls with her; together with the food and provisions for the week they were to stay onboard.

The day had been spent in a leisurely way getting everything settled ready for the start of their voyage the next morning. First they were going to visit Cowes and then their favourite Island harbour, Yarmouth, before passing through the Needles Passage and setting course for Cherbourg. After a day there they had planned to sail down to St Peter Port before, on the last day, making their way into St Malo.

He remembered how he had rowed back to the slipway for the last of the bags when a large Japanese four-by-four with trailer had roared up and a rather eclectic group of people had leapt out. Ian, at first, had not paid much attention to them, but they were an odd mix. The eldest was oriental, maybe in his mid forties, with terrible burn marks on one side of his face and walked with a limp; then came the strikingly beautiful woman, a strongly built man with Arabic features and a younger oriental man. A much younger oriental girl and a terribly English young man with a public school accent made up the group. Ian was amazed at the amount of stores and provisions they had brought and had assumed that they would all be leaving. He was therefore surprised to see that only three of the group actually got on board their Beneteau yacht, now laden well down to her marks, and had wondered how long their voyage would be.

The weather had been particularly unpleasant for late May but that evening, he remembered, was very beautiful and, though cool, pleasant enough to draw him and Sarah up into the cockpit to sit with arms around each other staring in rapture as the sun set, casting an orange glow upon the tower of Bosham church and waterfront. Thoughts of King Canute and his daughter, whose coffin lies beneath the lovely old church with the crooked aisle, had crossed his mind. Then Ian and Sarah had completed their chores to be ready for the morning tide. Checking around the deck to make sure all was well before turning in, Ian had become aware of continued and somewhat frantic activity by the three on the Beneteau moored just downstream of *Kiboko*.

The high tide was at six o'clock the following morning and Ian had been up, washed and breakfasted in good time. He recalled that morning had been absolutely still, the skylarks above the fields to the west providing the only movement and noise. The water in the creek had reached its highest point and it was as if Neptune, having breathed in, was just savouring the moment before breathing out again to create the ebb tide. That was how it had been before he slipped the pendant over the bows of *Kiboko* just seconds behind the departure of the strangers' yacht that he'd noticed was called *Umi Sama*. The three-cylinder diesel engine's confident beat under *Kiboko's* cockpit sole did little to disturb the peace and tranquillity of the moorings or Sarah and the girls, enjoying that lingering spirit of the dawn snug in their sleeping bags.

Using the depth sounder to help him, he had located the centre of the channel that wound past Bosham Quay. Looking up he realised that the yacht in front had missed the turn in the channel and was making straight for the spit, which was the old Roman road going west from Bosham, hard-fording the creek and forming a solid finger on the other side. Old timber pile stumps and ribs of wrecks, all of which were covered at high tide, edged the spit.

"*Umi Sama* look out!" he had shouted. "You will run aground there!"

The woman's head turned in the other boat only to disappear as she and her two companions were hurled headlong by the impact of the boat striking the spit. Ian had worked feverishly for the next ten minutes getting lines rigged across to the stricken yacht whilst Sarah, expertly at the helm, kept *Kiboko* on station waiting for the order to commence pulling the craft off. Then with both yachts, their engines pulling hard astern, the grounded vessel floated free.

When the two yachts had come alongside each other he had asked if they had heard much noise from below the waterline, as she came off.

"Yes, there was loud scraping noise," the Arab, who had just emerged from below, had said. "I think there may be bad damage."

"If you go back to your buoy it will be easier for you to have a good look," he had suggested.

"Please wait for few minutes then. We may need your help again," the Arab had requested.

Back on the buoy it had taken only two minutes before they had asked Ian to come aboard and offer his advice. Secured alongside, Ian had stepped onto the other yacht and gone below whilst Clare and Louise had gone onto *Kiboko's* foredeck, now dressed and kitted in their brightly coloured buoyancy aids. Both girls loved being onboard boats and were happy and excited at the prospect of having a holiday on this brand new vessel. In the main cabin of *Umi Sama,* the young oriental man was lying on the starboard settee holding his right leg, obviously in agony.

"He fell down through the companionway hatch when we went aground," the woman had told him. "He hurt his leg in the fall."

Going into the forward cabin, Ian had lifted the floor and saw immediately the intrusive bulge in the hull form with a star-shaped crack in the centre from which a steady stream of water was bubbling. His advice had been simply to take the yacht immediately to the old quay and beach it as high up as possible then get advice from a yard regarding repair.

"You definitely won't be able to put to sea with damage like that," he recalled saying. "That's going to knock a hole in your cruising plan, I'm afraid."

"Yes, it will," the woman had replied. "You also cruising with your family?"

"Not far, we only have a week, sadly," he had told her. "It's a delivery really, across to St Malo via Cherbourg and the Channel Islands."

After some discussion, Ian had agreed to escort them round and assist in securing the yacht in the right place.

Following the other yacht, he had been surprised that they had stopped so soon along the quay and after securing *Kiboko* had walked forward to help them warp *Umi Sama* along the quay until she touched bottom. As he arrived he was almost knocked down by the returning four-by-four with the young girl at the wheel and the older man alongside. Furious discussion followed and Ian, feeling ignored, was just about to return to *Kiboko* and get underway when he was again requested to inspect the damage and offer further advice.

"If we ran the bilge pump do you think it will hold until we get it down the harbour to a yard?" the Arab had asked whilst he had been engrossed in the inspection.

A test proved that the bilge pump could cope easily with the ingress of water.

Would he recommend a boatyard? How long did he think the repair would take?

As the questioning went on, Ian had become more impatient as each item for discussion became more trivial. Now, as he was recalling it, he realised the Arab had been increasingly tense and had kept taking side-glances towards the quay. It was only by chance that he had looked up and seen Sarah and the girls being roughly hustled into the four-by-four, his wife being held with a knife at her throat, and Clare and Louise carried kicking and struggling with their captors' hands clapped firmly over their mouths. The memory of it still filled him with shock and horror. At the time he had been frozen to the spot by the sight of it. That was when Arni hit him for the first time, a knockout punch straight to the jaw. As he came to he had found himself bound and gagged, lying on the berth opposite the oriental youth; struggling to free himself and sit up, he had been struck again, this time by the woman.

"You have choice," he was told. "You help sail your boat or you and your family die. What is it to be, eh?" she asked, ripping the duct tape from over his mouth.

"What have you done to them?" he had demanded to know. "What the hell do you think you are up to?"

Again she had punched him, this time hard in the stomach. "What is it to be?"

With no choice and still in shock, the words, "Where do I have to sail you to?" croaked out of his mouth as he had fought to recover his breath.

"You don't ask question, you just answer, sail boat, or die," she had replied.

Remembering the knife at Sarah's throat he had no choice but to agree. "Alright, alright," he'd said. "I'll sail but you harm them in any way and I will hunt you down and kill you."

With a sneering laugh she'd promptly gagged him again.

Around him the stores were being taken off the Beneteau and placed aboard *Kiboko*. The injured crewman lay deathly pale groaning occasionally with pain until the woman had appeared from the stern cabin with a hypodermic syringe and viciously jabbed the needle into the man's arm, injecting him with something that knocked him out almost immediately.

Sometime afterwards Ian recalled his bonds being cut and being dragged to his feet.

"One word from you and you will die. Now go onto the quay." Her words, though quiet, had held such menace in them as to make him shiver. Leaving the cabin he had looked down at the young oriental man on the opposite bunk and realised that the thighbone of his right leg was sticking out through a blood-soaked tear in his trousers. On the quay the Arab was waiting for him, a pistol barely concealed beneath his jacket. He'd looked around for Sarah and the girls, but they were nowhere to be seen.

"Wait for me in the cockpit," the Arab had said before giving him a hard shove in the direction of *Kiboko*. Thrown into the forward cabin of the yacht, he had again been tied up and gagged. He had lain listening to the frantic efforts of the group to stow everything aboard and had guessed from the level of conversation that other members of the group had returned. Ian remembered the low growl of the older man's voice giving orders.

"Why do we need him?" he'd heard the woman ask.

"Because," the Arab had replied, "this boat have no self steering so someone must be at the wheel all times."

"Can we not take steering from other boat?"

"That job takes many hours and too much risk. This is only way. When we at sea he will steer eight hours in twelve, I steer four and you act as his guard when I sleeping."

Then the engines had started and they had left the quay, *Umi Sama* leading *Kiboko* down the creek towards Itchenor. He had heaved himself into a sitting position and pressed his face to the starboard cabin window in the hope that someone on a boat would have seen his gagged face and take some action. Not for the first time he had wondered bitterly why so many boat owners left their expensive toys moored throughout the season unused or cared for. At the Christian Youth Enterprise Centre slipway four youngsters were preparing two dinghies; trying to keep his face against the window he kicked out against the hull desperate to attract their attention. Before he could deliver a third kick the woman had entered the cabin and given him a paralysing blow to his right thigh before leaving him rolled up in agony on the cabin floor.

Thinking back, her confidence in leaving the wheel and coming forward like that was impressive but bearing in mind the narrowness of the channel and the number of moored boats there were to hit, her action was probably inexperience.

He recalled lying in the forward cabin flexing his legs and watching the bulkhead compass spin then settle as they turned into the Chichester Channel. It was not until they had passed

25

Stockers Sand buoy and were on course for the Chichester Bar outer marker that he had recovered enough to get himself back onto the bunk and try to clear his thoughts.

Though outrage had still clouded his mind he was well aware of the threat he and his family were under and the need to now play safe if possible and await his chance. Through the cabin window he could see *Umi Sama* running under engine alongside them, with the Arab at the wheel, and had wondered how the leak was holding and why they had risked bringing the yacht to sea in the first place. Suddenly the engine revs died and the woman had come forward and with a wicked-looking knife cut his bonds. Standing back she had asked, "Do you still agree to sail this boat?"

He had nodded. "Yes, I don't have much choice, do I, with you bastards holding my family hostage."

The sneer returned to her expression and sliding behind the cabin table she'd ordered, "Get on deck and set sails."

Ten minutes later with the yacht running under a full mainsail and genoa, she had ordered him to sail in pursuit of *Umi Sama,* which, under engine, had pulled some distance ahead of them. Then she had gone below and radioed their departure details to Solent Coastguard. The message informed the Coastguard that the yacht *Kiboko* was leaving Chichester Bar for Cherbourg with two adults and two children aboard, ETA in 12 hours. Ian recalled cursing himself for mentioning their planned cross-channel trip. Moments later a similar message was sent from *Umi Sama* mentioning two adults on board and also destined for Cherbourg.

By 10 o'clock that morning, the north westerly breeze that had sprung up three hours earlier had increased to a force 4. *Kiboko* had overtaken *Umi Sama* and was leaving her far behind. It was then that the woman had ordered Ian to turn the boat and go back to join her companions. Now he understood why the Arab had led the way out of Chichester Harbour; the woman could steer a yacht but had no knowledge of pilotage or navigation. Alongside *Umi Sama* half an hour later, he'd put a reef in the main and rolled in a few turns of the foresail in order to slow *Kiboko* to the speed of the other yacht. By evening they had covered some fifty miles and in the failing light could just see house and streetlights along the hilltops of the Cotentin Peninsula. Under shouted orders from the Arab, he had brought the Victoria hove-to a short distance downwind of the other yacht. As nothing appeared to be happening aboard *Umi Sama,* his interest had switched to looking towards the French coast and a search for any other craft nearby. Looking back towards the other yacht he'd noted that the Arab had got the dinghy on deck and was busy with the foot pump inflating it. The next time he looked up the Arab had launched the dinghy, climbed down into it alone and by using the guardrail stanchions was hauling the dinghy along towards the bow. Suspicions aroused, Ian had known almost before he saw the heavy anchor in the Arab's hands what was happening – each brutal blow had him flinching as he watched the man smash a hole in the yacht's hull through to the forward cabin just above the waterline in a matter of minutes. Held by the drama of what was unfolding, he had watched fascinated as the Arab climbed back on board the yacht, so Ian thought, to help his injured friend to safety, but instead the Arab had lowered one of the two life raft cases into the dinghy, hoisted the yacht's sails and set the auto helm. Triggering the launch of the remaining life raft, he had scrambled into the dinghy and cast off, leaving the young oriental man on board the yacht to drown. *Umi Sama* had now gathered way heading towards Cape la Hague but was heeling and allowing water to enter through the hole in her port-side. Tearing his eyes away from the scene he had gone to protest, but turning to plead with the woman saw her nodding in satisfaction and approval. He had just stood there speechless, appalled and frustrated by his inability to prevent the man's murder. In the

27

time the Arab had rowed across to *Kiboko*, *Umi Sama* was sinking fast and as he had dumped the other yacht's life raft on the stern seat of *Kiboko,* there were only bubbles on the surface to mark the sinking.

Ian had stared at them in horror. "You left him on board to drown. How could you do that?" he'd yelled. "You've just murdered a man in cold blood. What kind of people are you to do that; why not at least give the poor bastard a chance in a life raft."

The memory of what he had seen brought back the feeling of fear and deep revulsion.

Both of them had just looked at him for a moment before going below to return moments later with Sarah's and the girls' clothes, which they dumped over the side.

"What are you doing now? For Christ's sake, people will think they are ..." he had stopped in mid sentence as realisation dawned as to what it was that he was witnessing. "You sick bastards, surely you don't think you can get away with this."

Suddenly the Arab had grabbed him by the collar and held a knife at his throat. "Another word and I slit your throat from ear to ear. You understand!"

He glared back at the man wanting so much to be able to hit back but had to reply, "Yes, I understand."

The knife dealt with the inflatable dinghy, its shredded remains carried to the sea bottom by the weight of *Umi Sama's* anchor. The Arab had then launched *Kiboko's* life raft, throwing Louise's teddy bear into it as a final touch. It was clear then that this pair wanted the world to believe that both yachts had sunk and all on board were lost. He had watched, thinking of Sarah's and his own parents' grief and the effect it would have upon them. His mind struggled with the enormity of what had happened and its impact upon so many people.

"Get up there and let reef out," the Arab had shouted at him. "Go. Now!"

Ian had stumbled along the side deck and, unable to concentrate, had twice let the main halyard slip, incurring the wrath of the Arab. Finally underway again, he had been ordered to sail a course parallel to the coast. Down below, the two had a long discussion, which ended with the woman rummaging in the cockpit's port-hand locker to emerge triumphant with a strange cone-shaped buoy. Meanwhile, the Arab had been recording a hysterical mayday message onto a miniature tape recorder. Coming into the cockpit, they had inflated the buoy and inserted a small radio transmitter into a waterproof slot in the cone section, pulled the aerial out to its full extent then carefully launched the buoy from *Kiboko's* side deck as the yacht passed due north of the Alderney lighthouse.

"What happens when or if the buoy is found and the recording replayed?" the Arab had asked.

"The acid capsule will sink it when the tape finishes."

"That is good. Is every one the same?"

"Oh yes. After each message is sent unit will sink," the woman had said, with a hint of pride in her voice.

Two hours later and some ten miles away the Arab again had appeared on deck and ordered an alteration of course to north aiming towards Portland Bill, pushing past him to remove the Red Ensign and replacing it with the French national flag. He had then realised that any vessel sighting them would have believed them to be a French yacht that had passed several miles south-west of the casualty, heading for the English coast. The Arab had removed the spray dodgers and using another radio device had apparently triggered the buoy to start transmitting the mayday message. The pair had sat listening with some satisfaction as the hysterical voice called 'Mayday, Mayday, Mayday' and went on as if in panic to explain that *Umi Sama* had rammed *Kiboko,* and both were sinking fast. The response to the mayday was impressive but met with silence, leaving the French Coastguard no alternative but to issue a request that all vessels in the area keep a lookout for survivors and debris and to send the lifeboat to the scene. He had desperately wanted to grab the radio microphone and send his own distress message but knew that to even reach for the radio would mean the death of him and his family.

It had taken an hour before anyone reported sight of anything; a French trawler, which had altered course for the area, reported that the life raft belonging to *Umi Sama* was found up-turned in the water and empty. Thirty minutes later, the dead body of the crewman was found and taken onboard the same trawler. As that news came through he'd studied the others' expressions and noted the woman's mild satisfaction. Dead men can't talk. Strong feelings of revulsion and hatred had overcome him and he had screamed at them a torrent of abuse and accusation, only stopped when the Arab, grabbing him by the throat, had threatened to puncture his left eye with the knife. As the Arab had backed off, he could remember standing, trembling uncontrollably, and feeling sick with loathing.

As dawn had appeared in the eastern sky, the radio reports confirmed that the search was concentrated within a small sea area associated with the body.

"Hey, you now tack and steer 260 degree," the Arab had ordered. "That should bring us clear of the French coast passing well north of Ushant," he added, speaking to the woman.

As Ian, again at the wheel, brought the yacht onto its new course, the two had sat in the cockpit openly discussing the likely effect of the staged sinkings.

"They will search, maybe for two days, then they give up," the Arab had said.

"So soon?" she had asked.

"When they find nothing more they will give up. The sea has often taken a ship and shown no sign, why not now, eh?"

After some time, they were both agreed that the rescuers would accept the basic evidence that two yachts had been in collision with each other, and assume that the lack of bodies was due to the severity of the impact and speed of sinking.

"Fate," the Arab had said, "is a remarkable thing, as now it has provided irrefutable evidence of our untimely deaths."

What was it she had replied? Ah yes, the woman had laughed and said, "How pleased the banker, Yamamoto, will be that the sea has apparently taken the stone from his shoe and what a shock when he learns that the stone has actually hit him in the eye."

The Arab had shared the laughter, adding that for all his brainy schemes, Yamamoto would not be remembered like they would be. "Nobody has ever held thirty million people to ransom."

Ian recalled his sense of shock and disbelief. Had he heard correctly, did they actually say thirty million people? Where were they going, what were they going to do? The thought was too baffling for his exhausted mind and he drifted off to sleep.

The kick in the ribs woke him. "Get on deck, you are wanted," the woman said, then watching him fumbling, still half asleep, into his clothes, she had yelled, "Come on, you taking too much time, hurry." Ian had only been away from the helm for three hours. Making his way aft, he realised what the problem was. The wind had got up and under full sail, with the yacht on a broad reach, she was dangerously over pressed. On deck, he saw the man struggling at the wheel to stop the yacht from being turned across the wind and broached. Taking the wheel, Ian started the engine and put it in gear increasing the revs, then picking his moment, as *Kiboko* slid down the back of a wave, he spun the wheel, turning the yacht almost head to wind.

"Hold her there," he shouted at the Arab, above the noise of the wind, as he reduced the revs again so the yacht was just making headway. The immediate danger took his full concentration, pushing his memories of the last few days to the back of his mind.

Working hard at the winch, Ian wound in the foresail, then, clipping his safety harness onto the jackstay, made his way forward to the mast and took in two reefs of the mainsail. Spray lashed him as he worked, stinging the facial cuts he had received from the beatings and soaking his clothes. Breathless from the exertion, he returned to the cockpit and hauled in the mainsheet. "As I let some of the foresail out again bring her back on course!" he shouted at the Arab who started turning the wheel. Within a few minutes the yacht was back on its heading, now under control. As Ian went below it started to rain and from the look of the skies, it was going to be a very wet and windy day.

"You can turn the engine off now," he said over his shoulder, descending the companionway steps, noticing the Arab's glare in response.

"Panic over?" Ian jumped at the sound of the woman's voice and spun round to see her lying in her bunk.

"Yes," he replied. "Tell me, what do I call you?"

"Hamaura-san," she said. "He is known as Arni," she continued, nodding in the direction of the cockpit.

"Hamaura-san," he repeated in a neutral tone and went forward to change into dry clothes and his heavy weather gear, ready to take the helm.

As he returned to the cockpit and took hold of the wheel, three rapid and hard punches were received from Arni, who then grabbed him by the collar again and dragged him up close to his own face, shouting, "You make no stupid funny comment to me, you hear? I do not like it. Now steer as you are told," he said, pushing Ian at the wheel and slapping him hard around the back of the head.

Dazed and bleeding from a cut above his right eye and swollen lip, Ian hugged his ribcage wondering whether the second blow had broken anything. He prayed that Sarah and the girls were not being treated like this. Sarah was fearless – would she react or would she try and stay out of trouble? One thing was for sure, these people had no regard for human life, so whatever her reaction, he just hoped that they were safe.

The weather had worsened and winds of force 7 to 8 had thrust the yacht further out into the vast ocean. The heavy rain meant that steering was done by compass bearing and an instinctive feel to combat any cross-seas. By midnight, when Arni returned on deck for his four-hour stint at the helm, Ian's concentration had failed twice and *Kiboko* had slammed into waves with bone-shattering force.

Now exhausted, his brain numb and his body aching, Ian said a quiet prayer for Sarah and the girls before trying to sleep. The violent motion of the yacht was hardly conducive to relaxation and Ian found himself wanting to return to the helm, purely to stop the punishment that Arni was putting the vessel through due to his bad handling.

Sleep must have finally taken over for he was woken by the heat of the woman's cigarette as she stubbed it out on the back of his neck, making him twist away and jerk defensively back against the yacht's hull.

"He is waiting," was all she said.

As he went on deck he found her sitting under the protection of the spray hood. Something in her manner suggested that she had not enjoyed the rough seas of the last few hours. Taking the wheel from Arni, he confirmed the course to be steered and then looked around for ships that might be near.

"I think someone should check the mast rigging and deck anchorages," Ian said after five minutes or so. "Can you take the wheel?"

"Why you need check?"

"Because during the last four hours this yacht has been badly steered and slammed into too many waves," he answered. "Yachts are not designed to take that type of punishment."

Reluctantly, she slid along the cockpit seat, then grabbing the wheel stood and peered forward.

"The course to steer is 235 degrees."

"I know," she said. "Now get on with what you need do and hurry."

He started with the backstay, then, with safety harness clipped on, worked his way forward to check the capping and lower shroud anchor points, bottle screws and each wire seizing. As he was conducting the inspection, he was aware that the yacht was veering off course frequently and almost gybed on three occasions.

So, he thought, the bitch doesn't have much sailing experience.

"Well?" she said as he transferred his harness clip to the cockpit 'D' ring.

"When things calm down a bit I need to put a turn on each of the bottle screws."

"Why you need do that?"

"The rigging is new and the wire has stretched," he answered. "If it starts to snatch with the violent motion, it will either break the deck anchorage or snap the wire. Either way, it could bring the mast down."

"Ah so," she said, with a nod of understanding.

"We don't have enough diesel to motor back to land."

She spun around to face him again, her eyes glaring at him. "Is that true?"

"Yes, I only fuelled up for the delivery across the channel. There is probably less than sixty miles of motoring left in the tank," Ian replied.

She stood staring at him for some time trying to fathom whether or not he was telling the truth. Deciding that he was, she sat, deep in thought, obviously rattled. When she handed over to Arni she demanded to know why he had not checked the fuel level.

"Why you not do job you are supposed to do, eh? Why you not make sure we have enough diesel?"

"I did job ok. Murata sending diesel with boat from Azores. Why you always claim against others?" Arni shouted back at her.

"Oh, is that so," was all she said before going forward to the heads to hide from making an apology.

The weather was easing as Ian's watch continued and near its end he was able to go forward with tools and make the adjustments required. When Arni arrived on deck to do his midday sun shot, it was quiet enough for full sail to be set.

Ian shuffled down in his sleeping bag, trying to find a way in which he could rest his body without the pain in his ribs disturbing him. Thoughts were beginning to enter his mind that his captors' sailing skills were not good enough to take them much further unaided; he was therefore probably safe for a while, especially if he could show up Arni's weaknesses.

Then, as previously, his thoughts returned to Sarah and the girls, worrying and wondering how they were being treated and whether they had been harmed. Finally, he dozed off into an exhausted dream-troubled sleep.

Chapter 2

After twelve hours of being shut down in the cellar, Sarah had dozed. Both girls were asleep, their little tear-stained faces pale with exhaustion and their bodies still tense with fear, laid with their knees up, in a foetal position. Tears ran down Sarah's face as she opened her eyes and looked at them, remembering the way they normally slept, bodies straight, arms wide across the covers, so relaxed and secure.

Footsteps outside riveted her eyes to the door, keys fumbled, the lock turned and into the cellar came the Japanese man with the facial burns and limp, followed by the young Englishman carrying a tray. Sarah, now pinned against the wall in fear, was slightly surprised when the Japanese, Murata, failed to goad her by holding the gun either to her throat or to one of the children's heads as he had done on previous visits. Instead, he stood by the door and with a grunt, directed the Englishman to put the tray down.

"When you've eaten, you will be taken to another..." Murata's shout stopped the Englishman apparently in mid sentence; he looked fearfully at Murata who waved him back out of the room by motioning with the gun. The shout had woken the girls, who rushed to the protection of their mother. Murata gave a contemptuous flick of his head and left the room, locking the door behind him.

Sarah recognised their captors' names as being Japanese and told the girls that not all people from Japan were like this. She told them of her university friend, Seiko Yamakawa, who she still wrote to after several years, and what a lovely friend she was. Calming the girls, Sarah encouraged them to eat, noticing as she did that the food was the instant package type, accompanied by packet soup. In spite of her own hunger she ate little, concentrating on helping the girls, taking them both onto her lap and feeding them herself.

"Do you think Daddy's alright?" It had been Clare, the eldest, who spoke.

"Yes," she had replied. "They need him to steer the boat, so they won't let any harm come to him." Her guess and confident statement belied her true fears for her husband.

"Where is Daddy going to sail them to Mummy, Japan?" asked Louise, just five years old.

"No, not Japan darling, that's a long, long way away. Probably just across to France or maybe Holland, I don't really know," she answered, stroking a lock of hair away from Louise's eyes.

Sitting, warmed by the food and soothed in the arms of their mother, both girls dozed until Murata and the Englishman came to move them. As they climbed from the cellar, Sarah noted the faint farmyard smells again. It was dark outside and the naked light bulbs showed up the stark interior of the house. They were ushered upstairs to a first floor bedroom that was quite large. A door in the far corner led to a bathroom with an old Victorian-style bath in the middle of the room and a large white china hand basin next to the window. The toilet in the corner had a high-level cistern, which flushed by pulling on a rusty chain with a hard rubber ball grip on the end. The windows had been boarded up from the outside long ago but the shiny new screws securing the sliding sashes to the frames to prevent them being opened were obviously very recent. Sarah looked around and saw that the door to the landing had been fitted with new bolts on the outside and a hasp and padlock. "How long do you expect to hold us prisoners here?" she demanded, standing erect, chin thrust out in defiance.

"Long time, so do nothing to make yourself uncomfortable," Murata replied, leaving the room.

Like a zombie, Sarah moved around getting the girls undressed and nestled into the blankets tossed on the floor for them.

"My friends don't go much for comfort I'm afraid." The voice had startled her.

"What do you want? Why have you taken us prisoner like this?" she demanded for the hundredth time. "What have you done with my husband?" Tears were now streaming unchecked down her cheeks; the girls in the corner clinging to each other were also in floods of tears.

"I can't talk much now as Murata will be back in a bit. One thing though, they had not planned this, it's only because our boat got damaged and Yoshi was injured." The public school accent sounded very out of place in these primitive surroundings.

The stomping sound of Murata's footsteps had the Englishman quickly leaving the room, padlocking the door behind him. Sarah heard voices then the sound of the two men descending the stairs. For an hour at least, she sat staring blankly across the room, her brain unable to hold thought. Finally she prepared her blankets and rolled herself in them but was unable to sleep.

Images of their kidnapping flashed before her eyes. It had all started so innocently as her lovely, friendly, helpful Ian had done what he always did when he saw someone in trouble, and that was go and help. Though their English was not good they had appeared grateful. It was when this fiend Murata had turned up at the quay that things had changed. Whilst Ian had been below in their boat giving advice, this hateful man and the hard-looking woman had been discussing and arguing with each other. She had been so surprised to see three of them come on board uninvited.

"Can I help you?" she had asked.

Then the gun had appeared and was held at Clare's head. Sarah recalled the sickening fear of that moment. She had gasped in horror, unable to grasp what was happening.

"Take that thing away from my daughter! How dare you do such a thing," she had screamed.

The woman had slapped her round the face and told her to shut up.

"We are taking your boat and your husband will assist in sailing it," the woman had said.

"No you will not," Sarah had replied defiantly, only to receive a second, harder slap.

The girls were now screaming, but only for a short time as both were grabbed and hands placed over their mouths.

Sarah had gone to attack the younger woman when her wrist was held in the vice-like grip of the man, who then produced a knife and held it at her throat.

It was then that she found herself being forced up onto the quay and towards the large black four-by-four. The girls were kicking and wriggling but could not break free and she with the knife pricking the skin under her chin was too frightened to put up further resistance. In the vehicle, the young woman had driven whilst Murata squeezed in the back seat beside them, holding a gun at little Louise's head.

Thinking of this now, Sarah burst into tears, her shoulders shaking, and covered her head with the blanket. God knows how this would affect the girls; would they ever recover from such treatment? Recover, she thought – would they survive, let alone manage to recover from this.

It was more the feeling of morning than any indication in the room that woke her. She looked at the girls still tightly curled up asleep. Tip-toeing to the bathroom, she washed, noting with surprise hot water from the tap. Clean now, she felt a little braver, and on return to the bedroom began to exercise gently to take away the stiffness from the hard night's sleep. Feeling more supple, she then decided to examine their prison more closely. If only she could find a gap to see through, but there was none; instead, as she turned off the lights, the darkness was impenetrable. Outside, she could hear the cackling cry of magpies squabbling. She stopped to listen, the sound of nature surreal and incongruous to her, locked away in this evil old house. Would she and the girls see the world as being normal ever again? She looked closely at the door only to find that it was solid oak. Plaster damage revealed that the internal walls were of lath and plaster. She pushed at it, hoping that it would be rotten as she and Ian had found whilst renovating their little house. But what would she have done if it had been? There was no way she could make a hole large enough for escape without being discovered. Despondent, she sat heavily back down on her blanket bed and prayed for a miracle.

The young Japanese girl brought breakfast. Sarah looked at her curiously as she shuffled across the room in that style typical of Japanese women she had seen in films. By the door stood Murata, gun in hand. Placing the tray on the floor, the girl turned to Sarah and in slow English, she said, "You stay here and not give trouble, everything alright, you understand?" her voice hard and staccato.

Sarah nodded then asked, "How long do you think you can hold us prisoner here?"

The girl frowned and snapped, "Long enough."

Alone again, Sarah and the girls ate the breakfast, aware now that outside the room someone was on guard.

After a little while the Englishman entered.

"What day is it?" Sarah asked.

"Thursday," he replied, picking the tray up from the floor. "I've brought you some reading matter, magazines and the papers."

Dropping the bundle of papers on the floor beside her, he looked confused at her expression of horror. Her face had gone quite white; one hand to her mouth, the other reaching for the top newspaper. 'Search for missing yacht crews scaled down.' Beneath the headline, was a photograph of Ian and her with the girls on holiday the previous year, aboard their old boat.

"Oh," he said, a little embarrassed, "I should have told you not to worry about that, it's all a fake you know." He held up his hand to silence Sarah before she could speak and listened for a moment to ensure that they were not being overheard. "You see, we couldn't leave our damaged boat at Bosham so we had to steal yours to do the crossing with, and Murata and Hamaura came up with the idea of sinking our boat and making it look as though both boats were sunk."

"You are telling me the truth, aren't you?" she said, still shaking with shock.

"Yes," he replied. "I swear."

"Where is Murata and your young lady?" she asked.

"Oh, gone off shopping," he said, "at least that's what they said when I came up here. They've gone out for food, I think."

"You seem very fond of her," Sarah said, trying to sort out in her own mind whether the young man in front of her was genuinely one of the bad guys or just being led by a pretty face.

"Yukiko, yes, I am," he replied, "we've been living together for over a year now. She's well educated you know, Tokyo University." Sarah remained silent, waiting.

"Read philosophy and politics; really committed to her ideals. Leaves me behind I'm afraid.

"Father hates her guts stupid old b..." Something in Sarah's graceful and refined demeanour stopped him from completing the swearword. "What do I care, they've only ever been interested in their world of politics, Alison and I were just to make up the correct family photograph."

"Alison is your sister?"

"Yah, poor Ali, as soon as she was old enough she was paraded like some prize cow around in all the right circles, until that halfwit Jamie stuttered a proposal, then she was forced to marry him," he said, shaking his head. "That's why they hate Yuki, she isn't county, y'know," he continued, in a mock aristocratic voice.

"Isn't your sister happy?"

"God no; who would be with that excuse for a husband," he said with a sneer. "Are parents concerned, huh, like hell they are. If my mother had her way I'd be saddled with Sophie Jameson and that stinking mare she rides."

"Oh surely not," Sarah said, surprised by her own response.

"Oh surely yes. You'd be surprised how many supposed representatives of the working class in the House of Commons are determined that their children are going to move up the social ladder several rungs."

"Even so, I'm sure they would be very concerned that your relationship with this girl has led you to become involved in violent kidnapping."

"Oh you bet they will," he said. "Not for me though; the old man will only worry that this would lose him his chance for a knighthood."

"If he did, that won't make them come to you and say sorry though, will it? Probably quite the reverse," Sarah said, wondering how much of this reactionary stuff he had thought out and how much had been fed into him by his Yukiko.

The young man shrugged and sat down, toying with the gun and watching the girls play some imaginary game in the corner of the room, while Sarah sat glancing through the article about the yachting accident.

Suddenly she sat up straight. "They've found the body of the little fat one who was hurt. It wasn't fake, it was real, look!" Sarah thrust the newspaper at him.

"No, really, it was all fake, Yuki said that he was set off in a life raft and it overturned, they were very sad about it."

"Life rafts don't turn over in those conditions," Sarah said angrily. "Either this report is true and both boats have been lost or that young man was murdered. Whatever way it is, Yuki or Yukiko, whatever her name is, is lying to you, can't you see that?"

"No, no. Yuki wouldn't lie to me," he said, sounding confident of Yuki's honesty and trust in him. "I tell you, she's not lying."

The slight sharpness in his tone had been enough to stop the girls in their play and have them looking concerned and nervous.

Looking across at them he suddenly felt a little embarrassed. Though he was not fully conscious of it, the violence of the kidnap had unsettled him and shown a side of Yukiko's character that he had not seen before, one that he was not sure he liked. He scrambled to his feet and muttering something about things to do, left the room, snapping the padlock closed behind him and leaving Sarah trying to work out whether this young man really was one of the gang, or just caught up in the thrill of doing something that would make 'daddy' suffer. Work on the 'hooray Henry', she thought, he's obviously got a soft spot for the girls, so somewhere in that selfish brat mind of his there must be a conscience she could work on.

As Sarah sat in her prison contemplating their fate, a supervisor and two maintenance men sat, just over four thousand miles away, enjoying the mid-shift break.

"Oh shit, does anyone want a pack of goddam anchovy and egg sandwiches?" As Mel Clements got no answer he hurled the pack into the trashcan in the corner of the lower control room. "Jesus, Anne-Mari, you stupid bitch. Goddamit, every damn day the same damn thing, never takes any goddam notice of what I

43

say, just sits in front of the damn TV." He continued to growl for a moment or two then stormed out of the room shouting back over his shoulder, "I'm going to the canteen to get a pizza."

"Have you seen his wife?" It was Stanislav, the instrument engineer.

"No," replied Yamada.

"She's weird. You know those fashions they wore in the nineteen thirties, well, she dresses just like that."

"Honestly? You're joking."

"No really, Burton was telling me. He said she was nuts, and sits and watches the old movie channels all day long. Mel has to do all the housework, all she does is make his sandwiches."

"Yeah?" said Yamada in disbelief.

"Yeah. Burton had to go round there one day when Mel was on leave and he saw her dressed all strange like, just sat there in the chair in front of the TV."

At that moment Mel Clements returned, a half eaten pizza in his hand. "Stanislav, when your break's finished, go to level five and start on checking those hydraulic pump gauges for the fuel rod actuators, okay?"

"Sure, Mel," said Stanislav, throwing a peanut up into the air and catching it in his mouth.

"One of these days you're gonna choke yourself doin' that," said Clements. "Yamada, you finish up here and clean up. I gotta go to a meetin' about commissioning schedules. I'll be back later."

Twenty minutes later, and now alone, Yamada removed the face panel of the heat sensor device transmitter that Mel Clements had been working on earlier. Carefully lifting the unit out, he placed it in his lunch-box and closed the lid. From the bottom of his toolbox he removed an almost identical unit and plugged it in, replacing the face panel. He stood back to admire his work – Yep, no one would ever know the difference.

Yamada, unlike the rest of Murata's group, was not a product of university left wing politics; his motivation was born of a deep resentment towards the country of his birth, the United States of America. His great-grandparents had come from Japan in 1915 in search of the American Dream and with hard work and astute investment his great grandfather became a respected Wall Street investor. October 1929, however, saw his wealth disappear in the Wall Street Crash and the depression of the 1930s brought the family close to destitution. During this period his grandparents had met and married, then came the Second World War and the family's internment. Separated from each other for the duration, the couple weren't reunited until 1947, his grandmother then in poor health. Post war anti-Japanese sentiment meant continued hardship for the Yamadas, made worse by the death of his grandmother whilst giving birth to his own father. The family tragedy was to continue when his father, now married, was drafted to Vietnam where he died from a drug overdose in a Saigon brothel after deserting his regiment, leaving Hiroshi and his mother to survive as best they could in his grandfather's home. After a childhood surrounded by bitterness and resentment, coloured by stories of internment and injustice, Hiroshi Yamada emerged a very troubled and troublesome teenager. At the end of an industrial electrician's apprenticeship, he surprised his mother and grandfather by joining the army. It was there that he found his niche and was soon selected for Special Forces duty taking part in several covert operations in Columbia and Nicaragua associated with anti-drug trafficking. On his last operation in Nicaragua, only months before leaving the army, he met Hamaura and was recruited by her into Murata's faction of the Japanese Red Army. Over a period of time this little group, enlarged by other like-minded individuals, became an embarrassment to the main movement, which ostracised them and eventually started to hunt them down.

It had been Murata-san who had ordered him to get a job with the TN (Nuclear) Corporation. He had been there two years now, as an electrician working on maintenance contracts for three PWR operators on the eastern seaboard. Devoted to Murata and carrying a passionate flame for Fumiko Hamaura, he had obeyed the rule to keep a low profile and stay out of trouble until the time had come to act.

After only six months the three had carried out a hold-up in a bank that brought them operating funds. Two more robberies and the group split, Murata and Hamaura left for Europe, where she got a job in an electronics factory, manufacturing instrument control units whilst Murata organised and planned. Then, this last Christmas, Yamada had received from Hamaura computer games that didn't fit into any game console. It was later in a series of letters from Hamaura that he learnt what the units were for and how he was to install them.

Mel Clements, back from his meeting, came and collected Yamada from the lower control room. They walked up to level five, where Stanislav was finishing off his work. Whilst waiting, Clements and Yamada leaned over the handrail and looked down onto the reactor area.

"To think so much power is housed in something that size blows your mind, don' it," said Clements.

"Never really thought about it before," replied Yamada, "don't even know how it works."

"Hell man, working on this team and you don't know how these little babies tick?" said Clements, his voice full of surprise.

"No, no-one's ever taken the time to tell me."

"Well as we got a moment or two I'll tell yer." Mel Clements drew a deep breath and started. "Inside that dome there is a reactor. Slightly enriched uranium dioxide is contained in a couple of hundred fuel assemblies, each about the height of the reactor core. The assemblies each have about two hundred and seventy fuel rods, arranged in a lattice-type array." He used his fingers to demonstrate the configuration. "The fuel rods are in a tube of zirc-alloy, which is an alloy of zirconium. Massive steel structures support the fuel assemblies in the reactor pressure vessel, and these direct the coolant water flow up through the fuel. Fifty clusters of absorber rods slide in selected fuel assemblies that ditch soluble boric acid, which controls the reactivity. The dissolved boric acid absorbs the surplus neutrons, controlling the reaction rate."

Yamada looked puzzled. "Why soak up the reaction by using this boric acid stuff?"

"Jesus," responded Clements, "that's like some wild horse down there; if you don't have her reigned in all the time, she'll stampede to destruction. Hell, without control that core would turn this place white hot in minutes."

"Hey, really?" said Yamada, impressed.

"Believe me, Yamada, if that son of a bitch ever got really cooking you could write off this entire state. Nobody could live round here for years, maybe even centuries. Shit, it don't bear thinking about." Mel Clements was always keen to promote an exaggerated picture of doom to his young engineers in order to keep them fearful of making errors or doing slipshod work.

Yamada stood there nodding his head in understanding. No doubt about it, Murata-san had been right, this would have them crawling on all fours.

"Okay guys, I'm all finished up here." Stanislav stood behind them with a grin from ear to ear. "Let's say we grab a beer."

"Sorry, not tonight," Clements said glumly. "Got things to do back home."

The three strolled to the changing rooms for a shower and their street clothes. Yamada was pleased that Clements had refused the beer because it would have meant him joining, and he had a message to pass. Once in the parking lot, he waited for the other two to drive off into town before he left the lot, turning in the opposite direction towards the Chesapeake. It was a long drive but eventually he came to the road leading out to the Potomac shore near to Sandy Point. After a few miles the tarmac ended and the road continued as a dirt track that judging from the ruts and potholes, had not seen any maintenance for years. Either side of the track was dense woodland that closed off the sky above, giving the impression that he was driving down some long dark tunnel. Cresting a rise, the road took a sharp left turn and suddenly he was on a wide sandy beach, at the head of which was an old timber shack painted in a dull maroon colour. Stopping the car before it reached the really soft sand, Yamada got out and swaggered across to the shack. As he approached, the door flew open, and framed in the doorway was a man who at first glance looked to be in his sixties, but on closer inspection could not be much more than thirty. The face could have been photographed in Belsen or Auschwitz – gaunt, haunted, with eyes that told of unmentionable torment, but it was not the horrors of Nazi Germany that had wrought this grotesque mask. It was heroin.

"I suppose you've brought the stuff?" Yamada spun round, surprised by the voice behind him.

The girl stood looking at him through beautiful dark brown eyes that held an expression of deep sadness and resignation. She wore a faded cotton dress with a frayed hem that hung over her slender body, her bare feet speckled with sand.

"Yeah," he answered, fishing in his pocket, bringing out a package and holding it out to her. The girl slowly took a pace forward and stretched out her hand to take the package but he snatched it away and threw a nylon bag at her. "In there you will find four Japanese carp flags. You will fly them from that pole from next Tuesday until 4th July."

"Why?" she asked.

"Why not?" he replied. "Just make sure my boss sees them when she sails by."

She shrugged and carried the package into the shack, stopping to comfort the man with the words. "It's alright Jake, he's brought your stuff."

Yamada followed her in, pushing the man to one side and crossing the room to unlock a large metal cabinet containing a radio transmitter. Carefully he inspected it all over, then pulling a test meter from his pocket he checked the batteries.

"No one snooping around here?" he asked.

"No," she replied. "We haven't seen anyone since you last called."

"Good," Yamada said. "You can't afford guests."

Yamada looked across at the man, seeing his hands trembling and the pain in his staring eyes. He returned the look impassively, got up, and leaving the shack went back to his car. From the trunk he lifted two boxes of provisions, which he took back to the shack. Inside, he pointed to the boxes and said to the girl, "This is for you, no point in me giving you money for food, you'd only spend it on more drugs for him. I don't want you getting caught and bringing the law back here, you understand me?"

She nodded and asked again, "You did bring the stuff, didn't you?"

"Yeah, here it is." This time he put the package in her hand. "You've gotta make that last until 4th July, you got that? I'll look in before then, but I won't be bringing any more stuff."

"How much is there?" she asked.

"Huh. Enough to keep him chilled 'til winter," Yamada replied with a sneer.

Driving away he found her face haunting him. She was his recruit, captured by her lover's addiction. A highly talented guitarist, he had swept her up, only to tear her heart to shreds as he became hooked on drugs. After two years of watching the downward spiral she had finally got him into a clinic where it was thought they had succeeded in curing him. Sadly, his return to the real world was too much for him to take and within weeks he was back into his world of oblivion. Yamada had met them in a suburb of Washington. She had been crouched over Jake, who was lying on the sidewalk stoned out of his mind, her tears and pleadings going unanswered. Yamada had seen guys in that state before and fancying his chances with the girl, had offered to help her take him off the street. Back in the room she shared with Jake, he realised her absolute devotion to the wreck of the creature he had carried. Aware that her love for Jake made her of more use to him than just casual sex, he had suggested that they get out of town to where she could see Jake through his last weeks or months.

The shack and beach he had bought with his army pay, along with part of the woodland. He had plans that some day he might build a house there. The group had used it before, its isolation and location ideal for their purposes. She had agreed, surprised that his only demand was for her to look after the shack and let no one in except him. It was only weeks before her money for drugs ran out and he had been able to offer her a supply, provided that she attended to small duties at the shack. These included the regular running of a small generator to keep the transmitter batteries topped up and his latest demand for the flags to be flown. She had also to guarantee that she would never take any drugs herself whilst she was staying there. The deal worked well and as the weeks passed she was feeling more and more beholden to him.

Back on the tarmac road, he gunned the engine, leaving a trail of dirt and dust behind him as he started back on his long drive home, satisfied that the pre-arranged signal would be in place, meaningless to anyone other than Fumiko Hamaura.

At the farm, the following morning, Sarah was washing the girls' underwear in the sink when the Englishman came in with some sandwiches and glasses of water.

"Do you think it is humane in any way to keep us locked up in this room without any proper exercise or fresh air?" she said, glaring at him. "Don't you have any influence over what these animals are up to?"

"Yuki is not an animal," he retorted hotly.

"She must be if she is allowing this to happen to two small girls," Sarah said, now finding it difficult to control her temper.

He went to say something, then decided against it and left.

Later in the day Yukiko came in. "Your children may play in yard for half hour. Any attempt to run away and they will be shot," she said, her voice hard and cold. "Make sure they understand only good behaviour will be allowed."

Clare and Louise were reluctant to leave their mother but eventually she persuaded them to go outside to play.

When they returned she hugged them with relief that they appeared unharmed. "What games did you play?" she asked.

"The man wanted us to kick a ball to him," Clare said. "But it wasn't fun like playing with Daddy."

"The lady kept shouting at us to stay near this house," said Louise. "I wanted to play hotels in the barn." Her lips pouted in disappointment.

"Come."

Sarah looked up to see Murata in the doorway. "What do you want?" she asked, feeling the grip of fear in her stomach.

"You exercise now."

Telling the girls that she would be safe and would not be long, she went out of the room and followed Murata down the stairs and out into the fresh air. Seeing Chichester Cathedral spire in the distance she knew roughly where they were. In the stress of their kidnap she had become disorientated and had believed that they had travelled much further than in fact they had.

"How long must we stay here?" she asked.

"Always you ask questions," he replied. "You will stay here as long as I think necessary."

"Our parents are not rich so if you are demanding ransom…" she started.

"I do not use you for such purpose," Murata interrupted angrily. "You are here in order your husband obey well our instruction."

They continued in silence walking round and round the yard, Sarah catching glimpses of the surrounding fields and far-off houses.

As the door to their room opened, Sarah saw two frightened little faces look back at her from the wall by the window. Hurrying across the room she crouched down and hugged them to her. Turning to Murata she said, "Would it have been so much of a risk to let us all enjoy the fresh air together? Or are you afraid that a woman and two small girls will overpower your guard?"

She saw in his eyes the thought to cross the room and strike her, but something stopped him. Maybe she thought, to hit a defenceless woman might mean loss of face.

Her words obviously had their effect, for the next day both she and the girls were taken down to the yard together. Murata and Yukiko stood guard with guns at the ready, whilst the Englishman tried to get the girls to play football with him. At the end of their allotted period, it was Louise who walked up to the young man and asked, "What is your name?"

Surprised, he looked down at her and said, "Er, Julian, my name is Julian."

"Oh," she said, and walking back to Sarah she announced, "His name is Julian so now we know."

Sarah almost burst out laughing. It was strange how names were so important to young children.

Chapter 3

A north-easterly wind, variable 4 to 6, constantly on their starboard quarter for the past 48 hours, had kept the Victoria 34 blasting along, covering a regular 130 to 140 miles a day. As Ian prepared to take the helm he applied dividers to the chart and estimated that another nine or ten days would bring them to the Azores.

During the last two days the storm that had swept them past Ushant had subsided. The sea, however, was still rough and there was a large swell that kept the helmsman constantly busy. Settled now into some form of routine, Ian concentrated on staying out of trouble and restoring his strength. The physical and verbal abuse that his captors had meted out had reduced him to almost total withdrawal and isolation, trying wherever possible not to speak to them and eat alone, serving his own food if he could and doing his own washing up. Though Arni did not seem to either notice or care, Hamaura did and would try to invite responses to her instructions.

"You are wondering where we are heading?" Hamaura asked after two hours of silence between them. Ian shook his head then mechanically checked the compass and reached forward and eased the foresail sheet a fraction.

"It is not the Azores; we will simply meet with another boat and take on more water and stores." Ian made no response, just stood and looked around the entire horizon checking for other vessels.

"Do not ignore me, shitabataraki, or I will punish you again," she said, her face becoming ugly with annoyance. Again Ian did not respond, gambling that she would not react but suddenly she leapt up and was about to strike him when a strong gust of wind hit the boat, making it heel over dramatically and start to broach. Ian, at the wheel, reacted immediately to haul the

53

yacht back on course, but Hamaura had been caught completely off balance and was sent flying across the cockpit to crash into the opposite combing, her right shoulder making heavy contact with the winch and her left ankle caught and twisted in the loose sheet tails. Within an instant, Arni's face appeared at the head of the companionway.

"What's going on?" he demanded, looking somewhat surprised to see Hamaura sprawled on the cockpit sole, struggling to untangle her feet. "What happened here?"

Something snapped in Ian's mind; whether it was the stress he was under, the justice of her accident, her sprawling undignified form, he didn't know, but it was enough for him to point and laughing shout, "Stupid bitch fell over, pity she didn't break her bloody neck."

"Look and listen well," Arni shouted back. "If she had broken anything you could have said goodbye to your family. In future you will be polite to both of us otherwise I will have your daughters tortured. Do you understand?"

Ian nodded. "Do you understand?" Arni repeated, this time in a frenzied shout, cleverly forcing a verbal response from Ian, reinforcing his subservience.

"Yes. I understand," Ian replied.

Glaring at Hamaura, Arni said, "You keep your temper under control or we will not get across this ocean. I can't sail this solo and you're needed to do other duties than steer, so no more accidents, okay?"

"Who do you think you are speaking to!" she replied, but it was too late. Arni had already turned away to go forward to his bunk, winning that exchange and showing Ian that the man had more to him than was at first apparent. Hamaura struggled to her feet, kicking wildly to free the sheet from around her ankle. Once free she considered following Arni in order to put him in his place but knew she had lost that exchange and must wait her chance to reassert her command status. Placing her full weight onto the twisted ankle brought a cry of pain and she staggered and sat down hard. As she pulled the trouser leg up to inspect the ankle Ian noted that it was already swelling nicely and if she didn't get a cold compress on it soon it would hurt for days. That would stop her kicks and punches, but he was sure that she would find some other method of inflicting pain.

Her loss of face had the effect of moving her below to continue with her game of recording things on tape. Ian could only guess that these were either records of the voyage or, more likely, new false messages for the buoys to carry and transmit.

The incident had produced one gem of information and that was their intention to cross the Atlantic, presumably to the USA. Try as he might, Ian still couldn't figure out why they were making the journey or whether they had a strict timetable to keep to. Their frantic departure from Bosham indicated that they could not afford either questions or delays and Ian wondered whether they were being chased. He had no doubt that the yacht *Umi Sama* had not belonged to them. Had it been stolen, why stage the elaborate sinking, why not just abandon the yacht at Bosham Quay? Probably it was chartered that way – yes, he could see the thinking behind it all. Their apparent drowning would effectively stop further investigation.

Ian's musings had taken his attention away from the horizon for a good while and now as he looked up from the compass, the scene gave him fresh cause for concern. Now well above the horizon were tall dark black clouds, a sure sign of another storm.

"Can you relieve me at the wheel?" Ian shouted down.

She looked up from her recording, obviously annoyed at the interruption. Ian noted with some satisfaction her heavy and painful limp as she came up into the cockpit, sitting herself down in the starboard quarter before grasping the wheel with her left hand.

"I say, that's awfully decent of you," he said with no little amount of sarcasm.

"Hurry, I've got work to do," she replied, scowling at him.

"Look over there, we have to prepare for that."

Below, he reset the barometer and checked the time then went forward to use the heads and have a good wash. Trying not to disturb Arni, Ian changed his clothes. Sauntering back to the chart table, he noted again the barometer reading. No doubt about it, they were in for a severe storm. He turned to the galley and lit the oven.

"What are you doing?" she screamed at him.

"I'm organising a meal," he replied. "Always try and face a storm on a full stomach, you need the energy to see you through it." She glared at him but made no response.

Tinned beef supplemented with carrots, peas and the last onion and served with tinned potatoes was not exactly haute cuisine but it was hot and filling. As Ian prepared to serve up the meal Arni emerged from the forward cabin in readiness for his watch.

He was surprised to see Ian preparing a meal and Hamaura on the helm. "Why are you helming?" he asked.

"He say storm is coming and we must have food," she replied. "So he can cook it."

"Oh." He paused at the companionway hatch, and said, "I was thinking, you recording all of these messages, what if Yamada not completed his work."

"Yamada-san very reliable, everything will be ready for us."

"How will we know?" Arni asked.

"Have no fear, we will know from very first action," she answered. "It will be on every radio station and TV channel."

Arni, leaning out into the cockpit, read the log and returned to sit at the chart table to bring the chart up to date.

"Are you eating down here or up on deck?" Ian asked.

"Here," Arni replied in his normal abrupt tone.

The two of them sat down together leaving Hamaura grimly at the helm struggling to cope in the rising wind. As they sat eating in silence, Ian pondered who Yamada could be and what it was that he was preparing for them. Also, why would it be on every radio and TV channel?

"It's blowing up for another storm," Ian observed.

"When you finished go up and take in a reef," Arni said through a mouthful of food.

"Only one?"

"Yeah, only one. You take more off later."

"Have you noted the speed that the barometer is dropping?"

Arni looked up. "What do you mean?"

"Have a look at the barometer readings for the last two hours and you will see what I mean," said Ian, not prepared to go into any more detail.

On finishing his meal Ian got into his wet-weather gear and climbed up into the cockpit. Out of the shelter of the cabin he was surprised at the strength of the wind; reefing wasn't going to be easy.

Looking around he assessed the sea state carefully then turning to Hamaura he said, with as false a smile as he could manage, "You can eat now. When you've finished, wash up and stow everything safely." The backhander from Arni, who was now standing just behind him, nearly knocked him over the side.

"Shut up and just do as you are told!" said Arni, grabbing Ian by the arm and thrusting him towards the side deck.

Clipping on, Ian carefully worked his way forward to the mast and signalled to Arni to turn the yacht into the wind. Quickly, he dropped a reef in and hauled the halyard tight again. Yet again he became aware of Arni's lack of experience. Here they were with the barometer dropping like a stone and Arni unaware of the need to prepare now for the extremes that would shortly be upon them. Now it was fear of the elements that made him act – he was determined that he wasn't going to die by drowning. What a ridiculous situation this was; to keep his family alive he must now work to stop these two, who were the biggest threat to them, from drowning in this vast ocean. Clambering back into the cockpit he faced Arni.

"What experience have you had of sailing a small yacht through a heavy storm on an exposed ocean? Be honest with your answer, otherwise we all die and I'm not ready for that yet." Ian's eyes fixed on Arni's searchingly.

"I've been through many storms," Arni replied, placed slightly on the back foot by Ian's questioning.

"On an ocean this big on a yacht this small?" asked Ian.

"No, not in a boat this small," admitted Arni, aware that he was talking to someone with obvious skill and experience.

"Okay, then this is how it's going to be…"

"You don't give orders," snapped Hamaura, standing holding her plate of food at the bottom of the companionway steps.

Ian regarded her coolly. "Your sailing expert Arni here, has just admitted that he has not experienced a real blow in a small boat. You, from what I have seen, have a strong stomach but that is all. You're going to need much, much more than that to get you through the night."

"He trying to fool you," she jeered at Arni. "You not going to fall for that, are you?"

"Let's hear what he recommends," retorted Arni. "For the love of Allah he's just as interested as we are in staying alive."

"You screw this mission up and I will make you pay!" Hamaura's voice rose in anger again.

"I screw up nothing, let us hear him out." Then swinging round on Ian he said, "Okay expert, what would you do, eh?"

"First of all I would start the engine then get the mainsail down and replace it with the tri-sail. Then we get the foresail in and put the storm jib on the inner forestay, using the engine to maintain speed. From the speed the barometer is dropping I think we'll see winds of maybe 9, gusting 10, before long, so we need to watch for big seas landing on the cabin roof. The danger is the hatches – if a big green wave falls on us and one of those gets smashed then we're in big trouble. I suggest you lash the spray dodgers over them and push the two horseshoe life belts under to act as a cushion."

Arni interrupted. "I'm not wanting to use the dodgers, we need protection here."

"They won't be much use when it gets up. If we stop a big wave over the side it could carry the dodger away and probably the stanchions as well," Ian replied.

"You reckon, eh?"

"Yes, I do. Also, we need to fill this cockpit up using fenders stuffed into the spare sails bags. Someone must tape seal the bags, in the dry, otherwise they could fill with water and defeat the object. Any volume they take up will reduce the weight of water if we get swamped. Down below, absolutely everything has got to be secured. Doubly so, especially things like the batteries. A couple of those airborne will cause untold damage." So the list went on, with Ian explaining in each case why such preparations should be considered.

The work took them an hour and a half to complete but even then Ian was not entirely satisfied. In that time the wind had risen in strength to around force 8, but still the glass was falling. The wind and seas now joined to present solid walls of water, marching in regular lines, to rush at *Kiboko's* stern, each one threatening to engulf her.

Finally, with only a storm jib set and poled out, the yacht was running before the wind, trailing as much mooring and anchor warp as Ian could find to act as a sea anchor to hold the yacht's stern into the wind. He had stopped the engine an hour ago when he had dispensed with the tri-sail and was now just checking around to make sure everything was secure before going below and battening down. He stared at the life raft for several seconds, debating on whether to launch it and make his escape. Hamaura and Arni were below and he knew that Arni wouldn't be able to sail back for him. Then memories of the 1979 Fastnet Race came into his mind, in which many of those who had abandoned their yachts for a life raft had perished whilst their yachts had survived. His thoughts drifted along the possibilities a bit longer until he remembered about the rendezvous near the Azores; if he escaped, news would get back to England and his family would die. It was then that he saw the name *Kiboko* on the Dan-buoy, the only thing the evil bitch had missed. In one movement it was over the side, to spin away astern and in moments be out of sight.

Ian smiled to himself, knowing that she would miss it and knowing that she would realise its significance if found. Looking around him, now clinging to the binnacle frame, he checked and rechecked the lashing of the wheel and sail bags. It was then that the sea decided to dump a large wave on them; knocked down, Ian blessed the sail bags and his safety harness. It took several minutes for the cockpit to drain, during which time more water had come over the stern but the bags were serving their purpose and little real weight of sea remained onboard, most draining immediately over the transom. Now lashed with spray, Ian clipped onto the 'D' ring by the companionway and, timing his entry, pushed the hatch forward as the boat crested a wave, removed only the top washboard, cleared his harness and climbed into the cabin, slamming the washboard home and the hatch closed in almost one movement. Hanging on grimly to any firm handhold, he made his way to the starboard settee and wedged himself in place to get his breath back before struggling out of his wet gear. Then swinging his way back to the companionway steps, he removed the cover and began pumping, thanking the owner as he did so for having the foresight to install a standby bilge pump in the cabin for such occasions.

As the wind increased above force 9 the waves began to really build, now reaching heights now of 30 feet, but in the open ocean forming a regular pattern with only occasional cross seas. Hours passed and through the cabin windows they could see the massive waves, white-faced with spume, careering past them with a roar that could be heard even above the screaming of the wind in the rigging. Ian, having claimed the starboard cabin settee, had rigged its lee cloth and settled himself down, closing his eyes and trying to rest as much as possible; occasionally he would eat a biscuit or two.

It was Arni who was the first to succumb to seasickness, making a timely arrival in the heads. To Ian's surprise it was only a few minutes after that, Hamaura made a dive for the bucket he had strategically placed under the cabin table. Ian looked over the lee cloth wondering whether the time had come when he could overpower them, only to see Hamaura's firm grip on her automatic pistol. It was a risk he couldn't take.

Dawn brought no let-up in the onslaught of wind and waves, but still the yacht soldiered on, keeping remarkably dry inside. Every hour Ian would go round the yacht checking for damage and thankfully finding none, yet fearing all the time that the storm would generate the ultimate wave that would break through the defences. The day passed, marked only by a slight lightening of the sky, and still *Kiboko* fought on, mast intact and standing proud.

With evening came the first signs of a lessening of the winds, though the seas still pounded them unmercifully. Ian started to regularly open the hatch to check, as best he could, the sail bags and helm lashing. Even timing the hatch opening carefully, each time his face was whipped by spray torn by the wind from the crest of the following wave. These moments of fresh air helped him keep his stomach under control and served to reduce the stench of vomit in the cabin.

By midnight, Ian judged it safe to go on deck again and, clipped on by two straps, he went forward on hands and knees, just in time to re-lash the main anchor that had been almost torn away from its deck blocks. Blinded with spray and twice washed back by waves that almost entirely covered the yacht, he thankfully regained the relative safety of the cockpit. During the next hour the wind began to moderate and in two hours had reduced to around force 7. Ian hauled in the warps he had trailed astern, set some mainsail and drop the storm jib to the deck after letting out some foresail. Standing behind the wheel again, he set the yacht back on its course of 235 degrees feeling a great sense of relief that he and the yacht had survived, but frustrated that he had been unable to catch his two captors unawares and deal with them. Looking up into the sky, he watched the moon skiing over the wind-shredded clouds, its light illuminating their torn tresses, the lines of the Alfred Noyes poem 'The Highwayman' running through his mind: 'The moon was a ghostly galleon tossed upon the cloudy seas.'

As dawn lightened the eastern sky, the hatch was pulled back and Arni's head appeared. He looked drained and exhausted, the sufferings of the last two days showing in his eyes. He looked at Ian for several seconds before nodding and shouting, "Thanks." Then he disappeared from view again. The thanks surprised Ian and marked a subtle change in Arni's attitude. Contempt and abuse were to be replaced by some respect for Ian's seamanship and willingness from Arni to divulge the skills of celestial navigation. As dawn broke, Arni took the wheel, sending Ian below to make coffee, sandwiches and get some exhausted sleep.

Ian was surprised to find that he had been allowed almost seven hours' sleep. Arni woke him with a shake, telling him to prepare some food; he still looked pale and had obviously not eaten any food or, Ian guessed, drunk any water. He refrained from giving any advice in the hope that dehydration would take over and render Arni incapable.

Ian's first chore was to clean up, a task he found far worse than the roughest sea. Eventually, with the cabin clean and the bilges smelling sweet again, he started making sandwiches and tea.

In the cockpit he found Hamaura and was shocked by her appearance. She looked at least ten years older with dark rings round her now sunken eyes. She was holding a bottle of water from which she was taking the occasional sip.

"Here," she said, handing Arni the bottle. "Drink some of this, it will make you feel better."

Arni took the bottle and drank half the contents before handing it back to Hamaura. "Shokran," he said and gave her a bow.

Cursing to himself, Ian took over the wheel as Hamaura and Arni slid to the forward end of the cockpit and Hamaura fell asleep. Arni however, remained watchful, obviously feeling better for taking on fluids.

After two hours Hamaura awoke and accepted a sandwich that she nibbled at cautiously. Finding that the sandwich had no ill effect the next one she ate hungrily before venturing below to make up packet soup. Returning on deck, mug in hand, she started to take in more of her surroundings. Ian was aware of what was confusing her; he could see she had detected that something was missing but could not quite work out what it was. Finishing her soup, she put down the mug and shuffled along the cockpit seat towards the transom.

"What goes in there?" she asked pointing towards a plastic tube clipped to the pushpit stanchion. "The Dan-buoy," answered Arni. "Where is it now?" he asked looking at Ian.

"We lost it in the storm," said Ian as casually as possible. "We took some heavy seas over the stern."

"What does it do?" Hamaura asked.

"If someone falls overboard you throw it as near to them as you can, to mark where they are. In big seas like this if you fell over the side, for example, unless Arni here threw the Dan-buoy near to where you were in the water, you would be lost from view in seconds. Look." Ian picked up the water bottle Hamaura had been drinking from and tossed it over the stern. The three of them watched it disappear over a following wave never to be seen again. "See what I mean?" said Ian. "Arni would probably see you for a few seconds more than that but unless he got the Dan-buoy over the side quickly, you wouldn't stand a chance."

Hamaura gave Ian a long thoughtful look. "Did it have yacht name on it?" she asked

"I would think so," said Ian. "In fact I'm sure it did, I remember checking it when I took the yacht over."

"You took letters off?" she asked Arni.

"No, you were doing that along with horseshoe lifebelts," he replied.

Hamaura sat in silence for a few moments then nodded. "Yes, I remember doing so," she replied, trying hard to make her voice sound confident.

Ian inwardly smiled at the lie. Hamaura was not the type to admit to making a mistake, especially one that could prove serious. He knew that she would now be worried, despite the fact that it would be a million to one against it being found.

Arni left the cockpit and made for his bunk, leaving Hamaura to sit poker-faced calculating the odds.

"Any chance of a hot drink?" asked Ian.

Without a word she went below and made some coffee and to Ian's surprise some more sandwiches.

"Here," she said, thrusting the three-quarter-full mug along the seat towards him.

"Thank you," he replied, surprised that she had not found an opportunity to scald his hands again.

Midnight came and went and it was almost one in the morning before Arni came on deck to take over. Ian crashed out on his bunk fully clothed, his body still aching and the cuts sore from the constant splashes of salt water, but he slept almost immediately. After only three hours' rest he was again shaken and summoned on deck, and found the sky as dark as night and the rain coming down in torrents.

That same dawn woke Stavos, a fat sweaty Lebanese who hid out from the rest of the world in a shack in the back streets of Horta. Beside him, still snoring gently was Fatia, his mistress and meal ticket. He fumbled in the dim light for the packet of cigarettes and his old flip top lighter. Blinking and yawning he pulled a cigarette from the packet and lit it, coughing and wheezing on the smoke. Hawking and spitting accurately into the bedpan on the floor beside him, he gave Fatia's rounded buttock a slap and between coughs ordered her to make coffee.

Without protest she got up and stumbled to the gas cooker in the corner of the room. Turning on the gas bottle, she struck a match and put it to the grease-covered ring, snatching her hand away as the gas ignited with a loud pop. Stavos watched her with affection as she busied herself spooning in the coffee and placing the pot onto the flame. Turning, she saw him looking at her. "What's the matter with you, hey? You look at your own body."

"We are getting old, Fa," he said wearily, "but the prophet has been kind to you, eh?"

"Shut up, you old fool and get dressed, the Japo will be waiting," she ordered, but with a kindly tone. His comment had warmed her even though she knew that her looks could still attract a regular trade on the street.

Stavos gave her a fond look, then scratching absently, he swung his legs over the side of the bed and pulled on a pair of crumpled trousers that had been dropped on the floor the previous night, hobbling across the cold stone floor to the wash basin, he turned on the brass tap. A spluttering noise preceded the trickle of water that slowly filled the basin and overflowed onto the floor as he plunged his face into it, rubbing with his hands. Straightening up, he groped for the towel on a hook behind the door and dried himself, his toilet for the day complete.

As Fatia poured the coffee he crossed to the small window and brushed aside the curtain, squinting through the torn fly screen and dirty glass in the early light at the storm clouds racing overhead. "The Japo won't be putting to sea in this," he grunted, removing the mug of coffee from Fatia's hand and taking a loud sip.

"How you know, eh? 'E sounded very determined when you told 'im abou' the storm," Fatia said, glaring at him with one hand on her hip.

"Well 'e 'adn't seen it then!" he retorted.

"Look, 'e is paying you more money than I can earn in a year; that means 'e will go! So be there!" Her voice had risen several decibels.

"All right, I go, and if I drown?" he asked.

"I will dance on your gravestone!" she replied.

"Ah Fa," he swung to face her, his expression showing hurt. "You don't mean that."

She smiled, relieving the hurt. "No, I don't mean that. God go with you and care for you, but go quickly!"

Stavos slurped at his coffee whilst getting dressed, then, oilskins on, he left, scrambling down the stairs and out into the rain-drenched and windy street.

Fatia had followed him down the stairs and was watching his huddled form as he half walked, half ran, down towards the quayside. Her expression showed both fear and fondness. The fear was the storm, maybe the Japanese man would insist on sailing in this awful weather. The fondness was for the only man

66

who had been honest with her and not tried to abuse her. She smiled; they made a strange couple, he a fisherman, small-time arms smuggler and her minder, she plying that risky trade, street walking.

Chapter 4

Phil Saints was not on duty when the passage details of *Umi Sama* and *Kiboko* were radioed in; it was only when he checked the station's 'Vision Systems' log at the start of his shift that the name *Umi Sama* made his eyebrows rise.

"I see that *Umi Sama* is out on charter again, Glen," he said over his shoulder to his watch officer. "She must be making the owners a bomb this year. I wonder how long it's out for this time."

"Wish I had the money to hire it," said Glen. "Large Beneteau; saw it in Haslar Marina a couple of weeks ago when young Jack was down. Got all the kit on it: radar, GPS and two life rafts. Must cost a fortune nowadays to fit out a yacht for charter."

"Yes, she is large; with just two people aboard they'll be rattling around like two peas in an oil drum." With that, Phil put the yacht from his mind and carried on down the list of contacts. He was always pleased when yachts checked in advising them of their passage plan. These traffic reports contained details of the vessel: its name, size and a brief description together with details of those on board, number of adults and children, etc. The reports were entered onto the computer for record purposes and unless the vessel's crew made contact with the station to advise them of safe arrivals or a problem, no further attention would be given to the craft. The exception to this would be if a relative of the crew or someone awaiting the yacht's arrival reported that they were overdue. Then the watch manager and his staff would assess the prevailing conditions and, if there was any cause for concern, review whether a yacht could have diverted to another port or turned back to its homeport. In both of these events, volunteer officers could be called on to make physical checks in the relevant harbours and marinas. Simultaneously the

Coastguard would issue a Securité broadcast, requesting vessels to look out for the overdue craft and report if seen. Should the land search not bring results, high headlands covering the estimated area of search would be manned, again by volunteers, and a lookout kept. At this time a full-scale search would be mounted, initially using aircraft.

On the day the weather was very fair, but being early in the season, few yachts were out. The commercial traffic was at its normal level and the usual crop of traffic information and navigation notices had to be dealt with.

It wasn't until nearly the end of his shift that the mayday came in. Both men looked at each other stunned as the details emerged of the collision and sinking of the two boats. Their French opposite numbers had reported the incident moments after the mayday had been received and directed vessels to the area to carry out a search for survivors. So strong was the mayday transmission signal that Solent Coastguard heard it direct, their direction-finding equipment locking onto the signal to give them a good idea of the location of the broadcast. The French Coastguard Service had similar success and was able to send a craft immediately to the scene, but could not find any trace of the incident.

As the shift changed and the new team took over, the information was handed to them, all contained in an incident log. "Strange one this; very unusual for both yachts to be damaged such that they sink; must have been going some at each other for that to happen," Phil Saints said to Alec, Katy and John, the night watch team. "Scary really. Glen and I were only talking about *Umi Sama* earlier on and saying that she had all the gizmos, then this."

"Doesn't surprise me much," said Alec. "The way some of these grotty yachty types carry on with next to nothing in the way of training."

"There he goes again," John chirped. "Wouldn't have happened if they had been stink pot drivers, I suppose. What have you got against yachts?"

"They're too complicated for amateurs to play about with," Alec replied. "A power boat has got far better precise handling, a gust of wind doesn't knock one of them off course."

"Can you stow it the pair of you, I want to get home," Phil chimed in before the debate could get heated.

"Sorry mate," said Alec. "I think we've got all the background we need; you on tomorrow?"

"Yes," said Phil. "The twelve to midnight again, see you."

With that he left to pick up Stella who should have been finishing her stint at the local hospital. As he drove into the hospital car park, he saw her hurrying down the steps of the entrance, waving goodnight to another nurse.

"Alright, my lovely?" greeted Phil in his best yokel accent.

"No, I'm not, Phil Saints; that wind cuts right through you as you cross the car park. Here's a cold nose for you." With that she leant across and kissed him before putting her cold nose on the side of his neck.

"That's not cold," he laughed, putting the car into gear and pulling away.

During the drive home she told him of her day with all its highs and lows. At home, a meal waiting in the automatic oven had them sitting down to eat half an hour after coming through the front door. In all that time Phil had hardly said a word.

"You're very quiet tonight, Phil, anything the matter?" Stella asked, looking concerned.

"No, it's nothing really. It's just that two British yachts collided ten miles or so north of Alderney and sank – something fishy about it that I don't understand. If it were just one yacht sunk it would make more sense, but both doesn't seem right somehow. Not in these weather conditions anyway," he said, with a puzzled expression on his face.

"What did the others think?" she asked.

"You know, old Alec started going on about 'It wouldn't happen to power boats'. While John looked as if he was going to come to the defence of the whole yachting fraternity, I made a run for it before it got heated," he replied.

"Weren't they curious as to why both boats had sunk?" she prompted.

"I didn't stay around to find out," he said. "If I had, you would have been dead with hypothermia before I arrived to pick you up."

With a chuckle she stood up and started to clear the table of dirty plates, taking them through to the kitchen.

The following morning the newspapers were full of the story and the apparent tragic loss of an entire family. None of the papers had found out much about the couple that had chartered *Umi Sama* except that they had recently flown in from Germany. Intrigue was growing regarding them, especially as the description of the body found did not match that remembered by the charter company.

The press were also speculating as to whether both yachts had in fact been run down by one of the large vessels in the east-bound shipping lane, that runs along the French side of the English Channel.

As Phil came on watch, he searched the incident log and started to read. The story was not much different from the previous evening in that the French Coastguard was satisfied that there had been a collision between the two yachts, in wind conditions where both could have been travelling at quite high speeds and possibly on opposite tacks. The lack of debris or survivors indicated the severity and suddenness of the collision and fitted the terrified sound of the mayday message.

Later in the log was the description of the finding of the upturned life raft and then the body. That was quite interesting as the body was that of an oriental male with absolutely no identification on him.

Later still, an initial post mortem revealed that the oriental male had broken his leg some hours before the sinking and that no first aid measure whatsoever had been applied. The Solent Coastguard was informed in case they had received a Pan Pan Medico request.

Though bits of debris from *Umi Sama* had been found, the only trace of *Kiboko* had been some clothes and its life raft that had remained upright and drifted some considerable distance away from the first one found.

Phil Saints read and re-read the report looking for something strange, coming up with only two points, but ones that he thought were very important. The first was that if both boats launched life rafts, why was only one body recovered? Secondly, why was the mayday located as being north of Alderney? They had both informed that Cherbourg was to be their destination, which tied in with the location of the body. He went into the RCCM's office.

"Have you got a minute, Harold?" he asked.

Harold Blakemore was sitting as normal, wedged in his chair poring over some paperwork. "What is it? Can't you see I'm very busy?" he said, trying hard to look important.

Blakemore was new to the station and rumour had it that he had only been moved there to give him a bit of a boost before retirement. At 55 years old and with long service, he was well past the age when such a promotion would have been made on merit. Unlike Phil and most of the others, he had no military background, coming into the Coastguard Service from the Department of Pensions, where he had enjoyed a brief career. With him, in Stubbington, had arrived his wife, Madeline, who had obviously expected to have been the wife of the Rescue Centre Co-ordination manager twenty years ago and was now making up for lost time.

"It's about the double sinking last night," said Phil. "There are a cou…"

"The French are handling that, there is no need for us to get involved," interrupted Blakemore. "I've already made that clear to the press, this station will not be making any statement on the incident at this time."

"I don't think it is a straightforward accident," persisted Phil.

"Write a report and I shall look at it when I've got a moment, which will be after I have completed my preparations for the conference next week." Blakemore accompanied his remark with a dismissive glare.

"Alright," said Phil, turning and heading back to his desk, seething at Blakemore's reaction and the way he obviously placed a conference in front of a serious incident such as this.

As his shift continued and no further news became available, Phil settled down and prepared his report, trying hard not to introduce his gut feeling as this would immediately give Blakemore a reason to dismiss the whole thing.

On reflection Blakemore was correct as far as procedure was concerned; the incident had occurred in French waters and they were just as capable of working things out as he was. HQ would also welcome Blakemore's frankness with the press as they always warned officers not to make uninformed statements.

It was nearly 1700 hours when Phil knocked on Blakemore's office door again, in the hope of handing in his report and discussing it.

"The report you wanted, Harold," he said.

"What report?" replied Blakemore.

"The one you requested earlier about the yacht sinkings off Alderney," Phil reminded.

"Oh that. Just leave it on my desk; I'll look at it when I get back on Friday. I'm up at HQ tomorrow," Blakemore said, with a vague wave of a handful of papers that he proceeded to jam into his briefcase.

Without comment Phil placed the report in Blakemore's in-tray and left.

Only a few minutes later Blakemore scurried out of the building, probably, Phil thought, for a briefing session from Madeline about what he was to say tomorrow at HQ.

In France too, the day had brought no further information regarding the yachts' collision. Three cross-channel ferries had formed a search team line abreast and made a three-sweep search along a corridor of sea in which it was felt that debris and any survivors would be. In such circumstances the ferry companies assisted, accepting the fuel cost and delay, and rarely suffered any passenger complaints.

French military aircraft and the Lifeboat Service had been in action but nothing else had been found. Interestingly, the incident had occurred when there had been a large gap in shipping in the area, suggesting that the newspaper theory of a run-down by a large vessel was incorrect. By evening the search was already being scaled down as the authorities moved into a waiting strategy.

Without further information for the press to feed on, and having had their theories of run-down refuted, the story soon left the front pages and had disappeared from the newspapers completely by the end of the week.

By the third morning, the police victim support personnel were beginning to move out from the Vaughan's parents' homes leaving the task of care to friends and relatives. All, in fact, much as Blakemore had anticipated in his personal report on the subject to HQ. "A very sad business, such a terrible loss. Such lovely children as well. I sometimes think that our yachtsmen take far too many risks with their families, tragic, truly tragic." His tone designed to convey a fatherly concern to the group of senior officers present.

Sitting on the train back to Fareham, Blakemore felt rather proud of himself. He felt that he had handled the day well and especially his report about the yacht sinkings. Idly he searched through his briefcase pulling his report out and reading it again, basking in the glow of a job well done. At Hamble, his briefcase slid from his lap spilling its contents onto the floor of the train. In picking them up he found Watch Manager Saints' report and almost put it back in the case with the other papers but decided instead to give it a brief look.

When Madeline saw him get off the train at Fareham station, she saw a man with a very troubled expression upon his face.

"What went wrong, Harold?" she demanded to know, missing any of the normal pleasantries of greeting.

"Nothing dear, in fact they all seemed quite impressed," he replied, without any real conviction.

"Well why do you look as though you have seen the end of the world?" Madeline asked, standing waiting for him to open the driver's door of their car for her.

"Oh, it's just that I read Saints' report on the way here in the train and I think he may have raised some awkward questions that maybe we should have considered," Blakemore's voice now almost trembling.

"Does his report go any higher than you?" she asked, glaring at him.

"No dear, not normally," he said, suddenly feeling a little more at ease.

"Well then," she said, her tone matter of fact. "It's cold meat and salad tonight. You can't expect me to provide you with hot meals and come all this way to pick you up. And your train was late."

"That sounds perfect, dear," he replied, closing her door and walking round to the passenger side and getting in. The ten-minute journey to Stubbington, which Madeline had described as 'all this way' was completed in silence, Blakemore staring out of the car window and wishing that he had splashed out on a meat pie at the station café in Southampton.

Leading Seaman Stanley raised his binoculars again to check what his last sweep had revealed. Sure enough, a Dan-buoy was bouncing in the choppy sea about three miles off on bearing 020. Turning, he reported his sighting to the captain. "Danbuoy sighted three miles 020, sir."

Lieutenant Commander Curtis stepped out onto the wing bridge and raised his glasses. "Thank you Stanley, well spotted. We'd better go and have a look." Returning to the bridge enclosure, he ordered, "Turn to starboard and steer 015 degrees helm."

"015 degrees it is, sir," came the response.

"Sub Lieutenant Gresham, we will exercise the men in recovering a casualty at sea. Organise a party and have the rib prepared," ordered Curtis.

"Yes, sir," replied Gresham. "May I ask who we are recovering, sir?"

"There is a Dan-buoy in the water ahead of us. We will recover that and any body that is with it, but it is to be done as if it was a member of crew gone overboard."

"Yes sir," said Gresham, saluting and leaving the bridge to get his rescue party organised and the rib ready for lowering.

Ten minutes saw HMS *Port Carrick* standing to windward of the Dan-buoy, the minesweeper's 600 tonnes and 60 metres of hull creating a windbreak shielding the rescue exercise. The order to lower the rib and her crew of four acknowledged, the whirr of pulley blocks was easily heard above the wind. Once in the water and cast off with the outboard running, the craft surged forward then turned in an arc towards the buoy.

"Take it easy Jones, we are supposed to be rescuing a member of the crew, not running them down," rebuked Gresham.

"Sorry, sir," said Jones, raising his eyebrows to his mate McBride, obviously not impressed or interested in the training.

Alongside the buoy, Sub Lieutenant Gresham took some minutes looking around for any hapless sailor then ordered the exercise to start. "Now I want you to treat this device as if it were a crew member and unconscious. We can assume that the man is wearing a lifejacket and that it is inflated and he is lying face up in the water."

Looking around Gresham picked on Jones again. "What do we do now, Jones?"

"Grab hold and pull it out, sir," Jones said, with something of a cocky smirk on his face and looking round at the others.

"No, Jones, we don't just grab hold and pull it out. Over the side with you, then as we get you back on board, I suggest that you listen very carefully to the instructions so that you can recite them when we recover the Dan-buoy," ordered Gresham, pleased with the opportunity to take Jones down a peg or two.

"But sir," Jones started, only to be stopped in his tracks by Able Seaman Kelsey.

"Get on with it, Taffy, otherwise the skipper will get annoyed and we'll all be in trouble." Kelsey's look left no doubt that in those circumstances Jones would receive more than a fair share of any punishment.

With a mumble of protest Jones slid into the water. "Jesus Christ, it's cold," he said, and then with a pop and a hiss his lifejacket inflated, taking him completely by surprise. "Shit, what's happening?" His face a picture of fear and alarm.

The others roared with laughter as Jones started to flounder about. "Pull yourself together, you big girl's blouse," Kelsey growled.

"Right, fun over," said Gresham. "Kelsey, you take hold of the collar and bring Jones to the side facing aft. Now take hold of him under the armpits, you'll have to sit straddling the side tank to get the reach, that's it. Atkins, you hold onto Kelsey to help pull the weight. Now McBride, you reach under his knees and raise him so that he's almost flat in the water; you'll also need to straddle the tank. Now both of you lift him onboard."

The weight of Jones when soaked caught them all by surprise and it was with some effort that they finally got Jones onboard. "There gentlemen, you can see that it is not the easiest of tasks," said Gresham. "There is a towel in that bag, Jones. Now quickly explain to the others what it is they have to do, then we can all get back to the ship and dry off."

His instructions given to Gresham's satisfaction and the Dan-buoy recovered, the rib motor was put in gear and with McBride at the helm, powered back towards the *Carrick*.

"Sir." It was Jones, muffled in the towel but holding the Dan-buoy and pointing to the name painted on the float.

"Yes, Jones, what is it?" said Gresham, half concentrating on Jones and half on their approach to the minesweeper.

"It's the name on this buoy, sir. I think I read about it in the papers back in Gib. The boat went down and a whole family drowned." Jones' voice was filled with awe by the thought.

"You sure Jones? I thought that happened in the English Channel," replied Gresham. "We can check when we get back on board. Easy there. Get that stern line, McBride."

"Casualty recovered, sir, and rib lifted in," reported Gresham fifteen minutes later.

"You appeared to take your time out there," commented Curtis. "Any problems?"

"No sir, I just thought it would be better if we recovered a real person and Jones volunteered, sir," said Gresham.

"Oh did he now. That's a first. Well carry on, Sub," said Curtis with a knowing smile.

"Just one more thing, sir. Jones says he recognised the name of the boat that the buoy came from," said Gresham. "*Kiboko.*" Does it mean anything to you, sir?"

"Yes, it does," replied Curtis. "It's the name of one of the two yachts that sank each other off Alderney ten days or so ago. The only reason that I remember it is that the name is Swahili for Hippo." He stood quite still, his hand to his forehead as if trying to recall something. "Yes, strange business, life raft and clothes recovered but no sign of much wreckage or, come to that, many bodies. Take over here, Jack, whilst I get a message to the Admiralty. By the way, was anything else floating about out there?"

"No, sir," said Gresham, and with a nod Curtis left the bridge.

Gresham watched Curtis leave, then, turning to Lieutenant Jack Gould, asked, "How did he know that it was a Swahili name?"

"His parents were British High Commission in Kenya when he was a lad. I remember him telling me one evening," Gould replied. "Shouldn't you be checking the stowage of the rib?"

The report Lieutenant Commander Curtis made to the Admiralty gave the position of the recovery and the tie-up with the yacht sinking in the Channel. Eventually the information was passed to HM Coastguard who in turn copied it to Solent Station.

It was John Longford's watch and on seeing the message come up on the screen, he immediately picked up the phone and dialled Phil Saints' number. "Phil, it's John," he said, speaking to Phil's answerphone. "Just got a message from HQ saying that the minesweeper HMS *Port Carrick* recovered a Dan-buoy from a yacht named *Kiboko* out in the Atlantic at position 45 degrees 21 north and 15 degrees 42 west. Thought you might be interested. Speak to you later." Putting the phone down he stood and was about to take the news through to Harold Blakemore when he realised that Harold was away at the conference and would not be back until the Thursday. Hurriedly he tapped into the web and getting up a chart of the North Atlantic, he pinpointed the position of the find and sat staring for some moments before printing off the chart and putting it into Phil's message tray. Thoughts about Phil's mystery would have to wait until later as the evening was proving to be very busy indeed with already two lifeboats out to vessels with engine failure in the rough weather. All three watch officers were fully committed. The helicopter 'Whiskey Bravo' was put on standby, in case the powerboat, in trouble off St Katherine's Point, got too close to the rocks before a tow could be passed. It had been nearly two weeks of bad weather with one storm front following another, more than enough to keep the country's Coastguard stations at full stretch.

"Yarmouth has got a line aboard that powerboat off St Kat's," reported Katy Masters, the station's one and only female watch officer. "Do you want me to stand 'Whiskey Bravo' down or would you rather wait to see what happens off the Nab?"

"We had better wait," said John. "Look at the rain lashing at that window – that'll knock Harold's roses about."

The waiting proved unnecessary as the other boat in trouble miraculously got her engines going just before the Bembridge Lifeboat came alongside.

"Who forgot to turn the fuel switch on?" sung Katy as she waltzed to make a round of coffees.

"We did ask about that, I hope," said John.

"Yes," said Alec, "as soon as they first radioed in, but I was not that confident that they knew where the switch was."

"Not a good time to go looking for it and then have to learn how to bleed the system," said John. "The sea gives you some hard lessons."

"Solent Coastguard, Solent Coastguard, Solent Coastguard. This is container ship Pulsar, Pulsar, Pulsar. Are you receiving me, over?"

"Pulsar, this is Solent Coastguard. If your traffic is routine go to channel 67, over." Katy's voice was calm and clear as she moved sideways to the AIS screen and clicked onto the flashing green arrow that indicated the transmitting target.

This latest device in their operations room had already proved its worth. Through a separate aerial the computer received transmitted signals from all large commercial vessels passing up and down the English Channel. These gave the ship's position, course and speed together with information about the vessel's size, her cargo and crew numbers. This information appeared overlaid on a chart of the Solent sector, giving the watch officers an immediate understanding of the vessel's location and the opportunity of ensuring a rapid risk assessment if the vessel was in trouble.

"Solent Coastguard, this is Pulsar going 67," replied Pulsar.

There was a pause then, "Solent Coastguard, this is Pulsar channel 67."

"Pulsar this is Solent Coastguard over."

Solent Coastguard, we have received wave damage to our cargo off Selsey Bill and have three containers loose. We are making for shelter off Isle of Wight but think we may lose some containers before reaching calm water, over."

"Pulsar, this is Solent Coastguard, your situation noted, is the cargo shift affecting or likely to affect your vessel's stability, over?" again her voice calm. Katy had received many calls of this nature.

"Solent Coastguard this is Pulsar, er, no, vessel stable at this time."

"Pulsar, this is Solent Coastguard, roger, we will continue to monitor your progress on AIS and via channel 16 and 67; if your situation worsens please call direct on channel 67."

Solent Coastguard was able to dual watch on both the emergency and call up channel 16, as well as the working channel of 67. By keeping a watch for Pulsar on 67 it avoided the repetition of channel redirection and would keep the all-important channel 16 open for other emergencies. In this instance there was not much more to be done, unless a container did go over the side, in which case a navigation warning to other vessels in the area would be issued. When the radio exchange had been completed, Katy phoned HQ to alert the duty surveyor and check on tug availability should Pulsar's situation deteriorate.

"Solent Coastguard, Solent Coastguard, Solent Coastguard, this is Bembridge Lifeboat, we are escorting motor boat Bonnie Lass into Bembridge Harbour, over."

"Bembridge Lifeboat, Solent Coastguard, message understood, out."

All three watch officers eased back in their seats and relaxed a bit but still maintained that professional monitoring of the airwaves, awaiting the next call.

Phil Saints returned to duty at 0400 hours on Thursday, and was sitting with John Longford for ten minutes, taking over the watch.

"Thanks for that message you left on the answerphone, by the way," Phil said. "If it's from the same yacht it would bear out my theory that the incident was not kosher."

"I printed out a chart of the sea area and marked the position the Dan-buoy was in when they recovered it," said John. "It's over in your tray if you're interested."

"Better look at it later; there is obviously a lot going on," replied Phil. "Who's following that missing dog walker?"

"Glen, he's monitoring the search team out there looking. What kind of idiot walks their dog along the cliffs at night in weather like this, I ask you?" John said, his exasperation with Joe Public showing through.

The cold front following the gales earlier in the week had brought cold conditions for the time of year, made more unpleasant by a series of heavy rainsqualls and gusty wind conditions. Typically small boats were using the gap between the storms to return to their home ports or make the dash away for a few days' early break. This frequently meant that the crews were not properly worked up after the winter break and items aboard, such as the standing rigging that should have received attention over the winter months, broke at critical moments. The result was the normal crop of call-outs for the RNLI to deal with as well as the inshore volunteer craft.

Like John, Phil found his shift to be a busy one, with no time to spare for the mystery of *Kiboko* and her fate until shortly after 1100 hours, when he took the opportunity of an apparently quiet five minutes, to grab a sandwich, a cup of coffee and look at the Atlantic chart John had printed off for him. He was unaware of Harold Blakemore standing behind him until he was tapped on the shoulder.

"Can you come into my office," Blakemore said with a tone of command, turning and leading the way before Phil could respond.

As Phil entered Blakemore's office at the head of the stairs, he was instructed to close the door but not invited to take a seat.

"Phil, I do not like to do this but I'm afraid I must. You have been spending time chasing shadows regarding that sinking two weeks ago. I told you at the time we are far too busy here to involve ourselves in matters that the French are more than capable of dealing with. So, I am ordering you now to forget about that business and get on with the job in hand. God knows there is enough on our plate at the moment." Blakemore delivered this seated at his desk, his right hand slapping the leather top to emphasise each sentence.

Annoyed at the totally unfair reprimand, Phil replied, "I was just taking the first break I have had since coming on at 4 o'clock this morning and was just going through the contents of my in-tray."

"Be that as it may, I do not want any of my staff wasting any further time on this incident," said Blakemore, obviously wanting to end the interview there.

"Did you see the report from HQ regarding the recovery of the Dan-buoy?" asked Phil, wanting to push the subject further to convince Blakemore that it was a suspicious incident.

"Yes, and I repeat that it is the business of the French authorities, not ours, now that is all," Blakemore retorted, opening a drawer in his desk, pulling out a file and starting to read it.

Phil was about to continue the argument when there was a knock at the door and Glen's head appeared.

"Just had news about the dog walker, Phil. Not good I'm afraid; he's been found dead in some bushes." Glen's expression was sad.

"I'll come straight away," said Phil, making for the door.

"See what I mean," said Blakemore, taking the opportunity to force his point home. "We have too much to do without chasing around making work."

Ignoring Blakemore, Phil followed Glen back to the operations room. "OK," he said. "Give me the details."

The dog walker had taken the cliff path as feared but had not fallen. Initial reports indicated that he had had a heart attack, collapsed and died, his body discovered near the path in some bushes by another dog walker. Phil sat musing on the report thinking of something that Katy had said some weeks ago – what was it now, oh yes – 'If you own a dog it's almost certain you will find a dead body.'

Chapter 5

The full force of the gale did not hit him until he got down to the harbour itself and now leaning into it he struggled to put one foot in front of the other. Glancing up to check the direction of his heading he caught sight of his client sheltering beside a quayside stall. On seeing Stavos the man moved from the shelter to join him. "You are late," he said accusingly. "I not like people who are late."

Stavos glared at the young Japanese who had hired him. After so many years of mixing with the dregs of humanity he had learnt not to try and understand their motivation. Most of them appeared to be reacting in fear rather than logic; with this one it was pure arrogance.

"Have you been to sea much before?" he yelled, his voice hardly discernible above the shriek of the gale.

"Yes – many time I have." The reply, obviously a lie, was spoken hesitantly.

"I say we wait two days," shouted Stavos, "for this to blow over. Then we can…"

"We go now!" The young Japanese turned on Stavos. "I pay you leave today, my people wait out there."

Stavos tried again. "It is too dangerous to put to sea in weather like this and we will draw attention to ourselves."

"Murata-san will be much angry you do not go, he rely on you, he say you are able seaman." Though shouting above the storm his voice conveyed a sneer that angered Stavos.

"Okay, we go. You sick on my bridge and I will kick you over the side."

The pair struggled on until Stavos stopped alongside a battered-looking fishing vessel. Old and tired as it looked, its engines were some of the best maintained in the Atlantic and for a vessel of its size there was nothing to beat its sea-keeping qualities. Built in Norway for operation off the Icelandic coast, Stavos had bought her for well below her real value when the British owner's business went under due to EU fishing quotas. Funded in advance for two of Murata-san's arms shipments, Stavos had got the engines into tip-top condition and improved the ballast ratio significantly, enhancing the stability in rough seas. The loss in catch quantity did not bother him as his 'fish' were generally of high value.

Leaping on board required excellent and practised timing, neither of which Teiji Yamamoto possessed. Following Stavos, he had leapt when the boat was on its way down, so endured a long drop before meeting the deck as it started to come up. Yamamoto's legs folded under the impact and he crashed in a heap, in danger of going over the side. Stavos grabbed him and dragged him to the foot of the bridge ladder.

"You been to sea many times, eh! You try to break your neck when you should stay ashore and help cast off." Stavos, shaking his head in disgust, stepped over Yamamoto and clambered up to the bridge to start the engines.

It took twenty minutes for Stavos to set up a single beam slip and cast off the bow and stern warps after clearing the springs. Back in the wheelhouse he scanned the quayside and Port Captain's office through binoculars to check if they had aroused any interest, but no one could be seen and he hoped that the weather had kept everyone at home. Descending the bridge steps again, he pulled Yamamoto to his feet and said, "When I say go, you undo the warp on that bollard and then pull all of it onboard, you understand?" A pale Yamamoto nodded and bent to pick up the loose tail of the warp in readiness.

After a few minutes of preparation and a careful study of the wave pattern, Stavos strode to the bridge wing door and yelled, "Okay, go!"

Furiously the youth hauled on the warp until it was all lying in an untidy heap on the side deck. Stavos put power to the bow thrusters, threw the port engine hard astern and pushed the starboard engine throttle lever ahead, forcing the vessel away from the harbour wall. Cancelling the bow thrusters and balancing both engines ahead, the boat slipped out of the harbour, climbing and sliding over the heavy swell hidden by the torrential rain.

Once clear, however, she was no longer the dominator of the element on which she rode; out in the full teeth of the gale she was like a rodeo cowhand trying desperately to stay on.

After his exertions with the warp, Yamamoto had struggled up the bridge ladder and stumbled into the wheelhouse. Spying a bucket in the corner, he rushed over to it and slumped down, already retching from the motion.

Stavos studied a piece of paper with latitude and longitude written on it that his passenger had thrust into his hand as they had approached the boat. Keeping a watchful eye on the sea he stole several glances at Admiralty Chart 1950 on the table alongside his steering position. "Allah preserve me, two hundred miles in this," he said, fumbling in his pocket and pulling out a bent cigarette which he lit before fixing his gaze on the tumultuous seas ahead.

In the corner of the wheelhouse Teiji Yamamoto heaved again and for the hundredth time wished he had not lied to Murata-san about his sailing experience.

Son of 'The Banker', Japanese Red Army leader Shigenori Yamamoto, Teiji was a mere shadow of his father. His relationship to the Japanese Red Army through his father kept him separated from a normal upbringing. He was a sensitive child who was open to bullying as he cried easily. Mercilessly goaded by his father, he hid from him whenever possible. At the age of twelve his father disowned him and he clung to his mother until her untimely death in the same hotel fire in which

Murata-san received his terrible burns. His mother's photograph he carried always, keeping the negative in a safe deposit box of a London bank.

Even after the split with his father the man's reputation with the enforcers of law and order worldwide dogged his own existence. After his mother's death he drifted to Europe where he was eventually taken on by Murata-san. The route to this employment had been pure karma. Arriving in London with little English, he was reduced to begging for a job as a barman/waiter in a Japanese restaurant in the city area where Japanese businessmen entertained influential guests. Quite by chance little Yukiko, lunching in the restaurant with her English boyfriend, had spotted him and reported his presence in London to Murata-san. Nothing would have come of it had the disaster at Bosham Creek not happened and the kidnappings not been forced on them. Murata knew that the risk of having Ian aboard was high and needed to replace him as soon as possible. Hence the operation to re-victual the yacht at sea and the opportunity to bring onboard a loyal crew member and dispose of a potential threat.

Onboard the fishing vessel the barometer was still falling, and as the stout craft battled its way northwards to the rendezvous point, Stavos threw a glance at the youth.

"You are here only because Murata sent you," he said, his voice a contemptuous tone. "Murata good customer of mine; we have shipped guns, explosives, even women.

"He pays well and until now never no fuss," he paused and then said, "had anyone else asked me to take you I would have handed back the money and told you to piss off."

For Stavos this was a strange shipment – no cargo to speak of except a few boxes of provisions, drinking water and diesel and two sail bags stuffed with second-hand sails. Then this useless boy, with a briefcase and sailing kit that had obviously never been worn before.

Stavos was first and foremost a seaman and despite the outward appearance of his vessel and carefully presented personal appearance, behind the facade everything was clean and shipshape. Over the years he had learnt that even officialdom does not come aboard if the decks have a few rotting fish on them and are happy to check papers over the side rail. Those that did make it to the bridge were never invited any further and therefore missed the warmth and neatness of his cabin and white painted spotless condition of the engine room. A natural part of his seamanship was the stowing of warps and he suddenly remembered that Yamamoto had taken onboard the last one. Picking his moment carefully he dived across to the starboard side and looked down onto the deck, diving back again to put the vessel port side to the wave train and set her up to lie ahull. His glance down had revealed that the warp was trailing in the water and risked being wrapped around the propellers or rudders. At any time such a happening would be dangerous, but in these seas it could be fatal.

The twelve steps down to the deck were more like twelve miles down a rock face; twice his feet were washed from under him before he could grab a loop of the warp and drag it back up the steps to the wheelhouse door. Bracing himself in the corner between the wing guard rail and the wheelhouse itself, he hauled in the warp, coiling it onto the deck before seizing the coil with the tail and dragging it into the wheelhouse.

Dropping the warp on the deck he rushed at the youth kicking him hard in the ribs and screaming, "You have never been to sea before. You are a landlubber, useless, stupid and bloody dangerous!"

The last sentence seemed to sting the youth for he flinched and then, with almost unseeing eyes went for a gun inside his jacket.

Even as the gun cleared the holster Stavos was there grasping the wrist and holding a knife at Yamamoto's throat.

"You don't talk to me that way!" Yamamoto screamed back totally unaware of the presence of the knife. "I am samurai, I will kill you if you speak to me like that again. You will show respect!"

Stavos ripped the gun from his hand, dragged the youth to his feet then hit him with a clubbing blow, letting him drop unconscious to the deck. Quickly he padded the youth over and removed a knife and hand grenade, together with wallet, passport and photographs of two women. Pocketing the gun, he hid the knife and grenade before studying the photographs and putting them, the wallet and passport back into Yamamoto's pocket.

Back at the wheel Stavos got the vessel underway again, then divided his time between steering a safe course and sorting through the contents of Yamamoto's briefcase. This was very revealing as it produced about $200,000 in used $50 bills, a series of Italian and French passports, all with American visas and two sets of yacht registration papers, one completed, the other left blank. A small packet at the bottom of the case held a box of typeset and a frame, obviously for completing the second set of registration papers when required.

Retching, the youth regained consciousness. Gathering his wits he then glared at Stavos before crawling hurriedly to the bucket. "You will pay for such action, gaijin," he threatened. "I am trusted member of Murata-san's special group, he does not allow such insult."

"I tremble at the thought," sneered Stavos. "Maybe you want to swim rest of way, eh?

"Why does Allah test me so much? Do I not keep Ramadan? Do I not pray?" cried Stavos. To him, what had looked like a good deal was rapidly turning sour. His thoughts skipped to Fatia, comforting his brain with her memory, only to be reminded that she was not onboard and he would have to cook only Allah knows what.

Laying the ship ahull again, he made his way down to his cabin beneath the bridge then to the port side into the galley. Hurriedly he grabbed a round loaf of bread, some cheese and a chunk of cold lamb and jammed them into a plastic container. Holding the container in his left hand, he clutched two litre bottles of water under his arm and made his way back to the bridge. Placing his hoard on the shelf above the chart table, he put the vessel back on course.

"Here, you will need to drink this," Stavos said, as he quickly passed a bottle of the water to Yamamoto.

North-east of Stavos and his hapless crew, Ian was just going off watch, Hamaura taking her turn at the wheel. As Ian peeled off his heavy weather jacket he studied the chart, noting the rhumb line drawn to a rendezvous about two hundred miles north-east of the Azores. His stomach went queasy as the implication of what might await him there dawned upon him. A rendezvous with another vessel could well mean a replacement member of crew and it would be very unlikely that he would be paid off in the normal way for his services. Now that Arni would follow Hamaura on the wheel, there was no chance of him steering the boat off course and them missing the rendezvous point. The stupidity of that thought struck him immediately; Arni would make absolutely certain that the two vessels met. To continue with a hostage aboard presented far too many risks. Ian's guess was that the two boats would be in radio range of each other by midday and probably alongside by early evening. His estimate of the timing was only slightly adrift as he was woken from his troubled sleep by the voice of Hamaura on the boat's VHF set at 1300 hours.

91

"Stavos, Stavos, this Kinoko Kumo, repeat Kinoko Kumo, over." Hamaura, sitting at the chart table microphone in hand, drummed her fingers on the tabletop impatiently. Her call-up received no response so she tried again. "Stavos, Stavos, this Kinoko Kumo, Kinoko Kumo, are you receiving, over?" When there was still no response she thrust the microphone back onto its clip, rose and stepped up the companionway ladder. "We are in the wrong place. There is no response from Stavos," she said accusingly.

"Why blame me every time?" Arni replied with some hostility. "You think always my fault, maybe this Stavos not so hot at navigation eh, you not think of that?"

"Murata-san, he says Stavos brilliant seaman and his boat has GPS so he won't be wrong." With that she turned and came back into the cabin. "Hakuchi gai-jin," she shouted, then threw herself down onto the starboard settee.

Ian, feigning sleep, was now trying to piece together what he had heard. When there was no reply his heart had soared, as this presented the possibility that Arni was not the great navigator he professed to be and they had missed their target. In fairness to Arni the weather conditions and movement of the boat did not aid accurate navigation, though Arni had been able to take a noonday sight with the sextant. Ian knew that as good as a sextant was, a one second delay in picking up the point of the sun's zenith could put them out a nautical mile in calculation of longitude, also, that the timing error could be several seconds on a boat sailing through large waves. The large seas would also make it difficult to measure the angle of the sun to the horizon, thus affecting the accuracy of their latitude.

"Stavos, Stavos, this Kinoko Kumo, Kinoko Kumo, are you receiving, over?" Ten minutes had passed since her first call. Ian listened anxiously but there was no response. After two more attempts she again gave up and sat cursing quietly to herself.

Ian was now thinking about how to stay alive. With the prospect that an eventual meeting would take place, he was pretty certain that he would be killed. His captors were both scrupulous in keeping their weaponry out of his reach; even when he was in the galley with the chance of stealing a knife his movements were closely watched. Even with a knife his chances of being able to strike a blow would be virtually nil, as both Hamaura and Arni had demonstrated their cat-like reactions and awesome hitting power.

On board Stavos's fishing vessel Teiji Yamamoto was in a bad way. In spite of instructions from Stavos he had not drunk any of the water and was now suffering from dehydration, exacerbating his seasickness. Stavos, though aware of this, was unable to leave the wheel for long enough to deal with Yamamoto and still get to his rendezvous on time. Only as the dawn had come did it appear that the wind conditions were easing and even then the seas were still mountainous. He knew that at 1300 hours Hamaura would start transmitting in order to help make the rendezvous, and he knew he was behind schedule. The vessel was only making ten knots over the ground and the rendezvous point was just over one hundred miles away. Assuming that the yacht was on schedule he would be unlikely to make contact until 1500 hours. Looking again at the slumped figure in the corner of the wheelhouse, Stavos prayed that the seas calmed quickly so that he could apply the autohelm and be free to attend to Yamamoto. Even if he got him on his feet again there was no doubt that he would be completely useless on a small yacht. What was he to do – should he warn Hamaura that this boy was of no use, or should he let her find out for herself? He glanced again at the youth and in the gathering light could not see any signs of life. Stavos took a chance and set the autohelm, watched for a couple of minutes to check that it was coping with the seas, then moved across to the boy and bending down to him, pulled his head up from his chest. The dull stare from the eyes said it all. Alive, yes, but in no fit state for a transfer at sea. Pulling the water bottle from behind the boy's shoulder, he undid the cap and tipped a mouthful or so into the boy's mouth. The effect was a choking cough that sprayed most of what had been swallowed back at Stavos. Cursing, he tried again, this time with more success. Over the next ten minutes he coaxed almost all of the bottle's contents into the youth before propping him securely back into the corner. Then disaster struck; the autohelm had been coping remarkably well with the confused seas but a double punch from two waves off the port bow left the boat open to the large wave which struck her squarely on the beam, laying her right over. The impact caught Stavos completely off balance and sent him flying across the bridge to hit the starboard side of the wheelhouse, knocking the wind out of him. In the same instant the youth was also flung across to the starboard side, his right foot striking Stavos high on his left cheek with such force that it instantly started to swell. Stunned and aware that his boat was not recovering, Stavos instinctively pulled himself up and, looking astern into the fish hold, he saw that the trawl beam had broken free of its securing hangers and was dangling only by its cable. As he watched, the vessel started to right itself but as it did so the trawl beam cable started to pay out from the drum as the beam disappeared into the sea. If he could not get to the brake in time to stop it paying out altogether it could well rip the cable drum and frame out of the deck and expose the engine room below. Using the railing along the wheelhouse stern to pull himself up, he gained the porthand wing door, then went out onto the weather side where he was struck by another large wave. Holding on for dear life he managed to reach the deck before the next wave to come on board washed him across to the starboard side. From there he made his way back to the cable drum. On reaching it he hauled on the brake lever as hard as he could; as the seconds passed smoke from friction on the brake pads billowed out of the housing. Eventually his efforts slowed the spin of the drum sufficient for it not to be dangerous and when the cable was finally run out the impact was small. He now had to get the cable wound in again, which meant returning to the bridge to start the deck drum engine, then a return to the deck to operate the cable lay lever that ensured the cable wound evenly on the drum.

Two hours later, after receiving several more cuts and bruises, Stavos was back on the bridge and able to get his breath back. The swelling from Yamamoto's flailing foot had all but closed his left eye, and the back of his head, where it had hit the wheelhouse side, had a lump the size of a walnut and was badly cut. Now breathing less heavily, he glanced across to where Yamamoto lay. A pool of blood indicated that the youth had sustained some significant injury when he had been flung across the bridge, but he was still alive and aware of his condition as he was holding his handkerchief in a ball against his right forearm. The seas, now much calmer than two hours before, meant that the risks of autohelm control were negligible, enabling Stavos to go below to his cabin for the first aid box. On his return he checked the GPS position and marked it on the chart, then turning to Yamamoto he moved the hand holding the blood-soaked handkerchief away to reveal a deep wide gash. Moving the arm to get a better view brought a yell of pain from the youth, revealing that the arm was almost certainly broken. Stavos, with as much care as he could, cut away the sleeves of the jacket and shirt then cleaned the wound. A ruler from the chart table provided a splint and, with a thick dressing to plug the gash and tape to secure everything in place, he stood back to admire his work. Not pretty, but it would do.

"I think you will be coming back with me," he said to Yamamoto. "No way could you be any help on a yacht." The youth looked back at him with a look of sadness that implied a deep sense of utter failure. For the first time since their meeting

Stavos understood the importance that this boy attached to the task that Murata-san had given him.

By 1500 hours, two hours after the rendezvous time, Stavos's boat was still fifty miles away from the meeting point. He now had a problem of fuel consumption, as throughout the previous day and night the engines had been working hard but progress had been very slow. The amount of fuel used meant that he now had to reduce speed to conserve sufficient for the return voyage. There was nothing he could do about it; they would just have to wait or anticipate his track and sail down it in the hope of meeting him. Decision made, he went below and prepared a meal.

At 1700 hours Hamaura unclipped the radio microphone again and thumbed the transmission button. "Stavos, Stavos, this Kinoko Kumo, repeat Kinoko Kumo, over." Again silence followed so she repeated the transmission. It was several seconds later that Stavos's voice was heard.

"Kinoko Kumo, Kinoko Kumo, this is Stavos, repeat Stavos, over."

"Stavos, Stavos, go to channel 8 and wait, over," instructed Hamaura.

"Channel 8 understood, over," he responded, reaching for the channel selector knob.

Switching to channel 8, Hamaura spoke into the microphone again. "Stavos, Stavos, give your position, over."

"I have been delayed by very bad weather and I have problem with passenger. So we now 27 miles south-west of meeting place on bearing 210 degrees, over." Stavos looked up at the speaker as if to see the voice response coming back.

"Wait one," was all he heard for some time then the radio crackled again and Hamaura came through. "We think you maybe ten miles south of us. We change course and will put up white flare in half hour's time, over."

"Which course you wan' me to steer, over?" Stavos replied.

Again a period of silence followed before Hamaura instructed, "Stavos, you steer 010 degree."

On the fishing vessel Stavos acknowledged the change of course then turned to check on Yamamoto. The youth was indeed very weak and had a greeny pallor about him that did not look good. Every time the vessel rolled he would let out a moan but he had stopped being sick.

"What do I do with you, eh? Do I send you over to yacht or do I take you back Horta." Stavos looked down at the pathetic figure at his feet. The mention of Horta had produced a shake of the head indicating that the youth still wanted to be transferred.

In the last few hours the wind had abated and already the seas were much calmer. Even so, going alongside the yacht would be out of the question and Stavos had already decided that he would load his vessel's rib with the stores and drift it downwind to the yacht first. Then if Hamaura still wanted the boy, he would haul the rib back and place him in it and stream the rib again.

Having thought the transfer through he returned to the bridge window and started to scan the horizon for the flare.

Exactly on the dot of the half hour Stavos caught in the corner of his eye the dying glow of the flare. Carefully he swung the vessel onto a course of 160 and increased speed. Setting the autohelm again, he reached for the microphone. "Kinoko Kumo, Kinoko Kumo, this is Stavos, repeat Stavos, over."

"Stavos, Stavos, this is Kinoko Kumo, did you see our flare, over?" This time it was a man's voice.

"I think I just saw so please do again." Stavos wanted to make absolutely sure before he went too far on the new course.

A minute passed, then straight ahead of him he saw clearly the flare go up and reported his sighting.

As the two vessels drew closer together Stavos explained his plan for the transfer and was pleased that Hamaura was in agreement. Then came the tricky business of explaining about Yamamoto.

"Kinoko Kumo, my passenger is not good stomach for the sea and has been very ill through storm. I think maybe best he go back with me Horta and you forget about him," he explained.

"We need him here, it is very important he take over some work for us," came the response from Hamaura.

"He will not be any use to you as I think he break arm in the storm and he no good sailor," Stavos said, now not wanting to get any blame for wasting her time.

"We will make decision when he come aboard," was her reply and with a shrug of the shoulders Stavos set about making preparations.

The rib was a semi-rigid inflatable made by Avon and Stavos was very pleased with it. Three and a half metres in length, it could take a twenty-five horsepower outboard and was very quick and stable. He loaded it with the boxes of provisions, two five-gallon cans of fuel and some spares as listed by Murata-san. Saving the second-hand sails and water for the second drift, Stavos linked up the davit frame ready to launch the rib over the vessel's side. Finally he attached a long painter to the rib's bow ring then, running the tail round the trawl beam streaming winch, left the coil on the side deck, tying the end to the spare net locker handle.

Back on the bridge Stavos switched on the aft deck lights and shaking Yamamoto, said, "It is time for you to get ready, we must be close to them now so you look smart, eh?"

The boy tried to stand but his legs gave way and he slumped back down on the deck groaning in pain. "They say you gotta go so you get ready and I will carry down to the deck," said Stavos, handing Yamamoto a wet cloth. "Wipe your face with this and clean up the front of your jacket." The youth wiped his face and dabbed at his sailing jacket, neither activity creating much improvement in his appearance.

Stavos scanned the horizon with binoculars, picked up the masthead light of the yacht and adjusted his course to bring the yacht downwind of his boat by twenty metres or so. The final approach seemed to happen quite suddenly and Stavos found himself having to do a hurried turn to avoid being carried down onto the yacht.

Aboard *Kiboko* Arni and Ian had prepared the yacht for the rendezvous, dropping the sails and streaming a sea anchor to slow their downwind progress. As the fishing vessel came and lay abeam upwind of them, Ian was surprised to see only one person working the davits and lowering a rib over the vessel's side. He watched in silence as the man on the trawler's deck used a boathook to release the davit frame and let the rib float away on the wind towards *Kiboko*.

With a shove Arni propelled Ian onto the yacht's side deck. "You take those boxes out of the rib and put them on the side deck," he ordered, reinforcing the instruction with a wave of his automatic. The only assistance he gave was to lift the fuel cans.

Climbing down into the rib, Ian was disappointed to find that it was engineless, even the oars had been removed. Timing his moves skilfully, he loaded the boxes onto the side deck as instructed, noting that it was mostly food stores, the fuel, a briefcase and a few spares. Climbing back on board the yacht he was ordered to take the boxes below and stow the contents. As he carried the third box into the cockpit he turned and saw the man on the trawler struggling down the ladder from the wheelhouse with a bright orange load flung over his right shoulder. Reaching the deck he put the item down, leaning it against the wheelhouse structure; it was then Ian realised that it was another man.

"Hey, get on with those boxes," came Arni's order accompanied by a painful kick in the thigh.

Obediently Ian returned to his task with a slight ray of hope. From the limited opportunity he had of assessing the newcomer it was obvious that he was not going to be of much use in sailing the yacht. Piecing together the little he had heard of the radio conversation and what he had just seen, Ian now thought he might survive a little while longer.

It was some time before Ian felt the rib thump the side of the yacht again and he had almost completed the task of stowing the food. On deck there was some commotion as Arni laid on the side deck to reach down and grab the two sail bags from the rib.

"Hamaura-san, you come and look at this," shouted Arni.

Hamaura had been checking through the spares, obviously searching for something in particular. "What is it, can't you do anything on your own?" she shouted back, not even looking up.

"This is important, come now," Arni insisted.

"Wait, I think some spares are missing," she responded. "They are very important." Opening another small box her expression changed and putting the box carefully into her toolbox, she shot Ian a glare and went on deck. "What is it now – oh my God."

"What do we do now?" asked Arni.

"We have no choice; we carry on with what we had before," she replied.

"OK, I send him back," Arni said, starting to wave to the trawler.

"No," Hamaura said, grabbing his arm and forcing it down. "He is useless and will be problem for Stavos at Horta."

"Well, he will be useless here," said Arni with some conviction.

"I know he will, that is why he won't be here," she said, stepping down into the cockpit and calling to Ian, "Come up here quickly."

Not having heard clearly any of the conversation on deck Ian froze, his legs almost giving way. Holding onto the galley he took several deep breaths before slowly making his way to the companionway steps, his mind racing with ideas that were rejected as soon as they appeared. He looked round, his eyes taking in the most incredible details of his surroundings, everything in the most intense colour. At that moment he realised that he felt no emotions at all, for now his wife and children would die also, and all he had tried to do to save them was worthless. With a feeling of complete emptiness he looked up into the cockpit and saw Hamaura waiting like the executioner at the block, and these few steps his walk to the scaffold.

On the second step she grabbed his left ear, dragging him fully into the cockpit and across to the port side where he could see into the rib. There, laid in the bottom of the craft, was an oriental man in his early to mid thirties. The sling on his arm showed he was injured and by the green pallor of his face and the state of his clothes, he was also very seasick.

As Ian stood awaiting the probable order to help get the man aboard, thoughts of how he could drown Arni if the two of them were to stand in the bobbing and unsteady rib were forming in his mind.

Then from the corner of his eye he saw Hamaura draw a small-bore pistol from inside her jacket and shoot the man twice in the head.

Turning to a stunned Ian she said, "You cause any trouble and you go same way." Then pushing past him she went below and picking up the radio microphone said, "Stavos, Stavos, this Kinoko Kumo, Kinoko Kumo, over." There was a few minutes' pause as Stavos was seen scrambling up the wheelhouse ladder to the radio.

"Kinoko Kumo, this is Stavos," came the breathless reply.

"Tell the supplier that his meat was rotten and had to be disposed of, out," and with that she hung up the microphone and ordered, "Let's get underway; we have wasted too much time."

In his wheelhouse Stavos stood holding the microphone and stared out of the window towards the yacht, where he could see someone hauling on the sea anchor warp as the vessel drifted away. He descended to the deck level and hauled in the rib. By the time it was lifted inboard, the yacht had its mainsail hoisted to the first reef and turning westwards, settled to its new course with the crew setting a foresail.

Taking his time Stavos stepped into the rib and removing the clothing from Yamamoto's body, heaved the corpse over the side into the cold Atlantic. This would be his last job he decided; he would take Fa to the Canaries and live comfortably with her like husband and wife. No more risky business; he was getting too old. He would keep the rib with the two spent bullets embedded in the fibreglass bottom as a reminder, just in case he was ever tempted back to the old life.

Chapter 6

A few draws on the stem and the pipe was glowing well, clouds of aromatic scented smoke billowing up to be lost in the general fug around the bar ceiling light.

"Hey Phil, are you still on about those boats?" The speaker, a thickset foreman from the local boatyard, was getting more than a little bored by Phil Saints' constant questions and conjecture about the loss, three weeks earlier, of two yachts the other side of the Channel.

Another draw on the pipe and slow exhalation; Phil's penetrating blue eyes gleamed like steel across the bar. "Barry, my boy, events will prove me right, you'll see." Then turning, he fixed his gaze back onto the punk-style youth across the table from him.

"You said the big Beneteau with the fancy radar gear went aground and the Victoria pulled it off." Phil's gaze now fixed on the youth's eyes.

"Yeah, that's right. They towed it off then after a bit of leapin' backwards and forwards when they was bofe back on the buoy, they's ups and goes round to the quay; I fort they was gonna beach 'er there."

The youth sniffed loudly and wiped his nose on his sleeve, returning Phil's gaze through brown dull eyes.

"What happened then?" Phil asked.

"Dunno, me mate told me to pull the ne..." His voice, embarrassed, tailed off. "Anyways it was nun off my fuckin' business; what you want to know for anyway, they sunk out in the Channel mate, not 'ere."

"Never mind lad, never mind." Phil got up, his interview with the youth at an end. No way could he get any more, now that the illegal net fishing had slipped out.

Phil left the thick atmosphere of the bar, carrying his pint out into the still, warm evening. On the veranda overlooking Bosham Creek, he found Stella sitting on the parapet wall, her long sun-tanned legs dangling down above the gentle lapping water that made to the wall at high tide.

Following her gaze he made a clucking sound. "That must be the third car this year to be left parked below the high water mark," he said, looking at the rescue van's efforts to tow a car out of the water.

She turned, and from beneath her jet-black hair the warm brown eyes threw their net of tender caring over him. "Has Sherlock finished his evening's detections?" she asked lightly, swinging her legs back over the wall and slipping her arms around him.

"Yep, I've got what I came for," he said. "From what our young friend tells me, *Umi Sama* was put on the putty opposite the slipway along there, and I wouldn't mind betting sustained some damage to the hull then. You know I reckon there has been an act of piracy committed and that the other boat *Kiboko* is still about. Why I think this I just don't know, but my gut feeling tells me that this stinks like rotten fish."

"Is there a Mr Saints here of HM Coastguard?" shouted the landlord gazing around the bar, a telephone receiver in his hand.

"'E's outside, mate." It was the punk youth Phil had interviewed earlier. A few minutes passed before Phil, having had the message relayed to him, reached the phone.

"Saints."

"Ah, Phil, found you. Harold Blakemore here. It's about your mystery sinkings." Blakemore paused as though searching for the right words. "It appears as though you could have unearthed something. Can you come back to the station? I will be here."

"OK, I'm on my way. Do you mind if my wife comes with me, as taking her home is in the wrong direction?"

"No, of course not. Oh, by the way, I've got a couple of men from the Anti-Terrorist Branch in my office." Blakemore rang off.

As Phil drove back to the Coastguard Station he explained to Stella the events that had led up to the evening's summons.

"Oh you didn't, Phil," she said, when he told her that only two days after Blakemore's reprimand he had sent his report and comments to the police. "Blakemore won't like that one little bit. Fancy going over his head like that." After a few minutes thought she said, "Wish I'd been a fly on the wall when the two ATB men turned up."

"That's the thing," said Phil. "Blakemore was at home pruning his roses from about five o'clock this evening, so they must have called him back to the station. Can you imagine what Madeline would have said?"

"Well, I suppose I could go onto permanent nights until you get a new job. Or would it be more sensible to emigrate and change our names." As she said this, Stella turned to face him, her expression not all humour.

"I'm sorry, luv, I seem to have stepped over the mark with this I know, but it just kept nagging away at me." Stella glanced at him and chose not to respond, out of devilment more than anger.

After a few minutes of silence between them, Stella turned to him and asked, "What exactly did you put in that report to bring two ATB men down here at this time of day?"

"I simply laid out the facts as I knew them. I pointed out that it was very rare for both yachts in such an accident to sink, even rarer for both to go down so quickly. I also stated that in my opinion, if life rafts had been launched from both craft it would have been necessary for at least one member of crew to be on deck in each case, therefore at least one other body should have been found during the search. The location of the wreckage was wrong in relation to the pinpoint we had of the mayday signal. We agreed with the French on the location, but even allowing for the wind and tide I felt the wreckage was too far east. I also pointed out that *Kiboko*'s skipper was a qualified yacht master and his wife qualified to coastal skipper level. When I spoke to the Vaughans' friends who had seen them off from the Bosham yard, they had mentioned that the Vaughans' were going to stay one, maybe two nights on the Isle of Wight. Their traffic report the next morning stated that they were going straight to Cherbourg. Why would someone of their experience change their minds without telling anyone ashore of their revised passage plans? Finally I pointed out that the yacht *Umi Sama* had been hired out to a woman, said to be of oriental appearance and a man of Middle Eastern appearance. In our Traffic Report they only mentioned two persons aboard, so what was the body of an oriental male, with a broken leg, doing in the water close to the wreckage?" said Phil.

"You mentioned to me something about a Dan-buoy being found," Stella said.

"Yes, that finally clinched it for me, not that Harold was interested."

After a few moments she asked, "Why did you report it to the Anti-Terrorist Branch?"

"I didn't. I sent the report to the police; they must have passed it on. So little checked out regarding the two that hired *Umi Sama*, even their passport details turned out to be false," Phil replied.

"Oh, you didn't mention that before. How did you find out?" she asked.

"After the sinking the charter company made enquiries. Sadly it may well invalidate their insurance claim." Steering their car off the M27 towards Fareham, Phil thought again about the coming interview.

"Just one other thing," said Stella. "Then I will shut up and let you think. Are you the only person who thinks this sinking is dodgy?"

"I hope not," replied Phil. "I know both John and Glen have their doubts about it, but I'm the only one to push it."

Stella was silent but in a form of response, reached over and stroked his upper arm.

Leaving their car in a space almost opposite the Coastguard Station they crossed the road, entered through the code locked front doors and climbed the stairs to the operations level. Leaving Stella to walk along to the Operations Room, Phil stopped outside the first door on the left, knocked and entered.

Blakemore immediately broke off what he was saying to his guests. "Ah, Phil, you got here quickly. Let me introduce you to Commander Campbell and Inspector Jackson, both from the Anti-Terrorist Branch. This, gentlemen, is my Watch Manager, Phillip Saints."

As handshakes were exchanged Phil assessed the two men. Campbell, short, wiry, with eyes like a ferret, missing nothing. Jackson, tall, tough, cruel blue eyes ruthlessly hard. Both men, impeccably dressed in dark suits of good quality; in fact everything about them was precise. They in turn assessed him.

"Your report made interesting reading, Saints." Campbell's friendly smile took Phil by surprise. "We had tied the sinking of those two yachts with the finding of Hiroshi Tanigawa's body, but after some thought believed it to be coincidence. Your information about the false position reporting and the finding of the Dan-buoy, however, got us back on track."

"You were able to identify the man, sir?" said Phil with some surprise.

"Yes, we were; you see he had a rather distinctive birthmark on his back," replied Campbell. "We know him to be the son of one of the original Japanese Red Army leaders, one

Makoto Tanigawa, currently in jail in Japan and hopefully never coming out."

At this point Campbell passed a photograph to Phil, showing a young Japanese man apparently passing through an immigration point. "Your report got us thinking more about the others on board this yacht and the question of why young Tanigawa ends up floating face down near the French coast with a broken leg and a large quantity of morphine in him. That's him passing through Heathrow two months ago in the company of this woman." Another photograph was handed over. "We think that she is Fumiko Hamaura, a one-time political activist in Japan with extremist views. She has been out of the limelight for a few years but we think she may also be connected to the Japanese Red Army."

"You're not sure of her identity?" Phil interjected.

"We are awaiting confirmation from Tokyo," replied Campbell. "For some years now there has been a split in the Japanese Red Army, something of a civil war has been going on and we are concerned that they may be bringing their battleground here."

"I don't think so," said Phil. "The Dan-buoy off *Kiboko* found towards the Azores indicates to me that this gang is heading across the pond."

"It's thinking like that," said Campbell, "that brought us down here. I want you to work through all of your thoughts with us to see if we can gain a picture of what exactly is going on."

"Can I use your phone, Harold?" asked Phil. Blakemore waved vaguely towards the handset, looking puzzled.

The landlord picked up the phone and in a harassed voice said, "Yes, what is it?"

"Phil Saints here, HM Coastguard."

"What do you want? I'm rushed off my feet here," said the landlord.

"Earlier this evening I was talking to a young lad named Brian Yoling, is he still there?" Phil asked, hoping that the landlord could hear him above the din in the pub.

"I hope this is important," said the landlord, craning his head to see over the crowd in the bar. Seeing the youth in the corner playing the fruit machine, he said, "Yes, he's still here, do you want a word?"

"No, not now. Can you ask him to wait? I'll be over in half an hour. Tell him I'll pay for his pint."

Putting the phone down Phil turned to Campbell. "Earlier this evening I was talking to a young lad who saw both boats leave their moorings. He told me that *Umi Sama* went aground on Bosham spit."

"That's interesting. What damage, do we know?" said Jackson, his steely eyes flashing with interest.

"I don't think he knew and I was unable to complete the interview. He may have seen more so I think it would be a good idea if we go and have a chat," said Phil. "By now the tide should have dropped sufficient for us to see the spit, which should give us an idea of the potential damage."

In two strides Jackson had crossed the office and was holding the door open for Campbell and Saints. Blakemore rose as if to join them when Jackson said, "Thank you for your time, we won't be needing your assistance any further," and with that closed the office door just before Blakemore's face turned red with indignation.

Back at the pub Phil found Yoling enjoying his second free pint. Steering him out onto the veranda Phil felt the lad tense the instant he saw the two policemen.

"Hey, wot's this about, I ain't dun nuffin'." The youth protested and started to pull away.

Taking a firm grip of the lad's arm Phil whispered into his ear, "Net fishing in Chichester Harbour is illegal, but we are not interested in that. Just tell us everything you saw the morning those two yachts left."

"Fuckin' hell, I told you the lot befaw." Yoling's voice took on a whiny tone.

"Look lad, this is more important than you will ever know," said Phil.

"Wot's it wurf," said Yoling, thinking to push his luck.

"Your peace of mind that you won't be prosecuted for net fishing and hounded every time you put your boat in the water." Saint's voice, still low, carried sufficient menace.

"Shit. You official bastards all the same, always wantin' somfin' for nuffin'."

Steered by Phil to a seat opposite Campbell, Yoling sat, and staring at Campbell through his dull eyes said, "Alright mate watcher wonna know?"

Phil Saints could only be impressed by the patience and cunning with which Campbell conducted the interview, to say nothing of the way his Stella had in so timely a manner calmed Yoling after Jackson had used his more direct approach.

"Look lad, you saw a damn sight more than you are telling us. We can finish this in Chichester nick if you like," Jackson had said, leaning over the lad threateningly after Yoling had given a slightly flippant response to one of Campbell's questions. Yoling had clammed up immediately then and was staring sullenly out over the harbour.

"Brian," Stella had said quietly, "I can call you Brian?" The youth had nodded. "We are desperately trying to piece together precisely what happened to those yachts and need every scrap of detail. Please, you can really be a great help in solving something of a mystery here." Her brown eyes and calm comforting voice had won the lad completely, to the point where his further answers to Campbell's questions were directed to her.

"Fascinating," Campbell had said, when the youth had reluctantly walked away from the pool of warmth of those eyes.

"Mrs Saints, thank you very much for your valuable assistance." His expression conveyed deep admiration.

Suddenly Phil leapt to his feet and chased after Yoling; after fifty yards he caught up with him. "Hey Brian, have you got your boat handy? It'll be worth twenty quid to you."

Yoling stopped at the words 'twenty quid', and came back with a smile on his face. "How long for, I ain't got all night."

"Half an hour," said Phil. "I want you to take us over to where that yacht ran aground."

"It's on the slipway; I'll just go and get the oars." Without waiting for any further instruction he went off through the village.

When Phil got back to the veranda the landlord was clearing the tables and closing up for the night. "Your friends have gone back to the car," he said, turning a bench upside-down and lifting it onto a table.

Phil, arriving at the car, found Stella sitting in the front passenger seat whilst Campbell and Jackson stood a few yards away in deep conversation. Walking over to them he said, "Yoling is going to row us over there, to where the yacht went aground. It might not tell us anything but it's worth a look."

"Excellent Saints, well done. Did it cost much?" asked Campbell with a wry grin.

"Twenty pounds for half an hour," replied Phil, returning the smile.

"Cheeky little toe-rag," growled Jackson, but his hard face also showed amusement.

The well-varnished clinker-built rowing boat was rumbled down the slipway and into the water, turned and brought back alongside the ramped concrete for the passengers to board. Phil settled himself in the bows, with Yoling taking the centre thwart and Jackson and Campbell on the stern seat. Quickly Phil checked his large torch-cum-lantern and then said, "OK Brian let's get underway." As the youth pulled on the oars with that strong confidence born of practice, he said, "You certainly keep this up together well. Do the varnish work yourself?"

"Yeah, I wouldn't let anyone else touch her; gets a good rub down and two coats every six months or so," Yoling said, his voice showing the pride he took in the work.

The creek at this point was very narrow and it was only ten full sweeps of the oars to cover the distance. Hauling on the starboard hand oar Yoling turned the boat in towards the spit and ran it aground. Phil stepped out followed by Yoling and both hauled the boat up the spit far enough for the other two not to have to wade through water.

Once on the spit the four men started to search along its northern edge. "It was furva over," said Yoling, "more in line wiv the upper channel."

Pointing the torch in the direction indicated, Phil immediately saw that one pile stood at a very different angle to the others. Striding across to it, he set his torch down and switched it to lantern mode. "This is it," he said, his voice showing excitement at the find. "Look at the way it's almost been broken off at ground level, and look, see that bright blue around the top, that's anti-fouling for sure."

"Would the impact have been enough to seriously damage the yacht though?" asked Campbell.

"Too right it would," said Yoling. "When they hit, it stopped 'em dead, 'ad 'em all going arse over tit, it did." He laughed at the memory of it.

"You saw it that clearly?" asked Phil.

"Yeah, as I says before, we was over there, see, and I looks up as you do like when the woman shouts out to let go. Then I just got back to what I was doing when I 'eard the bloke on the uvver yacht call out for 'em to stop. I looks over to see wot 'e was on about an that's when it 'appened."

"You said that there were three people onboard the yacht that went aground," said Campbell.

"Yeah, that's right. On the uvver boat there was a couple of kids as well, cause when they was messin' about on the buoy, those two was standin' in the bows waving to us."

Back on the slipway Campbell pressed a note into Yoling's hand and thanked him for his assistance. Yoling's gratitude indicated that his reward had been better than the twenty pounds agreed.

"Those types are remarkably observant," said Campbell as he sat sipping coffee in the snug lounge of the Saints' cottage. "All poachers rely on that sharp-eyed talent, to keep them out of trouble, normally."

Jackson looked up from his notes as Stella placed a large plate of sandwiches in the centre of the coffee table. "There's cheese and green tomato chutney and ham and tomato. The chutney's home-made. I hope you like it," she said.

"Cor," said Jackson. "I haven't had green tomato chutney since I was a lad when my Mum used to make it." He reached over, selected a sandwich and took a large mouthful. "Smashin'. You want to try some of this, sir."

Three hours later Jackson, now with his jacket off and tie undone, raised his hand and said, "To summarize then, we are going with your hijack theory," he glanced at Phil Saints, "based on the boat being damaged and possibly a member of their crew breaking a leg, which links in with the French autopsy on Tanigawa. You also reckon that this yacht, *Kiboko*, is crossing the Atlantic and was not sunk, as first thought, off Alderney."

"That's as I see it. They would have needed another helmsman as *Kiboko* didn't have any self-steering mechanism according to the builder's details; apparently the French buyer was going to use French kit," said Phil. "I am also convinced that anyone attempting that voyage in a boat of that size would not take kids along as well. I agree with both of you that the kids and possibly this chap Vaughan's wife are being held hostage to ensure his co-operation."

113

"So far in this picture we have only got possibly Miss Hamaura, Tanigawa and one other man in the team." Campbell sat staring straight ahead at some distant point. "If this is part of the Japanese Red Army civil war and if hostages have been taken, as we believe, then some person or persons are holding them somewhere. The 'where', is the most important thing at this time and the 'how many', the second." He looked at the other two men. "Your ideas please, on where you think the Vaughan family are being held."

There were a few minutes of silence whilst the three men sat looking at the notes they had made to see if somewhere in that information lay the answer. "My guess, and it is only a guess, is that they are close to Bosham," said Phil.

"A guess, you say?" said Campbell.

"Well, maybe a bit more. You see, the charter firm gave me the impression that when arrangements were being made, the two doing the charter only took a quarter of an hour to get to their offices. The address given to the charter company was that of an elderly couple who had been away staying with their son up north. I think they had found that out and used the address for the boat charter, but in fact were living somewhere else. Finally, I am sure they know that they are on the wanted list and would therefore not be living where there is even the slightest chance of them being recognised, like a hotel, or consider taking long journeys where they could run the risk of being stopped in a random police check or involved in an accident."

"Any ideas from you, Jackson?" Campbell asked.

"I agree with Saints here. Travel for them is a risk and so a nice quiet secluded spot nearby is what we should be looking for. There are plenty of those around here."

"Right," said Campbell. "Jackson, first thing in the morning I will contact the families and get the latest photographs of the children and their mother. I want you to make formal contact with the local police force and set up a temporary incident room away from Bosham but not too far." He looked down at a road atlas that Phil had been using to give them a rough layout of the harbour and coastline. Stabbing his finger at the page he said, "West Ashling, that'll do. See if you can find a hall or something there."

"You'll have to excuse me now, Commander, as I have to leave for work," said Phil.

"Good God, is that the time?" exclaimed Campbell, genuinely shocked. "We must leave. Can we call for our car?"

"Yes, of course and I'll wake Stella and get her to cook us an early breakfast," replied Phil, holding his hand up against the protest that Campbell was about to make. "She would be annoyed with me if I let you leave without any food inside you."

Fifteen minutes later Phil Saints re-entered the lounge carrying a tray of tea things and wafting the smell of bacon and eggs into the room. "The teddy bear," he said.

Campbell and Jackson looked at him curiously.

"The second life raft found was from the yacht *Kiboko* and contained a damp, but obviously much loved teddy bear. Where, I ask, was the child that went with it?"

"Excellent point," said Jackson. "I know my young Charlotte would have been hanging onto her teddy bear in a situation like that. If she had gone to the bottom with the boat, her teddy would have gone too."

"I see exactly what you mean," said Campbell. "That teddy bear was purely and simply a plant to have us thinking that all four supposedly onboard had perished."

Phil Saints nodded.

Stella's face peered round the door. "Breakfast is on the table if you care to sit up."

Two days had passed since the meeting in Phil and Stella Saints' cottage. Phil's return to work that morning had let him in for a grilling from Harold Blakemore who was furious that he had sent a report to the police without informing him. 'A black mark on your record', was the phrase used. All through that watch and today's it had been like he was walking on eggshells when Blakemore was around.

Meanwhile, at West Ashling village hall, Jackson had installed his team and just conducted a briefing of local senior officers. "Excuse me, sir, the Commander would like to see you." It was Campbell's pretty driver, WPC Tucker.

Jackson rose from his desk and walked across to the area that Campbell had partitioned off. "Come in, Jackson. We have just received a full report from Tokyo concerning Hamaura." Campbell leaned back in his chair, pushing a file across to Jackson. "We have also received some further bad news which is that Hamaura is now believed to be a close follower of one Todashi Murata who is the leader of one of the factions at war within the Japanese Red Army." Campbell reached for another file and opened it. "Murata is 'old school anarchist'; loves blowing things up and disrupting society in general, the experts reckon that he lost sight of any political goals years ago and is in it to fuel his sheer hatred of world order."

"Glancing through this, it seems that they are two of a kind," commented Jackson, scanning the file pages on his lap. "Do you think they are working together?"

"Tokyo seems to think they are and say their intelligence advice is that they are planning something big. It appears that last year the FBI was looking for them in connection with some bank robberies in the States which the Japanese think was to finance their next operation." Campbell banged the desk. "How on earth did they get through Heathrow? We even got her photograph on entry!"

"Saints said something interesting to me the other night in the car," said Jackson, looking at a point high up on the wall in order to concentrate on his recall. "I asked him why a terrorist would use a yacht as a means of transport and he said for easy entry through a small port. Maybe their next hit is France and that's the way they plan to get in unnoticed."

"What we need to know is whether that oriental black wizard, Murata, is aboard the yacht or whether he is the puppet master back here." Campbell's facial expression showed concern.

"Does it make much difference if he is aboard, sir?" Jackson asked. "I don't know much about this Murata bloke."

"Oh yes, it would change everything. If he is part of the hostage holding team, then getting them out alive will be very difficult and that is if we manage to find where they are being held." Campbell drummed his fingers on the desk. "On the loose here, we can't begin to guess his whereabouts. If he was on board the yacht and if the yacht is traced, then at least it should be possible to contain him until an arrest is made." Campbell stifled a yawn. "We also need to find out who this Middle Eastern male is that helped hire the boat. Maybe he's onboard the yacht."

"Are you having doubts about this local search, sir?" asked Jackson.

"No, I think we had to follow our hunch. Anyway the dice has been thrown, let's just hope that it stops on our lucky number, or I will look very stupid." Campbell got up and stretched.

"On the face of it, sir, I think we were right. Why not hold them locally? It's risky to travel far with them." Jackson had stood up to leave, sensing that the meeting was over and wanting to have a closer read of Hamaura's file.

Since midnight, the West Sussex police had been calling on deserted and isolated buildings, checking on occupants, and were shaken to have already uncovered a black magic coven and two drug raves, but no Japanese Red Army kidnappers. In the corner of the hall Jackson watched two WPCs talking quietly over the radio to search cars and team leaders. As information came in they passed it on to a mapping clerk, who identified the building searched and circled it on his large scale map in green, for cleared.

Suddenly at the door there was a small commotion. "Sorry, sir, even members of the press can't go in," the large sergeant was saying, barring the way against a crumpled-suited haggard-looking reporter and a tough-looking cameraman.

"Well, maybe you can tell me what's going on. Has there been a murder?" Then, ignoring the sergeant, the reporter shouted, "Hey Jackson! What's the Anti-Terrorist Branch doing in West Ashling? Has the PM come for a holiday?"

Jackson had instantly recognised the reporter as one Harry Parson, unaffectionately known as the 'Parson's Nose'. At the instant of sighting, Jackson had turned, heading for the back of the hall out of Parson's reach, but too late, the sharp-eyed Parson had spotted him and the call had been clearly heard by everyone.

"Bring him through, Sergeant." Jackson's voice expressed resignation.

When both men arrived Jackson glared at the sergeant. "They're not Siamese twins, Sergeant; I only need the talking piece of the duo."

The sergeant flushed with embarrassment and annoyance.

"On the other hand leave him here; then I can stop him wasting film." Jackson sat but did not offer a seat to the pressmen.

"Now Inspector, what a delightful cha…" Parson's voice petered out in the face of Jackson's raised hand and inhospitable glare.

"Parson, I'm not interested in which sewer outfall you and your sidekick have just crawled out of, and can only assume that your appearance here is just bad luck."

"That's not a very polite welcome for a public servant to make, Inspector," said Parson, puffing himself up in indignation. "May I remind you who I work for and the power they have over public opinion." Parson was now leaning threateningly over Jackson's desk.

"Maybe my welcome reflects the feelings of the Squad, who to a man, despise your sensationalism and twisting of the facts." Jackson had not had to raise his voice; its tone and his manner enough to have Parson step back, flinching. "Now, listen carefully, Parson," Jackson continued, his voice still carrying an arctic chill. "When you leave here in a few minutes' time, you will have forgotten everything you have seen and in particular that you have seen me, right!"

"You can't do that, Jackson; we have rights you know. The Police State you want to represent doesn't exist just now." Parson swung round and started for the door. "My public deserves to read about your lot's devious activities and cover-ups."

The camera flash blinded Jackson, its wind-on drive buzzing, then another flash of the communications corner and the mapping group. On the door the sergeant made to stop the two pressmen from passing. Parson, seething with rage and indignation, shouted, "Piss off out of my way, Sergeant. If you so much as touch me I'll have you for assault!"

The sergeant faltered, looking round for support, and finding none available said, "I only wanted to know your names and occupation details for the incident room record of visitors, sir." The voice sounded calm and pacifying and slowed the two pressmen.

Parson, his eyes still flashing with rage, swung to address his cameraman. "He makes it sound as if we were signing the Royal Yacht Squadron's visitors' book, doesn't he, Dave?"

"Stupid git," mumbled Dave.

"Precisely Dave. I couldn't have put it better myself." Then turning to the sergeant, he said with a sneer, "See, Commissar Jackson, he no doubt has files on us both."

At that moment a smartly dressed wiry man came up the steps to the hall. On seeing Parson his eyes lit up in apparent surprised pleasure at the unexpected meeting.

"Mr Parson, what an opportune time to meet with you." The opportune time Campbell mentioned had involved him in a quick sprint from his partitioned area out through the stage door and round the side of the hall. "I should be obliged if you would spare me half an hour of your time to assist us in preventing a serious act of terrorism."

Parson's jaw dropped. "Er, what did you say?"

Campbell patiently repeated his invitation and taking Parson's arm, he said, "If you would just come with me, gentlemen, I shall explain everything."

Parson, speechless and confused, allowed himself to be turned and escorted through the hall to an interview room that had been set up behind the stage.

"WPC Tucker, would you organise coffee for us please, er, black or white, gentlemen?"

Recipes given, the two pressmen had a few seconds to take in their surroundings. In the corner of the room were some old masks from last season's pantomime and ranged down one side wall there was a wide shelf, which had seen many make-up sessions, judging from the amount of rouge and base smeared over its surface. Above the shelf was a long wall mirror surrounded by naked bulb fittings, half of which were empty. Parson smiled and nudged Dave, his head nodding in the direction of an old poster pinned to the wall advertising 'An Inspector Calls'.

A folding table occupied the centre of the room, with two chairs on the side nearest the door and a long wooden bench on the other beneath a small window. Commander Campbell gestured to his guests to be seated on the bench, taking for himself one of the chairs.

"I'm sorry that greater comfort cannot be offered but you will appreciate that our occupation of these premises only commenced at 10 o'clock last night." Campbell's voice was warm and casual, a smile playing around his mouth. "Hopefully our work here will be ended before police bureaucracy allocates me a parking space and a three metre by two metre grade two patterned carpet."

Parson immediately warmed to this man with the confident manner and sparkling blue eyes.

"I suspect your status entitles you to fitted carpet and two paintings on the wall." Parson knew rank when he saw it. "Having the pretty WPC Tucker as your driver as well, I wouldn't be surprised."

Campbell waved his hand dismissively, ending the status negotiation, but inwardly impressed by Parson's observation and accurate guess about Tucker. "Anyway, Mr Parson," Campbell's voice now business-like, "my reason for wanting to speak with you is that I need you to camouflage a very important operation."

"What do you mean by camouflage?" said Parson, emphasising the last word. "My readers trust me to present the facts, not tell them fairy tales."

"I can assure you that your readers will hold you in much higher esteem at the end of this operation." Campbell's face hid the thought of holding the two pressmen until a 'D' notice could be served, preventing their paper from publishing anything they had seen today, but in reality he would not be able to present a sufficiently strong case for the action to work. "Let me explain the situation to you, then I am sure you will agree with the idea of camouflage."

Briefly he set out the background behind the operation and its associated local search. Campbell stressed again and again how dangerous Murata was and that the lives of two small children and their mother were most likely in extreme danger. "It

121

is essential that we find this man and his associates quickly and get them into custody. If they think that our search is in any way to do with them there is no knowing what could happen. Thus the need for camouflage."

Parson sat speechlessly on the bench, amazed at the man's honesty and slowly aware of his own great responsibility.

"All this is absolutely true, right?" Parson still couldn't fully comprehend what had just taken place.

"Absolutely," said Campbell, now more confident that he had made the right decision.

"Are you sure that this Japanese Red Army bloke Murata has got the Vaughan kids and their mother hostage?" Parson still needed to strengthen his grip on the facts of the story.

"We have strong reasons to believe this to be the case, but I confess, we have no firm grounds to believe that they are being kept in this area," replied Campbell, "that is just a hunch."

"Prisoner escapes from Parkhurst after bludgeoning two guards." Parson paused and then went on. "Police sources inform that in the early hours of yesterday morning Charlie Jones, or whoever, escaped from Parkhurst high security prison on the Isle of Wight after carrying out a furious attack on two prison officers. Though ports on the island were immediately watched and extra police put on standby to assist in the search, officials tell us that they believe 'Charlie Jones' has left the Island by stealing a small powerboat found last night in Chichester Harbour. Roadblocks are being set up and a search of the area is being conducted. Police say that 'Jones' could be armed and is very dangerous and the public should not attempt to approach him."

"Excellent, Mr Parson, enough to cover the search and justify roadblocks." Campbell sat back feeling a little more relaxed. "OK, Mr Parson, get writing and I want to check the draft before it leaves here. In fact I want it to go out from here."

As if by magic Parson produced a pen and notepad and started to write, stopping only to ask what name they should give the fictitious convict. In half an hour the story was complete and approved by Campbell.

Jackson entered the room looking curiously at his boss. "You wanted me, sir?"

"Yes," said Campbell. "Take this story that Mr Parson here has so brilliantly constructed and make sure that all of the newspapers get it, especially the local ones."

"What about radio and TV, sir?" asked Jackson.

"Of course, them as well," said Campbell. "Get one of the local boys to head the press briefings. I don't want our presence known about. Oh, and can you brief the Chief Constable and Prison Governor and ask them to back the story up on the island. They will know what to do."

"The bastard," said Dave with some feeling. "After you wrote it all, he gives it to the whole of the bloody street."

"Dave, shut up," said Parson turning on his cameraman. "If we were the only paper to put this out it would look odd wouldn't it? I'm sure that when the real story can be told, we will be the ones with the inside track."

"You are right, Mr Parson. You will be given first break on the real story," Campbell said, satisfied with the way things had gone.

"Sorry guv, wasn't quite up to speed there," Dave rumbled, looking and feeling as though he was in danger of becoming very confused.

"Now what we need is a couple of pictures to boost our spread," Parson chirped.

Campbell looked reluctant, then said, "OK, just one of the search plot, but strictly no ATB personnel."

"That's a deal." Parson stood grinning and extended his hand to Campbell, who shook it. "Yeah," said Parson. "Definitely fitted carpet and two pictures."

As they left the room Jackson turned to his boss and said with some venom, "That little bastard better play it straight."

"Oh, he will," smiled Campbell confidently. "He realises the responsibility that his new knowledge carries. And, that his future in journalism rests on him playing it straight with us; this time."

Chapter 7

Murata's body twitched and his hand moved as if in reflex to shield his face. The nightmare did not wake him, his mind now used to seeing the arc of the petrol bomb as it spun through the broken window and across the room. Yukiko, lying in his arms, woke and watched him as the nightmare took its course, whispering softly, soothingly to him. She gently kissed the livid scar across his chest and stomach, arousing him to wakeful passion.

Later, Murata lay awake staring at the ceiling, the girl alongside him in satisfied sleep. He thought back to that night five years ago in Kyoto when Shigenori Yamamoto's men had made their first bid for his life. On that night, the lady was much more beautiful; yes, indeed, Yamamoto's wife was a flower of rare beauty, whose artistry when coupling was unsurpassed. Before his eyes he saw the skin of the girl blacken, behind his eyes he heard a death-ridden scream. The image startled him into full wakefulness and his hand moved to stroke the girl's body as if to reassure himself that all was well.

It was his affair with Yamamoto's wife that was the real motivation behind the schism in the group, but it had brought out the differences in other areas, especially their operational direction. Yamamoto always wanted to hide behind bank fraud and economic sabotage, rather than keep with the highly publicised conventional attacks of the Japanese Red Army. The result had been a split in the organisation, with both sides more at war with each other than following their goals. Since the hotel fire bombing, four attempts had been made to take Murata out, all of which had failed. Similarly, his attacks on Yamamoto had failed, in the process losing Murata valuable men.

Now he was changing his approach by launching an attack on a large population group in America and making sure that

Yamamoto's name was firmly stuck to it. Even if the attack ultimately failed, he knew that the Americans would hunt down Yamamoto and destroy him. A sneer of satisfaction crossed his face followed almost instantly by an expression of frustration. After five years of gang war he had been forced to recruit from outside of Japan. Arni, though highly qualified, was gai-jin and therefore not to be fully trusted. Little Yukiko had introduced this Julian Makepeace, another foreigner who did not understand devotion and loyalty in the way of the Japanese. Only the beautiful and ruthless Fumiko Hamaura matched Murata's exacting standards for trust, but even here, her quick temper was a weakness.

How much of Hamaura's temper had been the cause of the Bosham Creek fiasco Murata did not know, but it had been a major setback and had caused him to make drastic and rapid plan changes. By now he should have been in Paris but instead he was holed up here in this derelict farmhouse, keeping hostages. He reviewed again his decision to steal the second yacht and its skipper. It was a reflex action caused by the obvious serious damage to the yacht Hamaura had chartered.

The original plan had been to charter a yacht for four months to 'cruise the Brittany Coast'. In actual fact they would cross the Atlantic, arriving and entering on false papers, conduct the attack and sail back, emerging again as peaceful yachting friends calling in at Brest on their way back to England. The yacht would enable them to smuggle in the electronic equipment required to execute the attack and was also a way of entry and exit that was not so well watched as the main ports and airports.

Now, of course, the plan had holes in it. They had been forced to stage the sinking of the charter vessel and the stolen yacht, making off into the Atlantic with a hostage aboard to replace the crew injured in the creek. Murata's mind lightened as he thought through the events that had brought Yamamoto's son into his grasp. That was a stroke of luck indeed and he would ensure that the youth's body would be left to further incriminate Yamamoto senior. How willing the boy was to help, believing that at last he would be treated as Samurai and feared, as he deserved. Such childish pride and weakness of character could not have come from his mother. Sending him via his trusted friend, Stavos, to a mid Atlantic rendezvous would indeed kill two birds with one stone. Murata was easing himself to a sitting position, idly contemplating the boy and wondering what had brought about such a personality, when his mobile phone rang.

"Mushi, mushi," he growled into the phone. A short pause, then he heard Yamada's voice at the other end ask, "Murata-san deska."

"Hi, hi, Murata desu," he responded.

"Just to let you know that the tree you sent has been planted and should blossom well on 4th July." Yamada was proud of this message which, if overheard, would not convey anything but nice thoughts.

"Ah so, that is very good news, thank you so much for telling me. Tell me, will the flags also be flying on 4th July?" Murata asked, his voice full of laughter.

"Oh yes," came the reply. "We have even put them up early," Yamada said, his voice full of pride at the reception of his news.

"Well done. I will be in touch nearer the time," said Murata, then pressed the button to end the call.

There, he thought, was a young man with the right attitude. Hamaura was very clever to pick him up.

On the landing above, Julian Makepeace sat at his post in contemplation. Since their arrival two weeks ago he had become more and more confused. Yukiko was moving away from him and try as he might to show his loyalty to the group, it made no difference. He still felt like an outsider, not to be trusted. Murata-san had never been welcoming, but since the Bosham Creek affair, was now plainly unpleasant. Only three days ago

Murata had changed the duty roster, placing him on guard at night alone instead of sharing his watch with Yukiko. He had wondered whether it was Yukiko who had asked for the change, as she was now becoming very distant. The change also meant that he no longer had a chance to play with the two girls in the yard, something that they did seem to enjoy. Mrs Vaughan had remained hostile but the two daughters, Clare and Louise, had taken to him and had started laughing at his clowning around.

Julian understood why the hostages had to be taken but could not see how they were going to be kept for the whole of the operation. The children in particular were showing signs that the experience was causing lasting damage. He also felt sure that Mrs Vaughan believed her husband to be dead, but she showed no sign of this to her daughters. Julian thought that she was a very brave woman and that she had also gained some respect from Murata-san, an achievement not easily attained, as he well knew.

Julian was suddenly wide awake and staring at the padlocked door. "What's up in there?" he asked in a low voice.

"I need a doctor." Sarah Vaughan's voice was only just audible.

"Is it the baby?" he asked, with a feeling of growing apprehension.

"Yes," she replied, "I feel so ill. I'm sure I'm going to miscarry. Please, please get help. I promise I will say nothing to the authorities."

Murata appeared at the foot of the stairs and looked questioningly at Julian.

"It's Mrs Vaughan," Julian said. "She feels very ill and thinks she is going to have a miscarriage."

"Ah so," was all Murata said, before turning back into the lounge that they were using as sleeping quarters.

"She needs a doctor now," Julian said, trying to make his voice sound firm and confident.

Murata swung round, and with eyes blazing, said in a loud voice, "No doctor, you understand! No doctor. Nothing will change my plan. If she loses baby she will have others." Turning on his heels he strode away.

"Did you hear that?" Julian asked in a loud whisper at the door.

"Yes, I did," she sobbed.

"Is it really bad or do you think a rest will help?" The suggestion sounded pathetic and he winced as soon as he had said it.

A groan followed by a weak, "Oh God, someone help me, someone help me," pricked his conscience and he moved away from the door to escape the soft sound of crying.

He sat for a further ten minutes not knowing what to do. Then, triggered by another sickening groan from the room, he began to creep down the stairs with some vague plan in his mind to try and fetch a doctor. Suddenly he knew what he would do. He would find a doctor's house and bring him blindfolded back to the farm to treat Mrs Vaughan, then take him out and set him loose, well away. To his mind the plan was sound and he was sure that Murata would accept it when he delivered the doctor. Retracing his steps, he searched his jacket and found a piece of paper on which he outlined his plan and tucked it behind the architrave surround to the doorframe where it would be seen. Again he descended the stairs, arriving at the bottom with aching lungs having held his breath for the whole descent. Calming himself, he crept the few feet to the lounge door and stole a glance in to see if it would be safe to cross the opening without drawing attention. The shock of what he saw almost made him cry out and give himself away. There in the middle of the room, a naked Yukiko was holding and caressing Murata in a sensual way that Julian had never enjoyed from her. Hate now welled up inside him and it was only his fear of Murata that prevented him from rushing in and striking the man. His back to the wall, and brain racing, he stood frozen for at least two minutes. Numbed and unable to think straight he closed his eyes tightly, trying to switch off the world around him, but what he had seen would not go away. Reality was dawning; Yukiko was the reason for him being there, and she was the one who had persuaded him into using his parents' property. Now it was obvious she had been using him all along, just like his self-centred parents.

Silently Julian climbed the stairs. On reaching the landing he saw light through a chink in the curtain and realised that the night was passing; if he was to do anything it must be now.

Recovering his note, then undoing the padlock, he slipped into the room and kneeling by Mrs Vaughan said, "I'm going to try and get you out of here. Do you think you can walk very far?"

"No," she replied and groaned once again.

Gently he woke the children, putting a finger to his lips seeking their silence. "Your Mummy's not very well, so I am going to try and get you all to a doctor. But we must not make a noise otherwise the other man will try to stop us." Their eyes, still full of sleep, looked up at him and in unison they nodded.

Clare helped Louise to get dressed and put on her shoes whilst Julian gave what little help he could to Mrs Vaughan. As in many of the old farmhouses, there was a back stairway leading down to the kitchen. Lifting Clare first, he carried her along the landing and down the back stair, leaving her under the kitchen table and whispering to her to remain quiet. His second trip brought Louise down to her sister; then the difficult job of getting Mrs Vaughan safely down silently to avoid attracting the attention of Murata. By the time he had finished it was fully light outside, and checking his watch, it would be only five minutes before Yukiko would come to relieve him.

He slid the bolts on the back door and gently eased it open wide enough for them to get through. Once outside he said to

Mrs Vaughan, "Take the girls across to that old bailer and hide behind it. I'm going to try and buy some time."

A flicker of a smile crossed her face and she thanked him.

Back inside he climbed the stairs again and resumed his seat outside the room. Only seconds passed before he heard Yukiko's footsteps on the stairs. It was then that he realised he had forgotten to fasten the padlock. Moving quickly to the door, he made to make it look as if he had just quietly closed the door and clipped the padlock home.

"What are you doing?" Yukiko asked, a frown on her face.

"Just doing a final check, actually," he said, turning towards her. Carrying on in a low voice, he explained. "Last night Mrs V. was not very well and that disturbed the children. They only got properly off to sleep about an hour ago. They are dead to the world in there."

"What you mean dead to the world?" she said, making a move towards the door.

Julian stepped in front of her stopping her progress and putting his finger to her lips said. "Ssh! You will wake them. Dead to the world means that they are very tired and are in a deep sleep and will not wake up for some time."

"How is Mrs Vaughan?" was her next question.

"I still think she needs a doctor, but at the moment she is asleep so best not to disturb her. See what she is like later," he replied, trying to sound nonchalant.

He could see that his assurance had not fully satisfied Yukiko so played another gamble. "I'm going to grab some fresh air out in the yard. Come with me. They won't be going anywhere for the next few hours." His invitation, issued with a pleading look, made her pause, obviously weighing something up in her mind.

"Okay," she said. "You wait here while I tell Murata-san." With that she descended the stairs leaving him waiting nervously by the door.

After a few minutes of conversation she returned to the foot of the stairs and looked up.

"Murata-san says it's okay but not too long," the nervous expression on her face sufficient for Julian to guess that she was about to tell him their relationship was over.

Quietly he descended the stairs making it look obvious that he did not want to disturb the hostages.

Outside, she walked a few yards before turning to him saying, "I think we should be just friends at moment. At least until this thing is over."

He put on a hurt expression and walked away from her towards the bailer and out of sight of the lounge window. "What is it?" he asked. "Have you grown tired of me?"

"No, no," she lied. "It's just that Murata; he likes team to concentrate only on job. When job over everyone can play."

"Oh, I see," he said, appearing to accept her explanation.

Casually he picked up a length of wood and a stone. Throwing the stone up into the air, he struck out at it on its descent sending it soaring off into the distance.

Instinctively, Yukiko turned to watch the stone's flight, oblivious to the second swing that brought the piece of wood with a crack down on her skull.

Catching her body before it hit the ground, Julian dragged it behind the bailer where Sarah and the girls were waiting.

Sarah looked at the girl, shocked. "Is she still alive?" she asked. Julian knelt to check for breathing.

"Yes, she'll be alright," he replied, looking round the side of the bailer to see that the coast was clear. "We must move away from here quickly. If we go off in that direction we will come to the Emsworth bypass and flag someone down, but we must hurry."

Gathering Louise up in his arms and taking Clare's hand he started off. Looking over his shoulder he saw Sarah Vaughan following, trying hard to keep up, but she was obviously in a lot of pain. Twenty yards from the embankment she fell and was unable to get up. Putting Louise down, Julian told Clare to take her sister and wait for him at the top of the bank behind the bushes. Seeing the girls set off, he raced back to Sarah Vaughan and kneeling beside her, tried to see how best he could help.

"I can't go any further. Save the girls. Go quickly." Sarah Vaughan's words came in gasps, her face terribly pale with exhaustion and pain.

Holding her under her armpits Julian dragged her to the field hedge that ran from the farm buildings to the embankment and did his best to hide her.

"I will be back as soon as possible. Try not to move or make a noise." With that he rose and in a low run raced to the embankment.

Scrambling up the steep slope, he reached the wooden fencing along the crest and started to climb over. As he swung his leg over the top rail he heard the screech of tyres under heavy braking. It was the last thing he heard. Murata's burst of automatic fire hit Julian in a line from his hip to his head, throwing his body over the fence and down onto the hard shoulder.

Seeing him fall, the two girls moved uncertainly towards where Julian lay. Before they could reach him, blue uniformed arms swept them off their feet and calming voices tried to soothe them as they were rushed back to the squad car slewed towards the bank thirty yards away.

"Darran, get on the radio and call for armed backup. That poor sod back there had about ten rounds in him. I'm going to take a look," and with that, PC Nic Forge ducked back out of the car and started to run back towards where Julian had fallen.

"Nic, don't be a prat. Get back here and wait for backup, you plonker!" PC Darran Archer yelled; but it was too late, Nic was well down the road.

"Control, this is PC Archer on patrol Emsworth bypass. We have found two girls matching description of missing pair. Also body of a man shot only a few moments ago. Urgently need armed backup."

"Wait one," came the reply. Darran looked over his shoulder at the two terrified young girls clinging to each other on the back seat. "Hi, I'm Darran. It's ok now, you're safe," he said, giving them his best friendly smile.

"They've got Mummy and she's not well," cried the elder one.

"Was the man down the road there one of them?" Darran asked.

Clare, with tears streaming down her face, nodded.

"Was he chasing you?" This time his question was met by a shake of the head.

Puzzled, he asked, "Was there anyone else chasing you?" Clare nodded again but was crying too hard to speak.

The car radio crackled again. "Backup is on its way. What is your exact position?"

"Control, we are 500 metres east of the Newel Lane road bridge, the road going north from the head of Bosham Creek. PC Forge has gone to investigate the shooting. We have two very frightened girls in the car who say that their mother is still being held by someone."

The radio crackled once more but this time a man's voice came through. "Can you confirm if the girls' names are Clare and Louise Vaughan, over?"

Darran turned to the girls and looking at the elder asked, "Is your name Clare?" She nodded. "Is this your sister Louise?" She nodded again. "And your full name is Clare Vaughan?" Again a nod.

Picking up the microphone he reported back in, confirming the information.

Meantime, Nic Forge had run back along the hard shoulder pumped up with the adrenalin rush of having caught sight of the shooting out of the corner of his eye. He had started to brake hard on seeing the two small girls jump down the bank towards the road. Then, just caught sight of the man falling, as if shot. As he neared the body his brain rationalised the event and he changed course, keeping low towards the fence. Now on all fours, he edged through the long grass to where he could look down the embankment on the other side of the fence. In the field at the bottom, a man dressed all in black was cautiously making his way along the hedgerow. PC Forge stood, instantly attracting the attention of his suspect, who started a limping run backward towards the farm buildings.

"Stop, Police!" Forge yelled. The response was dramatic; the man swung a sub-machine gun from his shoulder and hosed the hedgerow at waist height with a deadly hail of bullets. When the clip was exhausted he turned and ran stumbling across the field in the direction of the farmyard.

"Control, this is PC Forge. I have armed man in sight and am in pursuit." Almost immediately the response to his call came. "Maintain watch only, do not, repeat, do not approach suspect. I confirm you are not to approach the suspect."

"Understood. Suspect is making for farm buildings off Newel Lane." Nic Forge slid down the embankment and started out along the hedgerow. The man's intent was obviously to kill someone hiding in the hedge and from the way he was spraying the area it was certain that he had not known precisely where his target was. As he progressed along the hedgerow he could hear the sound of emergency vehicles apparently coming from all directions. His radio, quiet half an hour ago, was now constantly chattering with co-ordinated instructions to cars and search groups. The police helicopter was scrambled and was heading his way.

Fifty metres along the hedge he heard a weak cry from under the overhanging greenery. Checking on the progress of his suspect, he moved closer to the hedge and lifting the low branches saw the pale face of Mrs Vaughan.

Letting the branch drop back into place he thumbed the switch on his radio. "Control, this is PC Forge. We urgently need ambulance to come to scene on Emsworth bypass. We have seriously injured lady in adjacent field."

"Ambulance is already on its way," came the response.

With that he crouched down and lifted the branch again to study the unconscious form lying there.

Lulled by the weeks of quiet and inaction, coupled with the night of passion with Yukiko, Murata had given little thought to her request to go out into the yard with Julian. His thoughts had been more concerned with the success of the rendezvous in the Atlantic. He had every faith in Stavos, who had proved himself very capable in the past. It was Arni he was worried about – was he capable of such accurate navigation? Glancing out of the lounge window he had seen Julian turn away from Yukiko and walk out of sight. She, after a little pause, had followed him saying something. When they had not returned to view after five minutes he began to be concerned and went through the old kitchen, where he found the back door open. Quickly outside he had skirted the building, gun in hand, keeping low. It was only by chance that he saw Yukiko's trainer showing beyond the frame of the bailer. He had walked across expecting to find the two together but instead there was Yukiko unconscious on the ground.

Looking around, he just caught sight of Louise's bright blue jumper as she climbed through the fence at the top of the embankment. With a limping gait he ran out of the yard and into the field where he saw Julian scrambling up the embankment. Continuing across the field he was closing the gap fast and as the youth started to climb the fence Murata opened fire, satisfied to see the body jerk with the impact of the bullets and go crashing to the ground.

Not seeing Mrs Vaughan he assumed that she was either ahead of the girls or hiding in the hedgerow. Guessing that probably the second scenario was most likely, he had moved to the edge of the field and started searching for her. The quick arrival of PC Forge had stopped him only two yards away from her place of hiding. Fearing that more police were in the area he had retreated, firing into the hedgerow in the hope of killing her.

Back in the farmyard he found Yukiko sitting holding her head, tears rolling down her face. "Murata-san, I have failed you at most important time," she wept. "Please forgive. What can I do to make it right?"

"How did it happen?" he said, his voice rising in anger.

"He trick me when he pick up stick and hit a stone. I look away from him and he hit me." Her voice was trembling in response to his threatening tone.

"Get petrol can from barn. We must burn this place quickly," he ordered, moving towards the kitchen door.

Moving unsteadily across the yard, Yukiko entered the barn and found two plastic canisters marked 'petrol'. Struggling under their weight, she headed back across the yard and through the front door. As she set the canisters down Murata appeared, stuffing his wallet into his pocket and carrying the little wrist bag containing all his contact data.

Over his shoulder was slung the automatic and as his loose jacket flapped open she could see a pistol butt protruding from its holster. In his left hand he held a second pistol in a shoulder holster and he handed it to her. "Put this on and keep lookout across the field while I see to this," he said, picking up one of the canisters and making for the lounge.

Outside, gun in hand, Yukiko kept low as she moved across the yard to a point behind the low wall where she could look out over the field. In the distance she saw a figure crouching at the edge of the field. He was obviously concentrating on something in the hedge and did not present an immediate threat, so she chose not to shoot. Whilst she waited, four blue flashing lights appeared along the top of the high bank and men started sliding down it and into the field, spreading out to form a line before turning to make their way towards her. Two men, carrying what looked like a stretcher, were moving towards the crouched figure who, she guessed, had found Mrs Vaughan.

Inside the farmhouse Murata had almost finished pouring the petrol around, his brain devising an escape plan. The sound of police sirens appeared to be coming from all directions. Through the window he could see the line of policemen moving towards the farmhouse and wondered whether he had time to escape in Julian's four-by-four, remembering almost immediately that he had given the keys back to Julian the day before. He must make it to London where he would be lost in the crowd, but what about Yukiko-chan. Yes, she would be useful because she had many contacts there that could be of value. Looking round to check, he saw Yukiko's laptop, grabbed it and made for the door. Lighting a petrol-soaked rag in a bottle, he hurled the incendiary through a window and watched, amazed at the effect of the ignition. Calling Yukiko to him he started running out of the yard and down the lane. The sound of a police car approaching from the opposite direction had them ducking into a yard by the railway level crossing, where several old coaches were parked. Hiding behind one they sat and got their breath back. Murata was very puzzled – where were all these police coming from?

Ten minutes had passed and three police cars had driven past on their way to the farm; the fourth one, a van, stopped and six policemen got out. They were standing in a group, obviously awaiting instructions, when another unmarked vehicle arrived.

Murata, taking Yukiko's hand, guided her down the side of the coach and stopped to open the luggage compartment. Pushing her in, he followed, lowering the door gently behind them. Murata then took hold of the frame and gave it a sharp tug just to snap the catch in place. No one more than ten feet away would have heard their actions; all they had to do was lie low and wait.

Murata concentrated upon analysing their escape so far. The fire at the farm would have destroyed any chance of a police dog being given something of theirs with which to follow a scent. There was no chance that Julian was going to tell anyone anything, or the children for that matter. Mrs Vaughan, if she survived, could be a problem, but she had not seen their route on leaving the farm so she would be no immediate help to the police. Yes, he would just have to wait and hope that a chance would be given to them to get away. Just then he heard footsteps and taking the gun from his shoulder holster, turned to face the side of the coach, only to hear the driver's door open, someone get in and the engine start.

"Hey, Jack!" a voice called. "Have you seen anyone about in the last half hour?"

"No, Terry. You lot looking for someone then?" asked the coach driver.

"Yes, there's been some kidnappers using the old farmhouse over there," replied the policeman.

"Well it's news to me. I've been coming and going in and out of here every day and not seen a thing. I'll keep me eyes skinned for you though," and with that he crunched the coach into gear and it lurched forward out onto the lane, turning in the direction of the main road.

"Constable, did you search that vehicle thoroughly?" asked Jackson, the hard-faced tall one of the two ATB officers.

"No, sir," admitted PC Terry Mannings.

"Nothing moves around here without it being thoroughly searched and the search officers covered by armed men, do I make myself clear? We are dealing with some bloody ruthless criminals." Jackson's voice had that level of bad-tempered exasperation about it that implied he should not have had to explain that to anyone in this search group.

Turning to the uniformed sergeant alongside him he said, "Radio to the car at the end of the lane and get that coach stopped."

"Can't, sir. It's been called away to a traffic accident on the Dell Quay roundabout," the sergeant replied stiffly.

"Jesus Christ. What the... Oh never mind." Jackson turned away and kicked a stone hard into the hedge. "Get a description of that coach circulated and have it stopped and searched by armed officers now."

"Right away, sir. Mannings, I want a word with you." With a furious expression on his face the sergeant strode towards PC Mannings to first obtain a full description of the vehicle, then issue some career advice.

At the edge of the field the young paramedic was working hard on Sarah Vaughan. She had stopped breathing just as he had arrived and from the signs, she had been haemorrhaging for some time. "Can't do much here, Neil, we'll have to get her to the ambulance." Don Harding gestured to his mate to help him get Sarah onto the stretcher. "One, two, threee. Okay now, as quick as we can. I don't think we've got long for this."

Helped by PC Forge the two ambulance men got her over the field, up the bank and over the fence to the roadside where their vehicle was parked. Once inside Harding resumed his desperate attempts to revive the lady. After five minutes his efforts were rewarded by a flicker of the eyelids followed by ragged breathing. "Right Neil, let's go. Can you tell A&E we're coming and that we have a very sick lady onboard who has miscarried and is haemorrhaging and at this time I can't stop it. I think she has already lost about two pints." The sirens wailed and lights flashed as the ambulance picked its way through the group of police vehicles preceded by two police motorcycle outriders. Travelling behind was an unmarked car driven by WPC Tucker with WPC Tina Gillard in the rear seat cuddling two very tearful, traumatised children. Both women and Commander Campbell, at his fatherly best, had tried in vain to get the girls to talk but all to no avail. It was hoped that the grandparents might be able to help when they arrived at the hospital later.

As the little convoy disappeared into the distance Commander Campbell walked across to the body still lying on the hard shoulder but now hidden by a forensic tent.

Calling from the outside of the tent he asked, "Does he have any ID?" There was a few seconds pause then the tent flap parted and a young officer appeared dressed in white overalls.

"There is nothing in his pockets that tells us who he is, so we are going to have the laborious job of photo recognition. Fortunately the face isn't badly damaged so we shouldn't have to do a computer reconstruction." Hamish Baird waited for Campbell to answer.

"Take all the photographs you want but I don't want anything leaving the scene without me seeing it first," Campbell said quietly. "I assume that you can let me have a picture pretty soon?"

"We are just getting that set up, sir," Baird replied. "I'll bring them over as soon as I can, sir. Where will you be?"

"Over there with PC Forge," said Campbell, striding away to where PC Forge sat on the embankment holding a thermos top of tea and staring at the ground. Campbell sat down beside him. "You know, Forge, these flak jackets we issue are no damn use at all." Forge looked at him, an expression of incomprehension on his face. "Yes, a flak jacket folded neatly in the boot of your car will not stop a thing."

"Sorry, sir, it won't happen again," replied Nic Forge, wishing a large hole in the ground would open up and swallow him.

Campbell patted him on the back. "Come with me, Constable, and run me through the events of what happened starting with the sighting of the girls." Both men stood and with Forge leading the way, descended the banking.

One hour later Murata was producing a knife from the sheath strapped to his ankle and was starting to work on the catch of the coach luggage bay. On leaving the yard the coach had been driven down the lane to the main road and turned left towards Chichester. Eventually it had stopped, Murata guessed, amongst some other coaches, as the driver had got down and had stood alongside the coach holding a long conversation with several other men. After listening to a discussion about the rates for school journeys and the problems of getting CRB if you have ever worked abroad, Murata was beginning to think that they would be trapped forever in this hot metal box.

A whistle from some distance away attracted the group's attention and with mutterings of 'At last' they moved away.

It was only a matter of seconds before the catch lifted and he was able to slowly open the flap and peer out to check that the coast was clear. Slipping to the ground he waved Yukiko to follow him, then standing between their coach and the neighbouring one they brushed each other down. Now looking less dishevelled, Murata broke down the automatic he was carrying, removing the barrel silencer and shoulder butt. Putting both parts into a black canvas bag, he held the now pistol-size weapon beneath his jacket and leading the way, stepped out across Chichester Theatre car park towards the bustling town centre. Using the underpass beneath Oaklands Way they crossed North Street and turned down North Walls into Tower Street. At the County Library they stopped. Once Yukiko had checked inside, Murata entered and the pair made their way across to the bank of Internet linked computers. Finding one free, Murata instructed Yukiko to go through his server to find if any e-mail message had been received from Stavos in Horta. Within minutes, Murata had learned that Yamamoto had successfully contacted Stavos and they had been due to leave with the stores and spares the day the message was sent.

As the library staff member approached them to check their user cards, they rose and left before being challenged. Now out in the street again they separated, each now making their way independently to London and hopeful anonymity amongst its teeming population. In a town with many Japanese students the young Yukiko blended in easily and passed through the station ticket hall without attracting any attention from the two policemen watching the platform entrance. Murata was not sure of his escape route; unlike Yukiko he had a long criminal record and the scars on his face made him easily recognisable. As he slipped from side street to side street he found himself still troubled by thoughts of how quickly his hideout had been surrounded. The British police did not normally have that manpower available in such a short time. Had they been betrayed? Had that young gai-jin Makepeace given them away before the escape? If so, how much did they know? With these thoughts now rushing through his mind Murata almost knocked over a traffic warden as she stepped back from a car windscreen to admire her work. The collision with a uniformed official brought him back to the instant reality of his situation and had him hurrying for a side alley, the warden's angry cry of 'Oy watch where yer goin' ringing in his ears. Alone now, and in a shaded spot, he stopped. Leaning against a wall, considered his next course of action. Two words came to mind: 'lorry' and 'nightfall'. With that decision made he went off in search of a place to hide until it was dark.

Chapter 8

The shock of seeing the man shot dead as he lay in the bottom of the rib had Ian frozen to the spot, its impact upon his attitude to his captors profound. Up until now he had harboured some small glimmer of hope that eventually he would be released and could return to his family. The cold-blooded murder had changed all that; to stay alive he must escape.

Arni's shove in the back had Ian cowering, his arms raised in futile protection. "Go forward and get the sea anchor in." Arni's face was set in a cruel smile. "We don't only shoot sick dogs."

Ian moved forward and started to haul in the anchor. Once he had it aboard he fed the warp back into the locker then disconnected the sea anchor itself to be stowed back in the cockpit locker. As soon as this was achieved he was ordered to empty the fuel cans into the main tank.

"Where do you want the cans stowed?" asked Ian.

"Over the side of course, where do you think?" answered Arni.

As Ian finished pouring the contents of the first can, Arni grabbed it and throwing it high into the air, fired a burst from his automatic pistol, hitting the can and sending it in an erratic descent into the sea. Instantly Hamaura was peering from the companionway hatch, gun in hand. Comprehending what was happening, she shook her head in disgust and disappeared below again. Having given the second can the same treatment, Arni turned to Ian and ordered him to set the mainsail whilst he motored the yacht into the wind. Rain began to fall and Arni, always one to avoid a watch when there was a chance of getting wet, went below to read and relax, leaving Ian to set the foresail alone.

Studying Arni's course predictions a few days later, Ian noted that their intended course would take them in a sweep towards Bermuda, leaving the islands only a few miles south of them. So near and yet so far, he thought, as he checked the compass course. It was then that a second thought occurred to him – were they planning another rendezvous? If so, would this one have a more seaworthy replacement for him? Occupied for some time with this prospect, he was unaware of the time and only focused when Hamaura's raised voice cut through his thoughts.

"Why we take this big loop?" she was demanding to know. "Azores here, Bermuda there, why we go all the way up here?"

"You do your job. Let me do mine," replied Arni, his voice rising in volume to match hers. "You know nothing, you hear, nothing about navigation and you know nothing much about sailing boats. So don't shout stupid questions at me, just watch and learn."

"If you don't tell me, how do you expect me to learn?" Her voice was less aggressive than before.

"We go up here to stay in the wind. If we go much below 38 degrees we could lose the wind and we don't have enough fuel to motor, okay?" Arni was still annoyed at being questioned.

"Why you not tell me when I asked first time?" Hamaura's voice rose again, her bad temper never far below the surface.

Arni didn't respond but just turned away, going forward to sleep until it was his turn at the helm.

Again the mention of Bermuda stirred Ian's thoughts, until he remembered that Hamaura had only informed the trawler, that the replacement had failed, and had not requested that a second plan be put in place. Why then did they want to go out of their way by going south against the Gulf Stream to Bermuda instead of crossing at right angles around latitude 38 degrees and picking up less adverse currents near to the American shoreline?

His brain unable to fathom another explanation, he concluded that maybe Bermuda was their final destination. Alternatively, whoever pulled this murderous couple's strings would automatically set up a replacement to reach them from Bermuda. Watching the clouds gathering in the west he said quietly to himself, "There are about 1700 miles between the Azores and Bermuda, 15 to 16 days of sailing. A lot can happen in that time."

With the evening came the rain, not heavy, just wet, yet another thing to dampen his spirits. Hamaura's brief turn at the wheel whilst Ian ate meant that by the time Arni came on watch he was exhausted. Within seconds of lying on the bunk he fell into a deep sleep. The dream was like none other he had ever had before; in it he kept seeing the image of a baby in someone's arms and each time he would reach out to take it in his own, only to have the image disappear and be replaced by darkness. Time and time again the image would appear, only to be snatched away, leaving him with a feeling of sadness and utter despair.

Now programmed to the 0400 hours rousing from sleep, Ian was already stirring as Hamaura entered the forward cabin. Pushing himself up, his hand touched a damp patch at head level on his sleeping bag; he had been crying – it wasn't just a bad dream.

"Get up! You not only person who need sleep," shrieked Hamaura, giving him a vicious prod with the gun barrel.

"Oh for God's sake, woman, do you have to shout and inflict pain all the time?" responded Ian.

"It is all you deserve, shitabakaraki," Hamaura replied, eyes narrowed, the words spat at him.

By the cooker he found coffee and a box of cereals; helping himself he then took his breakfast on deck where he relieved Arni. In the east the sky was getting lighter, heralding the dawn of a beautiful day. Putting his breakfast down on the stern quarter seat Ian nodded at Arni, who relinquished his grip on the wheel and without a word went below.

As Arni replaced Hamaura to keep an eye on Ian, he emerged clad only in swimming trunks, plus, of course, a gun. From below he dragged a thin mattress, which he proceeded to place in the sun on the windward side deck. The second trip below brought suntan lotion, a book and two cans of soft drink. Set now for this arduous task, he lay on the mattress to sunbathe. This ritual was to become the daily routine with Arni giving up the space to Hamaura, whose complexion turned from a snow-white to the brown of a tanned Western woman by the end of the week. Strangely, Arni never seemed to take any notice of Hamaura's obvious physical charms; her shapely body and beautiful face appeared to have no effect on him at all. During the whole of the voyage Ian had been aware of a constant hostility between them; hardly anything could be said without it becoming contentious, even down to something as trivial as the menu. Try as he might though, he was unable to divide them or divert them from their goal. Each attempt only brought their combined retribution.

Part of the daily ritual was the noonday sight, which both Arni and Ian took whilst Hamaura helmed. As this came at the end of Ian's watch he would see it down to being plotted on the chart and recorded in the log. The conditions had been perfect and each day revealed that the yacht had covered between one hundred and forty and one hundred and fifty miles. The act of recording all this data had amused Ian, as it would reveal to any official the exact course the yacht had taken and therefore potentially link it with the false sinking report. That was until the day he idly turned back to the beginning of the log only to see that the passage had been recorded as starting in Nice, calling at Gibraltar and then Horta before gaining the credibility of their true course. Also he noticed that the remarks column had recently received some attention from Hamaura in the form of whale sightings and beautiful cloud formations, fish caught and meals eaten. In fact she had very cleverly turned the record of this hard, relentless voyage into a romantic, enjoyable lovers' cruise.

After ten days the perfect weather changed and as Arni and Ian took their noonday sightings, black clouds threatened to the south-west, indicating an end to sunbathing. "There's a nice cloud formation for you to record in the log," Ian said to Hamaura as he stepped down into the cockpit. The kick from Arni landed just below Ian's ribs and had him doubled up in pain on the cockpit sole.

"I will not warn you again," shouted Arni. "You will always be polite to us, next time I will shoot you, you understand!"

Ian nodded, pulled himself to his feet and went below, going straight to the forward cabin and lying on the bunk, fighting to recover from the blow. Waking after four hours of restless sleep he was aware that the boat was being sailed over-pressed. Typically, Arni was always reluctant to do the work of reefing down and as Ian struggled to get into his wet gear, *Kiboko* was slamming hard into waves, causing things on shelves to jump. Finally, as he pulled his jacket on, a particularly hard slam threw a black bound album at Ian's feet. Crouching, he picked it up and was about to close it and put it back in the pocket locker above Arni's bunk when his eyes focused on the pictures it contained. Revulsion rose within him as he stared in horror at the depraved pictures of small boys; now of course it was obvious why Hamaura held no interest. Putting the album back, he went on deck and immediately set about the now dangerous task of reefing down.

Kiboko was under control and sailing faster, now that her spread of sail and angle of heel had been reduced, and Ian felt more comfortable. As he carefully picked a course through the waves he could hear above the wind the strains of another row taking place between Hamaura and Arni. Snippets of it were encouraging; she obviously thought that he, Ian, had to be kept as Arni was only good for 'fair-weather sailor' and 'too scared to do deck work'.

Shortly afterwards she came up into the cockpit, a sure sign that her stomach was still not capable of taking a rough sea. The relatively sudden arrival of a trough of low pressure had produced short seas stirred up by a force 6 to 7 wind.

"In these conditions I cannot sail the boat to the course," Ian shouted at Hamaura who was sheltering under the sprayhood. "The closest I can get is ten degrees, so we will end up quite a bit north of where you want to be." His statement was a hidden question. If she showed concern it would indicate that there was a rendezvous to be met; if not, then at least that threat was removed. Also it would confirm a growing belief that they were not going to call at Bermuda.

She did not answer for several seconds and Ian wondered whether she was going to discuss the situation with Arni. "You sure you cannot steer course?" she questioned.

"Yes," replied Ian.

"Okay," was all that she said.

After a few moments had passed she stood up, steadied herself by grabbing hold of the spray dodgers and stared astern.

Ian glanced over his shoulder and immediately saw the reason for her concern. Off in the distance and slightly to starboard of them he could see a cruise liner. "No problem," he said. "It will pass some distance to starboard of us."

"We turn now," she ordered, taking up the slack in the port hand foresail sheet.

Ian stood looking forward at the sea, his brain calculating the odds of him being able to create a sufficiently sudden broach to knock Hamaura off balance and maybe overboard. No sooner had the thought flashed across his brain than he saw her hook her life jacket harness to the companionway 'D' ring and brace herself firmly.

Even timing it as badly as he did, Hamaura stayed securely in place and in no time had the foresail set.

Whether or not *Kiboko* was seen from the bridge of the liner Ian didn't know, but he doubted whether even if seen, any record of sighting would be made, even if they could read the name on the dodgers. Several times during their voyage from the Azores they had sighted liners but all of the previous sightings had been many miles away and had not raised any alarm. Why Hamaura was so concerned about them being seen was something of a mystery for a moment or two until Ian remembered that *Kiboko*'s mainsail still carried the French identification number of its owner. If they wanted the boat to have a different nationality and identity then the sail identification would have to be changed.

They stayed on the new tack for three hours before Arni, coming on watch, ordered Ian to take the yacht back onto its previous course before he went below to eat and sleep. Waiting for the kettle to boil, Ian made a sandwich then glanced at the chart, trying to estimate where they were. Picking up the divider he traced out what he thought would have been their speed and course made during Arni's last watch. Adjusting the divider again, he continued along the same course until the time of the liner sighting and then measured out his estimation of course made for the remaining three hours. This, though rough, gave him some idea of their position; approximately two hundred miles east-north-east of Bermuda steering just shy of due west.

As so often happens at night, the wind eased and Ian was woken half an hour early by Arni to get more sail on. On deck the sky had that brittle clarity often associated with a cold front and indeed the temperature was well down on the previous day. With the dawn returned the wind that drove a series of sharp showers over them. Ian found himself reefing down only to let the same reef out as Arni strove to prove that he could sail the boat properly. At noon, cloud prevented any position fix and Ian was relieved that this, unlike their approach towards the Azores, did not cause any anxiety. As Ian later crashed onto his bunk he overheard Hamaura ask, "How many days more of this, eh?"

"Maybe six or seven depending on the wind. We shall need to get ready for the new ID; I will make a start tomorrow if the weather improves." Arni's reply was the final brick in the wall; they were going to the east coast of America and would definitely not be calling in at Bermuda. As he lay on his bunk Ian prayed that they would continue this looping course that was now taking them southwards towards Bermuda and the prospect of joining the sailing route between there and the American coast. That would increase the chances of them meeting other boats that could present opportunities of escape.

"Romance Allemande," she said, handing the new identity documents to Arni.

It was 1000 hours, two days after the liner sighting; the previous day Ian and Arni had struggled for hours to change the mainsail over to the one delivered by Stavos and the late Yamamoto. The problem had not been getting the original fully battened sail off but getting the replacement sail on. Each luff slider had to be filed down to fit the slot and the slider nearest to the headboard changed to allow the board to sit properly when hoisted. Not large jobs but tiring and time consuming, reducing their achieved passage over twenty-four hours to a mere twenty miles.

Now underway again Ian noticed the difference the replacement sail was making. No longer could they achieve an average of six knots; they were now down to five and if Arni or Hamaura were at the helm only four.

"What does the name mean?" asked Arni.

151

"How should I know?" replied Hamaura. "It's what is written here, that is all."

"An 'Allemande' is a courtly baroque dance with interwoven or interlacing arms, so 'Romance Allemande' means a romantic courtly dance," said Ian.

Both turned and stared at him incredulously. "How you know that?" Hamaura asked, her voice almost polite in tone.

"I have a liking for classical music, you know Mascitti, Morin, Barbella, Bacilly and composers like them," said Ian, "not just the really great ones like Beethoven and Mozart."

"Ah so," said Hamaura. "Not just a sailor."

Arni just shook his head and started to undo the spray dodgers ready to stick on the new name. As in all Arni's projects, it was Ian who had to do all the hard work. The cleaning up of the dodgers after Arni's painted scrawling of the *'Naqah'* took four hours and a whole can of thinners. Ian had been aware that the name had been painted on the outside of the dodgers during their sail down the English Channel.

"What does *'Naqah'* mean?" he asked.

"It is Arabic for a female camel," informed Arni in an almost friendly tone.

"Ah, I see, ship of the desert," remarked Ian.

"Yes, that is so."

Eventually they were cleaned to Arni's satisfaction and were left tied to the cabin top grab rails to dry. Overnight rain removed the final suds of detergent used after the thinners, so by the following morning all was ready for the new name stickers. To Ian's surprise it was Hamaura who with care and some artistic skill applied the letters, leaving Arni only the job of replacing the dodgers either side of the cockpit.

No sooner had the task been completed than an American cruise liner bound for Bermuda came over the horizon and passed close by, to be waved at by Arni at the wheel and

Hamaura standing in the companionway, the gun out of sight pointed at Ian.

"Any attempt to signal and you will be dead, you understand?" she said, happily waving to the cruise passengers.

"Oh, I wouldn't dream of it," Ian replied straight-faced, inwardly cursing his inability yet again to hit back in some way.

His response brought a questioning look from Hamaura, obviously weighing up whether punishment was necessary. Choosing to ignore the remark she sat on the companionway steps looking at him eating his meal.

"Why you never asked what we are doing this for?" she asked.

"If I had, either one or both of you would have knocked me about again; I've had enough of that," Ian replied in a matter of fact way.

"Are you not curious?" The question sounded as if she was surprised at his not risking a beating to find out.

Sensing that she wanted to either justify her future actions or even make him feel more humiliated by not being able to stop them doing something horrific, he answered. "No, frankly all I want to do is get back to my wife and children and try hard to forget that this ever happened."

Standing, he moved over to the galley, washed up his plate carefully and stowed it away in the rack before completing the rest of the washing up. Turning to go forward and rest he noticed that she was still sat watching him. He returned her stare with expressionless eyes.

"You are interested," she said. "You're just saying that to hide fact."

"Really I could not care two stuffs as long as I get back to my wife and children. Honestly, I am not joking," he said, his voice weary and his face showing signs of extreme exhaustion but his mind aware of her disappointment at his lack of interest.

Going forward and removing his outer clothes to get into his sleeping bag, he was aware of her just behind him. Zipping the bag up he looked at her. "Now what do you want?" he asked, stifling a yawn. "If I don't sleep now I will probably fall asleep on watch."

"My brother and cousin are imprisoned in Japan. They must be freed," she said, her voice getting louder as she spoke.

"Oh really, must we talk about it now?" Ian yawned again.

"My brother Japanese Red Army, I am also," she said with pride at the admission of belonging to the illegal terrorist faction.

"I don't do politics," said Ian, his eyes now closing in exhausted sleep.

Arni's call to be relieved at the wheel brought this strange conversation to an end for the time being.

A thousand miles away Mel Clements sat with anchovy and egg sandwiches in hand staring towards some far-off place. Should he or shouldn't he have Anne Mari visit a psychologist? What was holding him back? Every week now she seemed to become more detached from reality; the apartment was in a mess, he was having to stand over her to watch her do the most basic things like wash herself and comb her hair. What a difference to the girl he had married all those years ago – young, vivacious, so full of life and energy. Then he had been called up to do his Vietnam duty, returning just one year later after the fall of Saigon, wounded but alive, to find her a changed woman. It was as though lights had been switched off within her and try as he might he could not get her to explain what had happened.

"What's doing this afternoon, Mel?" asked Stanislav. "I finished the metering units just before the break."

"You could give Yamada here a hand with the line change-over controllers," Clements replied.

"No need," said Yamada quickly. "I'm almost done, really."

"You sure, you only been on 'em a couple of hours," queried Clements. "I don't want any slipshod job done out here."

"I'm sure. I've only got ten more to do," Yamada replied, picking up his tools and climbing down from the truck.

"Okay then, you can help me check the ground earthing circuit Stanislav, improve your suntan," said Clements, smiling at the bronzed instrument engineer.

The three men split up, Stanislav going to the rear of the truck to fetch the meters and Clements to the cable drum to pull off a length of cable for the test, whilst Yamada walked across to the switching station building.

"Keen boy, that Yamada," said Clements. "Learns real fast, well qualified too."

"Like me though," said Stanislav. "Don't like working with others that much; get the job done faster on our own."

"Must say all the stuff I've checked on is good work," Clements said, stripping an end of the cable ready to solder to the test clamp.

Inside the building Yamada worked quickly, removing the Washington circuit breaker unit and replacing it with the unit he had brought in that morning. This was the eighth switching station they had visited in the last two months as part of the TN (Nuclear) Corporation contract. When the company started, they only concerned themselves with nuclear power stations, but now they were taking on grid work as well as looking after remote switching stations like this one. This was fine for Yamada as it meant that he only had to break into five remote switching stations at night, which were the responsibility of other contractors. Tonight would be his last one before returning to Mission Creek PWR, the newest build of them all, after which he would cross the border into Canada then fly to Europe, maybe never to return.

When Mel Clements came looking for him at the end of the day, Yamada was just putting his tools away.

155

"Thought you only had ten to do," said Clements.

"A couple of the springs needed replacing on the cage couplings," replied Yamada, showing Clements two that he had kept in his pocket for such an occasion.

"That's what I like," said Clements, "thorough workmanship. Now don't you go leavin' us, now you gettin' the hang of it all, will you."

Yamada shook his head. Over the months that he had worked with Clements he had grown to like him. Clements had never once mentioned his ethnic background or treated him any differently to the others he worked with. He also trusted his men to do the job and when he did check their work he always explained that it was demanded by the client and was not because he had any doubts. Karma is strange, thought Yamada; all his life in search of friendship and respect, only to have to destroy it.

"Stanislav, you drive the truck tonight. I need to close my eyes for a while," said Clements as they put the tools in the back.

The journey was conducted in unusual silence. "Is Mel okay?" asked Yamada back at the yard.

"I think it's that wife of his," said Stanislav. "He don't say much but I think she's givin' him a hard time, what with one thing and another."

Watching the two men drive off into the town centre, Yamada started his car and turned onto the road heading north.

It took him three hours to get to the site and find somewhere secluded to hide his car from view. Donning a black hood and overall, he carefully unstitched the chain link at a mid point between two security lights where the shadow was darkest. It was also the point at which the infra-red camera pole was positioned, therefore the only point the camera could not observe. Through his night glasses he could clearly see the two guards seated in their room watching the monitors. Something was gaining their full attention causing him to quickly check the

156

position of the other cameras. There it was on the other side of the compound; the gift that would allow him to enter the site with ease. Parked along the power line track was a Buick convertible containing a couple oblivious of the fact that their passionate lovemaking was being watched. Slipping through the opening, Yamada made his way to the switch room door and within two minutes had picked the lock and entered the building. Even though the building was windowless he worked with shielded torchlight to find the routes that Hamaura had identified from the information he had sent her. Doing the changeover was tricky, as he must not activate the breaker, which would raise alarms all over the place. It was different compared to normal maintenance conditions when the controllers knew that the team were working on the circuits and re-routed accordingly. It took him three quarters of an hour of careful nerve-wracking work to complete the changeover and, as he finally sat back to check with the torch that he had not left any sign of his visit, he realised that his hands were shaking. Leaving the building he locked the door, then checking on the guards, he swiftly regained the gap in the fence without incident and crawled through.

Now practised at the art, his re-stitching of the fence was achieved in only a few minutes. After checking his work he stepped back into the darkness. Through his night glasses he checked on the guards, then across at the Buick only to see the girl standing on the back seat totally naked, starting to get dressed. Making his way back to the car he almost stumbled over another couple amongst the bushes.

"Hey, get outa here, freak!" shouted the man, struggling to his feet and hurriedly adjusting his clothing.

Yamada broke into a run and within moments was out of range, camouflaged by his overall and hood in the darkness. Stopping and crouching down by a bush he listened to find out if he was still being pursued.

"Gary Berkley, you come back here right now and take me home, you hear!" Her plea was that of a frightened young girl. "Gary, come back. I'm scared stiff all on my own."

"Okay, okay. If I'd caught him I'd have taught him a thing or two. Damn freak. We won't be comin' out here again with his type around." Gary's bravado brought a smile to Yamada's face. There was no doubt that his training in Special Forces would have made him the teacher, not Gary.

Back at his car, he removed his black attire and sat for several minutes drinking a coke before starting the engine and heading back. It was late and the long drive would mean that again he would only get a couple of hours' sleep before reporting for work.

In the morning he was the last to arrive and on the journey out to the site fell asleep, causing some ribald comments, when, parked in the power station compound, they had to shake him to wake him up.

"That was some filly you were with last night I bet," Stanislav said, giving Yamada a shove on the shoulder.

Yamada felt strangely embarrassed and looked down at the ground, a sheepish grin on his face. "Look at him, Mel, ain't that pretty. I'm sure he's blushin' under there."

After some more teasing Yamada admitted to the scene he had in part witnessed from the switching station the previous night but casting himself in the athletic male role.

"You got more hormones than is good for you, young man," Clements remarked. "Now let's get a day's work done. Here's the schedule they want us to work to. We've got to team up for most of it on the turbine floor, but once we've cleared the thyrister cubicles and got to the control rooms then we'd best split, otherwise we'll go over time."

The meal break arrived and Clements disappeared as usual to the canteen, discarding his sandwiches without even looking in the bag. Returning with a pie, he sat apart from the other two, deep in his own thoughts.

"Hey Mel, you gonna join Burton's bachelor party next Friday?" asked Stanislav, eyes wide with enthusiasm.

"Sorry, what was that?" replied Clements.

"I asked if you wos gonna join Burton's party on Friday next," repeated Stanislav.

"I'd like to but I got a lot to do right now and Anne Mari, well, she's not so good," said Clements sadly.

"Oh hell, man, surely you can have one night off. It's not everyday Burton stands us a drink. You've gotta be there too, you young stud," Stanislav continued, giving Yamada a playful punch.

"I don't drink," replied Yamada. "It has a bad effect on me; I become ill."

"Hear that, Mel, he don't drink! Great man, you can drive. Weee ho, are we gonna have a party." Stanislav leapt to his feet and started to dance like some disjointed puppet.

The afternoon was spent checking number two turbine's generator coil insulation, a job that kept all three in conversation distance of each other. As maintenance crew, they had defined schedules and all three would be taking a two-week vacation at the end of the Mission Creek job.

"Where you off to next week, Yamada?" asked Stanislav. "I'm gonna go down to Florida and see what flotsam I can find on the beaches, if you know what I mean," he continued, not waiting for Yamada's answer.

"I am going south too," said Yamada. "I want to visit San Antonio and see the Alamo."

"I don't do that history thing much," said Stanislav. "What you doin', Mel? You takin' Anne Mari someplace?"

"Maybe," replied Mel. "I'm tryin' to book something up but it ain't that easy, what with her not bein' so well." In fact, the idea had only just occurred to him; he would check Anne

Mari into a clinic and stay nearby so he could just keep in touch with things. The inspiration brightened his mood and in the refreshment break had him in the payphone booth, ringing round in search of a place that felt they could help her.

The Thursday morning schedule had Yamada assigned to checking the heat sensor device transmitter as he had done on the previous visit to the station. Completing the standard circuit tests he filled in the maintenance data card, putting his initials in the last column. Next he moved to the bank of relays controlling the absorber rod clusters; here he reached into his toolbox, lifting out the top and middle trays to reveal the bottom compartment. Moving a yellow duster to one side and checking that the coast was clear, he lifted the substitute relay and placed it on top of the cabinet. Phoning the control room, he arranged for them to switch the system over to standby whilst he was conducting his tests. Then removing the main relay he replaced it with the substitute, putting the original into his toolbox. Returning to the cabinet he went through the standard tests on the replaced unit to satisfy himself that it would work as a normal relay, and signed it off with the initials MC. He then phoned the control room, this time to inform them that he was now moving over to the standby circuit. Replacing the standby relay he again tested the system to ensure that all would appear as normal, again signing off with the initials MC.

Two hours later he dropped his maintenance sheet folder onto the pile alongside Clements, who was sat hurriedly writing details of his credit card onto a form. "Shall I take these up to the office for you? You look a bit busy there?" Yamada asked, trying to appear helpful.

"Everything check out okay?" asked Clements.

"Yeah, no problem," said Yamada. "Do I ask for anyone in particular?" he continued, picking up the pile of folders.

"Oh yeah, just ask for a Mrs McDonald. If she's not there little Ruby will take them. Get a signature. The pad's on my toolbox," and with that Clements returned to completing his form covering Anne Mari's clinic visit.

On the long drive back to the yard Stanislav kept up his efforts to get Clements to the party the following evening, finally winning through with the proviso that Clements would probably leave early and get a taxi home.

The last day of testing was always the day that Clements did the random checks on the work they had carried out. Yamada stood nervously in the control switch room as Clements selected the absorber rod cluster control relay for test.

"Was there any record that these had been changed in the past?" Clements asked.

"No, why do you ask?" replied Yamada.

"Oh it's just they look a bit different to the others, but they check out ok," said Clements, leaving his finger marks on the relay case and closing the cubicle door and locking it.

Yamada had felt sick with shock when Clements asked about the change and had only just regained his composure when Clements turned to him and patting him on the shoulder, said, "Come on, let's get to that damn party and watch Stanislav make a fool of himself."

Back in his rooms Yamada tried to phone Murata but could not get an answer; in the end he sent a text message: 'All arrangements for the BBQ in place. Looking forward to meeting you again.' Smiling, he slipped the phone into his pocket and finished packing his bag. Satisfied that he was leaving the place without any trace of his activities there, he closed the door quietly, crept down the stairs and out into the street to his car. At the kerbside he removed his door key from his pocket and dropped it down a drain. After putting his bag in the trunk he drove off to pick up Stanislav who lived a few blocks away.

At the party it wasn't Stanislav who was making a fool of himself; he had soon discovered that the barmaid at O'Brien's was more worthy of his attentions than the beer. Clements however was definitely in party mood and with Burton, got amazingly drunk. When the lap dancer organised for the evening turned up, it was Clements she had to wag her finger at and say to him, "Ooo you're a very naughty boy. What would your wife say?" To roars of laughter from the assembled crowd.

Burton, his eyes glazed in an alcoholic stupor, put his arm around Yamada's shoulders and said, "I ain' seen Mel Cements ly this ever before, an' I've known him for nigh on ten years. Hell I bet Anne Mari's gonna have a job holing him back tonigh'."

It was one o'clock in the morning when Yamada, supporting Clements, left the bar having said goodnight to Stanislav who was waiting around for the barmaid to finish her shift.

Stanislav's not coming along worked well with Yamada's plans. Since the start of operation 'Kinoko Kumo', Yamada had been trying to find a way of diverting suspicion from himself when checks were made into the faulty working of the equipment. Obviously putting Mel Clements' initials onto the maintenance sheets would only work until Clements was questioned and then Yamada's name would be linked with the work. With the operation due to reach its climax in the next few days, he needed to delay the hunt that would inevitably follow as long as possible. If his name were brought into the frame too early, all his work would be suspect.

At the block in which Clements lived, Yamada parked the car in a side street instead of outside the entrance. In the back seat Clements snored in a drunken sleep. Reaching under the driver's seat Yamada pulled out an automatic pistol and silencer. Screwing the silencer to the barrel, he got out of the car and stuffed the weapon into the back of his trousers to be hidden by his jacket. Slapping Clements around the face, he roused him sufficiently to get him out of the car and walking round to the entrance doors.

"Hey Mel. What's your entry code?" Yamada asked.

"Can' remem," Clements answered, sliding down the wall Yamada had propped him against.

Yamada reached up to the intercom system, pressed number 34 and waited. A few minutes later he pressed the button again, this time leaving his finger on it for several seconds. After the fourth attempt a woman's voice asked who it was.

"I'm Yamada, Ma'am. I work with Mel. We've had a bit of a party and he has had a few too many beers. Could you press the button and let him in?"

"Who are you again?" the woman asked.

"Yamada, Ma'am, I work with Mel," he said, trying to keep his voice friendly.

The lock buzzed and Yamada pushed the door open, jamming his foot inside whilst he half lifted and half pulled Clements into the entrance hall.

When the lift stopped at the third floor, Yamada guided Clements to the door of his flat and helped him find his key. As the door opened Yamada saw, standing in the middle of the room, Mel Clements' wife in full evening dress. Something about her looked so sad, her eyes hardly seemed to focus on either of them but she was obviously not drunk, just in a sort of dream state. Yamada had not expected this; he had anticipated some untidy slut, not this tragic figure before his eyes. Stopping Clements from falling flat on his face, Yamada staggered with him across the room and let him drop into an armchair. Standing back trying to gather his thoughts he jumped as his mobile rang. Pulling the phone from his pocket he studied the screen. It was a message from Murata-san: 'Well done, make sure garden is tidy for the special day. Murata.'

Yamada reached for the pistol and pulling it clear shot Anne Mari between the eyes before forcing Mel Clements' mouth open and pulling the trigger again. Cleaning the gun he removed the silencer and placed the pistol in Mel Clements' right hand, closing the fingers firmly round the weapon. Then using his work's ID card to ease the door catch as it sprung home, he silently closed the door and left the building. With luck it will take some days before they come to this flat, Yamada thought, and maybe think it was some kind of suicide pact. Yes. The garden is now tidy.

Chapter 9

"You are unfortunate like me to live in a country where monarchy is held in high honour. Normal person treated like slave while Emperor live like God. We fight to change system and allow all people to live same." Hamaura had been trying for days to start what she thought to be a meaningful conversation with Ian. Each time he had rejected her approach, claiming disinterest in politics. In truth she showed little knowledge of other political systems, seeming to be obsessed by what she considered to be the unfair Japanese system in which the Emperor still had a position of respect and some power.

"I thought that your Emperor was like our Queen, in that he is a figurehead of state rather than a ruler," said Ian.

"He and his ancestors have crushed Japanese people for many centuries claiming that they are God and must be worshipped," she said, her anger surfacing. "We are dedicated to sweep away this injustice and bring proper government." From there she launched into a fanatical tirade condemning what appeared to be everything that stood for law and order in Japan as being some form of plot by the monarchy and government to subdue the population and feather its own nest. It was during this outburst that Ian considered the idea of apparent conversion to the cause and tried hard to appear interested in what she was saying and interject with sympathetic comment.

Arni, coming on watch to relieve Hamaura, was surprised to see her sitting in the aft lee quarter of the cockpit in earnest discussion with Ian regarding world order and the revolutionary changes she and her few enlightened comrades hoped to bring. Before going below she explained the link with Arni was due to his membership of the Popular Front for the Liberation of Palestine and the close association of the two organisations.

Before Ian knew it he was embroiled in another political presentation.

The ferocity of Arni's feeling towards the United States Government and every American was nothing short of terrifying and revealed to Ian a fanatical hatred in the man that he had previously totally underestimated. Here it became obvious that these two were more than willing to commit any atrocity in order to bring attention to their deluded beliefs, provided that they took many American lives as well. These two were not merely anarchists with hopes of rich pickings from the ransom they had spoken about earlier; they were out-and-out extremists.

During the following days Ian found it easier to work on Hamaura than Arni; hers was a political quest whilst his was strongly founded in religious dogma. Ian kept the subject alive by a series of questions about the origins of her discontent, unearthing some genuine grievances but mainly student propaganda that had been carried through into adulthood. With Arni, however, Ian avoided any further discussion, concerned that it might increase the man's resolve to destroy.

The discussions brought an end to the taunting and torture from Hamaura and Ian prayed that he had bought more time for himself. How small a change had been achieved in the relationship with her was soon to be borne out.

Arni was lucky to get the noon sunshot with the sextant. Ian, as was now the established routine, took the instrument from him and repeated the exercise for his own benefit and practice. Going below, Ian watched Arni run the calculations and mark their position on the chart complete with date and time. Working the tables using Arni's readings himself and transferring the position to the chart, Ian noted a large error.

"Do you really think we are that far away from the coast?" he asked.

Arni laughed. "You really have got to understand this, eh. I put error on chart to see how much you know."

Looking at the latitude and longitude that Ian had calculated Arni picked up the eraser and rubbed away his mark. "You're close enough," he said.

Ian raised his eyebrows, wondering whether in fact the error had been intentional, or had the long voyage and tiring watch system got to Arni as well.

The ever alert Hamaura heard it first, her eyes scanning the horizon searching for the source of the noise. Seeing the speck in the sky some miles off, she shouted down to Arni to take the helm quickly as there was an approaching helicopter. As soon as Arni had the wheel she was below and ordered Ian into the forward cabin to sit with his arms folded where she could see him, her gun enforcing the instruction.

"You stay very still and no attempt to make signal," she said with menace.

Ian nodded and took up a position directly under the clear perspex hatch.

"Further forward, wise guy," she said. "You think I am stupid, you think I should trust you because you appear interested in my ideals."

Reluctantly Ian shuffled forward on the bunk until his back came into contact with the anchor locker bulkhead, aware that his newly found interest in revolutionary politics was worthless.

"That's better. Now you just keep still and you will not get hurt," she said, backing up the companionway steps to the cockpit and sitting on the bridge deck where she could see the approaching helicopter and keep an eye on her prisoner.

Above them the HH-60 Jayhawk helicopter of the US Coastguard Service turned and descended to around fifty feet, marking time with them fifty yards off their port beam.

The aircraft had taken off from Elizabeth City in North Carolina on a routine patrol and training flight. One of thirty five in operation with the Coastguard Service, it had a range of 600 miles and was part of the screen looking for illegal immigration or drug smuggling operations in addition to the role of air-sea rescue.

As Arni gave a friendly wave the radio crackled with the voice of the pilot.

"*Romance Allemande, Romance Allemande, Romance Allemande*, this is United States Coastguard Helicopter off your port side, are you receiving, over?"

Hamaura descended the companionway steps and picking up the radio microphone responded. "United States Coastguard, this is yacht *Romance Allemande* receiving loud and clear. Do you wish to continue on channel 16, over?"

"Hold channel 16 and advise persons onboard, nationality, port of origin and last port of call, over," the pilot instructed.

"We are two persons, Arnaud and Fumiko Fernande from Italy. Our port of origin was Nice and our last port of call was Ponta Delgada, Azores, over," Hamaura replied.

"Please state your destination, over," the pilot's metallic voice requested.

"We are aiming to make landfall at Morehead City, over," she responded.

"You are both required to report to immigration within 24 hours of arrival, presenting your passports with visas. Then you must clear Customs, over," the pilot informed.

"Your instructions are understood. We have passports and visas prepared ready, over."

"Continue your present course, have a nice day, out." With that the radio went dead and the Jayhawk climbed away.

"Take the wheel again," Hamaura ordered.

Ian climbed off the bunks and made his way aft, taking the wheel from Arni. As soon as he could he searched the sky for the departing helicopter, sighting it some miles ahead of them just to leeward of their course. As he studied the aircraft it descended again as if to make contact with another vessel. Several minutes passed before the aircraft again rose into the sky and, climbing to a higher altitude, headed west. Ian's spirits soared; for here could be the opportunity he had been praying for if the vessel was another yacht. Fortunately Arni had changed channel on the VHF radio to pick up any coastal weather forecast, so had not overheard the radio contact to the vessel ahead. From a weak and crackly signal Ian understood that the night would be wet with winds of force 4 with occasional gusts of force 6.

Arni returned on deck. "You heard the weather forecast?" he asked.

"Yes," Ian replied. "Sounds a bit wet and windy."

"You got it right. See this here," Arni pointed to his bronzed forearms. "Well, that's suntan not rust, so you take a rest now eh. You can come back for a coating of rust later!"

"Thanks a bunch," replied Ian. "Hope you peel." Then handing over he went down into the cabin and found Hamaura stirring a pan of noodles.

"I get you through some pretty bad storms and helm most of the way across this benighted ocean only to learn that I will not be arriving upon the other shore," Ian said with some venom.

"Why do you think that?" Hamaura replied.

"I was listening to your friendly chat with the Coastguard helicopter. The presence of a third person aboard this boat was not mentioned, that's why I think my time is up." Ian's anger, that had been brewing from the moment he had heard her report over the radio, boiled over; now he knew that he had no future and felt strangely reckless.

"We have not decided yet how to get you ashore," Hamaura responded. "I was keeping our options open, that is all."

"Why should I believe that?" Ian asked.

"Because I said it," Hamaura said, glaring at him angrily. "If you want food eat some of this, if not get forward out of my sight."

169

Ian returned her glare before reaching out, and using a fork, helped himself to a portion of noodles. Returning to the cockpit he sat on the leeside under the sprayhood and sullenly ate. He felt reasonably confident that the lazy Arni would keep him helming through to midnight and even tomorrow morning, but he guessed his time would be up before they were in sight of the coast. Hamaura's statement was definitely no guarantee of his survival and he still had vivid memories of the fate of his replacement in the Azores. As he sat staring out across the ocean he wondered what would be the fate of his family. With him dead, what reason was there for his wife and daughters' survival? In his mind's eye he could see the image of that older man with the burn scars on his face; had he already executed them?

Finishing the food he went below again and placing his bowl in the sink, went forward to get into his sleeping bag. Sleep was impossible as his brain kept racing with more improbable ideas of escape. With a great effort he concentrated upon the prospect of closing on the craft ahead of them, assuming that it was a yacht and that Arni would continue to sail too close to the wind. Ian guessed that it would be only five or six miles away. The problem would be that if *Kiboko*, or rather *Romance Allemande* was sailing faster than the boat ahead Arni would undoubtedly see it and alter course to avoid it. The frequent flogging of the mainsail was some reassurance to Ian that Arni, trying to impress Hamaura again, was pinching too high on the wind and slowing the yacht down in the process. Keep it up Arni, he thought.

The real question was; what could he do if they did get close to another vessel? To call out for help would bring instant execution and would probably endanger those on the other craft as well. To convey any message would be a risk and would be too complex for it to be effective.

If there was a vessel and he was able to overtake it during his spell in the dark, would it be possible to slip overboard and use a flare to attract the other boat's attention? For that to be even slightly possible he would have to ensure that *Romance Allemande* continued on course for some considerable distance without alarming either of his captors. The whole reason for his being there was the fact that the yacht did not have self-steering and though she could be balanced and was capable of holding a straight course for some distance, a gust of wind or a larger wave would soon knock her off course and cause her to come up into the wind and stop. Again the risk was too high, particularly in the conditions forecast. Maybe if he could disable the yacht's steering somehow, that might work. As demonstrated before, if he went over the side he would be out of sight in a very short time. So if they did not see him go and could not steer the yacht, his chances would be improved until he struck the flare. He would have to work that out later; first was the steering and the problem of wrecking that without drawing attention to himself. Rooting under Arni's bunk Ian found the socket set and as quietly as he could, removed three of the heads that might just fit the wheel nut. Ignoring the ratchet lever he selected the simple folding one, slipping it into the trouser pocket of his wet gear. Half an hour before he was due on watch Ian went to the heads and enjoyed a good wash and general smarten up. His next visit was to the galley where he set about preparing a good meal using the last of the tinned pies and potatoes. Hamaura was still sleeping so it was easy to quickly visit the cockpit and tell Arni that a meal would be waiting for him soon. Grumbling as always about being kept waiting, Arni insisted that he would finish the cooking, relinquishing the wheel and going below away from the gathering gloom and spots of rain that were now falling.

It was three quarters of an hour before the plate of food was pushed onto the bridge deck. Leaving the wheel Ian stepped forward and recovered the plate just before the food slid off it onto the cockpit sole. He knew that if he was to try any form of escape he would need lots of energy and so for the first time in days consumed all that was on the plate, even though it was cold. Hamaura appeared at the foot of the companionway looking bleary-eyed and made no move to come on deck, which allowed Ian the opportunity to investigate how to sabotage the steering. The wheel itself had a central boss screwed into the wheel spindle that could be tightened to prevent the wheel from being turned. The boss covered the nut holding the wheel to the spindle; therefore, by removing the boss Ian would be able to take off the nut then replace the boss again without it being obvious that the nut was missing.

Ian could hear Hamaura busy in the galley area fixing a meal. Taking advantage of the lack of surveillance he undid the boss and slipped it into his jacket pocket before selecting a socket head and trying it on the nut to see if it fitted. The second one fitted exactly, so putting it safely back into the jacket he tossed the other two over the side and replaced the boss. All he had to do now was wait until dark and pray that Hamaura would stay down in the cabin and play with her tape recordings.

Rain had begun to fall and thicker cloud turned day into night in a matter of minutes. Ian, now fully sealed into his heavy weather gear, pondered upon how to get the yacht to stay on course long enough for him to go over the side and be out of execution range before it turned into the wind and stopped. Try as he might the wind, force 4 gusting force 6, frustrated his efforts and allowed only two or three cables lengths before the yacht drove up to windward. He toyed with the idea of reefing down, but if there were another yacht ahead of them the reduced speed would prevent him from catching it.

After an hour he gave up the effort to balance the yacht on course and concentrated on getting as much speed as possible whilst keeping a careful lookout. The question now was what to do if he managed to catch up with another yacht. First would be how to disable *Romance Allemande* sufficiently to enable escape without endangering those aboard the other vessel. Removal of the wheel alone would give only limited time and probably insufficient distance to ensure safety. Somehow he must work out a way of keeping the yacht on course and create other problems to delay his captors from giving immediate chase.

Suddenly inspiration came. "Hamaura-san, can you take the helm for a few minutes?" he called. Several seconds passed before her form appeared at the companionway.

"It better be important, I am busy." Hamaura's face was set in its normal responsive frown.

"The anchor lashings are working loose," Ian replied.

Five minutes passed whilst she donned her wet weather clothes and clambered into the cockpit.

"If you can hold this course I will only be a few minutes. I hope," Ian said as he clipped his safety harness to the jackstay and stepped from the cockpit onto the windward deck. Making his way forward he knelt, screening the anchor area from Hamaura's view. Instead of attending to the anchor he reached under the drum of the headsail furler and undid the knot forming the bitter end of the furling line. If he was able to remove the wheel and get over the side, Arni's first action would be to haul in the foresail, by pulling on the furling line. Ian guessed he would do that before searching for the emergency tiller, stored in the deep cockpit locker, to keep the yacht held pointing into the wind by the mainsail. Ian was confident that Arni would not consider laying the yacht hove to. With luck, as he pulled off the last few coils from the drum, the line would come adrift and the sail would unfurl again, providing further confusion with the possibility of the yacht bearing away. Quickly Ian retied the anchor lashings and started to make his way back to the cockpit when another idea came to him.

Moving across to the mast he removed the falls coil of the mainsail halyard and thrust it through between the tensioned halyard and the mast above the winch, forming a knot around the winch that was not immediately obvious. Retying the falls coil to the cleat, he made his way back to the cockpit.

"Why you took so long?" Hamaura demanded.

"Wet knots are hard to undo," Ian replied. "Try it sometime."

"What were you doing at the mast?" she asked suspiciously.

"Just making sure that the falls coil doesn't come undone and go over the side," he replied.

"Ah so," she said, studying him carefully.

As he took over the wheel again she surprised him by clipping on her harness and going forward herself. Satisfied with the anchor lashings she made her way back, stopping at the mast and pulling on the halyard falls coil before returning to the cockpit.

"Did it meet with your approval?" Ian asked.

She nodded and gave a flicker of a smile before going below out of the rain.

Ian allowed her time to take off her wet weather clothes and settle back into the absorption of her tape recording machine. Then he quietly raised the lid of the cockpit stowage locker to check that the emergency tiller was not easy to hand. As far as he could tell, in the dim light from his pocket torch, the tiller was well buried and it would be a major operation to recover it. His eyes then fell upon a large coil of thin rope that was something to do with the inflatable buoys that virtually filled the locker even when deflated. Carefully he eased the coil from the locker and sat on it to hide it from prying eyes whilst he gently closed the lid again and threaded the padlocks through the catch eyes.

After a quick check on Hamaura he took up the coil, hung it on the outside of the spray dodgers and tied it to the top guard rail where in the dark it would not be seen. With another three and a half hours to go before Arni came on watch, Ian returned to his quest for speed, straining his eyes against the rain, searching for a light that would indicate another vessel. The wind was for once helping his efforts as it had swung into the south, giving them a perfect beam reach on which to charge blindly across the ocean. The main question still remained; how to make his escape without condemning himself to death by hypothermia. If he were in the water, would another vessel have sufficiently good watch keeping in this quiet part of the ocean to see him or sufficient strength and training to get him onboard?

His eyes strained to see forward – nothing, only the baffling blackness of the night and the rain. Maybe he had strayed too far north, or probably the other vessel, if there had been one, was bound for Newport or some other port well off their course. During the next hour his desperation to sight the vessel grew. With it came an increasing feeling of defeat and frustration at being cut off and alone: a helpless prisoner. His thoughts strayed again, as they often did, to Sarah and the girls, his conviction that Sarah was dead weighing heavily on his mind. The emptiness of heart one feels with personal loss could only mean that. They had been so close, so capable of telepathy, each the other's right hand, mentor and balm against life's aggravations. Her support and understanding during the last few months had been marvellous, especially considering her condition. Tears of dejection and frustration started down his cheeks, his resolve almost broken.

"Wake up and steer correct course!" Hamaura's screamed order brought him back with a jolt. "Can't you do anything without going into a dream? The British disease, sleeping on job!"

Without waiting for a response, she returned to the dry comfort of the cabin, her eyes noting the return to course. Ian straightened up, forced his shoulders back as if standing to attention and looked ahead and slightly up forcing a smile onto his face. His dark mood broken, he once more set about finding his elusive quarry, aware that his foolish self-pity had drawn the attention he desperately didn't want. Refocused and intent now on doing everything he could to track down another vessel in the vicinity, Ian tweaked the sails. He needed to gain the best possible speed and ensure that the maximum sea area was covered before he came off watch at dawn, the chance of escape lost.

So intent was his concentration that her silhouette in the companionway and the call, "Soup," made him jump. His reaction made her suspicious again and she came up into the cockpit.

"I was concentrating and your shout gave me quite a shock," he said, trying to sound plausible.

"No, you were looking for something ahead. What was it?" she demanded to know, coming out from the protection of the sprayhood and scanning the darkness herself.

"Apart from the odd forty foot container or whale, what is there to look out for when you are on watch in the Atlantic?" he replied.

"You are up to something," Hamaura snapped back accusingly.

Ian sighed. "Have it your way."

Hamaura glared at him and sat herself at the forward end of the cockpit in the shelter of the sprayhood. For a full half hour she sat it out, obviously getting damp and cold. Finally she snatched up the soup mug that Ian had drained and went below only to reappear after a few minutes to check on him.

Ian cursed himself for not seeing her and reacting like a schoolboy caught playing truant. It was a further fifteen minutes and four visits to the companionway before she finally settled back at her tape recorder. All this time Ian kept up his careful watch, aware that if he sighted anything he must not show it.

Then suddenly a distant glow rather than a pinpoint of light appeared. At first he thought it could be the lights of some far-off ship but a check through the binoculars revealed that it was the cabin light of a yacht seen through the companionway hatch. For some reason the yacht had no navigation lights showing which was why he had not seen it sooner. Snatching glances of the yacht he began to build up a picture that gave him some hope. He guessed from the vague silhouette that the yacht was about the same length as *Romance Allemande* and, much to his relief, she had at least one reef in her mainsail and was sailing at only a slight heel. As he continued to inspect the yacht he realised that they were in fact quite close and that *Romance Allemande* was overhauling her very quickly indeed.

Ian steered gently to bring *Romance Allemande* slightly downwind of his target, aware that at any moment Hamaura might appear, having noted the alteration of course. As the two boats closed Ian could at last see into the other yacht's cabin, which was illuminated by a Tilley lamp hung from a line between two posts. Every now and again he could see the top of someone's head bob up as if they were working on something at the foot of the companionway steps.

He checked on Hamaura and, satisfied that she was now deeply engrossed in her work, set about dealing with the yacht's steering. Swiftly removing the locking boss he withdrew the socket head and lever, assembled the two, slipped them over the holding nut and applied pressure. He was now beginning to panic as the distance between the two yachts was closing fast and the nut was not budging. It was now or never. Standing close to the wheel, he gave the lever his full strength and after a few seconds was rewarded with the nut turning at last. Finally putting the nut in his pocket with the socket and lever, he reached over the spray dodger and recovered the long line. Tying one end to the four o'clock spoke and the other to the twelve o'clock, he streamed the rest of the line carefully over the side rail. It would be essential to his plan that the wheel came easily off the spindle, so Ian tugged at each side of the wheel alternately to loosen it.

The gap between the two yachts was closing fast but still the wheel remained firmly on its spindle. Then he detected the smallest of movements before the wheel slid back along the spindle and almost came off. A couple of nudges and the wheel slid back onto the shaft enough, Ian thought, not to fall off too soon.

With his heart racing and the sweat of fear trickling down his back he checked on Hamaura. Then turning the yacht onto its final approach course, he prayed that the crew aboard the other yacht would not see them coming and hail them. Everything seemed to go into slow motion as *Romance Allemande* came into the shadow of the other yacht's sails. The other yacht was apparently under wind-vane self-steering and Ian wondered what the effect on this would be as the yachts came close. At last the two were alongside and Ian was able to luff up slightly and in three quick steps pass from *Romance Allemande*'s windward deck to the leeward deck of the other yacht, by catching hold of her shrouds, without making a sound.

Now using the reins he had attached to the wheel he hauled hard, turning *Romance Allemande* suddenly to starboard, her speed carrying her round and bringing her stern through the wind. The yachts were now moving rapidly apart and with a painful jerk that almost pulled him over the side, both halves of the line came taut in his grip before coming free again as the wheel pulled off the spindle. It crashed onto the helmsman's seat then flew up into the air, clearing the pushpit rail before sending up a cloud of spray as it hit the water.

He heard Hamaura scream something as she began to haul herself into the cockpit, only to have the vision snatched from him as *Romance Allemande* crash-gybed through the wind, careering into a dramatic broach before recovering semi hove-to with her headsail backed but mainsail still driving. As he watched *Romance Allemande* disappear into the darkness, her masthead light soon obliterated by the rain, Ian smiled, then wondered how he was going to introduce himself to his new captain.

On board *Romance Allemande* Hamaura had been close to finishing her task of recording demand and threat messages. Suspicious that the Igirisu-gin Vaughan was up to something, she made a note to get Arni to check the anchor area and the mast ropes as soon as it was light. Though she had checked them herself she was sure that she had missed something. Glancing up she could see his hand on the wheel and the boat was holding roughly to the set course. It was just as she finished planting the trigger signal onto the tape that it happened. Suddenly the yacht altered course, pitching her sideways as it heeled heavily to port. Hauling herself up into the passageway she fell headlong over her toolbox as she went to move aft, striking her left shoulder on the corner of the chart table. She heard, as well as felt, her collarbone break, but ignoring the pain got to her feet and holding on only with her right hand, climbed the companionway steps to the cockpit. Realising that Ian was no longer at the wheel she screamed down to Arni to wake up and come on deck. It was then that she made the mistake of leaning forward to climb the rest of the way into the cockpit, for as she did so the yacht gybed, the wind slamming the boom across, the taut mainsheet coming with it, crushing her against the forward cockpit bulkhead. The force of the gybe was more than enough to break two of her ribs as her right side was smashed against the hard corner of the companionway entrance, realigning her already broken collarbone and breaking her upper left arm. Passing out with the pain, her lifeless body was held tight by the pressure from the mainsail, her head and shoulders on the bridge deck and her legs hanging down the companionway steps.

179

Arni had been in a deep sleep when her screamed order had penetrated his brain. Reluctantly releasing the small young boy of his dream from his degrading torment, he dropped the lee cloth and swung off the bunk still half asleep. Stumbling through the cabin he also tripped on the toolbox then trod on something sharp that made him yelp. The yacht, heeled over in a harsh broach, brought fear and the need for urgency. Holding on and standing on one foot, he pulled the screw he had trodden on from the sole of his right foot and cursed before stepping to the companionway steps down which the legs of the unconscious Hamaura hung. Struggling past her body he braced himself across the steeply angled cockpit and hauled on the mainsheet traveller, releasing Hamaura from the crushing jam. Her body, now free, slid rapidly back into the cabin, her head hitting the galley stove with concussive force. Freeing the foresail sheet that was pinning the yacht into the broach, he waited until it righted and took a quick look in the sea around for any sign of Ian. With nothing in sight Arni descended into the cabin and, propping Hamaura up with the seat cushions, did the best he could to make her comfortable and secure before racing back on deck to haul on the foresail furling line to roll in the sail. With only two more turns to go the line went slack and with the flailing sheet jammed in the track roller, the wind blew the sail until it had fully unwound again.

"You bastard, when I find you I will kill you!" he shouted into the darkness.

"Where is the wheel? What have you done with the wheel?" Arni's voice was now a scream of rage. He bent to pull the padlocks from the locker catches only to find that Ian had snapped them home. Down the companionway steps again, it took him five minutes to find the keys in the chart table draws.

"He's gone over side," Hamaura croaked at him.

"Maybe, but he sabotaged the headsail before he went and has taken the wheel with him, the bastard. Did you see any other boats about?" Arni glared at her. "You were supposed to be on watch with him, or were you still composing your cry for justice?"

Stung by his sneering comment she spat back at him. "I kept good watch and did my job, no sign of any boat, I look only few minutes before he jump."

The first thing Arni had done was to look for other crafts' navigation lights but had seen none. It must have been only a couple of minutes after her call that he had made the search and it was unlikely that a boat could move out of sight in that time even in this weather.

Returning to the cockpit, Arni recovered the emergency tiller from the deep locker and fitting it to the head of the rudderpost, got the boat under control again. Searching for Ian's body was going to be impossible, as he had no idea how far and in what direction the yacht had gone during the last half hour or so. Setting the vessel back on course, Arni began to ponder on why Ian had gone to such elaborate lengths to ensure that having gone over the side, he could not be rescued. The more he considered the question, the more convinced he became that Ian had survived and was probably aboard another boat. Then movement below reminded him of the injured Hamaura. Centring the mainsheet and hauling it in tight, he moved quickly forward with three sail ties and pulled in the foresail, tying it to the forestay as best he could to stop it catching too much wind. Though not the best way to hove-to, it would keep the bows roughly into the wind and enable him to assess Hamaura's condition.

Going below, he found her on the starboard settee in the cabin, obviously in great pain. It took him two hours to splint her arm and bind her ribcage before placing her left arm in a sling in an effort to get the broken collarbone back in line. Fortunately her broken ribs had not punctured the lung and the painkillers appeared to be working well. He was aware that what he had done was not that good and had to admit that Ian would probably have done it far better. One thing was for sure, there was no way that she could sail the yacht but, Allah be praised, they only had forty or so miles to go then she could see a doctor.

Ian stood for several minutes staring at the point in the darkness where he had last seen *Romance Allemande*. Any moment he expected it to reappear with a furious Arni at the helm and Hamaura taking aim to execute him, but the dark wall held and at last he had relaxed. Aware that he had made his escape, he sat on the cabin roof and cried as the sense of relief flooded over him.

Several minutes passed before he regained control of his emotions and started to seriously assess his current situation. Carefully he bent over and took a peep through the cabin window. Inside he saw a brunette, probably in her mid thirties, with glasses, standing by the chart table studying what looked like a wiring diagram. After a few moments she got down on her hands and knees and peered into the engine compartment. Ian moved carefully forward, checking to see who else was onboard; to his surprise she appeared to be sailing single-handed. He made his way round forward of the mast then down the windward deck, still checking for others onboard and assessing the situation. Moving aft alongside the sheet winches, he stepped into the cockpit and crouching where his face was clearly illuminated, asked, "Do you need a hand with that?"

Chapter 10

"Hello, Mrs Vaughan. My name is Campbell. I'm from the Anti-Terrorist Branch. Do you feel up to answering a few questions?" Campbell had applied his friendliest smile as he stood looking down at the pale, tear-stained face of Sarah Vaughan. He had been waiting for three hours at the hospital, and had just been given strict instructions that he only had a few minutes before Mrs Vaughan would be sedated again to give her body a chance to rest and recover from its ordeal of the last few weeks and the miscarriage.

Sarah Vaughan rolled her head on the pillow to face him and in a very weak voice said, "I will help if I can but at the moment things are a bit hazy."

"Can you tell me how many people were involved in your abduction?" Campbell asked.

"There were three that took the girls and me away. Then there was another three that took Ian," replied Sarah, her face immediately showing stress at the recollection of the moment she last saw Ian.

"Can you describe any of them to me?" asked Campbell, opening his notebook and withdrawing a pen from the inside pocket of his jacket.

"The leader is a man they call Murata-san. Everyone seemed very frightened of him," said Sarah, her voice weak and unsteady. "He had terrible burn marks on his face. With him was a young Japanese girl who her English boyfriend called Yuki or Yukiko and I think the Japanese man found dead off the French coast was called Hiroshi." She fell silent for a moment or two, her eyes closed as if trying to recall something. "I'm sorry, I don't recall any of the others' names. The people on the boat: this Hiroshi and a woman, also Japanese I think, but the other man looked Middle Eastern to me."

"I'm sorry, Commander Campbell, but I must ask you to leave now," said the nurse who had been keeping a close watch on Sarah Vaughan's monitoring equipment.

"Just one more question?" he asked.

"No, you must leave now," replied the nurse firmly, pressing a buzzer on the wall panel.

As Campbell turned to leave the door opened and a doctor and two nurses entered hurriedly.

Leaving the room, Campbell walked down the corridor to where Sarah Vaughan's parents were waiting. As he approached them, Jackson appeared around the corner, obviously in a hurry.

"We've got an ID on that bloke who was shot," he said. "You're not going to like this. He's the son of the Home Secretary, Oliver Makepeace. Julian's his name. He's the one that daddy said was being harassed by the protection squad the year before last."

"Ah, yes," said Campbell, "I recall the incident well: 'My son must be allowed to have some privacy', or words to that effect. As I recall, our young Makepeace had just left home."

"Another thing, sir. The farmhouse, that appears to have been the hideout, is owned by none other than Oliver Makepeace. I understand that he bought it from the liquidator of the previous owner, a farmer by the name of Wolven. Currently he's applying for planning permission. It's good to be in power, isn't it, sir." Jackson's eyes flashed as he delivered this piece of information.

"How long has he owned it?" asked Campbell.

"Six months, sir." Jackson's prompt reply indicated that he had more to tell.

"You have something else for me I suspect," said Campbell.

"Yes, sir. I have learnt from the local authority that the area is 'Green Belt', but it appears that the Minister for Housing and

Redevelopment is currently reconsidering that status." Jackson's eyes showed clearly his internal fury.

"My word, Inspector Jackson, what a remarkably convenient coincidence," Campbell said, his voice mild and calm. "It is so reassuring to find that political spin-doctoring aside, the tranquil and honest conduct of our masters continues undisturbed."

"We finally caught up with the coach sir, and it looks as though it was the means of escape. The driver told us that when he got back to the coach after he had left it parked in Chichester, near the theatre, he found the luggage compartment door open. I've got forensic to give it a thorough going-over."

Campbell looked up at the ceiling and blew out his cheeks. "I've just heard from Mrs Vaughan that it definitely is Todashi Murata leading this little stunt, and he is now footloose and fancy free in England instead of cooped up on a yacht where we might have had a chance of finding and isolating him. I want that constable carpeted, in fact the whole of that group. God knows this is difficult enough without idiots like that helping the terrorists." Campbell's voice had risen in volume, attracting worried stares from Mrs Vaughan's parents and some of the staff.

"I'll see to it, sir. By the way, who is going to tell the minister about his son?" asked Jackson.

"I'll discuss that with Sir Michael straight away," said Campbell. "He'll probably want me to do it, so could you find PC Tucker and ask her to have the car ready."

"She's already standing by, sir," said Jackson.

"Thank you, Jackson," responded Campbell as he pulled his mobile phone from his pocket and started searching for the number.

In a quiet corner of the corridor Campbell discussed the situation with the Commissioner and, as anticipated found that he was to be the bearer of bad tidings.

On the drive back to the search headquarters Campbell instructed Jackson to close down the rural search and concentrate efforts on roadblocks and railway stations, as Murata would obviously want to get out of the area. By morning he would probably be far away and therefore all of those involved in the search should return to normal duties.

"I was surprised," said Campbell, "Mrs Vaughan knew about the death of Hiroshi Tanigawa. I'm sure they would not have told her intentionally."

"By the way, I want everyone to be sure that the security surrounding her and the children is absolutely watertight." Jackson nodded affirmatively.

"I also want to see your favourite journalist in my office at 1000hrs tomorrow. I've got another episode of the story I want him to write," said Campbell, as the car swung into the village hall car park.

"He's standing right over there, sir," said Jackson, pointing in the direction of a group of reporters.

As the men got out of the car the reporters rushed over and started asking questions. Campbell held up his hand for quiet and said to them that a statement would be made within the next half hour. In the back room of the hall both men set about creating a cover story for the local Chief Constable to give about the shooting and a report on the successful arrest of the escaped prisoner. On finishing the briefing of the Chief Constable and section heads Campbell slipped out of the back door of the hall and made his way via the footpath past the church to the village shop, where WPC Tucker sat with the engine running.

"Westminster or the minister's home, sir?" asked Tucker.

"It'd better be his official home, I think, as it affects both him and his wife," said Campbell, searching for his mobile phone.

The minister's secretary was officiously frosty: "I'm sorry, the minister's just going to the House," was her response to Campbell's request to speak with him.

"I really do need to speak with him immediately," said Campbell.

"I cannot disturb him there unless it is a case of national importance, which I doubt that this is," was the icy reply.

"This is a matter of the gravest importance with regard to national security." Campbell's voice was showing signs of annoyance.

"If you would tell me what it is about, maybe I can pass a message to him," she said with a tone of resignation.

"No, Madam, I can't tell you what it is about, now just put me through to the minister and stop this damn-fool game," said Campbell, his voice loud for the second time that day.

"There is no need to shout and I am not playing a game," the secretary said in a haughty voice.

Instantly the line went dead as he was put on hold and several minutes passed before he was finally put through.

"What is it, Campbell, I'm just on my way to the House. Can't this wait until the morning?" Oliver Makepeace's voice was irritable over the phone.

"No, Minister, I'm afraid it cannot. I think you would prefer to hear this at your home and in the company of your wife," Campbell struggled to keep his voice cool and polite.

"Oh God, what scandal has that idiot son of mine got into?" Makepeace's voice now more tolerant.

"I would rather I gave you the details when we met Minister; this is an unsecured call," said Campbell.

"Oh, is it? Then I will be there in an hour." Makepeace, aware that many phone calls could be eavesdropped upon, wanted to finish the conversation as soon as possible.

When Campbell arrived at the Home Secretary's official residence, Makepeace and his wife were standing waiting for him in the drawing room. Stationing WPC Tucker outside the door with orders not to let anyone near or into the room, Campbell entered and closed the doors behind him.

"Thank you for seeing me, Minister. May I suggest that you both sit down." Once they were seated Campbell continued. "It is my sad duty to inform you that at approximately 8.15 this morning, we believe your son Julian was shot dead whilst climbing over a fence onto the Emsworth bypass near Chichester."

"Impossible," said Makepeace immediately. "He's in Italy with that Chinese girl he has in tow."

Campbell sighed and pulling a photograph from the envelope in his hands, asked, "Do you recognize this person as being your son?"

Makepeace glanced at the photograph then stared at it in horror. "Oh, my God. Oh, my God. What has he done?"

"Obviously I would like you to formally identify the body at the morgue as soon as possible, Minister, but I am afraid that there is little doubt that it is that of your son. I am most terribly sorry that I have had to bring you this news. Please accept my most sincere condolences."

Shaken by her husband's reaction, Mrs Makepeace leant across to take the photograph but was intercepted by Campbell, who said quietly. "I am sorry to say that the picture is very unpleasant and I think that your husband has established that probably it is of your son. I believe it would be far better that you remember him as he was the last time you saw him."

Makepeace sat ashen faced staring at Campbell, his mouth working but no sound coming out. His wife looked shocked, but there appeared to be no other emotion.

Campbell crossed to the drinks cabinet, poured two large brandies and handed them to Makepeace and his wife.

"Commander do you know why... er... what... how this happened?" Makepeace asked, still struggling with the incredulity of what he had just heard.

"We believe that your son was encouraged by his, Japanese, girlfriend to become a member of a terrorist group led by a man called Murata, who heads a faction of the Japanese Red Army. During the course of some attack they are mounting they abducted a family of four, and were holding the wife and two daughters as ransom to the husband's co-operation." Campbell paused to let that information sink in. "Reports suggest that for some reason your son was involved in the escape of the wife and two girls, but we cannot confirm this at the moment, as the lady is seriously ill in hospital and the two children too traumatised to interview." Campbell paused again. "Murata and your son's girlfriend escaped the scene and have so far avoided being identified and arrested. Before I inform you of further details I would like to ask you a few questions regarding what you knew of your son's relationship with this girl and whether they lived together, in fact anything that may help us find out more about her, and her possible friends and collaborators."

The interview lasted for a further two hours but at the end of it, Campbell felt that he had learnt little with regard to Julian Makepeace and his life. The parents' thirst for fame and wealth had obviously allowed little time for their son; they were genuinely surprised that he had even known about the farmhouse. They provided the address of his small flat in Chelsea but neither of them had visited the place or possessed a key. Having obtained their permission to break in and search the flat, Campbell then left to organise a warrant for the search and a team to do the work.

When WPC Tucker knocked at Campbell's front door the following morning, it was answered as usual by his housekeeper, Mrs Craven.

"Come in dear, the Commander's having breakfast in the conservatory. If you go through, I'll bring you a nice cup of tea."

"Good morning, sir. I hope I'm not disturbing your breakfast," Tucker said, as she stood in the doorway to the beautiful conservatory that ran the full width of Campbell's large Victorian house.

Campbell was seated at a marble-topped table amongst the raised beds of orchids and tropical shrubs. His pristine white shirt and blue silk tie were protected by an equally immaculate napkin. On the table were several newspapers, each neatly folded to reveal yesterday's press statement from West Ashling. On his plate were half-eaten scrambled eggs and mushrooms.

"Good morning, Tucker, are you early or am I late?" His bright blue eyes sparkled with humour; he was in a good mood.

"I am early, sir, the traffic was unusually light this morning," she said, returning his smile.

"Have you had breakfast?" he asked.

"Yes, sir," she said, remembering her hasty bowl of cereal eaten in her dark and dingy flat near Borough Market.

"Here, take a seat while I finish this," he said, indicating a chair on the opposite side of the table.

"Here's another pot of tea for you both, and there is an Inspector Sheppard to see you," announced Mrs Craven as she hurried into the conservatory with a tray. "Shall I ask him to wait in the drawing room?"

"No, send him through here, and would you be kind enough to bring another cup and saucer for him?" asked Campbell.

Mrs Craven gave him a look of disappointment then turned to carry out his request. Her sharp instruction to the young inspector left him in no doubt that he was not welcome and that he should have visited the Commander in his office.

"Sorry to bother you at home, sir, but I thought you might like to have the report on the search of Julian Makepeace's flat as soon as possible," said Sheppard rather nervously.

"Thank you, Inspector," said Campbell, taking the file from Sheppard's hand. "Take a seat. Pour yourself a cup of tea."

"Shall I wait for you in the car, sir?" asked Tucker, now a little nervous herself.

"No, no, you are as much a part of this investigation as anyone," Campbell assured her.

There was silence in the room whilst Campbell read through the report. Finally he put it down and looking up at Sheppard said, "Good work. How long will it be before you can get addresses to fit all of those phone numbers?"

"We were very fortunate there, sir, as the phone list was one of the first things we found, under the mattress of all places. I put a couple of my men on it straightaway; here are the details of all of the landline phones and those mobiles with contracts. The pay-as-you-go ones will take a bit longer I'm afraid."

"Excellent," replied Campbell. "Now let's go through this."

"There's one other thing, sir; the book itself," said Sheppard, taking a sealed plastic bag from his briefcase and two pairs of latex gloves. Handing a pair of gloves to Campbell, he donned his own and laying a forensic mat on the table opened the bag and took out Makepeace's address book. Opening the book to the XYZ section, he said, "Can you make anything of that, sir?"

In the left-hand column on each entry were either three or four clock-hand characters, each line ending with a very definite full stop, then alongside them, a series of letters. In the third column was a further set of clock-hand characters. Ten minutes passed without either man speaking, both intent on studying the page in front of them. WPC Tucker, curious as to what they were looking at, came round the table and peered over Campbell's shoulder.

"I thought at first that the left-hand column was semaphore, but the letters don't make much sense," said Campbell. "I doubt that they are people's initials as they don't go beyond the letter

'I' and the string of letters seem so random. They appear to have some formula in them by the way he's included some brackets surrounding some of the letters and the odd backslash. I'm not sure that this is anything to do with names and addresses."

"That's just what we thought, sir," said Sheppard, relieved that he and his team had not missed something obvious.

Again the group fell silent as each tried to crack the code. It was after some minutes that Campbell became aware that Tucker was writing furiously in a notebook, looking up every so often to study the Makepeace address book again, and copying down a code sequence from it.

"Don't waste your time on it, Tucker," he said. "The code boys at the yard will be able to fathom it out given time."

"But I think I've got it, sir," she said.

Both men turned to her in amazement. "What did you say, Constable?" asked Sheppard.

"I think I've cracked it, sir," she replied.

"Well come on then, let us have it," said Sheppard.

"Well, sir the first column is indeed semaphore but it is numbers one to ten, not letters, and he also rotates them so that 'A' equals one in the first line but two in the second etc, thus destroying any obvious pattern. I think that the first column is the exchange code number and that the accentuated full stop represents zero, indicating that the telephone code is written down in reverse. In the second column he is using the alphabet to represent numbers, so 'AS' would equal 119 or 'IU' would equal 921. Where he uses brackets, you multiply the two numbers, so '(EW)' would equal 115. So if we take this line 'DGMK/(TH)WD', it should read 471311/160234; the backslash indicates two numbers on the same exchange." Tucker stopped and stood up, looking a little embarrassed, and blushed.

"What do you make of the third column?" asked Campbell, looking at her as if for the first time.

"I'm just guessing here, but I think that he is using the whole of the semaphore alphabet, but is again rotating it on each line, so for line four here the 'W' would actually mean 'T' and the 'P' would mean 'M' in this case, Todashi Murata," Tucker said, now more confidently.

"Why did you pick line four?" Sheppard asked.

"He made the mistake of underlining it, sir, suggesting it to be important."

"Sheppard, photograph that page and get it e-mailed to my office as fast as possible. We do not have a moment to lose," said Campbell, leaping to his feet. "Tucker, let's get to work."

Tucker, driving with the siren blaring and lights flashing, carved her way through the rush-hour traffic without much bother. Arriving at the Yard she was about to pull away to take the car down into the garage when Campbell said, "Leave it there, I'll get one of the others to park it. You've got an important job to do."

In the twelfth floor corridor they met Jackson. "Good work on the papers. Is the meeting still on with Parson?" asked Campbell.

"Yes, sir, he will be here at 1000 hours as you requested," Jackson replied.

"Excellent. Now WPC Tucker here is going to be sitting in the conference room to do some code breaking and she will be coming out every so often with a telephone number which I want our people to trace," said Campbell.

"Oh right, sir," said Jackson with a somewhat surprised expression on his face.

In his office Campbell found the e-mail from Sheppard already on his desk. "Right," he said, handing it to Tucker. "Get started," and watched her leave the room.

"What is it that Tucker is doing, sir?" asked Jackson with a confused expression on his face.

"The search team from Julian Makepeace's flat turned up this morning with his address book, the last few pages of which he had entered in code." Campbell smiled and, gesturing in the direction of the conference room, continued. "To my great delight and amazement, WPC Tucker broke it in a matter of five minutes."

"Well well," said Jackson. "So she's a cracker in more than one sense then."

Campbell looked up, frowning, then looking through the glass panel into the conference room said, "Oh yes, I see what you mean."

"The rest of the girls think she's carrying a flame for someone, sir, but it's not one of the team. All of the bachelors have invited her out at one time or another and I suspect some of the married ones too. All have been politely refused," said Jackson.

"Really," said Campbell. "Well let's get on, how long 'til Parson gets here?"

"Half an hour, sir," replied Jackson.

"Good. While I make a telephone enquiry about the condition of Mrs Vaughan, can you go outside and get my secretary to arrange some flowers for her. Thank you."

Jackson, back in Campbell's office, waited until he had finished his call. "Parson is waiting downstairs, sir. By the way, how is Mrs Vaughan?"

"Hanging on by a thread. I had hoped that she would improve after some treatment. Have you checked that her security is tight? I don't think they will try to get to her or the children but I don't want the press to get there either," replied Campbell.

"Yes, sir, I checked this morning first thing and instilled the message that strict security is to be maintained. Even the hospital staff don't know her name."

"Right, let's get Parson up here. We are going to give him another story to print," said Campbell. "I thought at first that there was no point in keeping this quiet and that the more people we had looking for Murata the better. The content of that address book, however, has changed all that, so we are going to get Parson to continue with the screen story."

"Fitted carpet, three pictures and a cracking view of St James Park," said Parson as he crossed to Campbell's desk and held out his hand. "How are you this morning, Commander?"

Working together, Campbell, Jackson and Parson concocted a story linking the fictitious escaped convict with an unidentified man found shot dead at the side of the Emsworth bypass. According to the report, the police at this time believed that the shooting was related to the finding of a woman and two children close to the incident. Police had been unable to question either the woman, who was in a critical condition, or the children at this time. Police believed that the escaped convict had hidden out in a deserted farmhouse, which was destroyed by fire around the time of the shooting. The police would not release details of the location of where those involved were being held until further details were known.

Jackson said, "The press will have a field day about escapees committing further crimes."

The three men sat for some minutes considering the merits of what they were doing. Parson, briefed with the true story, was aware of the dangerous course he was taking in his journalistic career. If this went wrong his life as a reporter would be over.

"Mr Parson," said Campbell as they walked to the lift. "You stick to your side of the bargain and I can guarantee I will stick to mine. We will of course have to inform the other papers and media regarding this screen story we have concocted."

" Commander, I always knew you would have to give this type of thing to the media in general," said Parson. "I sense that this has a 9/11 feel to it. I hope to God I'm wrong, but if you, sir, and Jackson are onto it, then well, good luck, Commander. Parson left New Scotland Yard on a cloud. What a game to be part of.

The meeting with Parson over, both men went into the conference room only to find it empty. "WPC Tucker has gone to the canteen for her meal break." It was Campbell's secretary. "She's passed all of the numbers to the team in the Ops room."

"Thank you, Mrs Fitzgerald," said Campbell. "Oh, when she returns, can you ask her to wait in my office."

"Yes, sir," she replied. "Is there anything else, Commander?"

"Yes, can you get me some large-scale maps of the east coast of America from, say, Fort Lauderdale to New York and have them laid out on the conference room table. If WPC Tucker is back maybe she can give you a hand."

On the way down to the Ops Room Jackson said, "America, sir, that's a bit of a long shot isn't it?"

"All the time we were talking with Parson I was trying to work out why they were prepared to risk hostage taking if they were not in the process of making a strike," said Campbell. "I think that Phil Saints was right and that their target is the USA. If it were here, France or Spain, we would have known all about it by now. Either something would have been blown up or a threat and blackmail would have been received. The French haven't reported anything and as you know we have been keeping them up to speed with all developments. Their watch on ports is very good when it comes to this sort of thing."

"I thought they may have a go at a holiday resort like those on Madeira or Tenerife," Jackson replied. "An Atlantic crossing in a small yacht seems a damn difficult way of delivering an attack. What happens if they are searched by Customs? Where would you hide explosives?"

196

"I would lay money on the fact that they already have the device or devices in place and the yacht is, as Saints so cleverly observed, an easy way of getting the team into the States," said Campbell. "That's an idea. I would like you to get Saints up here today and book him into a hotel. We could do with his input."

"I'll get my girls in the Ops room to organize it straight away, sir," said Jackson, feeling that at last they were going on the attack and not just sitting waiting. It was that aspect of police work that he found most irritating: the waiting for things to happen.

In the Ops room the team had completed the task. It was no surprise to find that Murata's number did not tie to an address. The initials 'HT' traced to a cheap hotel near the centre of Reading, whilst 'YN' was an address in the Barbican. 'TY' was purely a pay-as-you-go mobile and the team were currently investigating phone records to see if they could get any cross ties.

"If we assume that 'HT' is Hiroshi Tanigawa, it is very doubtful that he would have left any traces that are important in his room, but it will be worth interviewing the landlord, just in case he had any visitors," said Jackson.

Jackson detailed two officers with the task of interviewing Tanigawa's hotel manager then studied the list again. "Who's getting the phone records for Todashi Murata?" he asked.

"Me, sir," responded a smiling, fresh-faced, plain-clothed man in the corner of the room.

"Right, anything overseas I want to know about straight away," ordered Jackson, his expression enough to take the smile off the young man's face.

"Got some info on 'YN', sir. She is apparently called Yukiko Nagano; we'll be getting the full records through in about an hour, sir."

"Thank you, Hamilton. Which one of you is tracing 'FH'?" Jackson scanned the room to see one of his more senior

197

members with his hand in the air talking on the phone. When he had put the receiver down Jackson said, "Well?"

"Interesting, sir. The phone was purchased and registered in Germany. The phone company want a formal application before they release the records."

"Damn, thanks Stevens," Jackson replied bitterly.

"There was one thing though, sir. I pushed and pushed and finally they confirmed that the phone hasn't been used for about four to five weeks."

"Well done, Harry," Jackson said. "Now can you get straight on to that application?"

"Already at it, sir."

Jackson gave Stevens the thumbs-up sign and turned to Campbell. "Do you want to say anything, sir?"

"No, everything seems to be going pretty well here. I want a careful surveillance put on this Yukiko Nagano's place and an application put straight to the Home Secretary for a phone tap."

"I'll deal with that myself, sir," replied Jackson with a hint of relish in his voice.

Campbell smiled. "I'll be in my office if you need me."

WPC Tucker did not hear Campbell as he came back into his office. She was standing by the window looking at a slightly faded photograph of a lady with the most serene face she had ever seen. "That's a picture of my late wife," said Campbell. His words took her by surprise and had her spinning to face him.

"I'm sorry, sir, I didn't mean to pry," she said, blushing furiously.

He smiled. "That's all right. Please take a seat and tell me how someone with your talents is still a WPC and detailed to drive me around."

"When my husband and both sons were killed in the Croydon Tower bombing, three years ago, I decided to join the police. I was finally accepted in March last year, and after the initial training, I applied to become a firearms officer and also did the driving course. All the time I was wanting to join the ATB and this was the first vacancy that was available for my grade, sir."

Just then the door opened and Mrs Fitzgerald came in. "Excuse me, Commander, but you told me to tell you the moment the maps arrived."

"I'll be right there, Mrs Fitzgerald. WPC Tucker, I would like to continue this discussion but it will have to wait for a later date I'm afraid."

"Yes, sir, thank you, sir," was all she could think to say. In fact she felt as though she had said too much anyway; he was the first person in the police force that she had told about Colin and the boys.

Stella shook him gently. "Phil, Phil, wake up. There's Harold Blakemore on the phone wanting to talk to you urgently."

Stretching and yawning, Phil Saints slowly awoke. "What did you say, Harold Blakemore on the phone? I was only talking to him," he looked at his watch, "three hours ago."

"Well he must like the sound of your voice because he wants to speak to you again," she said, putting the phone in his hand.

"Yes, Harold," he yawned, "what can I do for you?"

"I've just had the Anti-Terrorist mob on the phone. They want you to go straight away to New Scotland Yard to assist them with this dodgy sinking thing of yours."

"Assist in what way?" asked Phil.

"Something about sailing the Atlantic. I don't know this is most irregular. It means the whole of the shift roster has got to be changed." Blakemore hated any change to the routine. In addition, he was acutely embarrassed when it had become obvious that Phil Saints had correctly assessed the truth of the sinking off the French coast.

"They want you to pack a bag; you may need to stay up in London for a few days. It's a pity I can't just call up for someone to replace you."

"Did they say who I was to report to?" asked Phil.

"They just said get there as soon as possible and to get a taxi from Waterloo Station. They'll cover the costs."

An hour and a half later Phil was on a fast train from Southampton Parkway flashing through the Hampshire countryside at over a hundred miles an hour. At Waterloo Station he got a cab easily, as it was a glorious evening.

"HM Coastguard, eh," said the cabby, "you're a bit far from your lighthouse, mate."

"It's Trinity House that look after lighthouses," replied Phil.

"Oh," said the cabby, "watch you doin' up 'ere then?"

The cab pulled up with a jolt outside New Scotland Yard and Phil handed the driver a twenty-pound note. "Can I have a receipt, please?" asked Phil.

"Yes, sir, right away, sir."

Taking the change and receipt, Phil stepped out of the cab and turned to pick up his bag. "Actually I stole the tea money and have come to give myself up."

"Oh big stuff then. I don't fink my conscience would let me get away wiv it 'iver."

Phil laughed and tossed the cabby a pound coin from his change.

Mrs Fitzgerald had come down to reception to escort him and was now showing Phil into the conference room where, laid out across the floor, there was a map of the eastern seaboard of the United States. " The Commander will be with you shortly," she said. "Can I arrange some tea for you?"

"Thank you, that would be most welcome," replied Phil.

He stood staring for a time at the maps, then, reaching down into the side pocket of his bag, he retrieved the latest edition of the Atlantic Crossing Guide. On a piece of paper he wrote down some mileages and started to work out passage times for the various routes that could be taken.

The door opened and in came a short lady in a catering uniform, carrying a tray with tea things on it. "There we are, dear, I'll come back later and clear the things away," she said cheerily.

Phil poured himself a cup and was just about to resume his study when Commander Campbell entered the room, closely followed by Jackson and two other officers.

"Mr Saints, thank you so much for coming so quickly," said Campbell, shaking his hand warmly. "May I introduce my team – you know Inspector Jackson." Phil shook Jackson's hand and nodded. "This is Detective Sergeant Collard and here we have Detective Sergeant Weaver, who is our Japanese expert. I think that the best thing we can do at the moment is try to anticipate what this bunch of fanatics are attempting, so the first thing to do is guess where they are heading." Having made the opening statement Campbell stood back and waited for the others to put their views.

"I am aware of your preference for the USA being the target, sir, but I still think either the Azores, Madeira or the Canaries. I just can't see them doing an Atlantic crossing; it's just too risky," said Jackson. Secretly he had been persuaded by Campbell's earlier arguments but wanted the others to think outside of the box, just in case anything had been missed.

"I'm inclined to agree with the Inspector, sir. I've done an Atlantic with a couple of mates on their yacht and I don't think that we would have been up for carrying anything like explosives, especially on a yacht as small as 34 foot. As for setting up an attack," said Collard, shaking his head.

"Weaver, what about you?" asked Campbell.

"Well, I have no experience of sailing at all. In fact I get to feel seasick stepping over a puddle. I do, however, have some idea of Murata's mindset, and I take him to be a very ambitious man seeking lasting fame, or rather infamy. The war between him and the other factions of the Japanese Red Army has so far left him looking second best. Intelligence from Tokyo indicates that there is a major operation underway, but they have no idea of the target, except that for once it is not inside Japan. I've checked on any major international conference due to take place on any of the Atlantic islands and found that starting last Monday there is another session regarding global warming. It is being held in Madeira and came to an end yesterday. Apart from that I don't really know. I can't see someone like Murata hitting a soft target like a tourist hotel, but a conference venue he may be attracted to." DS Weaver looked apologetic.

"Mr Saints?" asked Campbell, looking at Phil inquisitively.

"Do we know who's sailing the boat, sir?" Phil asked.

"Yes, we do. Apart from Mr Vaughan, under duress, there is one Fumiko Hamaura and a man thought to be of Middle Eastern extraction," replied Campbell.

Phil frowned. "Isn't it strange to have a non-Japanese involved in a Japanese Red Army plot?"

"No," said DS Weaver. "For some years the JRA has had links with the PFLP."

"Who are they?" asked Phil.

"The Popular Front for the Liberation of Palestine," replied Jackson.

"Um, I may be making an amazing number of guesses here," said Phil Saints. "You say that they have links with this PFLP; would it be purely expertise?"

"Mainly that, yes," said DS Weaver.

"Ok then. I think that this Middle Eastern gentleman was brought into the team to act as skipper for the yacht and that the man found drowned off the French coast was just crew. We know the yacht they hijacked was not fitted with any self-steering or GPS type gear. So Ian Vaughan was an essential hostage if they were going to get very far." Saints paused and looked at his calculations. "With respect, DS Collard, I think that the team onboard that yacht are tough enough and skilled enough to do an Atlantic crossing. I also suspect that the terrorists amongst them are politically and fanatically fired up to make an attack immediately on arrival at their destination." He paused again before pulling from his bag a map showing the whole of the North Atlantic. Putting the tea tray on the floor he unfolded the map on the table. "Forget the supposed sinking; the most important event was the recovery of the Dan-buoy which was about here." Phil stabbed his finger at a point on the map. "Note that the location is well west of Ushant and only a little south, indicating that they were going out into the Atlantic, not moving south towards Madeira." Pausing again to look at his calculations he continued. "The Azores is some 1200 miles out from a line of, say, Falmouth, about the same distance as Madeira. That, in the conditions of the time, would be about fourteen to sixteen days sailing, say eighteen from Chichester Harbour for good measure. From there to the States is another twenty to twenty-five days. They left Chichester Harbour forty-five days ago. Do you think that they would risk hanging around for something like three to four weeks in Madeira or the Azores without making the strike?"

Phil Saints looked around the group, who to a man were shaking their heads.

"In that case I would agree with Commander Campbell and look more closely at the possibility of it being the States," said Saints. "According to my calculations. They should have arrived two days ago if they were taking the northern route. That, however would be very cold and has the risk of icebergs, plus fog and heavy weather around the Grand Banks area at this time of year. The shortest is the great circle route, but this has again the iceberg and fog risk, plus punching against the Gulf Stream. My favourite would be the southern route running north of the Azores, sailing if possible below the line of low-pressure centres, but staying in the wind on, say, latitude of 37 to 40 degrees. When you get to longitude 60 degrees you then cut across the Gulf Stream to the American coast."

"Where would that land you?" asked Campbell.

"Anywhere between Morehead City and Newport Rhode Island," replied Saints.

The five men stood looking at the maps on the floor.

"That's a hell of a stretch of coastline. You might as well have included the dark side of the moon," commented DS Collard.

"I'm going to invite our friends from the US Embassy over to update them. Mr Saints, I should be grateful if you would stay and repeat your excellent analysis," said Campbell, noting Saints' nod of acceptance. "Inspector Jackson, to make sure that we have missed nothing, I would like you to brief the authorities in Madeira and Azores on the potential threat, but I would be obliged if you would not mention the USA in your comments."

"Certainly, sir, I'll do it from my office straight away," replied Jackson, turning and quickly leaving the room.

Chapter 11

The brunette looked up casually at him then back to the diagram she was holding, and said in an absent-minded tone of voice, "I sure could do with a hand fixing this as..." Her expression then changed to one of terror and incredulity as she did a double take before passing out.

Hurriedly Ian lowered himself down into the cabin then picking her up gently, half carried and half dragged her onto the cabin settee. Praying that she had not seen the film 'Dead Calm', Ian crossed into the galley, soaked a tea towel in cold water from the sink, then rummaged around and found a mug into which he put some more water. The wet pad on the back of the neck brought her round. She looked at him with a mixture of shock, fear and deep suspicion.

Placing the mug gently into her hands, Ian said, "I'm very sorry that I frightened you. Honestly, I mean you no harm, here drink this, it's only water. Would you like me to make you a hot drink or something to help you get over the shock?"

"No. Who the hell are you and where did you come from?" she screamed, her voice rising to levels of hysteria.

"My name is Ian Vaughan and I have been held hostage on a yacht that is now some distance astern of us. It is in the hands of two terrorists who are planning to carry out some attack upon the United States. I have been forced to help them sail here from England on pain of death to my family if I did not comply."

"Crap!" she shouted. "That is the worst story I have ever heard. You're here on some pirate stunt to steal this yacht."

"If I was, I would not have risked boarding this yacht alone," Ian said. "Honestly, what I am telling you is true. If you go on deck and look around you may by some fluke see the masthead light of the yacht I have just left, but hopefully we are too far away."

She got up and peered through the cabin windows into the darkness. "You can't see a damned thing in this weather!" she yelled at him. "Your boat could be ten feet away and you wouldn't see it!"

For the next twenty minutes he tried his best to allay her fears and slowly she began to calm down, but retained a high level of suspicion.

"Look, I don't think we've got much time to play with here, I must radio the shore and send out some kind of warning to the authorities before those two get too far away," said Ian, the tone of his voice giving the sense of urgency.

"It's dead," she said, "like the rest of the damned electrics."

"So that's why you were not showing any navigation lights," said Ian.

"The 'so-called' expert surveyor failed to notice that the engine doesn't charge the batteries up," she said with bitterness in her voice. "Why is it that you pay someone to do a job and when they fall down on it you have no way of getting your hard-earned money back?"

"Sounds as though you've had a rough time of it," Ian said. "Can I look at it, to see if anything can be done to get the radio into operation?"

She studied him with some suspicion before nodding assent. "Okay. I don't suppose you can make it any worse than it already is," she said.

"Do you have a circuit tester on board?" he asked.

"Is that the thing in the middle drawer there?" she replied.

Opening the drawer, Ian pulled out the tester and knelt at the opening to the engine bay and peered in.

After twenty minutes of checking the circuits from the engine's alternator he straightened up. "I think that it's the blocking diode that's gone," he said, looking rather dejected. "Sadly I don't know enough about electrics to be that sure, it may be the alternator itself. Have you got the starting handle for the engine and we can see if the alternator is putting anything out."

"Port-hand cockpit locker," she answered.

Holding onto both sides of the companionway hatch opening, Ian swung his feet up onto the bridge deck and hauled himself through, out into the cockpit. The port-hand locker was tidily stowed and the starter handle easy to locate and remove. For some minutes he stood straining his eyes into the darkness, fearing the sight of *Romance Allemande*, but all he could see was the form of some nearby waves and the yacht's wash slipping away astern of them.

Back in the cabin he cranked the engine into life at the third try then applied the circuit tester. "Nothing I'm afraid, it's the alternator that's up the creek, do you have a spare by any chance?" Ian asked.

"No, I don't think so," she replied. "If I had, it would have been in that box over there."

Ian glanced at the box and shook his head before reaching into the engine bay and using the compression lever, stopped the engine. "No point in wasting fuel," he said before turning to the chart table to see what navigation had been done.

The marks on the chart told him that the batteries had given up only a couple of hours ago and their position had been competently estimated from then. Opening the dividers he measured off the distance and transferred it to the scale down the side of the chart; it indicated that they were some 35 miles out of Morehead City, some seven hours sailing.

He stood trying to imagine what actions Hamaura and Arni would have taken. It depended on how successful his sabotage had been and whether they believed him to have drowned or survived. Suddenly he became aware of her staring at him.

"Sorry, I was wondering what my former captors were likely to have done. I know they were aware of my departure while we were still within sight," he said, "but I am sure that

207

they don't know what happened or whether I am still alive even."

"Nice try," she responded. "What were you doing all of that time up on deck? It doesn't take that long to find the starting handle on this boat."

"I was looking out to see if their yacht was in sight," he replied. "If it was I was going to change course to make sure we were well away from it before they saw us."

"You must think I've just flown in from Mars if you think I'm going to believe you. What the hell are you up to and how the hell did you get on board this boat?"

"The wind's eased a bit," he said. "Can we shake out that reef?"

"You haven't answered my question," she said.

"I'll tell you the whole story when we've got the reef out," Ian replied.

The anxiety and fear in his voice seemed to persuade her After setting the cabin straight and replacing the companionway steps and engine cover, they set full sail, then, settled each one side of the cockpit, he started his tale. At first she scoffed at his story, and kept interjecting with sarcastic remarks about how far-fetched the whole thing was. It was getting light by the time he had reached the explanation of his escape, and still she listened with obvious suspicion. Suddenly he had an idea and standing he stripped off his clothes down to his waist. On his chest were the yellowy areas of old bruising and a burn scar on his shoulder from one of Hamaura's cigarette wake-up tricks, which matched others on the back of his neck, the inside of his right wrist and earlobe.

"Jesus Christ," she said, shocked by what she saw.

"I know you were concentrating hard on what you were doing when I came aboard, but I think you may have just heard Hamaura shout out when she discovered that I had jumped ship," he said, looking at her as she tried to recall.

"All I heard was the cry of a gull," she said.

"That was her shout," Ian replied. "Believe me, it sounded strange because she was shouting down into the cabin of the boat."

Her expression slowly changed from one of doubt to one of awe. "I'm beginning to think that you are for real," she said, her face still showing that she was not fully convinced. "Do you think that they saw my boat?"

"No, I don't think they did. She was below and had the cabin light on, so when she came up the companionway her night vision would have been almost nil. Arni was in the forward cabin, asleep if I know him, so it was unlikely that they had any inkling of your presence." They sat in silence for a moment or two before Ian said, "One thing is for sure, had they seen us they would have put up a white flare or shone the big torch at us."

There was silence again between them, each trying to work out what would happen next. She still was expecting some trick and he the sight of *Romance Allemande* bearing down on them.

"Ham and eggs," she said suddenly. "I can't think on an empty stomach."

"That would be great, thank you," Ian replied. "I'll maintain a lookout if you don't mind, just in case."

"Don't you go doing any altering of course without consulting me, you hear."

"Of course not," he replied, looking a little hurt at the suggestion.

"Say, when did you last eat?" she asked as he cleared the last mouthful from his plate, twenty minutes later.

"It seems like ten years ago. They didn't go in for great breakfasts," he said, giving her a smile of appreciation. "I'll wash up."

Back on deck, the exhaustion of the previous day and night caught up with him and he fell asleep laid out along the leeside cockpit seat.

They had just entered the Beaufort Channel, when she reached over and touched his shoulder, leaping back in alarm as he sprung away from her touch. "Sorry, I forgot the cigarette burns," she said in a tone of genuine apology.

"Where are we? I'm sorry, I appear to have dropped off."

She pointed to the land ahead and to starboard of them. "That's Shackleford Banks and over there to port is Bogue Banks. We slip between the two and head up past the oil terminal on Radio Island."

"I need to see the police as soon as possible," he said. "I can't tell you how important it is."

"Don't worry, honey, that's just what I intend to make sure of," she replied.

"I've suddenly realised that you are the first young lady to cook me breakfast, whose name I do not know," he said, with a slightly mischievous smile.

"Nancy," she said, returning his smile. "Nancy Schroder."

"How do you do, Nancy, what do you do for a living?"

"I write for a ladies magazine. What I like to call general interest articles."

"Married?" he asked

"Was, you?"

"Yes, a lovely wife and two daughters," he said. "That is if they are still alive." His face clouded over as he thought of his family and their plight.

"I'm gonna moor the boat at the marina by the bridge and get Grant Hamilton to give us a lift to the Police Department." She looked at him, trying to gauge his reaction.

"That's fine by me," said Ian with an expression of relief on his face.

In the hour it took them to sail up to the bridge and onto the pontoon, Ian had washed and cleaned up his clothes as best he could. He felt brighter even with two days' stubble on his chin.

Nancy brought the yacht alongside with great skill. "You've done that once or twice before," complimented Ian.

"Not with this boat," she replied. "I only bought her two weeks ago in Bermuda. This was her maiden voyage, so to speak."

"Hence the electrics," said Ian.

She nodded, then looking up at the wharf she called, "Hey, Callum, is Grant in the yard?"

Grant Hamilton turned out to be an amiable six foot eight ex-football pro, who, though carrying a few injuries, was still in shape. He made no fuss about stopping work to deliver this stranger to the Police Station and during the journey asked no questions.

The drive from Radio Island involved going in the wrong direction for a time, before joining the main road that passed back through the town centre. Morehead City appeared smaller than Ian imagined it would be and he was surprised as they drove down County Club Road, to be in what was almost a leafy suburb. The Chevy Blazer swung into Mansfield Road and after a couple of hundred yards pulled up outside the Police Department building.

"Thanks, Grant," said Nancy. "If I give you the keys to the boat can you have a look at the engine alternator for me?"

"Sure. You gonna be okay left here? You don't want me to hang around?"

"No, we'll be fine," she said, turning to follow Ian who was already making his way towards the front entrance.

Inside the building, Ian walked straight to the desk where a young fresh-looking constable stood alongside a craggy-looking desk sergeant.

"Good morning, my name is Ian Vaughan and I am a British citizen." He placed his passport onto the counter.

"What can we do for you, Mr Vaughan?" said the desk sergeant.

"I need to speak urgently to your senior officer as I wish to warn him of an intended terrorist attack," said Ian, the words spilling out in his haste to get things moving.

"Whoa, now, just slow down there, we need to get some details down before we start dragging people away from important work," the desk sergeant explained, pulling a notepad toward himself and taking a pen from the stand. "Right now, let's get the basics, name, address, age etc."

"Cut the crap, Jed, this guy is for real, you'd better get the Chief down here pretty damn quick," said Nancy, who had arrived behind Ian just as the desk sergeant had started the list of requirements.

"Hey, Nancy, you with this guy?" he asked.

"Yeah, now get the Chief and stop scratching around like some old hen," she said with a hostile expression on her face.

The sergeant studied her for a moment then picked up the phone and punched in a number.

"Annie, it's Jed on the desk, is the Chief busy?" There was a pause. "Can I speak to him; something important has occurred down here." A longer pause ensued before he said, "I'm sorry to bother you, Chief, but we have an English guy here who says he wants to warn us of a terrorist attack." Another pause came as the sergeant listened to his superior's response. "Yes, Chief, I thought he was a nut too but that magazine writer Miss Schroder is with him and seems certain that he is telling the truth." Ian heard the words 'You better be right about this', before the sergeant ended the conversation with, "We'll wait for you in interview room one."

"I'd better come along as well," said Nancy.

In a windowless room, Ian and Nancy were directed to two uncomfortable chairs set behind a table. As the sergeant sat down opposite them, Ian reached across and took the sergeant's notepad. "I think it will be quicker if I fill this in for the moment," he said. The sergeant shrugged and handed him the pen.

Writing quickly in clear block capital letters, Ian had completed all of his personal details and had started on his statement by the time the chief arrived.

As Chief Stankovic entered the room Ian stood. "This is Mr Vaughan," the sergeant introduced.

Ian Vaughan held out his hand. "I'm pleased to meet you, you are?"

"I'm Chief of Police Stankovic," he said, accepting Ian's handshake. "Now tell, what's this all about?"

It took an hour to tell the story of how he had found his way to Morehead City and even as he was telling it the tale seemed to sound so unlikely, even to him. Again it was the bruises and the cigarette burns that turned the tables and got their full attention.

It was then that Stankovic held up his hand for Ian to stop. Picking up the telephone said, "This is Chief Stankovic, get me the FBI in Washington on the phone, will you."

A few minutes passed, then the phone rang. "Stankovic," he said, then gave a brief outline of the situation. They all sat in silence as the chief was put on hold whilst the operator placed the call within FBI headquarters.

Then Ian heard a man's voice come on the line. "This is Morehead City Chief of Police Stankovic speaking," the chief said. Then scribbled down the name of the person he was talking to. "Okay, Agent Brumen, a Brit by the name of Ian Vaughan has just walked into our station here to warn me of a terrorist atta…" Stankovic stopped speaking, a look of surprise coming over his face. "He says he knows all about you and wants to speak to you straight away," said Stankovic passing the receiver across the desk to Ian.

"Hello," Ian said hesitantly. "Ian Vaughan speaking."

"Hi, Mr Vaughan I'm Agent Brumen of the FBI, are we pleased to be in contact with you. I am planning to come down by plane to pick you up and bring you back to Washington so that we can get the full details. I reckon to be with you in about two hours. Meantime can you start to write down all that you can remember about what they said either to you or to each other about their plans. Any detail would help."

"Certainly, yes, I will do my best, but to be frank they did not go into any detail, most of what I can tell you is pure guesswork on my part," replied Ian, realising for the first time how little he had learnt from his captors.

It was nearly three hours before the door to the interview room swung open. A smartly dressed thickset man strode into the room together with a swarthy-looking companion, together with Chief Stankovic and the desk sergeant.

"Mr Vaughan?" he asked. Ian nodded. "I'm Agent Brumen of the FBI and this is Agent Capello of the CIA, we have both been assigned to this case."

Reaching into their jacket pockets both men produced their badges and flashed them at Ian and Nancy. "May I have a closer look at those?" asked Nancy with a pleasant smile.

"Who are you?" asked Brumen, upset that his credentials had been questioned.

"May I introduce Nancy Schroder, the yachtswoman whose bravery and assistance enabled me to make good my escape and get here to warn you of an imminent terrorist attack," said Ian, not instantly impressed by Brumen's approach.

"Oh, I see, well here you are, Ma'am," Brumen responded, handing over his ID together with that of Capello.

Nancy studied both carefully as though she knew what she was looking for, then handed them back. "Do we pass?" Brumen asked. Nancy nodded and resumed her seat at the desk.

"I understand that you know who I am," Ian said.

"Yeah, we received a communication from the British Anti-Terrorist Unit, informing us that you had been taken by a terrorist cell operated by a guy called Murata, and that your family had been held hostage against your co-operation," said Capello.

"You said my family 'had' been taken hostage, does that mean they are now free?" Ian asked.

"Yeah, we understand that they somehow escaped and are currently under police protection," Capello replied, smiling at the expression of joy and wonder appearing on Ian's face.

"Are they alright, did any of them get hurt?" Ian asked, fear returning to his face.

"As far as we know, they are all fine," said Brumen.

"Oh, thank God, thank God," said Ian, breaking down in tears of joy and relief.

While Nancy placed an arm around his shoulders, the rest of the group moved away quietly and allowed Ian time to take in the news and compose himself again.

After a few minutes, Ian raised his head and pushing the pages of notes across the table said, "Here are the notes you requested, I will probably think of other things as time goes on."

"You say you have alerted the Coastguard and ports up and down the coast, to look out for this *Romance Allemande,* Chief," said Capello.

"That's right, as soon as Mr Vaughan had explained everything, we put the wheels in motion," replied Stankovic, pleased to be able to report that some action had been taken by his department. "Mr Vaughan estimates that they would have been only one hour, maybe two hours behind him if they were comin' here and we ain't had news of any other yachts makin' the harbour."

"Any ideas Mr Vaughan?" asked Brumen.

"My guess; and it is only a guess, is that they are not fully convinced that I have committed suicide and have gone north to lose themselves amongst the yachts in the Chesapeake. I'm also pretty sure that they would have changed the name of the boat and her papers," said Ian.

"You said suicide," said Brumen.

Ian took them through how he had made his escape by bringing the two yachts close to a collision, before stepping off and steering *Romance Allemande* away into a gybe.

"You managed to sail your boat close enough to just step over onto Miss Schroder's boat?" Capello asked suspiciously.

"Yes," replied Ian. "Fortunately both yachts were sailing close hauled at the time, so it was just a matter of getting close downwind, then luffing up a bit to close the gap. I must admit that I was extremely lucky to pull it off first time."

Capello stood looking at Ian for some time, trying to assess whether he was telling the truth. Ian returned the stare calmly, guessing what was on the man's mind.

"You don't really believe that it could be done, do you," he said.

"Frankly, no, I don't," replied Capello. "But I guess it's all I'm gonna hear from you and Miss Schroder."

Ian shrugged his shoulders and switched his attention to agent Brumen, who was reading through the notes.

"What's this, thirty million people held hostage by two terrorists?" he said, looking up at Ian with an expression of incredulity.

"That's what they were saying to each other," responded Ian. "It made me think of something nuclear as a device. Again, I'm only guessing there, but they seemed pretty confident of the numbers and they were definitely not out to impress me."

"Hell, that's the daytime population of Washington, New York, Baltimore State and New Jersey and some," said Brumen, now with an expression of outward disbelief.

"That's why I considered it to be some form of nuclear strike," said Ian. "As you were listing the population areas just then, it struck me that you were describing the eastern seaboard population from a line of Washington north. How many nuclear power stations do you have in that area?"

Brumen's expression changed yet again. "I don't rightly know but I can tell you that two terrorists won't be able to get into any one of them."

Ian didn't respond but just looked down at his notes thoughtfully.

"What I do know is that you have turned up here, after some miraculous escape from two supposed terrorists, with some story of nuclear disaster, that is way beyond the realms of probability and you obviously expect us to believe you." Brumen, having delivered the sentence, sat back in his chair shaking his head.

"Okay," said Ian. "Can you imagine any other way of holding so many people to ransom?"

Capello looked at his wristwatch and said, "We're wasting time here, let's get back to Washington, we can argue about it on the way." Then turning towards Nancy added, "We will also require you to come with us, Schroder, as I haven't worked out how you fit into all this."

"I don't fit, as you put it, into this plot in any way shape or form. I'm just the unfortunate bystander, who this guy selected to use for his escape, or whatever you like to call it," Nancy said, looking very put out at the prospect of a Washington trip.

"Maybe, maybe not," replied Capello. "Until we know for sure what is going on here, you're coming with us."

"I'm awfully sorry about this," said Ian. "I had no idea it would involve you like this."

"You weren't to know how the CIA works," she said. "They suspect everyone of being out to commit acts of terror."

Two squad cars took them out to Michael J. Smith Airfield, Brumen travelling with Nancy, and Capello in a separate car with Ian, each undergoing interrogation as the vehicles sped through Morehead City with sirens wailing. At the airfield Brumen and Capello went into a huddle, obviously exchanging Ian and Nancy's statements. Brumen placed a call to Bermuda and confirmed that Nancy Schroder had in fact purchased the yacht, a Vancouver 32, and had set sail single-handed for her homeport of Morehead City.

"Miss Schroder, we now think it not necessary to take you to Washington, I will arrange for one of these cars to take you back into town," said Brumen.

"Why, thank you so much," replied Nancy sarcastically, then turning to Ian she said, "Here's my card, call me on that number and let me know how you make out."

"Thank you, I will," said Ian. "Thank you for all you've done and thank you for being out there when I needed you." With that he lent over and kissed her on the cheek.

Nancy smiled, stepped towards him and returned the kiss. "It was an interesting and not too unpleasurable an experience. I'm thinkin' to rename my yacht 'Mid Atlantic Taxi', what do you think?"

"Sounds a great idea," said Ian, smiling. "You may continue to get some very dodgy fares though."

"There is one thing we require you to do before you go, Miss Schroder," said Capello, pulling a few sheets of paper from his briefcase.

"What is that?" she asked.

"We need you to sign a statement, sayin' that you will not discuss or disclose any information with regard to the events you have witnessed in the last 48 hours," said Capello.

"Oh shit, just because I am a writer. Hey, do you think I will even consider doin' anythin' like that?" Nancy said, with obvious indignation.

"Miss Schroder, please understand we must do this the formal way," interceded Brumen. "Our futures are on the line, as well as that of Mr Vaughan and his family."

Snatching the document from Capello's hand, she got back into the police car and read through the whole five pages before scribbling her signature in the designated box at the foot of the last page.

"When this is over, I want that damn thing torn up," she said. "God, we call this the land of the free. Huh."

At that point, Capello placed a hand upon Ian's shoulder and guided him towards the waiting Beechcraft 400A executive jet.

"You gentlemen travel in style," said Ian as he took in the plush leather interior of the plane. "I am lucky not to be paying taxes over here."

"It was all we could get at short notice," Brumen said defensively.

As soon as they were seated and buckled up, the aircraft started to taxi to the northern point of the triangular runway configuration. Turning a full 180 degrees onto the runway, the Beechcraft accelerated immediately, soaring into the late evening sky just east of Radio Island. Ian looked down towards the bridge and marina and thought that he could just make out Nancy's yacht tied up on the end of the pontoon. As they climbed over the harbour entrance, the plane turned and headed north along the coastline. Brumen and Capello sat behind him discussing his notes and trying to guess where the attack would be made. Twenty minutes later, a slight alteration in course brought the Chesapeake harbour bridge and tunnel structures into view, with what looked like a huge fleet of yachts in the area.

"Excuse me," said Ian. "Do you know why so many yachts are down there?"

Capello looked out of the aircraft window. "I guess they're gathering for the Cock Island Race. My two boys and a couple of their friends, are racing my boat in it on Saturday. Had you not showed up, I woulda been sailin' in it too."

"Is it an annual event?" asked Ian.

"Well it has been since I owned the boat," replied Capello. "Which is five years now."

"Are there many other events in the Chesapeake at this time of year?" asked Ian.

"Well yeah," replied Capello. "An' lots of folk come here this time of year in their boats just to go cruising."

"So Arni and Hamaura will blend in very well then," said Ian. "They can move about from Baltimore to Portsmouth or Washington and not appear to be anything other than good honest cruising folk."

"We think that they will move around on land once they have arrived here," said Brumen. "Yachts are a pretty slow form of transport."

"They won't be interested in speed," said Ian. "Their only concern will be anonymity. Throughout the voyage over here, Hamaura was recording messages onto a tape machine and I believe that these will be placed into small inflatable buoys and launched from the yacht, to be activated at a later time from a distance."

"To avoid their location being tracked, you think?" said Brumen. "You mentioned something about this in your notes. How many recordings did she do?"

"I couldn't say for sure," replied Ian. "She spent ages playing them back, then re-recording a message. At the end of some of them, there was a piercing whistle, like the noise you get if you misdial and get a company's fax machine number by mistake."

"What size are these buoys?" asked Capello.

"Oh about two foot six diameter, conical in shape. The one they launched in the English Channel had an aerial, and they plugged a machine into it via a pocket, then sealed the machine into the pocket with adhesive tape." Ian closed his eyes, trying hard to recall everything he could about that incident.

"Once they transmit, we should be able to plot the position ok. We'll have to recover one and find out how it works. Maybe we can jam the signal to trigger them," said Capello refastening his seat belt, as the aircraft's seat belt signs came on and the plane began its descent.

The car from the airport had darkened windows and was being followed by another car; from this Ian understood that they were taking him seriously. In the hotel, which they had entered via the kitchens, they took the service lift to the top floor. The suite they entered was something, the like of which Ian had never seen before, with a beautifully furnished lounge, a bedroom, bathroom and dressing room.

"You should be comfortable enough here," said Brumen. "If you want anything, call room service and they will bring it up. Whatever you do, don't mention your name or make any outside calls. We'll have a man down by the lift, but I don't think Murata's group is going to know you're here. I wouldn't go out dressed like that, by the way, as that will sure attract some attention."

Ian looked down at his heavy weather gear, in which he had been sweating all day. "I would like some normal clothes – I don't suppose there are any shops open at this time of day?" he said.

"We'll sort something out in the morning for you," said Brumen.

Capello, in the corner of the room, ended a call and put his mobile phone back into his pocket. "Wow, you sure travelled in some pretty dangerous company," he said to Ian. "The guy you call Arni is none other than Yunis Madadhah. According to our sources he's been linked to the Japanese Red Army for the last six months or so, but had effectively dropped out of sight in Europe. Three years ago, he was linked to the Croydon Tower bombing in England, then the downing of flight 297 into Tel Aviv a year later."

"I can understand why he goes under the name of Arni," said Ian. "He's just like the film star Arnold Schwarzenegger, big, strong and with a punch like a fourteen pound sledgehammer. Those are just his good points though." Ian paused and the other two men looked at him waiting for him to continue. "Apart from being all too successful in carrying out terrorist attacks, he's a homosexual pervert with a taste for small boys. He even carries a disgusting photo album around with him; do you know, the whole time he was on board and around Hamaura, he never once gave her an admiring glance, even when she was down to just the bottom half of her bikini."

"Is she good looking?" asked Brumen.

"I'll say she is," said Capello. "Even from the poor photographs we have of her she looks a real stunner." Capello moved across the room to Ian. "You say she was stripped down to her bikini bottom, why do you think that was?"

"When I first met her, she was traditional Japanese, snow-white skinned. In Japan it is considered to be very lower class for women to have a suntan. In America things are different and for a lady to move around in the yacht cruising circles, without drawing attention to herself, a suntan, I would think, is a prerequisite," replied Ian. "If I can see the photographs you have, I will be able to point out any other changes."

"You'll be seein' those tomorrow," said Capello. "We're leavin' now, you get plenty of rest an' we'll see you in the morning. Oh, and by the way, don't go shavin' just yet."

Missing the significance of the comment about shaving, Ian said, "I know you will want to ask some more questions about these two, but when do you think I will be able to fly back to my family?"

"We need to seek some advice on that," replied Capello and turned to follow Brumen out of the room, closing the door firmly behind him.

Ian picked up the phone and ordered a meal from room service, then went through to the bathroom for a quick shower. It wasn't until he looked in the bathroom mirror and saw the 'two-day' stubble on his chin, that he realised that the CIA wanted him to stay for some time and a beard would disguise his identity.

The meal, the first decent one he had eaten for weeks, washed down by several glasses of red wine, made him drowsy and within half an hour he was fast asleep in bed.

He jumped when Capello shook his shoulder to wake him. "Hey, it's ten o'clock, there's some breakfast waitin' on you in the other room."

Ian slipped out of the bed and put on the hotel dressing gown. As he entered the sitting room, the smell of ham and eggs wafted towards him combined with the aroma of freshly ground coffee. Brumen was standing by the window admiring the view and Capello sat at the writing desk, his mobile phone to his ear whilst writing notes.

After exchanging brief greetings with Brumen, Ian sat at the table and tucked into the breakfast. A knock at the door had both Brumen and Capello spinning round, glaring in its direction. "Come," said Brumen in a loud voice, and the door opened and a slightly dumpy girl came in smiling.

Brumen and Capello returned the smile. "Good morning, Agnes, here's a new challenge for you," said Brumen. "Can you take down all the dress particulars of Mr Vaughan here, then go out and buy him three pairs of everything, and I mean everything."

Agnes blushed, then, sitting down opposite Ian at the table, took as many details about his dress requirements as she could think of before leaving the room to search out and purchase the items listed.

"What did she do to deserve that?" asked Ian.

"Oh, just showed way too much enthusiasm as our section assistant," said Capello. "She even volunteers to help on stakeouts."

"Weren't you that keen in your early days?" replied Ian.

"Hell, no," said Brumen. "Now can you take us through this buoy-launching thing again."

Ian explained again how the buoys were set up, launched and then triggered. When he had finished, Capello placed in front of him a photograph of Fumiko Hamaura. "Is that the bitch that you sailed over with?" he asked.

Ian studied the photograph for several seconds. "Yes, that is her, but she has changed quite dramatically," he said. "She is no longer the skinny, flat-chested girl you see in that photo. She has filled out somewhat but still has that very beautiful face. Though the mouth is more cruel than shown here, and the hair is long now. She also has a much more expensive dress sense."

"Well," said Capello. "Our shot was taken probably ten years ago when she was still a student protester. She has stayed well out of sight since then."

"We think that her motivation is her elder brother, who is currently under lock and key in Tokyo," said Brumen. "He had a go at blowing up the headquarters of MITI."

"She said that he was in prison and ranted on about the corrupt system of monarchy and law in Japan," Ian said. "I got the impression that her brother was her idol."

"He led a lot of student protests in Japan a few years back, but like a lot of those guys, failed to mature in political debate and ideological development. It was only a matter of time before he was caught doing something really stupid and paid the price," said Brumen.

Within half an hour another member of Brumen's team had entered the room with a laptop and, with Ian's direction, set about reconstructing the image they had of Hamaura. It took over two hours to complete but by the end of the exercise, Ian was confident that the image bore a good likeness to the woman.

When the young man left, Ian turned to Brumen and asked, "You gentlemen now have as much information as I do with regard to this couple. So can I now get back to my family and leave this in your capable hands?"

"We're still awaitin' advice on that," said Capello.

"Look, you just can't hold me here against my will like this," said Ian, now showing signs of annoyance. "I have given you all the information I know, I can't see what else I can do to help and I have a wife and two daughters that I am desperate to see again. My wife is expecting our third child, I want to be sure that they are okay after what must have been some pretty awful ordeal."

"We appreciate your concerns about your family Mr Vaughan, but we still think that locked away in your memory, are things that can help us in this case," said Capello. "I promise that as soon as we can, we will get you reunited with your family, but in the meantime we have enough information to take this potential attack very seriously and need all the help we can get."

Ian sat down heavily in a chair shaking his head, frustrated at Capello's response. Deep down he knew Capello was right and that he had to stay on and help as much as he could; the stakes were too high.

"You have reminded me, however, that we need to keep the British ATB up to speed with what's goin' on," said Capello picking up a grey handset, which along with a miniature switchboard, had been installed in the room overnight. "Why don't you go through to the bedroom while I have a short chat with the guy in charge over there, then you can have a word with him to put your mind at rest. Ok?"

Ian nodded and, pouring himself another cup of coffee, ambled through to the bedroom and sat on the bed awaiting a signal to pick up the phone. When he had finished his conversation with Commander Campbell, Ian returned to the sitting room.

Capello looked up at him and saw a cold and steely expression on Ian's face that had not been there before. "Everything okay?" he asked.

"No, it bloody well isn't," replied Ian, tight-lipped. "Those bastards have killed our unborn child. God knows how Sarah must be feeling at this moment." He looked away, out of the window, tears in his eyes. "I'll stay for as long as it takes to hunt them down and kill them."

As Ian stared sightlessly at the Washington skyline, Yamada stood, his eyes fixed intently on the departures board at Toronto Airport. Travelling under the name of Yoshi Miyake, he had crossed the US Canadian border the previous day, purchased his ticket for London and was now awaiting the instruction to proceed to the gate ready for boarding. He had treated himself to business class and checked in with just a smart new briefcase and a holdall. He figured that with just cabin luggage, he would attract less attention at the London end, appearing to be just over on a short business trip.

To his surprise his mobile phone rang. "Mushi mushi," he said.

"Yamada-san?" Fumiko Hamaura asked.

"Hi hi," he replied, "Fumiko-san desu-ka."

"Do not leave, do you understand? Return to flagpole where you will be required to help complete our work," she said briskly. "I have had accident and need your attendance here."

With that, the line went dead leaving Yamada looking both puzzled and pleased. He would be in at the kill and see the effects of his revenge and be able to tell his family waiting in the next world, that their suffering had been avenged.

Chapter 12

Jack Drummond swung down from the high sleeper cab of his Scania R 500 tractor unit, unlocked the filler cap and inserted the fuel nozzle into the unit's tank, then squeezed the nozzle trigger and locked it open. He produced a large handkerchief from his pocket and loudly blew his nose.

Away to his right, hidden behind a small hedge, Drummond's every move was being carefully watched. The figure had been standing there for over two hours watching lorries come and go from the filling station. Each time the shadowy figure wondered whether the driver would leave the cab door unlocked whilst he went to pay for the fuel.

As the pump meter passed the two hundred litre mark, Drummond freed the nozzle trigger and hurriedly put the unit back on the stand before sneezing. Reaching in his pocket again for the handkerchief he walked across the filling station forecourt, blowing his nose, and entered the shop.

"Evening, Jack," said the cashier.

Drummond raised his hand in a half-hearted wave as he scanned the shelves for something to help with his cold.

"Got anything for a cold?" he asked, his eyes streaming and his nose bright red.

"Yes, Jack, just to your left in the green and yellow packet. Yeah, that's it," said the cashier helpfully.

Jack dumped the cold cure, some crisps and a bottle of lemonade on the counter. "Better pay cash for these, otherwise the books get buggered up. Put the diesel on my account."

As he walked towards the door the cashier called out, "You got a dolly bird in the cab, Jack?"

"No, mate, gave up that lark years ago. Too damn risky nowadays, there's too many nutters about."

"Oh, I thought I saw a movement, that's all," the cashier replied.

"Na," said Drummond. "The only bird that gets up in there is the missus and tonight's her night for bingo."

Climbing into the cab Jack Drummond gave a casual glance around before pulling a flask of hot water from the grip alongside him and making up a sachet of the cold cure. Ten minutes later he started the truck and with the hissing of brakes, powered the unit off the forecourt and onto the A27, pulling a trailer load of bagged new potatoes behind, to be delivered to Covent Garden market in the early hours.

The blue flashing lights ahead had Drummond braking and dropping down through the gears. He was surprised to find that it was a roadblock.

"Got any passengers in there?" said a young constable climbing up the steps and flashing a torch around.

"No mate, you lost someone then? Oh, you mean that nutter who escaped from Parkhurst."

The policeman didn't answer. "Can you get down? We need to have the trailer opened up."

"What! Oh Jesus Christ, it takes bloody ages to open up the sides of this," Drummond moaned.

Reluctantly he climbed down and opened up the trailer for the search. Murata, hidden in the cab, lay tense with all muscles taut, pistol at the ready. During the day he had seen billboard headlines warning the public of an escaped criminal and, slipping into a back street newsagents, he had bought a paper. The front-page item filled him with fury; why was it that a criminal should bring the police in large numbers at this time of all times. Now he was on the run instead of tracking the Vaughan woman and killing her. Why had he listened to

Hamaura and kept them hostage? Why had he not killed them as soon as the boats were at sea? He could be hidden in Paris now, not running like some petty thief.

Twenty minutes later Drummond was back in his cab muttering obscenities before, engaging the five hundred horsepower engine and pulling away. The journey along to Portsmouth then up the A3 was, for a change, trouble free and he arrived too early for the market to be open.

Drummond reached again for the flask and made up another sachet of cold cure, sipping at the hot liquid as he peered out across the deserted lorry park. The drink finished, he screwed the cup back onto the top of the flask and for the fiftieth time pulled a tissue from the box on the dashboard and blew his nose. His nasal passages cleared for the first time in two days and he enjoyed that moment when the sense of smell returns, except the smell that caught his senses was not pleasant. If there was one smell that Jack Drummond disliked, it was the smell of mothballs, and somewhere in his cab there was something smelling of just that.

Todashi Murata lay still, eyes watching the back of Drummond's head carefully, whilst remaining hidden beneath the blankets and sleeping bag in the sleeper section of the truck's cab. Apart from the two-hour wait at the filling station, Murata's journey to London had only been troubled when the lorry was stopped at the roadblock. Even that had worked well, as he had guessed that it would. The cursory inspection of the cab was typical of someone doing a job in which repetition and boredom produced laziness and carelessness. He had even dozed as the lorry had droned monotonously along the highway, but was now very awake and alert. Unlike Drummond, Todashi Murata, in keeping with many Japanese, liked the smell of mothballs and normally packed some in his case when travelling to give his clothes a scent that he appreciated. Something in the way that the driver was sniffing told Murata that he was seeking the source of a smell rather than preventing his nose from running. Slowly the man rose and twisting round, started to rummage through the items in the sleeping quarter, testing each item with a sniff. Inevitably he lifted the sleeping bag, revealing the head and shoulders of Murata, and froze in disbelief and shock. Murata, already anticipating discovery, was poised to act instantly and before Drummond was aware of what was happening, had one hand on Drummond's chin and the other holding the back of his head. With a sudden and violent jerk he twisted the head round until a sharp crack was heard as the neck broke. Drummond's body slumped back into the driver's seat, his hand still clutching the sleeping bag, dragging it and the blankets down covering most of his torso.

Murata surveyed the scene, then slipped down into the passenger seat and leaning across, arranged the blankets to make it look as if the man was sleeping with his head facing the back of the driver's seat. Ensuring that he had left no obvious signs of his presence, Murata checked that the coast was clear, then opening the passenger door, lowered himself to the ground and slipped away into the dim lighting of the South London streets. He was sad to have been forced to kill someone who he had no grudge against, but had the man raised the alarm, all would have been lost.

In her small flat in the Barbican, Yukiko Nagano was sleeping soundly when the phone rang. Instinctively she reached over to pick up the handset but stopped just in time. The phone stopped ringing and now wide-awake, she sat up in bed and waited. Two minutes passed before the phone rang again; she counted the number of rings before it stopped. Four ring-tones meant that Murata had arrived in London and was at the meeting place.

Hurriedly she washed and dressed, then carefully placing a latex facemask in her handbag, she left the flat and hurried away, initially forgetting to check whether she was being followed. It was only when she had reached Cheapside that she remembered Murata's warning and careful instructions. Crossing the road she turned right and entered St Paul's tube station. Standing for a moment as if to study the ticket machine destination list, she bought the cheapest ticket and went through the barriers to the deep escalator. At the bottom she turned left through the first arch onto the platform, before turning sharp right, then right again through the third arch back towards the escalator, hiding herself amongst a group of tall commuter businessmen heading off the platform.

DS Tracy Gorman and DC Garry Featherstone stood little or no chance of maintaining the tail. Even though they had been only ten people behind her on the escalator they had been unable to spot the cunning double-back. Realising that they had lost contact with their quarry they had divided, with Tracy checking the platform and Garry taking the train for the next six stops until he had checked every carriage and watched out at every station. In all, twenty minutes had passed before the Yard learned that the tail had been lost and orders were given for both officers to return to the Barbican and resume watch on the flat.

Yukiko, actually unaware she had been followed, exited the tube station, turned left and entered a souvenir shop where she purchased a walking stick. Leaving the shop she doubled back, turning down the side of the tube station entrance to join the path through to St Paul's cathedral yard, where she stopped and sat for a few minutes checking on whether anyone else was loitering. Satisfied that those around her were intent on arriving at their places of work on time, she got up, walked along the front of the cathedral, down the steps and crossed the road. On the other side she loitered again, looking at reflections in windows, trying to see if anyone was taking much interest in her or acting suspiciously. Again happy that no one was following her, she turned down the path that led to the Millennium Bridge. On the bridge itself she followed Murata's instructions to the letter by first walking to the centre of the bridge then, pretending to receive a mobile phone call, turned back, retracing her steps to the north bank.

Murata caught up with her as she walked back towards St Paul's cathedral.

"Did you bring the face?" She jumped, surprised, as she had expected him to approach her from in front, not from behind. Murata had in fact been observing her since she had crossed the road at St Paul's. He had also been looking out for anyone following her.

"I have it in my bag, Todashi-san," she said, smiling with pleasure at seeing him again. "You gave m…"

"Give it to me quickly," Murata said, his voice edged with annoyance.

Hurriedly she reached into her handbag, pulled out the plastic bag containing the latex facemask and handed it to him with a polite bow.

Snatching it from her, he said, "Sit over there and wait for me."

Yukiko obeyed though felt upset by the cold greeting. As she sat down on the bench she saw Murata disappear into a public toilet. It was about ten minutes later that an old man shuffled up to her seat and slowly, painfully, sat down. At first Yukiko paid no attention to him, then as realisation dawned, she turned to the old man and asked, "Murata-san des-ka?"

"Yes, it is I. If you are asked, I am your grandfather."

Yukiko giggled, then getting up, turned and helped her 'grandfather' to his feet to start a slow and circuitous route back to her flat. En route they stopped at an internet café, as Murata was now anxious to know of the successful rendezvous in the Atlantic.

The message from Stavos had been sent over two weeks after the rendezvous. Aware he would excite curiosity if he were to return with an empty hold, he had actually done some fishing, arriving back with a good haul. Added to this was his fear that Murata would blame him for Yamamoto's injury. Eventually it had been Fatia who had composed and typed out the message.

Murata was not too surprised to learn of the failure of Yamamoto; his only worry concerned Vaughan, and Murata hoped that he would be executed before they sighted the American shore. The good news was that the vessel's identity could be changed and those of Madadhah and Hamaura. Still, it was a troubled Murata who emerged from the café and hobbled away towards the Barbican.

In Chichester Murata and little Yukiko had discussed where to hide in London and had concluded that her flat, which had been the communication hub for the group, was still safe, especially as only she and Murata knew where it was. During her relationship with Julian she had always lied about where she lived, and after moving in with him, it didn't occur to him to ask. Daily she had gone to the flat telling Julian only that she worked for a small import business based in the Barbican. For his part, Julian was so smitten with her that he would never have pushed or questioned. Any meetings of the group had been in the back rooms of small restaurants or in one of the London parks. So it was with this feeling of security that the pair made their way back across the city, unaware that the location was known to the ATB.

"Here she is," said Featherstone. "Looks like she's got some old bloke in tow." A few moments passed whilst he focused in the camera's zoom lens and took a couple of shots. "There's something not right about that old bloke," he said.

DS Gorman stood up and crossed the room to stand close behind the constable and train her binoculars on Murata. "That's not Murata, that guy's old enough to be her grandfather," she said.

"I've got a fiver that says it is Murata in disguise," said Featherstone. "Take a good look at that leather jacket and tell me that's what an old man would wear."

DS Gorman looked again. "I'm looking at the face and hands and those tell me that he's not our man."

DC Featherstone raised his eyebrows. The pairing had not been a comfortable one and he for one would be eternally grateful when DS Gorman was promoted out of the way. "Ok, have it your way. We had better report it in," he said, reaching for the radio.

"I'll do that," said Gorman, abruptly taking the radio out of Featherstone's hand.

"Base, this is DS Gorman. Subject has returned in company with very elderly male who we think is a relative."

The radio crackled and the station acknowledged the report, and requested that they maintain a close watch.

Across in New Covent Garden the local police were putting up a tape barrier around the Scania 500 as a police doctor climbed into the cab from the passenger side to inspect the body. Nearby two rather shaken market porters were talking to a WPC.

"We've known Jack Drummond for years. We fort 'e was asleep see, an' Dave 'ere says to me, 'Old Jack's gonna wake up wiv a bleedin' stiff neck'. Don't seem so bloody funny now." Mick Grayshot looked down at the ground with embarrassment.

"Finkin 'e was havin' a nap we left 'im then when it was arf past ten and 'e still adent woke we banged on the cab door, see," said Dave. "When he still didn't budge well we opened the door. 'Scues me, can I sit down a minute. I don't feel so good."

At that moment a van sped across the car park and a television crew leapt out and started setting up.

North of the Thames, at New Scotland Yard, WPC Tucker was watching News 24 and sipping at a cup of coffee. "News is just coming in about a brutal murder of a lorry driver at New Covent Garden Market. We are going over now to James Thurlston, who is at the scene," said the newscaster. The screen showed the reporter and Tucker listened to his description of the events, confirmed by the police inspector in charge. The event didn't really catch her attention until the cameraman panned round and focused on the side of the lorry, which had in large letters 'Drummonds of Chichester' and a telephone number. On her feet now, she hurried to the lift and pressed the button for the twelfth floor. She almost ran down the corridor to Jackson's office, to find the door open but no one there. "He's with Commander Campbell," said DC Connors from his desk in the outer office.

"Thanks," she replied, turning and hurrying away.

"He said he didn't want to be disturbed," called Connors after her.

"He'll want to hear about this," she called back over her shoulder in reply.

Mrs Fitzgerald knew when something was important enough to interrupt a meeting. Normally, on something that did not tick the right boxes, she would slip into Campbell's office, receive a shake of the head and then come out to make an apology. When the right boxes were ticked she would use the intercom. Over the years Campbell had come to trust her judgement and would either come out to see the visitor or get them sent in.

As WPC Tucker entered she felt both nervous and excited. "Yes, Tucker, what is it that you have come to amaze us with now?" said Campbell with a smile.

"If you turn on your television to News 24, sir, you will see a report about the murder of a lorry driver at New Covent Garden. I believe that the murderer is Murata and he got from

Chichester to London stowed away on the lorry." She stood feeling a little silly as instead of asking for more details both men looked at her straight-faced, saying nothing. "The lorry had Drummond's of Chichester on the side," she said.

"Anything else?" asked Jackson.

"No, sir."

"Inspector Jackson, can you find out whose patch that is and who is in charge of the case and inform them that we want a full report ASAP complete with the forensic data and post-mortem report," requested Campbell.

"The person in charge of the case is a Detective Inspector Withers, sir," informed Tucker.

"There we are, Inspector," said Campbell with a mischievous grin. "Tucker here has done half the job for you without leaving the office."

Jackson laughed as Tucker blushed bright red.

"It looks pretty certain that the old man seen by the Barbican team is definitely Murata then," said Jackson. "We had better reinforce the surveillance."

"Good idea, can I leave that with you as well?" asked Campbell.

"Yes, sir," said Jackson, getting to his feet and heading for the door closely followed by Tucker.

"WPC Tucker." She turned to face Campbell. "Thank you, that was a valuable link you made there," said Campbell.

"Oh, er, right, sir," she replied, returning his smile.

It was just after eight o'clock that evening that Inspector Jackson rang the doorbell of the flat. A rather horsey-looking woman opened the door and Jackson introduced himself.

"They've set themselves up in my bedroom," she said. "I'm just making some coffee, would you like a cup?"

"No, thank you, Mrs er, Cranston," replied Jackson. "I've just had a cup, thank you."

The woman smiled and pointed in the direction of the bedroom door.

Gorman and Featherstone had moved their surveillance point from a flat overlooking the front door of Yukiko Nagano's to one that looked into the rear windows.

As Jackson entered the room Gorman leapt to her feet. "Good evening, sir."

"Good evening," replied Jackson. "DC Conners has nothing to report from the front of the flat. Is there anything happening here?"

"Little Miss Nagano's been buzzing about but we haven't seen movement from Murata, sir," replied Featherstone.

"Murata, huh," DS Gorman sneered.

"You have reason to doubt that it is Murata holed up in that flat, Sergeant?" asked Jackson.

"Yes, sir, the man I saw was very old and hunched with a very wrinkled face and hands," she replied. "I would guess that it is the girl's grandfather."

"A light's gone on in the bedroom," reported Featherstone, adjusting the angle of the telephoto lens. "Bloody hell, those curtains are thin. They might as well not bother with them."

Gorman threw a cursory glance in the direction of the flat, then reaching down for the plate of sandwiches, picked it up and offered it to Jackson. "Something to eat, Inspector?"

Jackson shook his head and stepped up to the tripod with the binoculars mounted.

It took him a couple of minutes to readjust the focus to his eyes and retrain the glasses. Now concentrating on what he could see, he recoiled, shocked and with DS Gorman standing just behind him, a little embarrassed.

"Your theory about the grandfather's been blown," said Featherstone. "The bloke I'm looking at now is maybe forty and is humping young Nagano like a raging bull."

DS Gorman pushed Featherstone away from the big lens and looked through the eyepiece. "He must have already been in the flat," she said. "He definitely wasn't the man that we saw earlier."

"Make it a tenner if you like, Sarge," said Featherstone, upping the wager.

Gorman glared at him but didn't take the bet.

"DS Gorman," said Jackson. "Can I have a word with you outside."

On a raised walkway away from the flat Inspector Jackson turned to face the now apprehensive DS Gorman. "In future when you radio in reports, avoid placing any bias on them that is not fully shared by your colleagues. Your report gave the impression that you had a reasonable belief that the elderly man you saw was a relative."

"But, sir," Gorman interrupted. "We are still not sure that there is only one man in that flat."

"I am absolutely sure," said Jackson, his voice hardening with annoyance. "Had it not been for some astute lateral thinking by a WPC at the Yard, this surveillance would not have been reinforced to allow coverage of this side of the building and Featherstone would not have had the opportunity to confirm the presence of Murata in that flat." Jackson glared at the sergeant for a few moments whilst his angry words sank in. "Now get back to your work and keep a special eye out for anything like communication or preparation."

Back in the flat, Featherstone glanced up at her. "Anything wrong?" he asked.

"No, he just wanted to make sure we looked for signs of them making communication or preparing for something."

"Oh," said DC Featherstone, his eyes now back against the lens and a smile spreading across his face.

"There's a call for you from the States, Commander," informed Mrs Fitzgerald, her head peering round the conference room door. It was late the following afternoon, Saints and Campbell had been working out the probable course that the yacht would have taken and possible landfall made.

"Excuse me, Mr Saints, I'd better take this in my office," said Campbell, leaping to his feet and hurrying across the room to the interconnecting door.

Picking up the receiver he said, "Campbell here, who am I speaking to?"

"This is agent Capello of the CIA speaking. We've, er, got your guy Ian Vaughan. He sailed into Morehead City yesterday and reported to the City Police there."

"Excellent news, thank you very much for telling me. Where is he now?" Campbell asked. "What about the other two, have you got them as well?"

"Mr Vaughan is sat right alongside me now. He managed some spectacular escape, however, we have no idea where his captors would have gone," replied Capello.

"That is a great pity," said Campbell. "We have their leader Todashi Murata under surveillance and we have a tap on his phones but so far he has not had any communication with the rest of his gang."

"Why not bring him in and lean on him?" suggested Capello.

"Our expert here in Japanese criminal activity advises us that leaning on the man, as you put it, would definitely not work and could lead to triggering the attack early," replied Campbell.

"Well, it's your operation over there but if it goes on much longer then we'll be wantin' him. In fact we think we've got enough to apply for extradition now," said Capello, obviously unimpressed by the softly-softly approach.

"That's up to you," said Campbell. "We will of course keep you up to date with events here. Now may I have a few words with Mr Vaughan?"

There was a pause and Campbell could hear some background conversation before Capello came back on the line. "Vaughan is just going through to another room to take the call; I need to keep this line open. We are very anxious to keep him here until this is cleared up so I would be obliged if you avoid giving him any news that will lead to him demanding to return home just yet. I understand his children are fine but how about his wife?"

"I'm afraid there has been little improvement there and she has not responded to any treatment as yet," replied Campbell.

"Oh well, if you could put a gloss on that somehow, he's very stressed about them all. If you hold on I'll have you put through." With that, the line switched to music for a few moments, then Vaughan came on.

"Hello, is that Commander Campbell?" Ian Vaughan asked.

"Yes it is," Campbell replied. "Mr Vaughan, I understand that Agent Capello and his team are anxious that you stay with them for a while to help with their search for Fumiko Hamaura and the other man. Your family, I am pleased to inform you, are all safe and your daughters have been quite wonderful. You should be very proud of them. So we all would be very grateful if you would stay on a while and see this through. Our information from Tokyo is that this is planned to be a major attack carried out by a team of determined and ruthless individuals, so your valuable assistance would be greatly appreciated." Campbell did not feel comfortable doing this sort of thing and could not find the phrases he needed.

"You mentioned my daughters but said nothing about my wife," said Ian. "Is she and the baby ok?"

"I'm sorry to have to tell you that she lost the baby and is currently recovering from that ordeal," replied Campbell. "She is being given the best care possible, as are your children." There was a long pause and Campbell decided it best to wait and allow his news to be absorbed and evaluated.

"Thank you for being so honest," said Ian at last. "Can you arrange for me to speak to my parents? I will need to explain to them why I can't come back right away."

"Of course I can. I will get that done straight away," said Campbell, pressing the intercom for Mrs Fitzgerald.

"Mrs Fitzgerald, when I have finished talking to Mr Vaughan, can you arrange for him to receive a direct call from his parents in Portsmouth?"

Campbell talked to Ian Vaughan for a further thirty minutes about his experiences and escape – a conversation that he recorded. By the time he hung up he was truly amazed by what he had heard.

A knock at the door reminded him that Phil Saints was in the next room and he went straight over to see what he wanted.

"I hope I didn't interrupt, sir, but what I think is a rather important thing has just come to my notice," said Saints.

"What is that exactly, Mr Saints?" said Campbell.

"I hope you don't mind, but on a whim I asked Mrs Fitzgerald to go onto the web and look up sailing events along the coastline that we are interested in. There's nothing going on in Morehead City but there is a large event called the Cock Island Race taking place in the southern end of the Chesapeake this weekend," said Saints. "These events are wonderful things to hide amongst."

Just then Jackson entered the room. "We've just intercepted a call to Murata, sir," he said.

"It was quite short and in English, a man's voice with either an Indian or Middle Eastern accent."

"Well, what did he say?" asked Campbell.

Jackson looked down at his notepad. "He said, quote, 'Vaughan was lost at sea, maybe took his own life, we don't know but just after he goes Hamaura is injured and will need time to get well. Can we have Yamada join us,' unquote. Then Murata said 'Okay but be quick he leaving, Hamaura-san knows how to contact.' Then he said 'Kinoko Kumo must go ahead on schedule you understand, on schedule.' With that he hung up on the other man."

"Does anyone know what 'Kinoko Kumo' means?" asked Campbell.

"According to DS Weaver it means mushroom cloud," said Jackson.

Phil Saints gave a low whistle. "If that doesn't mean some form of nuclear attack I don't know what does."

"Was it land-line or mobile?" asked Campbell.

"Land-line, sir," replied Jackson. "From the background noises it sounded as if it was being made from a café or restaurant. We didn't have long enough to run a trace."

Campbell crossed to the intercom. "Mrs Fitzgerald, can you get me Agent Capello in Washington please. I'll take it in here."

Within five minutes Capello was on the line and Campbell was informing him of the intercept and details of what was said. "Can you ask Ian Vaughan whether he recalls them using the phrase 'Kinoko Kumo' at any time?"

There was a delay whilst the question was relayed then Capello was back on the line confirming that Ian Vaughan had heard them using the phrase during their radio contact with the supply vessel north of the Azores.

"According to our expert here it means mushroom cloud," said Campbell. "We take that to indicate that the attack planned may involve a nuclear device."

The response was both loud and crude, causing Campbell to take the receiver away from his ear and glare at it. "Quite so, Mr Capello. We also think that Hamaura and the man, – sorry, can you say that again?" Campbell listened intently. "Ah, Yunis Madadhah, yes, we know all too much about him. Well, we think that they used the Cock Island Sailing Race crowds to hide out in and cover their arrival." Campbell listened again. "Oh, Ian Vaughan was thinking along the same lines was he? That's good."

Twenty minutes passed before Campbell put the phone down and turning, smiled at Jackson. "You probably heard that our old adversary Yunis Madadhah is the Middle Eastern man onboard with Hamaura. Mr Saints, for your understanding, he was the leader of the cell that carried out the Croydon Tower bombing." Saints gave a nod. "It appears that Agent Capello requires us to keep a close watch on Murata and report any message received or sent. He appears to no longer require us to bring him in and beat information out of him."

"The last time I looked at my pay cheque, it was in Pounds Sterling," said Jackson, "not US Dollars."

"The same thoughts were crossing my mind," said Campbell. "Nonetheless we had better increase our surveillance and make sure we leave nothing to chance. If you have any doubts about DS Gorman, have her sent back to City and get someone in there who does the job properly."

"I'll get on with that as soon as we have finished here, sir," said Jackson. "I thought it would be a good time to scale down the Hammersmith enquiry and re-deploy half of that team."

"Only those working in support; I don't want to see any of the core team taken from that operation. I am still sure that there is a risk there," said Campbell.

"Alright, sir. Maybe a few from there and some from the Stratford Street work."

"That sounds fine, thank you," replied Campbell. "Before you go, Inspector, you may like to hear this. I was most amazed at the man's ingenuity."

Campbell took both men through Ian Vaughan's escape story, turning at the end to Phil Saints and asking, "What would have been the effect of losing the steering wheel on a yacht under sail?"

"Well, under normal circumstances, where a yacht's rudder is only a few degrees off the centre line, the vessel would just turn her bows into the wind and come to a stop, unless the waves were constantly pushing the bows off. As I understand it, he made sure that full lock was on, and that would cause the yacht to gybe. In other words, cause the mainsail boom to slam from one side to the other." As he spoke he drew a sketch on his notepad to show both men. "That quite often causes damage and can bring the whole rig down if the wind is strong. I bet the other two were in a panic when it happened, as they would have had little, if any, warning," said Saints with a mischievous grin on his face.

"Could they steer the boat other than with the wheel?" Jackson asked.

"Yes, most yachts carry an emergency tiller to cover in case of steering linkage problems. I would expect one to be aboard that yacht. Retrieving it from the locker may not be the simplest of tasks though," answered Saints, still grinning. "I take my hat off to Ian Vaughan; sailing that close to another yacht then pulling a stunt like that takes great skill and courage, and from the sound of it, he didn't even get his feet wet."

The intercom buzzed and Mrs Fitzgerald informed them that the American Embassy were on the line requesting that the senior officer in charge take part in a video conference at the Embassy in one hour's time.

Jackson looked at his boss. "Your bag I think, sir. They would be very upset if we fielded the second team."

"Nonsense, I'm sure you are much more at ease in front of a camera than I am, but I think that the politics requires my attention," replied Campbell with some reluctance. "Mrs Fitzgerald, can you arrange for my car to be downstairs in half an hour's time please."

The request acknowledged, Campbell strolled across to the maps laid out on the floor and looked down upon the area of the Chesapeake. "Mr Saints, Agent Capello believes that Hamaura and Madadhah have gone ashore somewhere and that they will pursue this attack from the land. Vaughan, however, is of the belief that they will remain onboard the yacht as they have buoy devices that will transmit messages from a location remote to the boat. What's your opinion?"

Saints crouched down by the map and considered the question for a few moments. "I would go with Vaughan's assessment, sir. If you were on land, a series of roadblocks would inevitably contain you, or if you ran into one, would probably expose you to arrest. Afloat, you would be more likely to pass off as a couple cruising for pleasure and be better situated to launch these buoy devices you mentioned. Also, as you can see from the map, the Chesapeake is basically a large creek with a series of rivers running into it and hundreds of inlets and bays in which a yacht could hide. In a boat you can change your location by only a few miles, which by car would take hours of motoring."

"There's another aspect to this as well, sir," said Jackson. "I've been studying the information Tokyo have sent us on Hamaura, which, though, isn't much, does indicate that she is a survivor not a martyr. Yunis Madadhah is of the same breed; both sadists and ruthless but neither remotely prepared to give their own life for the cause. My guess is that whatever they are planning will be triggered such as to allow them to be safely out of harm's way. If they can trigger this attack remotely there is no reason to stop them being well out to sea, whereas if they were ashore, to leave the US would mean passing through some security checkpoint at either a border crossing or airport."

"Thank you, gentlemen, you have put forward a very strong case," said Campbell thoughtfully. "Mr Jackson. When you have completed your surveillance disposition, would you telephone me at the American Embassy with the details? I feel the need to impress Agent Capello and others across the pond with our efforts and efficiency."

As Campbell got into the car he felt strangely disappointed that it was PC Wheatley at the wheel and not Caroline Tucker. Putting thoughts of her out of his mind, he opened his file and started to read through his notes again to make sure that he had the sequence of events and details firmly in his mind.

It was the third time Campbell had met with James Alexander Beaumont, the American Ambassador, and found again that he liked and respected him. Their conversation, though serious, had the tone of two friends discussing a problem of mutual interest rather than a cold report of facts. During the subsequent videoconference with the States, Beaumont had been very generous with his praise for Campbell and his team. This had been prompted by Jackson's telephone report on surveillance progress.

What was very clear, was that all of the information had gone right to the very top, and everyone on the American side was aware of President Huckle's pressure on both the FBI, and CIA, to bring in their most senior staff to run the investigation. Agents Capello and Brumen were now just foot soldiers responsible for looking after Ian Vaughan and passing on any further intelligence he might recall.

Back at his desk Inspector Jackson had been sitting for some time studying the transcript of the intercepted phone call. Something was there in the wording that had alerted his brain, but what it was he could not identify. Needing to clear his head he left the building, and walking down Tothill Street he crossed the road at Queen Anne's Gate and entered St James Park. In the early evening the park had that strange mixture of homeward bound office workers, tourists and courting couples. Returning to the Yard half an hour later, he decided on a canteen meal and was pushing a lukewarm shepherd's pie around his plate when DS McKenzie joined him, complaining about the downsizing of his operation at the Stratford Street enquiry. "Really, sir, I just manage to get all the manpower I need there and I'm told I've got to give some of them up."

"That's it!" shouted Jackson, stopping all conversation in the canteen. "This Yamada bloke is there and is about to leave, not here! He is in America and was probably the man delivering the device! Thank you, McKenzie, that has helped a great deal."

Jackson leapt to his feet, leaving the meal half eaten, and hurried back to his office with McKenzie calling after him. "What about my enquiry team size, sir?"

In his office Jackson snatched up the transcript sheet and hurried along to Campbell's office. Late in the evening there was no one in the outer office, so Jackson knocked and entered to find Campbell just putting on his coat and hat.

"Yes, Jackson, what can I do for you?" asked Campbell.

"It's more what I can do for this investigation," replied Jackson. "Ever since that phone call, I have been niggled by the possibility that it contained more information than we first thought. Then just now in the canteen it came to me. This bloke, Yamada, they referred to, is already in America but was about to leave. My guess is that he is the man who has delivered the device and the 'A' team have arrived to trigger it."

"Is that the transcript you've got there?" asked Campbell.

Jackson handed the sheet to him and waited whilst Campbell read then reread the passage.

"I think you may well be right. Let me run the name past Ian Vaughan before we get our American friends too excited. I've got some more positive news for him regarding the condition of his wife, which Mrs Fitzgerald obtained this afternoon."

It was Brumen who answered the phone and happily passed it to Ian Vaughan when he heard that the message was in connection with Vaughan's wife's condition.

"Commander Campbell, you have some news regarding my wife?" The anxiety clearly showed in Ian Vaughan's voice.

"Good news, I am pleased to tell you that during the day your wife has made great progress and the hospital say that she could be released within a couple of days if she carries on like this. My secretary was able to speak with her earlier on and has learnt that your wife is keen for you to help in any way possible."

"Thank you for passing that news on, Commander. For obvious reasons I cannot make phone calls to the hospital from here, so any news coming in is most welcome. When my parents phoned they told me that Sarah supported my decision to stay on over here as long as I am of use, but I think I would be of more use at home."

Campbell let the conversation continue about Vaughan's family, working from briefing notes that Mrs Fitzgerald had left him. He gave up-to-date information regarding Clare and Louise and the affection his protection squad had developed for them. The question about the name Yamada he left until the end of the conversation.

"Mr Vaughan, do you recall either of your two captors referring to someone called Yamada?"

"Yamada, Yamada, oh, you mean the man mentioned in the telephone conversation," replied Vaughan. "No, it didn't ring any immediate bells."

"We think he may have been their man in America preparing the device for them," said Campbell.

There was a few moments' silence then Ian Vaughan said, "Wait, I am trying to recall something they said, when was it now, it wasn't off Cherbourg. I know, it was just before the storm when I dropped the Dan-buoy overboard, yes, that was it. Just a moment, I am trying to get this straight in my memory."

Campbell could hear Ian Vaughan talking to himself at the other end of the phone, working his way through an incident that had taken place on board the yacht.

"Yes, Commander, I do remember now. It was your comment about him getting something ready for them to use that did it. Hamaura stressed that Yamada was efficient and would have everything prepared for their immediate use once they arrived. She seemed to have great faith in the man."

"Did she use any words like, 'plant' or 'place', in her description of this person's activities?" Campbell asked.

"I'm sorry, I wish I could remember more clearly what she said," replied Vaughan. "I'm sure I would have noted it had she used such language, as it is normally indicative of placing a bomb."

"Mr Vaughan, after what you have been through I am amazed at what detail you can recall," said Campbell. "Thank you very much and be assured that you are of great value where you are. Now could you hand me back to Agent Brumen, please."

There were a couple of clicks then Brumen's voice was heard. "Yes, Commander, what have you got for me?"

"The message we relayed earlier referred to someone called Yamada. We believe that this person is already in your country and has been for some time. We suspect that he is the man who has prepared everything for Hamaura and Madadhah to trigger when they arrive."

"I'm looking at the transcript now, Commander," said Brumen. "I see what you mean."

"If you speak now with Mr Vaughan he will inform you of a conversation he overheard whilst onboard the yacht," said Campbell. "By taking these two bits of information together, my fear is that the device or devices are already in place and that the attack could be triggered just as soon as this Yamada rejoins the other two."

"Commander, thank you so much for that," said Brumen. We're tryin' Vaughan's idea that they are operatin' from the boat. If you have any other ideas please contact at any time."

"Have you considered asking Mr Vaughan to help with the waterborne search? He is an experienced sailor and could well recognise the yacht they are using," suggested Campbell.

"He did volunteer to do just that, but we thought it would place him in too much danger, Commander. I'll see what my superiors think of the idea before invitin' him to the party," said Brumen. "I doubt if they will buy it, somehow."

At length the conversation ended and Campbell, accompanied by Jackson, left the building for the night. Neither of them spoke on the way down in the lift, each occupied in their own thoughts as to how to close a net on this gang and avert a massive disaster.

Chapter 13

As Arni attended to Hamaura's injuries, they had discussed their options. She had accepted his concerns that Ian Vaughan may not, as she first thought, have committed suicide. This meant that under no circumstances could they risk entering the USA formally, as she had indicated to the Coastguard helicopter. Instead they set a course directly for the Chesapeake, changing again the ID of the yacht, by removing the sail numbers from the mainsail and rearranging the stick-on spray dodger letters.

This operation took Arni the rest of the night and as the sun rose, he was for the third time using a light line to stitch the dodgers back onto the guardrails alongside the cockpit. Below, Hamaura was painfully forging new American ship's papers under the name *Melodrama Clan*. She looked at least twenty years older, her eyes dark rimmed and face drawn with pain. It had taken her two hours to compile the anagram from *Romance Allemande* and as she finally placed the ship's papers into the briefcase, she was on the point of collapse.

They came in sight of land as the sun was setting and for the first time, sailed on through the night without showing any navigation lights. Around 6 o'clock the sun, streaming through the cabin windows, woke Hamaura from her restless sleep. Cautiously rising, she managed to boil some water to make up soup for Arni and herself. The agony of raising her right arm high enough to place Arni's mug at the top of the companionway, had her feeling faint. She sat heavily on the chart table seat, noting that no navigation had been done overnight. Remembering that they must contact Murata and request Yamada's help, she elbowed up the top of the chart table and rummaged around in search of her mobile phone, finding it eventually, jammed in the outer corner, by a copy of English Channel Pilotage. Finally, she took the phone and a tin of biscuits back to the starboard settee, where she had to sit for some time in order to recover. Now, focused again, she tried to switch the phone on but the screen remained blank. Cursing, she threw it to the other end of the seat and morosely sipped at her mug of soup. A movement on deck caused her to turn and look up into the cockpit. Arni, exhausted from lack of sleep and constant helming, had momentarily fallen asleep and slipped off the cockpit seat, waking himself as he did so.

Hamaura for once did not shout any accusation, instead she struggled to her feet and painfully climbed up into the cockpit to keep Arni company and help him see the voyage through.

"You any idea how far we have to go?" she asked.

"No, I am following coastline until I see Chesapeake Bridges," he answered. "We have company." He jerked his head in the general direction of two yachts sailing a parallel course, about half a mile off their port bow. "I'm guessing that they are also aiming for the Chesapeake."

"You have done well," she said. "I steer for a bit while you rest, I have one arm that is ok."

"We see how you manage while I get some food for us. If you can cope I will sleep over there," he said, pointing to the opposite cockpit seat.

The food when it arrived was consumed with three strong painkillers, that after half an hour provided some relief, enabling her to steer a course, edging the boat nearer to the coastline and into the track of the other yachts.

By eleven o'clock the effects of the painkillers had worn off and every movement of the yacht resulted in stabbing pain from the broken ribs. One in particular made her cry out and wake Arni.

"Painkillers not working?" he asked

"I apologise, but please can you get me some more and something to drink?" she requested, feeling that she was losing face through her weakness.

253

Arni got to his feet and froze, staring out astern of them.

Hamaura, painfully, turned to see what was holding his attention, to be faced with a large US Navy ship scything through the seas some distance away. At first they thought that it was making straight for them, then they could see her port side coming into view. She swept past them some five hundred yards away, without reducing speed or apparently taking any notice of them. Two miles in front of them, she began the turn that would eventually bring her on a course to enter the Chesapeake and the base at Norfolk. Relaxing, Arni went below and brought back the painkillers and a soft drink, before preparing a dish containing rice, tinned tuna and some peas.

As they started into the great gap that leads to the Chesapeake, the tide was making and in the more sheltered water, helped by the tide, their speed increased to eight knots over the ground.

Now sailing close inshore, they passed Cape Henry's Old Lighthouse and swept on across Lynnhaven Roads. As Hamaura looked around, she could see they were amongst many yachts, all criss-crossing with each other, as Arni steered them towards the inlet and under the Lesner Bridge. On arrival at the dockside marina, Arni checked in at the office. The reception clerk was slow, inefficient and obviously just going through the motions. Arni relaxed, he had feared that their arrival would excite interest and suspicion but on the contrary, the clerk didn't even ask where they had come from. Paying for three days, he left the office and crossed the road where, in the foyer of a restaurant, he found a phone booth and made the call to Murata. When Murata hung up on him, Arni stood for several seconds glaring at the phone.

"Why do I have to work with someone born to a donkey?" he grumbled to himself as he left the restaurant and returned to the yacht.

Stepping down into the cabin, he found Hamaura waiting for him with a mobile phone in her hand.

"What are our orders?" she asked.

"You are to contact Yamada immediately. He say you know how, then he put phone down. Who does he think he is dealing with, eh?" replied Arni, eyes blazing with fury at the way Murata had acted.

"Of course he is annoyed! We have lost Vaughan and possibly endangered operation. He has been planning for this long time now and at last step we have failed him!" she said, her old hostility returning.

"You failed him! You were person supposed to be on watch!" he shouted back at her.

Hamaura held up a hand to bring a stop to the argument. "This is getting us nowhere. I need to contact Yamada now, then contact doctor I know."

"You say your phone not working," said Arni in a quieter voice.

"This one belongs to Vaughan, it has signal and should work," she replied, her thumb working the keypad.

With both calls completed she said, "We sleep now, doctor not arrive until maybe eight o'clock, he has long way to come."

Without a word, Arni went forward to his bunk and was almost instantly asleep.

Being midweek, the marina had remained deserted and quiet throughout the rest of the afternoon and evening, so the clatter of leather-soled shoes on the pontoon's timber decking woke Arni in an instant. Moving with the stealth of a cat through the cabin, he passed Hamaura who had also roused to the sound.

It was no surprise to Arni to see in the lights of the marina, a little man of oriental features hurrying towards him.

"Is Miss Hamaura aboard this boat?" the man asked.

Arni did not reply.

"I am Dr Higashi, she phone me earlier requesting I come," the little man said, making a small but polite bow.

Arni reached out his hand for the doctor's bag. Taking hold of it, he placed it on the cockpit seat and opening it looked at the contents with the aid of a torch.

"Come onboard," ordered Arni.

Doctor Higashi struggled to climb aboard, but eventually stepped cautiously down into the cockpit.

"Stop," said Arni taking the doctor's wrists and forcing his arms above his head, frisking him in search of a gun or other weapons.

With a sigh Doctor Higashi said, "Miss Hamaura and I have known each other for many years. It is I who did most of treatment for Murata-san. Never before has anyone felt need to search me!" The comment had started off mildly but the last sentence left no doubt as to the doctor's annoyance.

Unimpressed, Arni merely pointed towards the cabin. "She is down there."

Dr Higashi's careful and thorough examination of Hamaura, revealed the need to have her taken to his private clinic, to have the broken arm reset along with the collarbone. The plan was for Arni to clean up the boat after its Atlantic ordeal, replace the wheel, then sail to the marina at Allen Point, in Long Cove, where Hamaura would rejoin the yacht and see through the final part of their attack. Arni carried her bag to Dr Higashi's car and saw them off, happier now that he was alone and away from her continuous aggression.

The conversation between the two boys woke Arni early. Pulling on some shorts, he made his way into the cockpit and looked forward to see them standing, throwing bread to some gulls.

"Hi guys, are you having fun there?" he asked.

The boys turned and looked at him suspiciously.

"Where do you get bread around here?" Arni continued. "I like to buy some."

The shorter of the two started to say something when the other gave him a dig in the ribs. "You know what Mom says about talking to strangers."

"He only wants to know where the store is," said the first, returning the dig.

"Just the same, she said we shouldn't coz of what happened to Jake Freeman, remember?" the taller boy retorted.

"Yeah, I remember, but I can't see why just telling a guy where the store is can be wrong," the shorter one continued.

The exchange was stopped by a woman's call from the corner of the car park. The boys turned and hurried away, leaving Arni feeling strangely rejected and frustrated.

Aware that Hamaura would expect the yacht to be sorted and awaiting her in Long Cove, Arni set to on cleaning up. A long search of the waterside marina shops and workshops eventually produced a replacement wheel. He even enquired about an autopilot for the yacht but it would take too long to fit. Finally after three days of hard work *'Melodrama Clan'*, polished and sparkling, lay alongside the pontoon with Arni loading the last of the stores.

"Did you find the bakers, sir?" The boy's small voice made Arni jump; he had not heard the lad approach.

"Er yeah, was that your brother you were with the other day?"

"Yeah, I wanted to tell you where you could get bread but he said Mom didn't want us talking to strangers."

"Where is he today?"

"Oh, Mrs Watts kept him back in school for pinching Maria's butt in class. Mom's waitin' on him at the school gate, is he gonna be in trouble."

Arni laughed. "How long is the detention?"

"Oh, about half an hour, then Mom's picking me up here. She will be here in a minute or two I guess."

Arni looked up at the car park area, his mind busy calculating the odds on whether he could get the boy aboard and get underway without attracting any attention.

"Do your parents own a boat?"

"No, we've only got Mom and she don't earn enough to own a boat. Dad was killed in the Iraq War, see." The boy looked away, his eyes filling with tears.

"Would you like to see aboard this boat?" asked Arni giving the boy his warmest and friendliest smile.

"I better not, Mom gets a bit freaky about people we don't know," the boy replied with a tone of disappointment.

"Ah come on, you're only just stepping on board to have a look," said Arni, his voice calm and somewhat persuasive.

The boy stood for a moment or two weighing up the odds on whether he could just take a look and get off before his mother arrived.

"Come on," said Arni, "I've got some cold Coke below."

"Well, just a quick look before Mom arrives," said the boy and nimbly stepped onto the toe rail and through the porthand gateway.

Making his way to the cockpit, he stepped down to stand behind the wheel and grasping it with both hands played the part of helmsman.

"Come down and get your Coke," said Arni, standing below in the cabin, alongside the chart table, holding the can up enticingly.

The boy raised a suntanned hand to shade his eyes and studied the quayside and car park in search of his mother. As there was no sign of her, or his brother, he stepped around the wheel and excitedly clambered down the companionway steps into the cabin. "Say this is ne..." was all he managed to say before a strip of duct tape was clamped over his mouth and his arms forced behind his back and bound tightly.

"...Beach Police Department are wanting to talk to Mr and Mrs Fernande, the owners of the yacht *Romance Allemande,* in connection with their search. They believe these persons could have seen Jason Schulkens shortly before he disappeared two days ago," the newsreader announced. "Farmers are predicting low grain yields this ye..."

Hamaura switched the radio off, her eyes blazing with anger. The WBT broadcast at first seriously troubled her, but then she realised that the yacht's name was wrong. It was almost certain that the animal she had been forced to work with, had checked the boat in using the wrong name. If that was the case then the police would be looking for a ghost ship.

Still in considerable pain, she reached for Ian Vaughan's mobile phone and punched in Yamada's number. "Yamada-san deska?"

"Hi, hi, Yamada des," came his response over the noise of a car engine.

"We have damaged goods which we have to dispose of," she said. "Purchase the necessary equipment and collect me from Dr Higashi's clinic as soon as you can."

"Hi watashi-wa wakarumasu," Yamada replied, "I will be there tomorrow evening."

"Domo, domo," she said, pleased that he was obviously not far away. "Sayonara."

Putting down the phone she rang for Dr Higashi. As he entered the room a few minutes later she announced, "I will be leaving the day after tomorrow and Yamada-san will arrive tomorrow evening; please could you arrange bed for him in here?"

"You will not be fit to sail yacht for some weeks," the doctor replied.

"I know, but I have to make adjustment to the team and it must be done straight away," she said. "Then I think we can manage without hoisting sails, just using boat motor."

Dr Higashi studied her for several seconds, then nodded and sat down on the chair beside her bed. "May I assume the adjustment you speak of is the Arab?" he asked.

She nodded.

"Please be very careful, Hamaura-san," he said. "That one is very strong and dangerous."

"Yes, I know, he is as dangerous as a snake. But Yamada-san is like a cat, and as you know, a cat can strike faster than a snake," she said, with a cruel smile spreading across her face.

Not for the first time in her company did Dr Higashi feel a shiver passing through him. Carefully, he listened with his stethoscope to her ribcage around the break area.

"You must avoid exertion, otherwise these rib fractures will never mend," he said firmly.

Nancy Schroder had also heard the radio broadcast, whilst she had been preparing lunch aboard her yacht, moored at the Portsmouth Boat Club pontoons. On a whim she had sailed up the coast, and into the Chesapeake and was just in time to watch the Cock Island Race and do a few interviews with the participants. Her editor was delighted as these were interviews with the wives and children that had taken part.

It was the name of the yacht, which had caught her attention and had her rushing to the forward cabin to retrieve her mobile phone. A second search of her sailing jacket produced Agent Brumen's card with his contact details. Hurriedly she dialled the number. "Brumen," the voice answered. "Who is this?"

"Nancy Schroder, we met a few days ago in Moorhead City," Nancy said.

"Yes, of course Miss Schroder, what can I do for you?" asked Brumen, his voice now brisk and alert.

"There's just been a news flash down here issued by the police, requesting that the owners of the yacht *Romance Allemande* make contact with them. Wasn't that the name of the yacht Ian Vaughan was on?"

"Yes, indeed it was. What was the connection, did they say?" Brumen sounded puzzled. "When we left we made it very clear to the Moorhead Police, that they were to leave the rest of the investigation strictly to us and not make any press comment."

"Oh, it was not the Moorhead Police, I think the radio mentioned Virginia Beach Police Department," Nancy replied.

"Oh right, that is very interesting. Did they say why they were looking for it? Brumen asked.

"They want to speak to the owner in connection with a missing boy. They think he or she may have seen the boy shortly before he disappeared." Nancy informed him.

"Where are you at the moment, Miss Schroder?"

"Portsmouth Boat Club covering the Cock Island Race. It's all right, I cleared it with the Moorhead Police before I sailed," she said defensively. "They said it would be fine."

"That's fine," said Brumen. "I was just interested should we need to come and see you again, that's all. I'm just goin' to circulate this around the team and will get back to you if we have any more questions."

"How is he?" she asked.

"How is who? Oh you mean Vaughan, he's okay, you want a word?" asked Brumen.

"Er, no," she replied feeling unusually shy. "Just say I asked if he was alright."

"Sure," said Brumen. "We'll be in touch if we need anything more."

Brumen slipped the phone back into his pocket walked across the room and sat down opposite Ian. "That was Miss Schroder, she called to say that the yacht *Romance Allemande* has been mentioned in a local radio news statement made on behalf of the police."

Ian looked up from the paper and gave Brumen a questioning look?

"It appears they want to speak to the owners in connection with a missing boy," Brumen informed.

"Arni must be up to his tricks, the bastard," said Ian with some venom. "He, or they, must be pretty confident that I am dead."

"Why do you say that?" asked Brumen.

"Well for a start, abducting a small boy is bound to result in questions being asked and secondly, they don't appear to have changed the name of the yacht."

"It's not certain that they hold them responsible for the boy's disappearance, but I see what you mean," said Brumen, sitting back in the chair and staring thoughtfully at the ceiling. "From what you found in Arni's possession on the boat and bearing in mind the apparently uncontrollable urges of these perverts, there is a strong chance that he is responsible."

"Not wanting to overplay the plight of that poor boy, I think that the time has come for me to be of much more use to this investigation, out there on the water, helping to look for these two," said Ian. "It's obvious that they think I'm dead and no threat to them. The sooner they are identified and caught the better for all. If they get wind that the law is searching for them, they may well go to ground and we will not find them until it is too late."

After three hours of phone calls, arguments and pleading, Ian Vaughan found himself in a helicopter, between Brumen and Capello heading for the Air Force Base at Virginia Beach. He sat in silence as the two agents conducted a shouted conversation over him. He was so deep in thought about the conversation he had with Sarah, just before leaving Washington, that he hardly heard a word of what they were saying. He couldn't work out whether it was the length of time that had passed since he had actually spoken to her, or that the trauma she had endured had changed her. She assured him that she was making good progress and feeling fitter every day, and that the girls were well but missing him a lot. Behind, however, was something else, something missing. The warmth that had been so much of her personality, even over the phone, was not there; she sounded emotionally dead. The bitterness of her farewell, 'Go find the bastards and kill them' shook him in its severity and hatred. Never before had he heard her utter anything so hostile or with such cruelty of tone. Nor had she asked him to be careful or take care; it had been just a bare order to an executioner. He wanted so much to be back with her and help heal her wounded heart.

Darkness had fallen by the time they landed and he was hardly able to make out any of his surroundings, as a black car whisked them across the tarmac, past many uniforms and bright lights, all blurred by heavy rain on the car's windows. He felt strangely uncomfortable about being driven on the right side of the road, with cars in the opposite lane appearing to pass close to his left shoulder.

"You still up for this?" asked Capello, digging Ian in the ribs as he asked the question.

"Oh yes, I really can't wait to get started," Ian replied. "I trust this Navy launch is steel hull and not fibreglass. I don't fancy approaching either of these maniacs trying to hide behind something they can shoot through."

"You can pull out, you know, we won't think you're chicken or anything, these people won't hesitate to kill you if they see you before you see them."

"Yes, I am aware of that, but with this beard I doubt if even my wife would recognise me, particularly with Agnes's grey tints added."

"Yeah, that was a neat move on her part, makes you look about ten years older," said Brumen.

"Let's hope they don't wash out in this rain," said Capello as he reached into his pocket to answer his mobile phone.

"Capello," he said, then stiffened as he recognised the voice on the other end.

After a few minutes, during which he listened intently to what was being said, he turned to Ian and shook his head saying, "This guy is our eyes. He knows the boat and the people, and without him in on this we are as good as blind. Both he and we know the risks but unless we take a few, we're never gonna catch these terrorists."

The voice at the other end took over the conversation, and from the tone and the look of frustration coming over Capello's face, was making significant changes to the operation.

"Okay, sir, Brumen and I will do the best we can. We'll arrange for Vaughan to stay in a hotel here, so as to be close if ID confirmation is required," said Capello without much enthusiasm. "We'll have to use Agnes to baby-sit, there just ain't anyone else available." More comments from the other end followed. "Yeah, she has been on the course and passed," replied Capello. "Right, sir, we'll keep you informed of progress."

Capello thrust the phone back into his pocket.

"Goddam it, these legal bastards. They want you to do the job and crap all over you if it don't get done, but as sure as hell turn everything into 'Mission Impossible'. Shit, I sometimes wonder why I ever leave my desk."

"Don't tell me," said Ian. "They've changed their minds about me helping with the search, just in case I get taken out and can't act as a witness in court, right?"

"You got it," replied Capello. "The only up side is that we know the name of the yacht."

"What happens if they also heard the broadcast and have changed the name?" Ian asked.

"We will be working from your computer likeness of Hamaura and a year-old photograph of Madadhah," replied Brumen, producing the pictures from his briefcase and squinting at them in the poor light inside the car.

"Did I hear you say that Agnes will be coming down to look after me?"

"Yeah, they insisted that you had a bodyguard at all times," said Capello. "You'll be okay, they said she was a good shot."

"Well, she is good at buying clothes, I give her that," said Ian. "So I just hope that she is multi-talented."

The car swung through the entrance to the base and stopped at the head of a pontoon ramp. Capello leapt out and ran through the rain to the gate office. Five minutes later he was back with instructions as to how to get to Ian's hotel.

It was lunchtime the following day before Agnes arrived, complete with suitcase full of clothes, make-up bags, even curlers.

"Are you sure you don't mind this idea of sharing a room?" said Ian. He was inwardly cursing his luck. As mentioned by Brumen and Capello, she was way too keen to become involved with fieldwork, and was likely to ruin his plans to conduct his own search for Hamaura and Arni.

"I can hardly protect you from down the corridor now, can I," she said, trying hard not to show enthusiasm in her face. This, she thought, was her big chance to prove that she also was field agent material.

Ian smiled. "Okay, I'll take the first watch this evening, you've been travelling since dawn."

Just then there was a knock at the door. "Who is it?" Agnes asked, pulling the largest handgun Ian had ever seen from a holster in her suitcase and moving swiftly to the hinge side of the door.

"It's Brumen here, Agnes, just open the damn door will you."

Waving to Ian to go into the bathroom, Agnes reached across and turned the catch, pulling the door open. Brumen struggled into the room with four rolls of charts under his right arm, his right hand gripping a life jacket and harness. In his left hand he carried his briefcase.

No sooner had he entered than Agnes had the door closed behind him.

Dumping his burdens upon Ian's bed, he turned to say something to Agnes when he froze, staring at the gun now casually held in her right hand pointing towards the floor. "For Christ's sake, Agnes, what the hell are you doing with that?" he demanded to know. "Have you ever pulled the trigger of a hand gun that size?"

"Well no, but I've been down on the range with a 38 and scored well with that," she replied.

"Put that damn great thing in your case and carry this service 38," he said taking a comparatively small automatic from his briefcase, complete with shoulder loop holster. "Don't go losing the damn thing 'cos I signed for it, got it?"

"Jablonski reckoned that the Magnum was the right deal," Agnes said, somewhat defensively.

"That idiot would issue you with a tank if he had one in store. Who did he think you were? Dirty Harry! God knows how he keeps that job," replied Brumen. "Must be something to do with his Polish ancestry. You know on one job, a couple of years back, there was a chance that we would be involved in a car chase, so Jablonski only wants to hand me an antitank weapon to, as he said, 'Take the whole goddam lot out in one go'."

Ian entered the room saying to Agnes, "Is it safe to come out now?"

She glared at him as Brumen snorted with laughter.

"Do you want a hand adjusting that life jacket and harness to fit?" Ian asked.

"Can yah, I ain't used to these contraptions."

Half an hour later Brumen left, after giving Agnes strict instructions regarding the safety of Ian ending with, "He ain't to go anywhere on his own except the john, you got that?"

Agnes stood by the window of their second-floor room and watched as the black four-by-four roared out of the hotel car park and turn right towards the naval base.

"Maybe this ain't gonna be as exciting as I thought it would be," she said with a sigh.

Two days had passed with no positive sightings of the yacht and with each passing hour, Ian was behaving more like a caged lion. "This pacin' around an' snarling at me ain't goin' to find this yacht any quicker," said Agnes, now really fed up with the task she had been assigned.

"I'm sorry, Agnes, but the longer this goes on, the greater chance this pair have of completing what they have planned and the longer it will be before I get back to my wife and family."

"Well I don't think that there is anything useful that we can do, other than wait for the boss to find the yacht."

"On the contrary," said Ian. "I think we can have a very interesting and important interview with this missing boy's mother and brother."

"Weren't you listening to the boss the other day?" she said, a little sharply.

"The only restriction I heard, was that you had to escort me everywhere except the john," said Ian. "I know what he intended but that was not what he said."

Agnes sat down and studied Ian for several seconds then she asked, "What will be achieved by interviewing this lady and her son?"

"A great deal, first we may be able to confirm that the people are in fact Hamaura and Madadhah, secondly we may be able to confirm that the yacht is still under the name *Romance Allemande,* as I find it difficult to believe that they would have taken that risk after I had jumped ship."

"Virginia Beach Police were quite sure about the boat's name," Agnes retorted, "and that was good enough for the boss so I still don't see the point of asking the same questions again."

"Look, it's just a feeling I have that what we have been told doesn't fit properly with the way these two work. For a start, I can't see Madadhah abducting a boy with Hamaura anywhere around, so if it is him they must have split up for some reason. In which case we should be looking for individuals not a duo," said Ian.

Agnes got up and walked around the room, pausing at the window looking out on the sunbathed car park. "I'll have to clear this with the boss," she said, going over to her handbag and taking out her mobile phone.

Much to her surprise, Brumen agreed on condition that she cleared it with the local police. That done they set off in a hire car and found the Schulkens' house in a quiet but slightly run-down area set back from Virginia Beach.

A neighbour answered the door, opening it just wide enough to peer round. Ian noted the two chains preventing the door opening fully, "You the press, she don't want to talk to anybody right now," she said firmly, making to close the door.

Agnes held up her badge. "I'm Agent Gleeson of the FBI, we'd like to speak to Mrs Schulkens and her son."

The woman studied the badge then reluctantly released the chains and opened the door to let them in. "Don't know what else she can tell you, all the hours of questions ain't found her boy yet."

Mrs Schulkens was sitting alongside the telephone in the lounge diner, her face pale and tear-stained, her dress creased from having been worn for days and her hair knotted and unkempt.

Agnes did the introductions and explained that Mr Vaughan was going to ask her some questions. She just nodded and pointed to the sofa opposite for them to sit, staring blankly at them emotionally exhausted.

Agnes sat down but Ian picked up a small stool and carrying it across the room sat down close to the arm of Mrs Schulkens' chair and gently took hold of her hand.

"Hello, Mrs Schulkens, please call me Ian."

Dull eyes turned and settled on his face. "I'm Paulette," she replied, making no attempt to take her hand away.

"I understand that this all happened just after you met your son at the school gate," Ian said quietly. "Can you take me through the events from the moment you left home to meet him."

"I wasn't at home, I was at work, I do letters for an insurance broker, name of Rivers," she said. "He gives me half hour off to get the boys from school, then they normally sit an' wait till my finish time doin' their school work."

"But that wasn't what happened that day, was it," Ian said.

"No it was not, thanks to that misbehaving critter in the corner there."

For the first time Ian and Agnes were aware of a boy sitting head bowed on a beanbag in the corner behind the door.

Ian gently squeezed her hand. "Can you take me through what happened from when you left Rivers?" he said.

"I crossed the road; I park my car in the marina car park. Then I drove along to the school and found Jason waitin' on me but wilful Willie there had gone and got himself a detention so I

269

had to wait," she explained, glaring at her elder son in the corner.

The boy leapt to his feet and made to leave the room.

"Sit back down there where I can keep an eye on you!" she screamed.

The command stopped the boy in his tracks. Turning away from his mother to hide his face, he slowly retraced his steps and sat heavily down again.

Ian waited a few moments then asked, "Was that when you let Jason walk back to your office?"

Paulette nodded. "He said he was just goin' to feed the gulls then come straight back into the office. Both of them had done that before if I was not able to meet them for some reason," she said, obviously feeling guilty for allowing the boys the freedom of a relatively short walk in a respectable neighbourhood.

"How long did you have to wait for William?" Ian asked

"Oh I guess it was about a half hour, give or take five minutes. Say, I've told all this to the local cops, what do you expect me to say that's different?"

"Paulette, I know this is just repetition for you, but for me it is all new and I need to get the sequence of events and detail fixed in my mind," Ian said, giving her his warmest smile. "Were you delayed any further from getting back to the office?"

"Yes I was, how did you know?" Paulette looked at him questioningly.

"Please, just tell me what happened," he said.

"Well, I was late anyway and the car needed gas so I dropped by the station and put ten dollars' worth in. Then my card wouldn't work, so I ran down to the office and borrowed ten dollars from Jean, rushed back to the garage, paid for the gas then drove back," she said.

"Did you explain that part to the local cops?" Agnes asked.

"Well no, I guess I forgot. You see when I got back to my desk, Mr Rivers was complainin' about me takin' so long," Paulette explained, looking downcast.

"When you drove back you didn't park in the marina, did you," Ian said.

"Well no, I saw Dave Cosby's space outside the office was empty and knew he was out seein' a client so to save time I parked the car in his space. Say, you seem to know a hell of a lot about what I did," she said, with an edge of suspicion in her voice.

"No, not really, I'm just guessing," Ian said. "You see my wife does a lot of running around after our two daughters and has similar problems when things don't quite run to order. I'm going to guess again that it was not until you finished work that you learnt that Jason had not come back to the office." Paulette nodded. "And poor William here was too concerned about what Mr Rivers would say if he came and distracted you from your work again," said Ian looking across at William for confirmation.

"That's right, Mom," the boy said, raising a tearful face towards her. "I didn't know what to do as maybe Jason was just talking with Lester in the marina office or maybe he got talking to the guy we saw there the other day."

Ian turned to face the boy. "Come over here a minute. Now sit on your Mum's lap and tell me all about this guy you saw the other day."

"It was nothing really, honest Mom, me and Jason were feedin' the gulls like we do and this guy asked us if we were havin' fun and where did we buy the bread from." William paused, waiting to be rebuked, but his mother just nodded her head for him to carry on. "Jason was all for telling him but I said you didn't like us talking to strangers and then you called us from the parking lot and that was it."

"Tell me William, or do I call you Willie?"

"Only Mom calls me Willie, all my friends call me Will," the boy said, his face serious, almost stern.

"Tell me, Will, what did this man look like?" asked Ian.

The boy shrugged.

"Was he tall, strong-looking, did he have a moustache or was he bald?"

"Yeah, he was big like Dad was an' yeah, he had a moustache." The boy was now squinting, trying to recall what he had seen.

"Was he sun-tanned like me?" asked Ian, pulling up the sleeve of his shirt to expose a walnut brown arm.

"Yeah, he was just in shorts an' he was the colour of that table all over."

"Did you see which boat he was on?"

"Yeah, he was standin' on a yacht when he was talking to us."

"Was there anyone else on board do you know, a lady perhaps?"

"Didn't see no one," Will answered.

"Can you remember the name of the yacht?" Agnes asked.

"No, I didn't give it much of a look." The boy paused. " It was something 'Clan' I think, but I ain't sure," Will said, realising that what he had missed was probably important. "I'm sorry mister, I didn't think to look properly."

Ian reached up and ruffled the boy's hair. "You've done just fine," he said. "Did you tell all of this to the police?"

"They ain't spoken to him, they only questioned me," said Paulette. "Neither of the boys said anything about this man they spoke to, this is the first I heard of it."

"Do you think this man could be responsible for Jason's disappearance?" Paulette asked as an afterthought.

"It is possible, yes," said Ian.

"You see what you dun, not bein' there to look after your little brother!" Paulette shouted, pushing the boy off her lap.

"Paulette, I understand it was a beautiful sunny afternoon when Jason went missing," said Ian. "Probably had Will here been out of school with his brother you would have let both of them go and feed the gulls."

"Well yeah, I probably would have," she replied. "He would then have..."

"Paulette," Ian interrupted. "If Jason has been abducted by this man and if he is of the type I fear he maybe, then it is quite likely that both of your sons would have been missing. Believe me, this is not Will's fault or yours, sadly in this world evil people exist."

Paulette's face crumpled as tears poured down her cheeks. Agnes crossed the room and sitting on the arm of the chair took Paulette into her arms to comfort her. Ian stood and went through to the kitchen, where he found Paulette's neighbour staring out of the window dabbing tears from her own eyes.

"We will have to leave shortly. Would it be possible for you to stay on for a while and comfort them both?" he asked.

"Yeah, I've been here ever since it happened an' my Dave said to stay until the boy is found," she replied. "I guess she could do with a hot drink right now."

"I think they both could," said Ian.

As Agnes turned the car to head back to the hotel Ian said, "I think we should also have a chat with Lester at this marina."

"Why do you want to see him?" she asked. "Do you think he's got somethin' to do with this?"

"I don't think he's responsible for the missing boy, but I do think he's responsible for giving the police wrong information about the name of the yacht," Ian replied. "I think we will find a marina office only manned during the day by an idle oaf, who is too lazy to go and do the rounds and check which yachts are paid up to date."

Ian's description was spot on and the visit proved to be conclusive. Lester probably scaled in at two hundred and fifty pounds and had the unhealthy pallor of someone who has not seen the sun for many months. Even though the office was air-conditioned to just above freezing, Lester was perspiring freely.

When asked how many times a day he patrolled the marina, he replied that he could see all the yachts from his office, and the night watchman went round first thing when he came on and in the morning to check the boats' moorings.

It was when they checked the entry for *Romance Allemande* that the breakthrough came. In the 'Owners Name' column was the name Arnaud Fernande, the very name used by Hamaura when in contact with the Coastguard helicopter.

"That's definitely him," said Ian explaining when and how he had heard the name. "We must wait for this night watchman and see if he can remember boat names."

When the man arrived at six in the evening, he confirmed that his role was purely to check the mooring warps evening and morning then just keep an eye out for anyone trying to climb round the ramp head gate, which at night was closed and could only be opened by knowing the keypad number.

"Do you remember seeing a yacht named *Romance Allemande* moored on the outer pontoon?" Agnes asked.

The watchman shook his head. "No, lady, I no see boat with that name."

"Are you absolutely sure of that?" she asked.

"Si, I am sure coz it is nice name for yacht and I would remember that."

"How about a yacht with a first name then the name 'Clan'?"

He stood with his hands covering his eyes for several seconds then said, "Yes, I remember something like that but I do not recall well coz not so nice name."

Ian and Agnes waited patiently as the man stood muttering to himself.

"I think maybe first word was Mel... sumting but I not sure, I sorry, is this to do with lost boy?"

"Yes," confirmed Agnes. "Did you know him?"

"Si, he an' his brother sometime here in evening, when their momma working late over there," he said, pointing towards Rivers' offices.

Neither Capello nor Brumen were pleased to learn that for three days, they had been searching for the wrong boat. "Is that the best that crap marina can come up with?" Capello had shouted down the phone. "Don't they check anything?"

Ian was asleep when Agnes shook him, saying, "I've got it, I've got it."

"What, what have you got?" mumbled Ian.

"They peeled the letters off and rearranged them," she said excitedly.

"Do you know what word they made?"

"No, I just had the idea."

"Great, wake me up when you've found the word," said Ian turning over to sleep again.

"Wake up, we've got to work this out ready for the boss in the morning," she said, giving Ian a hard prod in his back.

Chapter 14

Yamada arrived at the shack shortly after dawn; there was no sign of anyone as he slammed the door of the Cadillac CTS and stepped back to admire the most expensive thing he had ever owned. The loan company had wanted a sizable deposit even though his job with TN (Nuclear) Corporation gave him a good credit rating.

Birds were singing in the trees as he trudged through the soft sand to the door of the shack. Pushing it open he saw her knelt, softly crying, alongside the mattress in the corner. Guessing what had happened Yamada walked quietly across the room, gently lifted the girl into his arms and carried her out into the early morning sun.

She sat, her forehead buried in her hands, crying with both sadness and relief. Since Yamada's last visit Jake had just craved for hit after hit, no amount appeared to take him to the heights he yearned for. Unable to stop the cycle, she had watched helpless as he stumbled around rambling and muttering, staring strangely at the world around him, unaware of her tears and desperate sadness as she witnessed his final descent into oblivion.

"Would you like me to bury him in those woods back there?" he said, jerking his head in the direction of the trees.

"It's ok, I guess I can manage that," she replied. "Do you think anyone would mind if he was buried there?"

"I own the land here and I don't mind, I'll give you a hand," he said, feeling a strange desire to protect her.

They sat on the sand for several minutes longer, each deep in their own thoughts.

"When did he die?" Yamada asked.

"Last evenin', just as the sun was settin'," she sobbed.

"You got carp flags in the right order," he said looking up at the flagpole. The sight of the flags reminded him why he was there, which was to pick up the weapons he had hidden behind the transmitter and to get to the clinic.

The sudden change of subject had the effect of motivating both of them to get up and walk into the woods. They found a suitable spot in a clearing near to his boundary and spent the rest of the morning digging the grave. When he returned to the shack and picked up Jake's body it was just as if he were carrying a skeleton. Kerry Anne followed behind bringing Jake's guitar.

No words were said over the grave, both just stood looking down at Jake's body, its arms draped around the guitar. They filled the grave in and hauled a tree trunk over it, to stop animals from digging down. Kerry Anne stuck three bird feathers into the bark of the trunk above Jake's head, stepped back and waved saying, "Bye Jake, go fly, my love."

Yamada left her standing there, returning the tools to the shack, he opened the radio cabinet. Undoing the screw fixings down the left hand side, the unit swung away from the supporting frame to reveal a sizeable space behind. Reaching in, his hand gripped round the barrel of an AK47 assault rifle, which he removed and stood against the cabin wall. A second search produced a black plastic case containing two automatic pistols and a third search two boxes of ammunition and the pistol holsters. Something made him hurry his haul out to the car before Kerry Anne returned. For some reason he didn't want her to see him with the implements of war.

She emerged from the woods just as he was returning to the shack. "You can stay on here if you like," he said. "I will not charge you any rent, just keep the batteries topped and those flags flying."

On leaving he gave her a couple of hundred dollars for food and clothes that she promised she would pay back as soon as she got herself 'straightened up'.

Driving along dark roads towards the clinic and, he felt, his destiny, thoughts of Kerry Anne faded from his mind. Now he was focused on the fight for the cause and sweet revenge for his forefathers.

The night porter invited Yamada to sit whilst he put out a call for Dr Higashi. Looking around the reception, Yamada was surprised to see that the clinic was also offering beauty and complementary therapies, such as Reflexology and Reiki. Classes in Tai Chi and Yoga were also listed. When Dr Higashi arrived the two men greeted each other with formal bows. "Konban-wa Yamada-san o-genki desu-ka."

"Konban-wa Higashi-san, hi genki-des, anta-no genki desu-ka,"

It was quite late and Dr Higashi had come from his private quarters and was dressed in dark blue soft silk pyjama-like attire under a light cotton yukata.

"I am quite well, thank you, but I am very worried about Hamaura-san. She has been badly injured, the delay in receiving treatment has meant that she has had to endure more pain following our resetting of the broken bones," the doctor explained.

"Please can you try to persuade her to rest one more week here to give her injuries a better chance to heal."

Yamada bowed on receiving this request, enjoying for the first time in many years the respectful formality of Japanese etiquette. "Doctor, I will try my best to persuade her, but she is leader and I am very junior member of her team."

They quietly entered Hamaura's room and found her sleeping soundly. "I have administered a sleeping draft so please, do not disturb her until morning," whispered Higashi as he directed Yamada towards a bed set up under the window.

Careful not to wake his patient he bent to listen to her breathing then, moving towards the door, bowed and left.

Yamada, heeding the doctor's request, stripped off and quietly got into bed. Sleep evaded him for a time and when he did finally drop off his dreams were filled with grotesque images of Mel's wife and his own mother screaming some message that he could not hear.

He woke at 7 o'clock to find Hamaura still fast asleep. On tiptoe he left the room and found a bathroom with shower further down the corridor. A hot shower washed away the dreams of the previous night and he returned to the room feeling refreshed and hungry. To his surprise a traditional Japanese breakfast was brought in for both Hamaura and himself. This he found very strange, as for most of his life his diet had been American. He tried the miso soup and struggled with the chopsticks, endeavouring finally to pick up the piece of fish that was the main part of the meal.

A Japanese nurse had come in to help Hamaura take a shower. When Hamaura returned she greeted Yamada briefly then sat quietly by her bed eating her breakfast.

It was not until the meal had been cleared away that she opened the conversation. "We must dispose of Madadhah immediately, the fool has abducted a boy and police wish speak with him," she announced.

She spent a few minutes explaining Vaughan's disappearance and their arrival on US soil. "As soon as my back is turned he does this and brings police search, only his mistake with boat name stops the boat being found and all its equipment."

"But they know his name?" asked Yamada. "So you think he can be identified anyway?"

"No, we used the name of Fernande but boat name of '*Melodrama Clan*'," she replied.

"Hamaura-san please forgive me but I have never sailed yacht before and you are not able to, so maybe I find Madadhah and hide him until you are well."

"The attack must start day after tomorrow and each day we strike until either they give in to our demands or we turn their Independence Day into Total Dependence Day." Her words cut through the air like whiplashes that had Yamada almost flinching, the obvious deep hatred implied by her tone so much stronger than his own.

"You plan many separate attacks?" Yamada asked.

"Yes," she replied. "Each day we will issue our demands by radio buoy; then each night, if they do not obey we will strike at their power network."

"Then today I will find Madadhah and we take name off boat just in case," he said. "I will explain why to him. Where have you arranged to meet him?"

"Long Cove, there is marina there. Pass me that case, there is map inside."

After a long discussion Hamaura finally accepted that it would be best for her to stay at the clinic until the final phase. Yamada was to meet up with Madadhah, but not accuse him of the abduction, just explain that Hamaura required any boat name to be removed.

His drive to Long Cove was uneventful and he reached the marina just as the small workshop was closing up for the night. A breeze from the main channel had set a halyard slapping, a noise that sent the berthing attendant out along the pontoon in search of the errant cord. Yamada watched as the youth made his way to a yacht on the outer finger and climb aboard. Within a minute the slapping noise had ceased and the youth had vaulted over the yacht's guardrail and was making his way back.

"Can I help you?" the attendant asked Yamada.

"Well, yeah, er, has a yacht called '*Melodrama Clan*' checked in here recently?"

"No, sir. No yacht by that name in here," the youth replied. "There hasn't been much wind out there today, so maybe it's delayed."

"Is there somewhere to eat around here?" Yamada asked.

"Only Murray's round the head of the creek there. There's no way through along the shore, but if you go out the gate and take a left down to the fork you'll see it."

The walk to Murray's took Yamada half an hour but he had not hurried; instead he peered, wherever possible, at the properties bordering the creek. He decided that if the US government paid up he would spend some of his share on something like them. Maybe he would replace the shack with a nice house and pier for a powerboat.

The word 'only' in the berthing attendant's description had misled him into thinking it was just a burger joint, where in fact Murray's was a classy restaurant with a superb shore-side location. Yamada sat waiting for his meal sipping at his soft drink and running his eyes over the rest of the clientele. Everywhere he looked, the men and women sat relaxed in the comfortable surroundings, expensively dressed and enjoying sophisticated conversation. Smart uniformed waiters glided between the tables taking orders and delivering plates of food with what could only be described as artistry. So this, thought Yamada, was the American dream, the one that had been denied to his honest, hard-working forebears, the one denied to him, the one he was about to shatter. The thought of terrorising these smug, arrogant, self-satisfied bastards appealed to him and brought a smile to his face.

Leaving the restaurant Yamada made his way back to the deserted marina. He strolled around for a while before making his way back to his car and was just closing the car door when he saw the masthead light of a yacht entering the cove. Getting out of the car again he walked across the parking lot and over the bridge to the pontoons. The pontoon section lights bathed the moored boats in a gentle light, bright enough for him to read their names as he casually made his way out to the visitor berth area. He was some yards away as the yacht glided past the pontoon head, the helmsman studying the layout before making a final approach. Yamada watched as the yacht was turned into the wind and brought to a stop, whilst the helmsman hurriedly tied fenders to the guardrail and prepared shorelines. Positioning himself in the shadow between two large powerboats he studied the yacht closely trying to make out its name, then as the wind gently pushed the bows round he could clearly make out '*Melodrama Clan*' on the spray dodgers.

Yamada waited in the shadows as Arni brought the yacht alongside and hurriedly secured it. Stepping into the light he was impressed to see that Madadhah was instantly aware of his presence, but had avoided looking straight at him. Instead he had gone backwards along the yacht's side, appearing to adjust a mooring rope, before leaping nimbly over the guardrail to regain the protection of the cockpit.

As Yamada approached the yacht he knew that Madadhah had a gun concealed by the spray hood but trained upon him.

"Madadhah-san?" Yamada asked respectfully.

Arni just looked at him. "I am Yamada, Hamaura sent me."

"Why is she not here?" Arni replied.

"She is too badly injured to sail with us just yet. If I can come on board, I will explain in more detail," Yamada said, looking about to indicate that he did not want their conversation to be common knowledge.

Arni nodded and stepped back onto the yacht's small stern deck so that he could see every move Yamada made.

Down in the main cabin Yamada explained the full extent of Hamaura's injuries and the agreed plan. Emphasising the need to remove the yacht's name he also added that from here on they were to anchor overnight instead of visiting marinas.

Whilst Arni prepared himself a meal Yamada told him of his work in planting the radio-triggered control units. As the evening went on the two men found themselves more comfortable in each other's company. Arni gave his account of the Atlantic crossing, relegating Ian Vaughan's part to merely deckhand and occasional helmsman. They discussed Ian's possible suicide at length, but could not conclude for sure that he had died.

They both went ashore to get Yamada's kit from his car, returning on board to go straight to their bunks and sleep. Waking at four o'clock, the first stage of their plan was put into operation with the removal of the spray dodger lettering. They had a quick breakfast, before Yamada left to drive back to Sandy Point on the Potomac. Arni was tasked with sailing the boat round to meet up with Yamada late that evening.

Thin smoke from the fire spiralled up into the night sky. Yamada shifted his position and, leaning forward, turned a piece of steak, cooking on the griddle over the fire. In the hot ashes were potatoes and a can of beans. He turned away from the fire, to check that the roving lamp from the generator was still shining up at the flagpole. As he did so, he saw Kerry Anne coming down the beach in her new tight-fitting jeans and crisp white blouse. At first he didn't recognise her and was just about to shout a challenge when she lifted her head and, for the first time since he had known her, smiled.

"What do you think?" she asked.

"Makes you look a very different lady," he replied. "Very er, you know, er, pretty."

They both exchanged embarrassed smiles then looked away to busy themselves in preparing the meal.

The splash of the anchor surprised them both; neither had seen the masthead light approaching. The sound of oars ten minutes later indicated the arrival of a visitor and Yamada walked down to the water's edge, and with his flashlight identified Arni.

"I expected you earlier," he said. "Must have been further than we thought."

Back around the fire brief introductions were made, but no explanations. Arni and Yamada hurriedly ate their meal and left in the dinghy, to spend the night aboard the yacht, leaving Kerry Anne alone on the beach staring thoughtfully into the glowing embers of the fire. Yamada had said he would be back in a few days; she would wait then decide what she should do with her life.

On board the yacht Yamada produced a notebook with their instructions for the launch sequence of the buoys. Hamaura had laid great emphasis on this aspect of the attack, saying that they must achieve their aims for the release of prisoners and payment of money. Only if their demands were not met in time should the ultimate attack be made. Arni, working from the charts of the Potomac and Chesapeake, planned their course for the next five days.

"*Melodrama Clan*," shouted Ian.

Agnes looked over his shoulder at the notepad with lots of names and crossings out written on it.

"It would fit with what that night watchman suggested," she said. "We've got his phone number, I'll wake him and ask."

Ten minutes later she was being patched through to the launch on which Brumen and Capello were conducting their unsuccessful search.

"Your mobile is out of signal, so I got the Navy to patch me through," she said.

"Okay, what's the panic," asked Capello.

Agnes explained about the probable name change and how they worked it out and confirmed it.

"Good work, Agnes," said Capello.

"It was my idea but it was Vaughan who cracked the anagram," she admitted.

"Is that right, now," said Capello. "Tell him we're glad he stayed around."

On board the launch a hurried meeting was convened to assess the effects of this latest piece of information to their search plans.

The young officer in command of the launch had the most logical answer straightaway. "We must retrace our steps, visiting every marina to see whether the yacht has been checked in," he said with a tone of professional authority. "Then we work our way out from that point based upon the known timing. That way we will get a much clearer sense of the direction they are heading and the distance we can expect them to have travelled." Brumen and Capello agreed and immediately the launch was turned and headed back down the Potomac.

At the confluence of the Potomac and Chesapeake the launch turned southward towards Long Cove and, by mid morning, had reached the marina where Yamada and Arni had first met.

"*Melodrama Clan*," said the marina manager. "Nope, ain't got that name down here. Hey, Seb, you heard of a yacht called '*Melodrama Clan*'?"

The berthing attendant frowned with concentration whilst repeating the name to himself. "Yeah, there was a guy came in late, oooh mustabeen day before yesterday, askin' whether that yacht had checked."

"Can you describe this man?" asked Brumen.

"Yeah, oriental, about five eight, five nine, slim. Directed him to Murray's over there," answered Seb.

"What car was he driving?"

"Dunno, he was on foot when he left here."

"Did the yacht show up?" asked Capello.

"Can't say, it weren't here in the mornin' and the night guy didn't note anything, not that he ever does."

The launch had been standing off and slid back alongside the pontoon whilst Brumen and Capello jumped back on board.

"My guess is that the fella he spoke of is this guy Yamada," said Capello. "Betcha that the yacht came in here and picked him up without that night guy noticin'."

As he spoke the radio operator shouted up from his desk in the chartroom below the bridge. "Hey, listen to this." Over the bridge speaker came the voice of Fumiko Hamaura. "...unless the United States uses its influence to release from Japanese prisons Yoshi Hamaura and Hiroshi Kimura plus provide the sum of thirty million dollars we will be forced to take action against you. You have until eight o'clock this evening to confirm your willingness to obtain their release."

"What channel was that on?" asked Capello.

"Forty-Eight, sir, a military wave band, sir," answered the radio operator.

Brumen was down on the deck level making his way to the bows, away from the engine noise, frantically punching numbers into his mobile. His conversation confirmed that both the FBI and CIA had heard the broadcast and that an assessment meeting was being called and the Chiefs of Staff alerted.

Two hours later the department head of the FBI broadcast a statement, refusing to negotiate on behalf of any terrorist organisation. Just before eight o'clock that evening his message was repeated.

The blackout of Baltimore caught the authorities completely by surprise. They had been expecting some bomb attack on a government building and were caught completely off guard. So unexpected was the load shed, that it caused a domino effect to occur within that sector of the grid, blacking out a far larger area than either Hamaura or Yamada had thought possible. In the eight hours it took to restore power to the city, many people had died. Some in road junction accidents, immediately following the power cut, others through falls on darkened stairways or escalators and several through heart attacks, whilst trapped in elevators. Criminals took advantage of the darkness and confusion, which put more pressure on the police forces and other emergency services.

The press had a field day, printing wild accusations about poor maintenance and shoddy work practices; strangely, only one paper suggested a terrorist attack. Eastern Seaboard Power issued an immediate rebuttal of all the accusations, and stated that an immediate and thorough investigation was being carried out. Confused, the authorities threw enormous manpower into guarding power installations. The power companies demanded talks with unions, amid fears that recent labour disputes had become militant.

At eight o'clock the following morning the second threat was received, in which Hamaura claimed responsibility for the Baltimore attack, and gave the US Government until eight o'clock that evening to respond positively to her demands. It was to be the President himself who responded, informing that he had passed the message to the Prime Minister of Japan, and that this was a matter in which the United States of America could not provide any further assistance.

The unusual nature of an attack that did not leave any obvious sign of a break-in at any of the installations, nor involve the use of explosives, was frankly baffling to both power companies and the US Government. Had it not been for Ian Vaughan's warning and the knowledge that a terrorist cell was in the country, the threat and blackout would have been considered a coincidence.

The switching station, where the fault was believed to have originated, had been checked during the day and all circuits tested and found to be working normally. This in turn suggested that a station operative had accidentally caused the problem. Throughout the day operatives were being questioned and the station logs checked all to no avail. As always in this type of enquiry minor management infractions were exposed, but nothing that would cause such a massive blackout.

By early evening the enquiry was centring upon Highfield Switching Station, which had been under the maintenance contract of Crabtree Power Engineering. Senior engineering management and crew supervisors were called in, and the process of maintenance schedule checking begun. Simultaneously a maintenance crew from TN (Nuclear) Corporation had been called in to physically recheck and test the Highfield circuitry. For the top management of TN (Nuclear) this presented an opportunity to promote a further expansion of their grid maintenance contracts. With their scheduled working crews fully committed they had resorted to calling in those on leave. The first team to be approached was that of Mel Clements, but with no response from his phone the next on the list were contacted.

Exactly at eight o'clock that evening, the naval establishment at Annapolis received a second message, stating that the US Government's actions were not enough and the country would again be punished for its failure. Instantly following the message Annapolis itself was plunged into darkness, along with the towns of Bowie and Columbia. Again the authorities struggled to cope with the panic and disruption, and again there was a death toll. By dawn everyone, from senators to the man in the street, were demanding answers. It was now that the Government was forced to admit that acts of terrorism were taking place, and that the country was being held to ransom.

This in turn brought a general clamour for more information that the authorities nimbly sidestepped, claiming that at present there were too few leads, but that both the FBI and CIA were working hard to identify the group concerned. The National Guard were called out and police roadblocks appeared all around Washington, Baltimore and along the highways in-between.

That morning the authorities awaited the terrorists' next move. It didn't come until midday when a sneering triumphalist message was broadcast promising far worse retribution unless the demands were met in full.

Brumen and Capello, frustrated that their search, and that of other waterborne teams, was proving to be like looking for the proverbial needle in a haystack, were returning down the Potomac.

"My guess is that they ain't usin' regular marinas," said Brumen. "Each one they called at would have demanded at least the name of the boat."

"Yeah, you're right," sighed Capello. "We just gotta have Vaughan searchin' with us; on our own we have no chance at all."

Both men raised their binoculars as another yacht came into view anchored in a small bay close to a private pier.

"Look at that, not even a name on the dodgers, in fact I don't see any name at all," said Capello. "How many boats have we seen without any goddam name displayed? Hey, can you go alongside that yacht over there."

Capello boarded the yacht and stepped down into the cockpit to find that all was locked up. The padlocks, he noted, were of good quality and made by Chubb UK Ltd. Interested now he went forward and looked at the roller reefing gear, which was also a British make. Kneeling down he tried to look through the cabin windows but found that the curtains were too tightly drawn to afford any view of the yacht's interior.

"Hey you! Get off my yacht!" shouted a portly man in his mid fifties standing on the end of the private jetty.

"Is this your vessel, sir?" asked Brumen, who had been standing on the launch's deck, covering Capello with a pistol hidden under a folded jacket.

"Yeah, it damn well is, now get your friend off it."

An hour later they left a contrite Mr Steiner, having checked very thoroughly the vessel's ownership papers and house, gardens, cars and studio.

"I thought we had it there," said Capello. "Everything about that boat fitted what we are looking for, even where it was built. Damn it, I'm not searchin' any more unless we have Vaughan with us. I don't care a damn what Metcalfe says, we can't keep stepping on and off yachts just on the off chance. We need someone who would recognise which piece of white plastic to look for."

"You can be the one to take Metcalfe on," said Brumen with the air of someone who knew the opposition well.

"Like hell I am," replied Capello. "I'll let him know when it's over."

"He'll have your badge," warned Brumen.

"If he wants it he'll get it. Frankly I'm just too pissed off with this to care what that bastard will do," snarled Capello. "Every damn case we've worked on he's stuck his nose into makin' life difficult. Then when it's handed to him on a plate he's the one to stand in front of the press claiming to be the main man."

With that, Capello turned and opened the door to the chart room and strode across to the table, pulling his mobile phone from his pocket as he went.

"Agnes, this is Capello, I want you to check out and then get the Navy to fly you and Vaughan up to the Quantico Marine Corps base on the Potomac. Got that?" he ordered. "Once you get there, go to the marina just north of the base, I think it's on Potomac Avenue, we'll meet you there."

In the hotel room Agnes finished confirming her orders, then turned to Ian Vaughan with an excited grin on her face. "We are gonna join the hunt. Get your stuff packed quickly while I arrange our transport."

"About bloody time," said Ian with some feeling. "I wondered how many power cuts it would take before someone saw sense."

It was dark as they flew at 800 feet above the countryside just east of Richmond. Ahead they could see the lights of Washington away in the distance, looking like some strange nebula in the moonless darkness beneath them.

"There is something magical about flying over a country at night with all the lights," said Ian, looking down on Richmond. "It's almost as good as sailing at night under clear skies, when you can look up and see the Milky Way like a ribbon of misty light across the heavens."

"I've never seen that," said Agnes. "You don't see much of the night sky from city streets."

"Sweet Jesus, what in hell's goin' on," yelled the pilot.

Two of the switching stations, visited by Yamada during his night-time sabotage activities, had been triggered simultaneously. The load-shed had caused two power stations to come off line and go into shut-down routine. Stations linked to other routes on the grid could not support the sudden load demand and had been forced to sector limit supply. In addition the devices installed by Yamada had been designed to ignite thirty seconds after being triggered. Their location being central to the relay banks, and the intense heat emitted by the incendiary material, had damaged other route relays, expanding the blackout.

Ian and Agnes looked forward following the direction of the pilot's amazed stare. Where only moments ago had been the bright lights of Washington was now total darkness. As they watched, inhabited areas either side of the Potomac were being blacked out, as the grid shut-down followed the massive load-shed.

As they flew on, buildings with standby emergency power, such as hospitals, lit up to form small points of light in the velvet darkness. Road traffic could be seen moving and many flashing lights of emergency vehicles were in evidence.

Inside ten minutes the helicopter was making its approach to the base, a flight deck captain waving them down with glow battens. Once on the ground Agnes impressed Ian by requesting a base launch to take them the short distance to the marina.

"On the way in, I saw that the traffic outside the base was gridlocked, and we don't have time to waste waitin' on that bein' sorted," she had answered angrily, when her request had been questioned.

The response had been positive and immediate; within a few minutes a semi-rib with two crew had been launched ready for them. Brumen and Capello were surprised by the waterborne arrival of Ian and Agnes.

"Nice move," said Brumen giving Agnes a broad smile. "You're getting the hang of this field game."

"Seaman Abbots here will show you to your quarters, such as they are," said Capello. "We'll meet here in ten minutes and get a plan sorted."

Back around the chart table, Capello showed Ian the course the launch had taken, marinas visited and location of yachts boarded. "So that's it to date," he concluded.

"What time of day were these broadcast threats made?" asked Ian.

"The first two were around 0800 hours, then just before the second blackout there was one, the latest was around midday," Brumen replied.

"Umm. Who picked the messages up? Were they heard by many receiving stations or just one or two?"

"Why do you ask?" queried Capello.

"It's just that VHF works in line of sight, so often only some sectors will hear a transmission, especially if the transmitting aerial is small and low down. There are some

292

anomalies in that theory, but generally it holds good," replied Ian, noting a nod of agreement from the duty radio operator.

"Well, as far as we know, FBI and CIA monitoring picked up the first two messages as did we onboard here. The next one was only picked up by the Annapolis Navy Base and today's was again ourselves and the agencies," informed Brumen.

"Did Annapolis receive today's?" asked Ian.

Brumen turned and gave the radio operator a questioning look. "I'll check, sir," the operator said and turned to issue a call. Within minutes it was confirmed that Annapolis had not heard the day's threat on any of their monitored wave bands.

"Can I see your tide table for the Chesapeake?" Ian asked. The ensign on duty stepped forward, and reaching into a cupboard below the chart table produced the book and placed it on the table, opening it up to the correct month. Ian studied the times of the high tides over the last four days, then turning to the back of the book unfolded the tidal map of the area. For several minutes he stood deep in thought, then straightening up, said, "My guess is that they are sailing up and down in this area, at the confluence of the Chesapeake with the Potomac, and in the early hours of the morning, before dawn, they launch one of their radio buoys then sail off and hide up for the day in one of the myriads of inlets and creeks."

Ian took them through the procedure that Arni and Hamaura had adopted in the English Channel, the night the false mayday had been transmitted.

"You see they can remotely trigger the transmission from the buoyed radios and that can be done, when they are several miles away," he said. "I suspect that the delay in the fourth message was due to their signal being obscured at first."

The discussion continued for some time until eventually all were convinced that Ian's assessment was the most plausible.

"We need to patrol the area during the hours of darkness, then concentrate on the inlets during the day," said Ian.

"Obviously that vast area will require at least three launches on parallel courses at night. In the day I would suggest two checking the inlets and one out checking yachts underway."

"It is possible for us to reach the search area by 0200 hrs, clear the area at dawn, and go to Lexington to refuel ready for tomorrow," said Captain Westlake. "I better report all this in and get full clearance."

"No!" shouted Capello. "They are monitoring military wavebands; if you radio this in they will simply go somewhere else."

"Have you been reporting in by radio?" asked Brumen almost casually. A blushing Captain Westlake nodded.

"Well, tonight report that we are going to search the upper reaches of the Potomac tomorrow. We don't want to disappoint them by withholding our plans," said Brumen.

"I suggest we take the opportunity of getting our heads down until we arrive in the Chesapeake," suggested Capello.

As the meeting broke up Ian noted that Capello and Brumen lingered by the chart table no doubt to point out to the young captain the error of his ways.

Stopping to wait for Agnes at the bottom of the companionway steps Ian smiled, saying, "There's one pair of shoes I'm glad I'm not wearing at the moment."

"Same here," Agnes replied. "Capello can melt metal when he gets goin'."

The three hours it took the launch to make its way down to the Chesapeake seemed to Ian strangely short. He had slept and was surprised when Agnes woke him and handed him a mug of coffee.

"We're there, and the boss wants you up on deck," she said. "You're really cool, you know that? All this excitement and you can just put your head down and sleep as though you don't have a care in the world."

"A clear conscience Agnes, that's all," he replied straight-faced.

"I've got one o' them," she said. "And still I can't switch off like that."

"Really?" Ian asked with a mischievous grin.

"Now you just stop that. You're getting as bad as Agent Brumen," she replied, wagging a finger admonishingly at him.

He found Brumen, Capello and Westlake on the bridge.

"Okay," said Capello. "Tell us what you think we should be looking for."

"Any yacht underway in a sector ten miles north from here and within the navigable width of the Chesapeake," said Ian. "I would also suggest that we check all lit sources against radar contacts to avoid missing any unlit craft."

"He agrees with you, Captain, so let's get started," said Capello.

Captain Westlake and the radio operator picked up mobile phones and made contact with the other two launches in the flotilla. Westlake briefly explained to Ian the search pattern he had arranged with the other two vessels, during their assembly voyage. They all then stood and waited for their first contact.

By 0500 hours they had completed the first sector without finding a single yacht and immediately extended the search pattern ten miles further north. At 0640 a yacht was challenged by the third launch in the chain but did not fit the profile, as it was ketch rig with a family of six on board. Four other sightings were made, but none were even close to being what they were looking for.

On the dot of 0800 hours the terrorists' next chilling threat message was received, and this time two of the launches were able to get a bearing on the transmission location. Ian drew the two bearings on the chart.

"There we are guys, 37deg 52 min 45 north by 75deg 57 min 28 west roughly, about two and three quarter miles east of

Upper Trump Bank south of Herring Island, but of course they won't be there now."

"That puts them the other side of the Chesapeake," said Brumen, in a frustrated tone. "Shit, we've spent days looking for these bastards on the west side and up the Potomac."

"Captain Westlake, you said that you needed to take on fuel," said Ian. "May I suggest that we do that and you send one of the others to search that area for clues, such as a free-floating black buoy."

"You don't think that they are in the area any longer then?" said Brumen.

"Not if they are following the same practice as they did in the English Channel they won't be," replied Ian. "They activated the buoy about two hours after launching it and must have been at least ten miles away by then."

Capello was on the phone immediately requesting emergency scrambling of helicopters to patrol the waters of the Chesapeake at a radius of ten miles from the co-ordinates estimated as being the transmission point. Each was to report the sighting of any single masted, white hulled yacht and its heading.

The response was even more spectacular, two US Marine AV-8B Harriers were being put in the air. After some discussion it was agreed that they were to radar target 'spot' yachts within the profile only and report. Launches would then follow up and check out each vessel.

Ian had been right. Arni and Yamada were lounging in the yacht's cockpit, gloating as they listened to the message being broadcast from the buoy eleven miles astern of them. Unlike the previous messages this was transmitted simultaneously from two buoys, one broadcasting on public wavebands and picked up by hundreds of boats and many radio stations, the other on the military waveband.

"People of America, your President has been given four warnings and each he has ignored at your cost." Hamaura's voice was strong and clear over their yacht's radio. "His failure to protect you and the failure of your puppet Emperor in Japan to meet our demands will now cost millions of your people their lives and the lives of many in the years to come. For you, tomorrow will no longer be called Independence Day but by our justice and that of the true democracy of Japan and the true faith of Islam it shall be renamed Dependence Day!!! The day when America will pay for its interference in other nations' affairs and its crimes against their peoples. From tomorrow there will be a new world order when Japan will be relieved of the parasite who still thinks himself to be a god and the people of Palestine…"

At the end of the broadcast both men in the cockpit of the yacht spontaneously raised their fists in salute.

"How you able to hear military waveband?" asked Yamada, after a few moments' contemplation of the speech and the immediate future.

"Hamaura worked in German electronics factory which made NATO communications equipment," answered Arni. "She stole the chip which allows this radio to pick them up." Going down into the cabin he turned the radio back to channel 16 and came back on deck. "We are now just entering the Potomac so should be at Branson Cove in good time to pick up Hamaura."

"It is good she will be with us for final stage," said Yamada. "She has worked for years to achieve this. Murata-san should also be here, but we had to make sure he is able to take the crown from that coward Yamamoto."

"Did Hamaura mention Yamamoto's son?"

"Yes, she told me he had failed," Yamada replied with some contempt. "It has not been an easy path to reach this goal. One must be strong and loyal at all times, he showed the weakness of his father."

In the short time he had been aboard the yacht Yamada had learnt a great deal about the hatred that motivated his companion. Arni's life path, though very different to his own, had, according to Arni, been blighted by the American-backed politics of the Middle East. However, Arni was also a man who had achieved success in his fight against Christian and Jewish cultural domination, with the bombing of the Croydon Tower in Britain and the Tel Aviv strike. Operation 'Kinoko Kumo' though, would be his finest hour, a single strike that would bring this nation, which was considered to be the most powerful in the world, to its knees. How much Arni had contributed to the operation previously Yamada did not know, but he was aware that the precision in the launching and triggering of the buoys had been critical to this phase of the attack. Without Arni's skill in working the tides and currents it was unlikely that half of the messages would have got through to the intended target.

Yamada had become acutely aware that he knew nothing about sailing and had struggled to grasp the multitude of skills required. Each deck task seemed to him to require a complex knot to be tied; bowline, clove hitch, round turn and two half hitches were all foreign to him. As for controlling the sails and steering the yacht when under sail, that filled him with fear, especially when a gust of wind laid the yacht over.

His greatest problem was how to explain to Hamaura that he could not replace Arni especially as she would be unable to use her left arm at all.

Arni flicked the switch of a small portable CD and radio unit, tuning it to a local chat show station. The host was appealing for calm and stating that their switchboard was jammed with calls about the terrorist message. As they sat and listened they became fascinated by the way fear and panic was spreading. Roads were becoming jammed with people wanting to escape the threat but not knowing which way to go. A car door slamming would have people ducking and running for cover, fearing gunshots.

Unbeknown to Yamada and Arni, FBI trained negotiators were issuing broadcasts indicating that progress was being made regarding the release of those held but further time was required. Hamaura responded using Ian Vaughan's mobile phone as she started her journey from the clinic to Branson's Cove. Taking care with each call so as not to be traced, she pushed for guarantees and was told that these could not be provided until late that evening. Picking a busy roadside diner, she, accompanied by Dr Higashi and the nurse, sat watching the constant news speculation broadcasts of the TV stations. With all eyes focused on the screen Hamaura pulled out the mobile again and dialled her contact in Japan. In the short conversation that followed they informed her that all arrangements had been made for the release and that it was only awaiting a call from the US State Department for the prisoners to be freed.

Armed with this knowledge it was easy for her, in a series of short phone calls made from different locations, to place the necessary pressure for the release to take place at midday Eastern Seaboard Time, reinforced with the threat of bringing the attack forward if the State Department failed to comply. Now all she could do was complete her journey and await results.

Chapter 15

Burton slammed the door of his pick-up and crossed the pavement leading to Mel Clements' apartment. His young wife Allison had been far from amused at having her honeymoon interrupted after only five days. It was not until they had arrived back from Hawaii that they realised the urgency of the situation. His boss, Packard, had been trying to contact Mel Clements and had sent Burton to the apartment block to see if any of the neighbours had any contact details. TN (Nuclear) were desperate to prove that they could staff up to meet this level of emergency.

"Why in the hell did Mel Clements think he could just disappear off the planet like this? Jesus Christ, all team leaders know they gotta leave contact numbers for times like this," Burton muttered to himself.

As he approached the doors an old lady was letting herself out. "Excuse me, Ma'am, but do you know Mel Clements in apartment 34?" he asked.

"Why, you're from the same company, I recognise the overalls," she said by way of a reply.

"Yes, Ma'am, I am. We're needin' Mel to come and help us an we don't know where he's stayin' at present," Burton said. "Maybe he or his wife said where they was goin'."

"Oh, I wouldn't know young man, I live two floors above him and sadly only get to see him if I have a light bulb go. He's such a nice man and does so much to help the older ones in the block, you know only three weeks ago he…"

"Sorry, Ma'am," Burton interrupted. "This is very urgent, I best try his neighbours." With that he stepped past her and made for the elevator.

On the third floor the elevator doors opened onto a small 'L'-shaped landing providing access to four apartments. As Burton took in the surroundings he became aware of a sweet sickly odour pervading the corner by the stairwell. There was no response from 34, 33 or 32 but eventually a lady in number 31 answered her door.

"Yeah, what do you want. I ain't buyin' nothing so don't go wastin' yer time," she said, making to close the door.

Burton quickly explained his quest.

"I got no idea where they been an' gone to. All I know is that they maybe left the fridge door open and somethin's gone off," she said. "We all checked and it ain't comin' from nowhere else."

"The smell you mean, Ma'am?"

"Yeah, that damn smell. We been leavin' the windows open day and night and it still don't clear it," she said. "Called the landlord but they don't do nothin'."

"Have you tried the police?" Burton asked.

"Hell no, anyways they be chasin' around after these terrorists," she replied.

Left on his own Burton was about to press for the elevator when he stopped, and walking back to Mel Clements' apartment door, knelt and put his nose to the thin gap at the bottom. The smell was so intense it made him retch and jerk his head away. Then he could hear it faintly through the door, the sound of a TV or radio playing.

It took three hours for the police to arrive. "Are you the guy that called us over here?" the fresh-looking constable asked. "If so it better be worth it because we're damn busy at the moment."

"I think there maybe someone dead in there," said Burton.

"What makes you think that?" asked the older one of the pair.

"Just put your nose down there," said Burton pointing to the bottom of the door.

The officer sighed and got down on his knees and took in a deep breath. "Urrrr, shit. That's a corpse all right," he said, moving to the open window and taking in some hurried breaths of clean air.

"You goin' in, Jack?" asked his young partner.

"No boy, we are goin' in. You're gonna get your first taste of an ole stiff."

Under normal circumstances the finding of a suicide would not have attracted the FBI, but as Mel Clements was working for a power company, in the area where terrorist activity was known, things were different.

Burton had been physically sick when the door had burst open and the scene revealed. Now sitting on a dining chair, reluctantly provided by the neighbour, he was still trying to control his stomach. Crouched alongside him was Agent Baghurst of the FBI. "You told the police that you worked with this guy Clements."

"We work for the same company, that's all," replied Burton. "He runs one of the maintenance teams and I run another. We're rarely on the same site together."

"When did you last see him?" asked Baghurst.

"My bachelor party, I guess. He surprised everybody by turning up, then amazed us by getting as drunk as a skunk," Burton answered. "Young Yamada had to damn near carry him out to his car."

"Yamada, you say?" Baghurst said with sudden interest.

"Yeah, he and Stanislav work with Mel," informed Burton.

Within twenty minutes Burton found himself back at the TN (Nuclear) office trawling through Clements' team's work schedules and maintenance sign-offs.

As Burton had been entering Clements' apartment block that morning the two Harrier AV-8Bs had each searched the area and reported seven potential targets. As the information was coming in, the locations and projected courses were marked on the chart in the launch's wheelhouse. Brumen, Capello,

302

Westlake and Ian Vaughan stood staring at the plot trying to imagine which of the yachts plotted would be most likely to have been at the estimated buoy launch point three hours ago. Three were heading north in their direction, two others were making their way up the eastern shore and one making south for Cape Charles, assuming that it maintained its present course. That left one entering the Potomac, which more than likely had come up from the south.

"I want those two stopped and searched by the launches checkin' out the buoy site," said Capello, "and we'll check these three on our way south to head off that lone one goin' down to Cape Charles."

"You think they're making a run for the open sea now that they've dropped the buoy?" said Ian.

"Yeah," replied Capello. "That's just what I think."

Ian remained thoughtfully looking at the chart. After a few moments he was aware that the others were looking at him.

"What's wrong?" asked Brumen. "The idea sounds good to me."

"What I keep struggling with is how a signal sent from a buoy, that we know has reception limitations, can trigger an event so many miles away behind hills," Ian said thoughtfully, still staring at the chart. "I thought at first that they had accomplices ashore, maybe in the power station staff, but somehow that just doesn't fit. There are just too many people around for it not to be obvious who is responsible. There are no signs of break-ins which reduces the chances of it being the direct act of saboteurs." He stood looking at the deck head. "No, I can't crack it but there must be some other device they can trigger which causes all this."

With that the meeting broke up and orders were issued to clear the fuelling pipes and get underway. Moving at high speed they had quite quickly identified their three target yachts, none of which resembled their quarry. They were just blasting across

303

the water opposite the mouth of the Potomac when Capello's phone rang, "Yeah. We picked up the message you sent out to them," he said. He listened for a few minutes to the voice on the other end then gasped. "They what, used Vaughan's goddam phone to conduct ransom negotiations. Did you get a fix?" There was another long pause while he listened, then moved back to the chart table, opened a road atlas and started tracing with his finger across it. "You're sure it was her voice?" Another pause. "Okay, that puts a whole new light upon things, yeah, er, thanks."

"Hey, you're gonna lu-uv this," Capello said. "After this morning's threat message FBI negotiators broadcast a response designed to start negotiations. It worked and Hamaura used your mobile to push for the releases they want. She made several calls and though they couldn't trace exactly where she was, it was obvious that she was on land and movin' up from the Richmond area to somewhere along the southern shore of the Potomac."

"As I recall from the video conference with your London Embassy our ATB people have her and Madadhah down as survivors not martyrs," said Ian.

"Meaning?" asked Brumen.

"Meaning that she is travelling to a rendezvous with the yacht," replied Ian. "Our target should be the yacht going up the Potomac not the one south of us."

"No," said Capello. "I'll put my money on that southerly yacht, there's a hundred different ways Hamaura can leave the US. They could even have arranged to pick her up further down the coast."

"Look," said Ian. "At the speed this thing goes at we can take a look at the yacht and still have time to get down the Chesapeake before the other one reaches the ocean."

Capello gave a questioning look at Westlake.

"Providing we don't start looking at other craft, yes, we would have time," Westlake said.

"Okay, let's do it. Three rounds of whisky if you're wrong."

Ian smiled. "You're on, three rounds."

The change of course obviously woke Agnes who appeared bleary-eyed at the head of the companionway steps. Ian noticed her first. "Why, it's sleeping beauty," he cried. "What woke you? We thought you were there for a hundred years."

Agnes poked her tongue out at him. "When the boat tipped over back there I fell out of my bunk. God, that floor's hard."

"Come with me to the galley and I'll make you a cup of coffee," said Ian. "Anyone else fancy a cup?"

In the galley Ian set to work making coffees and sandwiches. "Say, you're rather good at this," observed Agnes.

"Training in support of two daughters, packed lunches, you know the thing. Flying around early in the morning checking that the homework was done, especially the youngest, getting breakfast fitted in and as I said, doing the packed lunches. Most times Sarah, my wife, did it all, but I got enough of a share to learn the art of rapid sandwich build."

"Why the change of direction back there?" she asked.

Ian explained about the mobile phone call locations and his take on the direction of the target yacht.

"Oh, I see. You sure it is them?" she asked

"No, but I'm more inclined to take a look at that yacht than the other one," he replied. "No, I'll be honest, I am pretty sure this is the right target, which is why I came down here to get people fed. You know before the battle of Trafalgar the entire British Fleet Captains ensured that their men had a good meal. The French and Spanish were not so well organised. When you're in a fire-fight good energy levels are essential. I believe that we are just about to go into a fire-fight." His expression throughout this comment had been very serious. "When we catch up with this yacht Agnes I want you to take good care, don't stand in the line of fire, you got that."

She half smiled and nodded. "I'll take these up," she said, picking up one of the trays of food.

Aboard the yacht Arni was really enjoying himself. The southerly breeze that had sprung up shortly after they had dropped the buoy had freshened slightly to a force 3-4 giving them the perfect beam reach and sending the yacht skipping the wavelets at a little over seven knots and bringing them to Branson's Cove an hour ahead of schedule. Rolling in the foresail Arni started the engine and motored into the cove looking for a suitable spot to anchor whilst they waited for Hamaura.

"There she is," said Yamada, pointing to a staging near the southern tip of the cove. "She has Dr Higashi with her."

Careful to keep his eye on the depth of water, Arni edged the yacht alongside the staging. The two men held the yacht steady alongside and watched as Hamaura carefully made her way, one step at a time, down a ladder to deck level then stepped on board.

"Konichi-wa Hamaura-san, o-genki deska," said Yamada in greeting.

"Konichi-wa Yamada-san, hi genki desu," she replied, returning his formal bow.

"Is he coming too?" asked Arni, jerking his head in the direction of Dr Higashi.

"No," she replied curtly.

Arni allowed the breeze to take the bows of the yacht away from the staging before gently easing the yacht's engine into gear and getting the boat underway. Yamada and Hamaura remained on the foredeck bowing to Higashi in farewell, then went into a deep discussion. It was obvious to Arni that Yamada was suggesting something that Hamaura did not agree with; eventually it appeared that he had got his way and both then made their way back to the cockpit.

"Your arm and ribs fixed ok?" Arni asked.

"Yes, thank you. Did you enjoy the boy?"

Arni was taken by surprise. "Please?" he said.

"You know, the one you stupidly abducted at the marina," she said, giving him a hostile glare. "You endangered whole operation; police are hunting for you now."

"I do not know what you are talking about," lied Arni. " Do not know anything about abducting a boy."

Yamada appeared from below and handed a small trainer to Hamaura. "You must have very small feet then," she said holding up the trainer. "Yamada-san found this in the forward cabin under the mattress the day he arrived onboard."

"It probably belongs to Vaughan's children," Arni replied, now not so sure of himself.

"Oh really. That is why it has J Schulkens written inside."

"If anyone has endangered this operation it is you. What have you been able to do since Vaughan went over the side, eh? Tell me that," he shouted back at her. "You stop this now and we get the job finished."

Hamaura was just about to say something more when Arni turned to Yamada. "You. Take the wheel while I get the mainsail down. We will go back to the shack under engine. Come on, quickly!"

As Yamada took hold of the wheel Arni leapt out of the cockpit and down the side deck to the mast. After the sail was dropped Yamada brought the yacht back on course. Arni, still on deck was taking his time flaking the sail neatly.

"Are you fit enough to steer?" Arni asked, glaring at Hamaura.

"Yes," she replied.

"Yamada, in that locker is a blue mainsail cover, bring it here, help to put it on," Arni ordered.

Yamada looked at Hamaura for confirmation; when she nodded he reached down and opened the locker. It took him only a few moments to find what he was looking for and to close the locker lid again. Behind him Hamaura was keying in a number on a mobile phone. It seemed that as soon as the connection was made the call was answered.

"Are they free?" she asked.

The voice at the other end was equally brief.

"Ah so," she responded and switched the phone off.

Yamada looked at her questioningly. Staring back at him her serious face slowly turned into a smile and she gave a contented nod of her head. "Pass me the last buoy," she ordered.

Yamada looked confused. "Hamaura-san they have given you what you have demanded?"

"No," she lied. "They have not, so they will pay the full price for their arrogance." For three years she had worked towards this moment; this chance to show the world that it is she who is the movement's real leader. Not even Murata-san could stop her now.

Practised now, Yamada had the buoy ready for launching in minutes. Hamaura, with his help, inserted the last tape player and loaded it, then, without ceremony, Yamada launched the buoy over the yacht's stern and watched it twirl away in the boat's wake.

"Hey!" shouted Arni. "Sail cover!"

They took their time rolling the cover along the boom and hooking the shock cord in place to close the cover completely around the sail. Arni then moved to the front of the mast and facing astern started to lace the sail head section of the cover in place. His legs and those of Yamada, who was now leaning on the boom and staring out across the Potomac towards its beautiful shoreline, obstructed Hamaura's view forward. The launch, travelling at high speed, therefore got to within half a mile before Arni heard it and shouted a warning. Yamada went to return to the cockpit but Hamaura's shout stopped him.

"You stay there, I will pass you the guns," she said, locking the steering and moving forward to reach under the sprayhood to retrieve two semi-automatics. From a pouch hung just inside the hatchway she pulled a hand grenade and slipped it into her pocket. Then, stepping back a pace, she handed the two weapons up to Yamada who in turn passed one forward to Arni. Turning back he saw Hamaura holding up two spare clips of ammunition and reached down to take them from her. "If anything happens and he and I are hit you must go to shack and press red button behind glass panel. That is activation signal device," she instructed.

"Hi wakarimashta," he replied with a bow.

With that she returned to the wheel and unlocking it made an adjustment to bring the yacht back on course.

"That's them," shouted Ian, lowering his binoculars and pointing towards the yacht one hundred yards away and twenty degrees off their port bow. "I'd recognise that bitch anywhere."

It was as the yacht changed course to starboard slightly that her head and shoulders had come into Ian's view.

Westlake turned to the helmsman. "Go round their stern and come up along their starboard side."

"Aye aye, sir."

Capello turned to Ian and said, "If you get hurt my pension's on the line so you go below and for God's sake stay out of sight."

Ian sighed and reluctantly climbed down off the bridge and entered the wheelhouse. "I've been ordered below, Agnes," he said. "Don't forget what I said, stay out of the line of fire."

"I'll behave," she said with a nervous smile.

Below, Ian moved forward to the sleeping quarters steadying himself as the launch made the sweeping turn. Sitting on his bunk he idly looked around whilst trying to work out what was going on above. It was then that his eye lighted upon

Agnes's travelling bag. Checking that the coast was clear he reached over and rummaging through the stack of T-shirts and underwear he found the large handgun that Brumen had been so derogatory about. A further search revealed a box of ammunition, from which he took a shell and, opening the gun, checked that it fitted a chamber. Satisfied that he had got the right match he loaded the other five chambers, stuck a handful of shells in his pocket and closed the gun, checking that the safety catch was on.

On the bridge Capello turned to Brumen. "Did I say three rounds of whiskey?"

Brumen nodded. "You sure did, pal. Vaughan should be doin' my job, he's definitely got the thought processes required." He raised his binoculars again studying the yacht's crew. "If that ain't the bunch then the Pope ain't a catholic."

"You got a tannoy system aboard this boat?" asked Brumen.

Westlake reached sideways and passed him a microphone. "Speak into that," he said.

Brumen held the microphone to his mouth. "This is the FBI, you are to stop engine and prepare to be boarded."

Hamaura didn't even turn round, she just kept going.

"Yacht *Melodrama Clan* this is the FBI you are to stop engine and prepare to be boarded."

Still there was no response and the launch was now closing fast. A seaman armed and in a flak-jacket moved forward into the bow and another went to the stern. Amidships a third flak-jacketed seaman stood brandishing a large boat hook with Capello beside him.

"Fumiko Hamaura and Yunis Madadhah, you are both under arrest. Stop engine immediately and prepare for boarding, or we will open fire," Brumen ordered.

Hamaura reached forward and pulled the throttle back into neutral then hard astern. The effect was to bring the yacht to a standstill very quickly, too fast in fact for the launch helmsman to respond without also putting the engines to hard astern. As the two vessels came alongside each other the seamen at bow and stern raised their weapons covering the terrorists.

"Put your hands in the air where we can see them," shouted Capello.

Both Madadhah and Yamada were standing on the other side of the yacht to the launch close to the mast and boom, so when Madadhah raised his hands, the left one was obscured by the mast concealing the gun he was holding. Yamada seeing the situation developing had slipped his gun under the sail cover out of sight but within easy reach.

Whether Hamaura had planned the sequence was never known but its effect was spectacular. The sudden reduction in speed of the fast moving launch meant that the following stern wave would quickly catch up with it, causing it to heave stern first, throwing all those onboard off balance. This coincided with Agnes opening the wheelhouse door and stepping onto a wet and slippery side deck. As she appeared the seaman with the boathook staggered sideways into Agnes causing her to slip and fall to the deck. Simultaneously both armed seamen reached for the guard rail to steady themselves and Capello fatally took his eyes off Yamada and Madadhah to look at Agnes.

Those on the yacht had seen it coming and had braced themselves ready and as the opportunity presented itself opened fire. Arni's first few bullets hit the seaman in the bow of the launch knocking him into the water. Yamada with a single shot killed the young seaman in the stern then turned his attention on Brumen and Westlake by spraying the bridge with bullets. Capello recovering from the lurch of the launch was getting Yamada in his sights when Arni's second burst of fire hit him killing him outright. It was Agnes who got the first few shots away, the third one hitting Arni in the groin, the fourth going through the top of his head as he bent double. That was the last thing she was to see as Yamada's second long burst of fire swept across her and the unarmed seaman killing them both. At the same instant the grenade that Hamaura had thrown expertly through the open door exploded in the wheelhouse killing the helmsman and wounding a fourth seaman.

The whole fire-fight had lasted less than thirty seconds in which time Ian had moved from the forward accommodation to the bottom of the companionway steps to the wheelhouse. He arrived a fraction after the grenade had gone off, his ears ringing from the blast, and saw immediately a fire breaking out that appeared to trap him below. Frantically he searched for an emergency hatch, eventually finding one in the engine room. Throwing the catches off he lifted the hatch and carefully peered out. The launch was dead in the water but the yacht was beginning to move away. Scrambling on deck he rushed down the starboard side deck using the wheelhouse as cover. Peering round the front he saw Hamaura at the helm of the yacht looking back at the launch with a look of triumph on her face. Raising the gun he fired, the shot smashing the binnacle compass. The second hit her in the left shoulder spinning her round to face him. As she focused on him an expression of recognition dawned on her face just before Ian's third shot smashed through her cheekbone and out through the back of her head.

The tug of a bullet as it ripped through the flesh of his left shoulder had Ian dropping to the deck and slithering backwards behind the wheelhouse again. Looking up he could see Yamada throw the empty magazine into the water and reach for the spare. Ian raised his gun and fired, fired again and, as Yamada raised his reloaded gun, fired the last shot and ducked out of sight opening the gun and frantically emptying the spent shell cases onto the deck. He dropped two fresh shells before he got a grip of himself and concentrated properly to reload the weapon. He was aware now that there had been no return of fire. Carefully he stood and stole a glance at the yacht only to see it some way off making good its escape.

A cry from the wheelhouse had Ian pulling the starboard door open and grabbing the fire extinguisher from the bracket just inside, the blast of hot air taking his breath away. He pulled the clip clear and squeezed the trigger. Foam burst from the unit's nozzle and he directed it at the flames, driving them back from engulfing the wounded seaman. The extinguisher fortunately lasted until he could reach the one by the porthand door before giving out. Triggering the second one he managed to complete the job and turned to see what he could do for the sailor. The man's injuries appeared to be mainly fragment wounds, loss of hearing, concussion, a broken arm and some broken ribs but apparently nothing fatal. He had luckily been standing protected by the binnacle and helmsman when the grenade went off. Carefully Ian helped the man to his feet and got him below and onto a bunk. Returning to the wheelhouse he stepped out of the porthand door and almost stepped on the body of Agnes, her eyes staring vacantly at the sky. The bodies of the seaman and Capello were slumped together in a pool of blood. Stepping past them he turned and climbed the steps up to the bridge where he found Brumen checking the body of Westlake. Brumen turned and looked at him, blood dripping from a wound on his forehead and his right arm hanging limply at his side. "Jesus Christ, what a mess, they just took us apart," he said, tears of frustration appearing in his eyes. "The captain's dead and the radio guy, Manning."

"So are Agnes, Capello and four of the crew. There's only you, me and Abbots left alive and he is quite badly wounded," Ian informed him. "Now let's have a look at you, that right arm of yours doesn't look too good."

"What about Hamaura and Co?" Brumen asked.

"Madadhah's dead, face down in the water just over there," said Ian jerking his head in the direction. "I shot Hamaura, but this guy Yamada got away, I might have hit him but I'm not sure. He winged me in the shoulder."

"Where is he?" asked Brumen.

"Last seen heading east down the river. If you can help me launch the rib I'm going after him, because this launch ain't going anywhere and Agnes and Capello didn't deserve to be on the losing side," said Ian with some bitterness.

"No," said Brumen. "I'm gonna call the cavalry, let them handle it."

He fumbled in his right-hand pocket with his left hand and eventually produced his mobile.

"Mr Metcalfe? We need backup immediately; we are just east of a place called Coles Point on the Potomac. There has been a gunfight and we have sustained many losses including Capello and young Agnes." There was a pause and Ian could hear Metcalfe shouting on the other end of the phone. "Yeah, I know it's a goddam mess but you shoutin' down the phone ain't gonna stop the guy that got away from completin' what they set out to do, so take your head out of your arse and get us some help!" Brumen shouted back, then hung up.

Brumen turned to Ian and struggled to his feet. "Oh shit, that bureaucratic dipstick ain't gonna summon help in time. I'm comin' with yer. It may well be the last time I do any work wearing an FBI badge."

"Hold it there, let's take a quick look at that arm before we do anything else."

Ian helped Brumen out of his jacket and shook his head. "I can see where the bullet went in but there isn't an exit wound so I guess it was stopped by the bone. You're staying here and waiting for help."

It took twenty minutes for Vaughan and Brumen to launch the rib, which miraculously had escaped damage during the

314

onslaught. Brumen, ashen-faced, slumped to the deck only just holding fast to the painter whilst Ian lowered himself over the side of the launch and into the rib. Being a military craft it had a simple list of operating instructions on starting and operation that took only a couple of minutes to work through before the 70-horsepower engine roared into life.

"Hey wait up," shouted Brumen. Getting to his feet he staggered across to the portside deck and searched through Capello's pockets until he found the mobile phone. Returning to the starboard side he went down on his knees and passed the phone to Ian.

"If you scroll through the caller list you'll find me but the important one I suppose is under COMIC. It stands for Commander In Charge and will get you through to Metcalfe. Don't ask, it was just Capello's sense of humour."

Ian smiled and looked up at Brumen. "I'll see you later."

As Brumen threw the painter into the well of the rib Ian opened the throttle and the rib accelerated away across the water in the direction the yacht had taken. In a very short distance the rib had climbed onto a plane and was skimming along the Potomac at close to forty knots. He had expected Yamada to try making his escape to the open sea. He tried to work out how long it had been since he saw the yacht motoring away, half an hour, no much more than that, probably over an hour. On the southern windward shore of the Potomac, the water, sheltered by the shoreline, was almost flat calm, therefore he considered that the yacht could easily have travelled six miles, maybe nearer seven.

Ian had taken the rib out towards the centre of the river and was just level with Ragged Point Beach when Capello's phone in his pocket started to vibrate indicating an incoming call. "Vaughan, this is Brumen. Metcalfe's been back on sayin' that another message was received, first of all from Madadhah sayin' a lot of Jehad stuff then Hamaura finishes it off sayin' that as we haven't met their demands thirty million people will die. Metcalfe has had the President breathin' down his neck and the Chief of Staff. When or if you find the yacht phone Metcalfe and tell him where to send the troops if you can. The Marines are getting two choppers up and headin' this way with a third carrying a field medical unit droppin' in here."

"That's good. I'm travelling down the centre of the river almost," said Ian. "Haven't seen any sign of the yacht yet but I expect to sight it in about seven, eight minutes or so."

"For God's sake, wait for the cavalry. Don't, whatever you do, take on that killer. Did you hear that?" Brumen shouted.

"Right, yes, understood," said Ian pressing the button to end the call.

After five minutes of high-speed chase Ian slowed the craft and picked up the binoculars to study the horizon. It was on his third sweep that he saw a yacht very close in on the southern shore. Altering course he increased speed again and headed in its direction. Fears were now crossing his mind as to how he was to make the approach without coming under fire. A direct high-speed approach wearing a flak-jacket was going to make it obvious who he was, on the other hand, this yacht might be totally innocent and by not checking it out quickly might allow Yamada time to escape. Taking off the jacket he decided on a flashy slalom approach as if he was showing off to some girl on board. The final two miles or so seemed to take forever to complete and as he got within half a mile he started to point at imaginary things on the shore throwing the rib from side to side in big sweeps making it leap off the small waves and throw up large plumes of spray. To complete the picture he undid his shirt letting it flap wildly out behind him to expose his suntanned chest. At a hundred yards from the yacht he could clearly make out blood smeared down the port side abreast of the mast. His next wild sweep opened up a view of the beach previously hidden from view revealing the figure of Yamada hauling himself out of the water, one hand lifting his upper body, the other brandishing the automatic pistol.

Spinning the rib round in a circle Ian took in the fact that Yamada was unable to stand and had obviously been hit in his left leg. Flashes appeared from the muzzle of Yamada's gun and spurts of water were thrown up just short of the rib causing Ian to duck low and turn the rib to obtain the cover of the yacht. Cutting the throttle he brought the rib alongside *Melodrama Clan* and making the painter off on the midships cleat scrambled aboard careful not to raise his head above the cabin roof. Yamada had just run the yacht aground in his haste to get ashore. Another burst of fire from the shore tore holes in the spray hood and ricocheted off the mast. Lying flat he pulled his way towards the cockpit and took a quick look in. Hamaura's body lay along the cockpit sole, her head and shoulders propped up against the bridge deck. The back of her skull was missing and all around the cockpit was covered in blood. Another burst of fire from Yamada ripped through the fibreglass hull and wood lining of the yacht's starboard side causing the vessel to shake in spasm from the impacts. Ian heard a girl's scream and ventured a quick look at the beach. He saw that Yamada was now about halfway between the water's edge and a shack up close to the tree line. He was waving a girl back but she was ignoring him, looking about, trying to comprehend the danger.

Ian raised his pistol and fired, narrowly missing Yamada. The girl stopped in her tracks and shrieked in fear. Ian fired again sending up a feather of sand close by Yamada's left foot. The return burst would have proved fatal for Ian had it not been for the yacht's radio and switch panel above the chart table. Realising that the next few seconds could be his last he slipped back over the side and into the rib moving astern so that the yacht's engine block was between him and Yamada. He remembered the flak-jacket and stooping picked it up and put it on. Moving to take another look at the beach he was hit just below the heart by the first round of another burst of fire. The impact sat him down onto the outboard engine cowl. Carefully he felt under the flak-jacket, removed his hand and studied it in a rather dazed state. Recognising, after some moments, that there were no signs of blood he looked down and inspected the neat round hole in the front of the jacket.

Ian sat for what must have been a full minute waiting for another hail of bullets, then he remembered Brumen's instructions. Pulling Capello's phone from his pocket he scrolled down to COMIC and pressed the dial button. Metcalfe answered the phone almost before the ring tone started.

"This is Ian Vaughan. Yamada has made it ashore about five miles east of your Navy's launch. He is wounded in the leg but is making his way up the beach to a shack with a flagpole near it flying Koi flags," he said.

"We have two units of highly trained Marines heading your way, they should be with you in about ten minutes."

Ian bobbed up to check on Yamada's progress to find that the girl had reached him and he was now limping, with his arm round her shoulders, towards the shack.

"That will be too late," said Ian to Metcalfe. "He will have triggered the device by then."

Raising the pistol he fired again. The range had opened up to fifty yards and he was aware that hitting a barn door at that distance would be a fluke.

Yamada hopped round to face him and raising the gun squeezed the trigger but nothing happened, the clip was empty. Hopping back he pointed with the gun in the direction of the trees to the left of the shack. In their shadows Ian could just make out a car. Undoing the painter he put the rib in gear and rounding the bow of the yacht gave it full throttle, aiming at the shore. The semi-ridged rib skidded up the beach, the outboard tilting forward and its shaft leg leaving a gouge in the sand.

Leaping ashore Ian struggled to run in the soft sand. Stopping he took aim and fired at the retreating couple. He saw the girl drop like a stone, hit in the centre of her back dragging Yamada with her. His last shot missed Yamada and he found himself again panicking to empty and reload the pistol's revolving chamber.

Gun loaded, Ian realised that Yamada was making to the car to get rearmed, and firing almost blindly in Yamada's direction set off as fast as he could towards the shack. Kicking the door open he rushed in, turning as he did so, checking for other accomplices that may be there. Establishing that he was alone he swiftly returned to the door and squeezed the trigger again to find that it made just a dull click. This time he took more care reloading and was able to take aim on Yamada, as he was only feet from the vehicle.

Yamada pulled himself up to open the trunk of the car as Ian, standing in the doorway of the shack, opened fire again. Realising that his only chance was to get away, he limped round to the driver's door, got in, and turning the ignition drove the car off down the woodland track. At the far edge of the wood he stopped the car and opening the door he went to get out and go to the trunk for the AK 47 he had left there, but was stopped by the distinctive sound of military Chinook helicopters. He guessed, quite correctly, that they would be full of heavily armed troops and decided that he would wait his time before avenging the deaths of Fumiko Hamaura and the girl he knew only as Kerry Anne. He waited until he could hear that both aircraft were on the ground and shutting down before he drove the car clear of the tree screen and down the track to the highway.

Ian had thought it better to keep by the protective walls of the shack rather than risk Yamada finding a gun in the car and catching him in the open. He was surprised to hear the engine start up and the vehicle race away. Firing at it through the trees he raced to the track only to see the car disappear out of sight. Turning back to the shack he stopped and reaching down turned the body of the dead girl over. Her eyes were wide open with shock, sand speckled the tanned cheeks and he thought that at one time she must have been very pretty.

The sound of helicopter rotors broke in on his thoughts and walking out into clear view he waved at the two helicopters with both arms.

As the first made its approach to the beach Ian was aware that he was being covered by a machine gun set up in the helicopter's side door. Taking no chances he dropped the pistol and keeping his hands in full view stepped back out of the dust storm that the helicopter had set up. The second helicopter was making its landing as three soldiers appeared out from the dust cloud and made their way towards him.

"Mr Vaughan?" Ian nodded. "I'm Lieutenant Travis of the US Marine Corps. I understand that you were chasin' a terrorist?"

"He took off in a car down that track, three, maybe four minutes ago. The dead girl over there was helping him get away," informed Ian, aware that the troops were setting a perimeter and checking the shack.

"There's a radio unit of some sort in here, sir," called one of the men.

"Don't touch," the lieutenant called back. "It could be booby trapped. In fact, Sergeant, seal off that building and make sure nobody else goes in there until we can get some experts in here."

At that moment it all caught up with Ian and he suddenly sat on the beach and put his head between his legs to try and stop himself from fainting. The adrenalin that had kept him going had run out leaving him feeling sick and exhausted.

"Medic, some glucose tablets and water over here quickly," ordered the lieutenant as he knelt down beside Ian. "Bring some dressings as well," he shouted. "This guy's wounded."

By the time the medic had arrived Ian was shaking as the realisation of killing two people and the sight of the dead and wounded on the launch hit him. Like many in the heat of battle the heightened adrenalin produced by fear had insulated him against the horror, but now it was all too real.

Back in the TN (Nuclear) offices FBI agent Baghurst was reporting in on progress.

"I've had a word with the chief engineer here, who's a guy called Packard and he's told me that his entire team of engineers and maintenance men are going to replace all the parts worked on by this guy Clements and his team startin' with that done in nuclear power stations."

Metcalfe, at the other end of the line, queried whether the men could be trusted and how long it would take.

"Packard is arranging to split the work crews out with other companies like Crabtree Power, that way it should avoid any other member of the gang operatin'. I asked about the time it would take an' he reckons about three days," replied Baghurst. "By the way, that guy Stanislav showed up here, he's the third member of Clements' team, we've got him in bein' questioned. I'll get back to you on that."

In London Commander Campbell had waited until the second power cut in the US had taken place before moving in on Murata. Inspector Jackson had planned the details and briefed those involved and now stood again in the flat owned by Mrs Cranston, behind DC Featherstone.

"If you hold the team for maybe twenty minutes this could be one of the easiest takes in the annals of the ATB, sir," said Featherstone with a grin.

"What do you mean by that, Constable?" asked Jackson.

"Well, sir, little Miss Nagano and Murata are getting all amorous again and if things go to their normal schedule they should be completely engrossed by that time."

Jackson stepped forward and peered through the binoculars on the stand. "Um, I see what you mean," he said thoughtfully.

Stepping back from the stand he picked up his hand-held radio and said, "Connection Operation Power Strike. We will use the locksmith route in."

Across on the landing leading to Yukiko Nagano's flat, expert locksmith Albert Temple stood nervously between two firearms officers who were dressed in full body armour uniform.

"Albert, it's your show today," said the one to his right. "Don't worry, all you have to do is get the front door open without making too much noise, which for you I'm sure is no problem."

They stood under the stairway awaiting the order to go. Albert Temple never minded the actual work, it was the waiting he hated. The hours he had spent hanging around in the freezing cold or early hours of the morning waiting for a search warrant to be issued. Normally it was a drugs raid when the police needed to get to the pusher or distributor before the evidence was flushed away. Once it had been a big counterfeit bust. Tonight's though was something very different, because no one was letting on what it was about.

Albert's keen hearing picked up the sound from the accompanying officers' earpieces and he had actually started to walk before they gave the word. Kneeling in front of the door he produced from his overcoat pocket a chamois leather rolled instrument case and laid it gently on the ground, then reached in his other pocket and withdrew a pencil torch and jeweller's eyepiece. Holding the eyepiece to his eye he flicked the torch on and held it up to shine a fine beam of light on the lock whilst moving close to conduct an inspection. Just a short glance was enough and putting the torch and glass away he unrolled the case and selected two fine instruments and inserted them into the keyway. With one gentle movement he twisted the two bright tools in unison and the door quietly opened. Reaching down Albert picked up his tool case and standing, stepped back, as the two officers followed by two of their colleagues slipped silently into the flat. Neither Yukiko Nagano nor Murata heard them come into the room. It was only when Murata's arms were grabbed and a gun barrel pushed into the back of his neck, near the base of the skull that they realised they were caught. Two female officers came in and checked Yukiko's clothes before she put them back on. Then they handcuffed her and led her away. Murata received similar treatment from the first two firearms men. What was faintly surreal was that not a word was spoken until Inspector Jackson walked into the bedroom and informed Murata that he was being held under the anti-terrorist laws and in connection with the murder of Julian Makepeace and Jack Drummond. Murata just glared back at him saying nothing but hoping inside that his cast of hawks had struck their quarry the fatal blow.

Chapter 16

The glucose at first made him feel a little queasy, but soon Ian felt his energy return and reaching into his pocket retrieved Capello's phone and rang through to Metcalfe.

"The Marines have sealed off the shack for the moment. It's got some sort of radio unit in it. I'm sorry, but this guy Yamada got away, the only consolation was that he didn't get to the radio unit so he was unable to trigger anything from there," said Ian as soon as Metcalfe picked up.

"Okay, you've done a great job. We've got the rest covered," replied Metcalfe.

"Are there other members of the gang here then?" asked Ian.

"No, what I meant was that we now know that Yamada had got himself on the maintenance staff for one of the power companies and we're checking through all his team's work over the period that he has been employed,"

"Ah, I see, were any of the sites nuclear ones?"

"Yeah," said Metcalfe. "In fact the last site they worked on was the new PWR station at Mission Creek. Why do you ask, does that ring any bells with you?"

"The station name doesn't mean anything, but what keeps niggling in my brain is that conversation I overheard about holding thirty million people to ransom," Ian replied. "Also those messages that I heard being recorded on the boat had a piercing whistle type signal at the end of them," said Ian. "I now believe that was the trigger signal to this shack radio unit we've just discovered, which, in turn transmits a delayed activation signal to the device's controlling power circuits."

"You think so," replied Metcalfe. "Hell, that sounds mighty complicated to me. Surely it would be someone in the shack doin' that at a set time after the message was transmitted."

"There was a girl at the shack," said Ian. "She was trying to help Yamada, who was wounded, get up the beach." He paused seeing again in his mind's eye the girl drop to the ground dead. "I shot her."

"Well, there we are," said Metcalfe. "She would have been the one to operate the transmitter, if that was how it was done."

"That's what I thought at first," replied Ian. "Then just now it dawned on me that had she been such a key player in the gang she would have been armed."

"Probably she was caught by surprise," ventured Metcalfe.

"Hang on," said Ian. "Sergeant!" he shouted; the sergeant turned his head.

"Sir."

"Did you find any weapons stashed in the shack or amongst the personal items there?" Ian asked.

"No, sir, place was clean, sir," the sergeant replied.

"Thank you."

"Metcalfe, I've just checked with the marine sergeant who was with the search unit and he confirms that there were no weapons in the shack," said Ian. "Also I heard their radio operator say that he was quite impressed with the unit they've found. It appears to be very powerful."

"Where is this leadin' us, Mr Vaughan?" asked Metcalfe.

"I would like to meet with the power station engineers and anyone of your people who heard the transmissions in full," said Ian. "Preferably at this Mission Creek power station."

There was a long pause whilst Metcalfe discussed the proposal with someone at the other end.

"We can't see what you can do that isn't already covered by the staff at the station," said Metcalfe finally.

"Look, this may sound strange to you, but it is likely that at some point during the voyage I overheard something that did not make sense at the time, but may register whilst I am talking to people who have a detailed knowledge of how the reactor works or is protected. I'm sorry I cannot be any more specific than that," Ian said.

"I'll think it over and get back to you," said Metcalfe before hanging up.

The sound of rotor blades heralded the arrival of a third helicopter, the sand storm forcing Ian to take shelter behind the shack. He emerged to find that a bomb disposal team had arrived to check out the shack and the radio unit. A fresh-faced young captain walked over with that casualness of an expensive education and family wealth. The lieutenant stood to attention and saluted.

Returning the salute the captain nodded towards the body bag containing Kerry Anne. "One of theirs, I trust?" his voice sounding almost English.

"Yes, sir," replied Lieutenant Travis. "May I introduce Mr Vaughan."

The handshake was firm, the brown eyes friendly. "I am pleased to meet you, Mr Vaughan. I'm Captain William Fraser Fawkes Jnr, I understand that one of them got away?"

"Yes, he was wounded, but got away in a car along that track," replied Ian pointing in the direction the vehicle had taken.

"He left a fair amount of rubber on the road where the track joins the tarmac. We could see the marks as we approached," said Fawkes. "Probably miles away by now judging by his take-off. Was he the only one or are there more about?"

"Our preliminary search indicates that he and the girl were on their own, sir."

"Thank you, Lieutenant, I'll get my men to work."

The shack proved to be clear of any explosive devices but had revealed long-term habitation by the girl and a man. The remains of the last supply of heroin were found beneath the floorboards but the girl's body showed no signs of drug abuse. The finding of the grave provided the first glimpse into the last chapter of two young people's sad lives. Half an hour after their arrival, the two electronic experts were given the go-ahead to check out the radio. With great care they inspected then removed the outer cabinet, then cut out a section of the shack's rear wall so that they could clearly see into the back of the unit. Then started the careful visual identification of all the visible parts followed by the introduction of the sniffer equipment to detect explosives.

As the bomb disposal team worked Ian sat amongst a small group of soldiers talking to the lieutenant.

"Do you think it is possible for me to go out to the boat and see if any of my personal kit is left on board?" he asked.

"Sure. Sergeant, you and these four give us a hand to re-launch that rib."

Lieutenant Travis accompanied Ian out to the yacht. The cockpit was a complete mess with virtually everything covered in blood. Flies buzzed around and were settling upon Hamaura's body. Ian noticed the plaster cast on her left arm and wondered how she had sustained the injury. Below they found the boy's trainer on a bunk in the forward cabin. Ian sorted through the personal gear he wanted to take with him, sitting for several minutes looking at his photographs of Sarah and the girls, wondering how Sarah was coping with the loss of the baby. He hoped that she was not worrying about him. She, of course, would not be aware of his closer involvement with the hunt. Looking at a photograph of his little girls his thoughts moved to how they were feeling after their imprisonment. Sarah and his little stars, how lovely and self-assured they had been, would that now all be changed?

A shout from the shore demanded the attention of Lieutenant Travis, but Ian, deep in his thoughts for his family, paid no attention. Finally as he left the forecabin with the last of the items he wished to take with him he picked up the trainer and Arni's grotesque photo album and handed them to the lieutenant.

"The police will find that this trainer will link Yunis Madadhah with the abduction and probably the murder of Jason Schulkens. The album here will link him with many other crimes against innocent children. His death was far too easy and quick. That vicious sadistic bastard deserved a very painful and lingering end to his miserable life."

Travis didn't reply immediately and Ian, sensing the lieutenant's concern, asked, "What's up?"

"Our Captain William Fraser Fawkes Jnr was way too optimistic when he suggested that Yamada would be miles away by now. My guys have found his car hidden in an old barn just beyond the trees. They are combing the area now to see if they can flush him out."

Ian raised his eyebrows. "Persistent little bastard, isn't he. Let's hope he doesn't open fire on this again. You can see from the recent air-conditioning vents that the hull doesn't stop bullets very well."

As the car hurtled down the track Yamada had been beating his fist against the dashboard trying in a vain attempt to vent his frustration. The anger generated throughout his life seemed to collect in a ball of intense and vehement hatred that was now being turned against one man, the man with the beard. It had been he who had shot dead Fumiko Hamaura, the woman Yamada held in his heart and mind above all others, it was he who had shot dead innocent Kerry Anne. The man with the beard was the one that had stopped him from triggering immediately the final signal.

At the tarmac he stopped the car and got out. Looking back down the track he forced his brain to think clearly about getting back and through the ring of defence he knew the marines would deploy. It was now more than ever before that his Special Forces training and experience were needed if he was going to kill his bearded enemy to balance the scales of justice, as he saw them.

If he could also trigger the final signal so much the better; if not it would still work at midnight, they would never find a way round his shielding without themselves setting the reactor disruption and meltdown process in motion.

Half a mile down the tarmac road he had seen an abandoned barn at the end of a short track near to the tree line. He would hide the car there and cut back through the woods to the Potomac shore. Getting back into the car he spun the wheels as he accelerated down the road leaving a burnt rubber scar along the road's surface, but made sure that he braked gradually and avoided creating obvious ruts in the track to the barn. Reversing the car into the dark enclosure he got out and searched for something to cover it with. Two bales of straw in the corner served his purpose and cutting the binding twine he spread the straw over the vehicle's shiny bonnet. Satisfied that it would be missed by casual inspection he opened the trunk and donned again his black overall and hood. Lifting the AK47 from the trunk he checked the gun's magazine, then putting two spares into his trouser pocket, slipped from the barn and using the long grass as cover crawled unseen back into the wood. Run-off from the fields had cut a ditch through the wood to the shore and squirming on his stomach he made his way along this and through the picket line to the beachhead. To his right he could just make out the two helicopters on the beach and was just about to make his way towards them when the sound of the third aircraft had him dropping down close to a fallen tree trunk to avoid being seen. As the machine kicked up its dust storm on landing he advanced again using the trees as cover until he reached the point where the tree line stepped back away from the water's edge making way for the wide sandy beach in front of the shack.

Groups of soldiers were working around the shack itself checking for booby trap explosives. He watched with amusement as the electrical team moved in and started to probe the radio set-up. All the time soldiers patrolling the cordon of sentries were passing within feet of where he lay hidden by the undergrowth, waiting for his opportunity to strike. His primary target, the bearded man, was sitting in the middle of a small group comprising of a lieutenant, a radio operator, two medics and four soldiers used as runners. Twice he had a clear sight only to be prevented from making the shot by the passing patrols. Columbia had, if nothing else, taught him patience in such situations so he relaxed and waited.

Suddenly the group stood and, walking as a body down to the rib, picked it up and launched it. Yamada raised the AK and followed the group's progress but always the bearded man was hidden from clear sight and he knew he would only get one shot.

Only the lieutenant and his target got into the rib with again the lieutenant blocking his view. Steered by the man with the beard the rib went out to the yacht tying up to the porthand side away from him.

At that moment a patrol returning to the base was coming close and forced Yamada to slide down out of sight. With the coast clear again he looked up but could not see his target and guessed that both of the men were now down in the yacht's cabin.

"Hey, Sarge!" It was the radio operator. "Caffrey and his boys have found a car covered over with straw in a small barn the other side of the trees."

The sergeant waved an acknowledgement and passed a shouted message out to the lieutenant who had stepped back out into the yacht's cockpit. "Okay, Sergeant, reinforce the perimeter then I want to conduct a thorough search back in centring on this part of the beach. If that is clear turn the line around and search again back out to the edge of the tree line and five hundred yards either side of the shack."

"Yes, sir!" shouted the sergeant, saluting and then turning to start organising his men.

330

Yamada slid from the bush he was hiding under, crossed the path scuffed out by the patrolling soldiers, and half crawled down the gently sloping woodland floor to the tree edge by the water. He knew that the searchers would have a good chance of finding his trail, left by his dragging wounded leg, and therefore he had to make his move whilst the search line was still out on the perimeter. Peering through the trees towards the shack he could see that a guard had been set at each corner to protect those working inside whilst onboard the yacht the lieutenant had gone below once more.

Hiding the AK and ammunition in a hollow tree trunk he slid down the bank to the beach and into the water. Once away from the shallows he dived and swimming along the bottom got almost a third of the way to the yacht before needing to surface for air. Down again he went, this time ensuring that as he broke the surface it was on his back to avoid his head coming too far out of the water. Carefully he raised his head and looking around, saw that nobody was paying any attention to the water as all eyes were on the wood. The final dive brought him alongside of the rib, into which he hauled himself. Eyes concentrating on the gap between the sprayhood and the side dodgers he cleared the commando knife from its sheath and instinctively ran his thumb over its blade to check its sharpness. Breathless from the swim and exertion of boarding the rib he lay in the well of the craft for several minutes before rising and peering into the yacht's cabin windows. Inside he caught a quick view of the bearded man putting items into a bag as if he was packing his own case ready for a journey. Yamada experienced shock at the realisation that the bearded man was the man Vaughan. How he had survived was indeed amazing to Yamada; Hamaura had been quietly confident that Vaughan had drowned. It had only been Madadhah who had argued that he was still alive.

Crouching again in the well of the rib he assessed his next move. Reaching up he ran his fingers across the bullet holes his automatic had made earlier. If only he had such a weapon with him now. He had never liked using a knife; it was difficult to use unless the victim was totally unprepared for an attack. Against a trained opponent a knife had limitations and it was those that now occupied Yamada's thoughts. A movement around the companionway hatch had Yamada moving close to the yacht's hull. Someone was shifting something in the cockpit, and then he heard the porthand locker being lifted and the clatter as the person searched inside it. Carefully Yamada stood and peered aft to see who it was and saw the camouflage covered shoulders of the lieutenant. The leg wound was now extremely painful; the swim had washed away the thin scab that had formed and caused bleeding to start again. Putting his upper body beneath the lower safety line he used a press-up motion to drag the rest of his body onboard. Another heave and his upper legs were on the deck, and then with a final push he was in a position where his right leg could be used to get him upright.

Measuring the distances carefully he stood and took one limping step nearer to his target and launched himself forward in a dive at the man below.

Ian had not noticed the movement of the yacht as Yamada had heaved himself aboard thinking that the motion was caused by Lieutenant Travis's search of the locker. It was the movement of Yamada standing up that took his attention away from the task of packing his sailing bag. The blood soaked trouser leg he saw through the cabin window made him call out.

"Lookout Travis, Yamada!" he yelled, just as Yamada had made his move.

Travis, alerted by the shout, straightened and rolled to his left in one move just in time to use his left hand to deflect Yamada's knife. The impact of the terrorist's body however, knocked him backwards bending the yacht's wheel with his right shoulder and knocking him unconscious as his head hit the stern seat. Yamada was also slightly winded by the impact and took precious moments to recover and prepare to stab the lieutenant through the heart. Pulling his arm back to strike the blow he was grabbed from behind by Ian Vaughan and fell back writhing to try and break the hold.

Furiously the two men grappled and twisted, pummelled and butted, in their attempts to gain advantage. As the struggle went on Yamada crowed about the victory that would soon be his.

"Even if I die... my...spirit will... be happy because... the... reactor will explode and cripple America forever."

"Not if... your... radio is switched off... it won't."

"Any tamper with... the radio... will trigger the... signal, gai-jin."

As he spat out the last phrase Yamada twisted violently breaking Ian's hold, and staggering, fell back against the open locker lid. As he fought to regain his balance Ian Vaughan searched frantically for a weapon or something to defend himself with. Just in reach was the steel emergency tiller that Travis had taken from the locker only minutes before. Yamada now upright lunged at Ian with the knife as Ian picked up and swung the tiller in his right hand whilst grabbing at Yamada's knife hand with his left. There was a sickening crunching sound as the tiller boss smashed through Yamada's temple popping the left eye from its socket and compacting the cheekbone. Instantly Yamada's body collapsed in a heap at Ian's feet, the knife dropping from his grasp.

The struggle had attracted attention from the shore and already men were arriving at the yacht intent on rescue. The sergeant was the first into the cockpit and stood dripping wet and dumbstruck for a moment or two as he took in the scene. "Jesus Christ, what the fuck happened here?"

333

Pointing downwards, Ian said, "That is Yamada and the body under his is Hamaura. I think maybe Lieutenant Travis is just knocked out."

As he said it Travis moved and reached up with his left hand to feel the back of his head. Bringing his hand away it was covered in blood.

"Jeffries, take the rib and get both medics over here on the double," ordered the sergeant.

As Ian Vaughan trudged back up the beach the captain approached. Lieutenant Travis lying on a stretcher tilted his head towards him. "Sorry, lieutenant but we dare not touch that piece of kit, it's just covered with anti-tamper shielding. We thought that maybe we could cut off the power supply but they've even got that covered. It seems that to touch any part of it would either blow the whole thing to bits or trigger a transmission, probably both."

The lieutenant looked thoughtful for a few moments. "Do you know what type of explosive they've used?" he asked, wincing with pain.

"We think it's probably something like C4 and enough of it to take out everything for a quarter of a mile. Looks like we will just have to leave it alone until someone above us wants to throw the dice."

Ian Vaughan sat down heavily rubbing his face then massaging the back of his neck. "I wonder how long it takes to shut down a nuclear reactor?" he asked to no one in particular.

"You are sure that is the target?" asked Fawkes, his eyes studying Ian intently.

"After the conversation I had with Yamada during our little struggle I am absolutely certain," said Ian with dry humour, returning the intent look then reaching into his pocket for Capello's mobile. "Damn and blast, this bloody phone's been broken," he shouted, throwing the device to the ground. "I must get in touch with Metcalfe at the FBI headquarters."

Captain Fawkes took a phone from his pocket and hit one button. "Ah, Lieutenant Petter, I want you to contact an FBI man called Metcalfe at their headquarters who is heading up the terrorist plot investigation that caused all of the power cuts. It is essential he reach me on this number in the next five minutes. You got that, FBI, Metcalfe. Right."

It was twenty-five minutes before the captain's phone rang and Metcalfe came on to speak. "Please hold, Metcalfe; I've got Mr Vaughan who needs to speak with you urgently."

"Metcalfe, Yamada came back, I think to take me out but that's not important now, what is important is that they have somehow managed to plant something or some things that will cause the power station reactor to go into meltdown," informed Ian. "From what I could see in his eyes he was very certain that this would happen."

"How did he get back?" asked Metcalfe.

"I don't know and it's not important," replied Ian somewhat testily. "What is essential is that you contact the power station at Mission Creek and get them to do an emergency shutdown."

"Emergency shutdown, you say?"

"Yes, an emergency shutdown as soon as possible, as every minute counts."

"The cost of doing that could be enormous."

"Nowhere near as much as a nuclear winter. For God's sake, they managed to cause enough panic and deaths with the power cuts and nobody seems to know how they achieved those, so I wouldn't take any chances with this."

When the conversation ended Ian handed the phone back to Fawkes.

"The ambulance has arrived for you and the lieutenant, sir." It was the tall medic who had applied the first dressing to Ian's shoulder.

"Thanks, I guess there is nothing more I can do here." Ian got up and shook hands with all those around him then walked alongside Lieutenant Travis, as he was stretchered to the vehicle.

"It's been interesting meeting with you, Mr Vaughan," said Captain Fawkes as Ian went to climb up into the ambulance. "Here's my card, I would really appreciate you looking me up the next time you are over." The handshake was warm, double handed and the smile genuine.

As the ambulance doors were closing Ian could hear the captain giving orders for everyone to withdraw to a safe distance from the shack and await further instructions.

Metcalfe found himself in conversation with the station's chief engineer Steffan Etchells, inside fifteen minutes.

"One of the neat things about APWR's is their stability in operation. You see the whole reaction can only accelerate under increased pressure and density. When the reactor coolant flow, which is simply water, gets hotter, its density reduces and that in turn reduces the atomic particle activity. In addition the coolant water, which flows over the fuel rods, has varying levels of boron that absorbs neutrons. Within the fuel rod assemblies, there is the potential to introduce boric acid that has a similar moderating affect," Etchells explained. "Really, I can't at the moment see your concern but your comments do remind me that, at those switching stations, this gang managed to bypass some pretty foolproof technology, so I'm not going to take chances. What I'm going to do is conduct some control adjustment tests to confirm that we have full command of the reactor zone."

"That all sounds very reassuring," said Metcalfe.

"One other thing about the APWR as opposed to the standard PWR is the secondary containment around the reactor. Though it would not prevent the wider effects of a meltdown it will contain some significant level of radioactive emission."

Putting down the phone on completion of his talk with Metcalfe, Etchells sent out instructions for team leaders Burton and Cleeves to meet him in the lower control room with their respective crews.

As Etchells was making his way down to the lower control area a stiff breeze had sprung up blowing down the Potomac. Sand on the beach blew up onto the walls of the shack. The trees that provided such a beautiful backdrop to the water's edge were no longer motionless and had begun swaying in response to the invisible hand upon them. A strong gust lifted the wooden panel that had been removed from the shack wall and flipped it round then dying, let it drop across the battery leads to the transmitter.

The shielding damage instantly triggered the signal, followed after two seconds by detonation of the charges. The explosion was heard twenty miles away and was enough to create a twelve-foot deep crater and fell every tree for three hundred yards around.

On entering the lower control relay room Etchells found Burton's men unpacking their tools ready to start.

The desk phone buzzed and Etchells reached over and picked it up.

"What was that?" he asked. "No, I don't think they've had a chance."

"Hey guys, the upper control room want to know if anyone here has done any adjustment to the coolant temperature?"

There was a general shaking of heads.

"Control, is the pressure rising in the reactor? Yes, how quickly? Right."

A technician opened one of the control bank cages and stepped back in alarm. "Shit, the whole of this bank's relay casings have melted and bonded to the frames. We're never gonna get them out in a hurry."

"What system is it?" asked Etchells, replacing the phone.

"The coolant rod actuators," the technician replied.

"This one's the same," another technician shouted.

Burton looked around at the faces of the engineers and saw fear.

"This thing's going prompt critical," yelled one of the technicians over by the reactor temperature panel.

The desk phone rang again. "Etchells."

"Metcalfe here, I've just heard that the signalling device has blown up and we suspect that prior to the explosion a transmission of some sort was made."

"I know, we have lost direct control here, can't talk now, must take emergency action," replied Etchells, slamming the phone down.

Alarms were sounding throughout the station and non-essential staff started to leave and assemble at their designated places in the car park where all of their passes were being checked and their presence recorded.

Meantime inside the lower control room Etchells had begun to lose control of the staff. Fear was gripping even some of the very experienced controllers and maintenance men. He looked around for Burton.

"I want you to pick four of your guys that are likely to keep their nerve then get the rest outa here," he said. "We need only those that can keep a cool head."

Burton himself was beginning to feel panic rising as he watched the temperature gauges creeping higher and higher.

"Craig, Jimmy and Sam. I want you to drop what you are doing and go through the turbine hall and fuel storage bunker and make sure that all of the other TN guys are outside in the zone 'B' assembly point," said Burton. "Give me a call when you get there."

None of them hesitated, leaving the room hurriedly, relieved that at least they were moving away from the primary

338

containment area. With them went two of the control staff without invitation, all five men running as fast as their legs could carry them.

Those that remained looked nervously towards Etchells and Burton for instructions.

"Hey, Etchells, I thought APWRs could not go into prompt critical," said Burton.

"This one's been designed with a higher than previous fissile content in the fuel rods in order to respond more quickly to a rapid increase in load demand," replied Etchells. "With the coolant rod actuators out and the boron level held low a chain reaction might just be possible."

"What can we do? These bastards have managed to sabotage almost every control circuit."

The control desk phone rang again and Etchells leapt across to pick it up. "Etchells," he said briskly. "Great, I'll get two men down there to collect them."

"The coolant rod actuator relays have arrived. Mac, you and Prior build a frame on the outside of the cubicle and lift the floor panels. We'll strip the incoming and outgoing feeds and bypass the cubicle that way." Etchells, now in control again, was finding planning and decision making were coming much more easily. "PD, you and Timber get down to the reception and bring back the relays, look sharp."

"We've got to somehow take back control of the water pressure pumps. If we can lower the pressure we will limit the reaction rate, that should get the temperature back down," said Etchells. Looking at Burton, he said, "You and I will take the short straw in the pump room."

In the pump room the noise was deafening and the temperature almost unbearable. Working together Burton and Etchells assembled a stand-alone relay frame and wired in the relay and a manual controller. In the extreme heat the work took a long time and both men were in danger of losing consciousness by the time the frame was completed. With sweat pouring into their eyes, both men set about opening each of the six pump control panels and connecting their controller. Finally they disconnected the mainframe control circuit wiring to each pump. To minimise pipe and reactor vessel potential deformation they gradually reduced the pressure generated by the pumps.

In Washington the President, his family and all White House senior staff were assembled and taken by coach to the airport where Airforce 1 and three other chartered jumbo jets were on the tarmac ready to take off. Members of the Senate and Congress who had not returned to their home states for the Independence Day celebrations were contacted and asked to also make their way to the airport. The national emergency plan was swinging into operation with senior civil servants, fire brigade officers, the police and of course hospital staff all placed on alert. In emergency centres senior staff were assembling and predictions were being made based on a potential meltdown and massive radiation cloud emission. The weather was good with a clear sky and a twenty mile an hour stiff breeze from the south that would carry the cloud across nearly all the major cities. Assessments regarding mass evacuations were being considered and rejected in favour of advising the public to seek a room in their homes where they could effectively seal themselves off. Not since the Cuban missile crisis did the authorities appreciate how little effective protection could be offered to the general public in the event of massive radioactive contamination.

The Canadian Government were contacted and advised of the current status. Their reaction was similar to that of the United States. In London the Prime Minister called an emergency cabinet meeting at which chiefs of staff and senior civil servants were in attendance.

At Mission Creek the reactor core temperature had reached one thousand and fifty degrees before Etchells and Burton had won back control. The effect of lowering the pressure was, as predicted, to reduce the nuclear activity and that in turn reduced the temperature. Bypassing of the sabotaged absorber rod controls had allowed rod insertion and boric acid to be dispensed. The high temperature and excessively high pressure though, had caused minor deformities to the reactor casing and pipework permitting radioactive leakage to take place under cooling. Though the primary containment area had been compromised the secondary containment remained secure, however, the station's operating life was at an end. It had been a close call, a very close call and the potential for meltdown had been narrowly avoided. The United States of America had been only minutes from a cataclysmic disaster.

Emerging from the pump room both men collapsed and were rushed to the radiation clinic on site before being transferred to a military hospital with specialist treatment facilities.

By five o'clock the following morning meetings were being held on site regarding the sealing of the primary and secondary containment areas and the permanent closure of the station. Chernobyl had taught everyone that a rapid response was essential when a primary radioactive containment area had been breached.

For most Americans the celebrations normally reserved for the 4th July went ahead as usual and the President's schedule of engagements was only slightly delayed. Newspapers were, however, receiving their biggest story of the year, each struggling to outdo the other for the most reader-grabbing headline. TV channels normally locked into traditional celebrations were rapidly changing broadcast schedules. Throughout the nation there was an initial sense of great relief followed by a feeling of intense vulnerability. Not since 9/11 had a terrorist attack come so close to succeeding. Cool-headed analysts were predicting that any country was open to such assaults and only the best of international co-operation would help restrict those intent on destruction.

Chapter 17

Ian Vaughan finished his breakfast, stood up and walked across to the window of his hospital room. He looked out over Tappahannock without really seeing it, his mind a jumble of the events of the last few days. Sarah and the girls came into his thoughts again and he wondered how they were. He turned at the sound of someone knocking on the door.

"Come in."

A tall, slightly built man with glasses entered, his expensive well-cut suit a stark contrast to Ian's dirty and bloodstained apparel thrown over the back of the chair by the door.

Behind him stood a seaman holding Ian's sailing bag and the soft case containing his new clothes and wet weather gear recovered from the launch.

"My name is Metcalfe," said the tall man with a serious expression on his face.

"We've spoken a few times over the phone, it is nice to meet you," responded Ian, "Did the attack go ahead on the power station?"

"Yes, curiously the radio transmitter you found blew up, but that was just after it triggered some rather clever devices that had been installed in place of the correct ones at Mission Creek."

"What happened?" asked Ian. "Did any more people get killed?"

"As you suggested the attack was aimed at the reactor and had you not flagged up that possibility the power company say that there was every chance the reactor would have passed point critical and the chain reaction produce a meltdown."

"They got to it in time then."

"They stopped the process moments before disaster became inevitable," Metcalfe said. "Sadly two members of the staff suffered radiation exposure and are currently under treatment for radiation sickness. Their prognosis is not good I'm afraid. One of them was only recently married, so I'm informed."

"Where would you like these, sir," said the seaman lifting the two bags.

"Oh, I'm sorry. Just under the window if you wouldn't mind. Thank you very much for bringing them over."

"That was no problem, sir, in fact it was a pleasure coz it allows me to thank you for savin' my brother's life back there on the launch. He said had you not put the fire out he wudda bin barbequed." Putting the bags down he turned, and grabbing Ian's hand shook it, stood back, snapped to attention and saluted.

"How is Abbotts? When I left him he was in a bad way."

"The medics reckon he'll be okay though he looked pretty groggy when I saw him."

"Let's hope they're right, far too many good people have been killed trying to stop this bunch."

The young seaman nodded in agreement, smiled and left the room.

"There will be many more people wanting to do that," said Metcalfe, allowing a smile to flicker across his face. "Please forgive me, I've been going on here and not asked how you are and what's the state of your wounds."

"They say the split eyebrows, lip and broken nose will heal without obvious scars. It looks a lot worse than it is," said Ian with a lopsided grin. "The left shoulder will have a gouge in it but that will be the only permanent reminder. How is Agent Brumen?"

"I checked on him before coming over. He'd like to see you before you go home," said Metcalfe. "The doctor's coming in a few minutes to check you over and if he gives you the all clear then we'll whisk you past Brumen then onto the BA flight to London."

"Wake up, honey, you got visitors," said the nurse with a smile that exposed the whitest teeth Ian had ever seen.

Brumen's eyes opened and then a large smile of welcome took over his expression. "Hey, buddy, howya doin'. Shit, your face looks a mess."

"Thanks, you're not exactly a work of art either, how's the arm?" replied Ian, returning the smile.

"You were right, the slug hit the bone, shattering it, hence the plaster cast and frame. They said they may let me get up later."

"How much later, I was counting on you carrying my bags at the airport."

"They're gonna bury Agnes and Capello next Monday," Brumen suddenly said with tears welling up in his eyes. "I'll say goodbye to them for you. You've gotta get home to that family of yours."

"I've written this letter to Agnes's parents and this one to Capello's wife and family, would you mind passing them on for me?"

"Sure, I know they will appreciate it so much," Brumen replied, biting his bottom lip hard to try and keep his emotions in check.

The three men chatted for maybe half an hour, with Metcalfe adding a few comments here and there. When it was time to go Brumen handed Ian his card with his private address on it demanding a promise that Ian visit him and his family.

At the airport all formalities were waived and Ian found himself sitting in first class with the cabin staff affording him special attention. His arrival at Heathrow was equally smooth, being ushered off the plane before anyone else and met on the air bridge platform by Commander Campbell.

"Ah, Mr Vaughan, I am delighted to meet you at last," said Campbell proffering his hand. "My name is Campbell, we spoke on the telephone."

Putting his hand luggage down, Ian grasped Campbell's hand in a firm handshake. "I am pleased to meet with you also," replied Ian. "Tell me are my family here as well?"

"Yes, they are waiting for you down on the tarmac," Campbell replied. "We have arranged a police car and escort to take you home, but before we join them, I would just like to ask whether myself and a colleague can visit your home tomorrow to receive your full account of what happened?"

"Could I not have a few days peace with my family?" asked Ian, a little annoyed at the intrusion into his plans for the homecoming.

"I am sorry but we do need to get this done as soon as possible. Pressure from the Prime Minister and Home Secretary I am afraid," replied Campbell, feeling more than a little embarrassed. He had vigorously opposed the instruction from Downing Street, but had literally been ordered to comply.

"Oh well, if you must, I suppose it will get it out the way."

"Thank you for being so understanding. Shall we go through here and down the steps to meet your family now?" Campbell said opening the side door of the air bridge platform.

Sarah was standing near the foot of the steps holding hands with Clare and Louise. Ian almost fell in his haste to meet them, dropping his bags at the foot of the steps and crouching with his arms open to receive the two girls as they rushed to greet him. Standing with one in each arm he squeezed them and kissed them whilst receiving their cries of how much they had missed him, and enquiries about the cuts and bruises on his face. Putting the children back down he stepped between them to greet Sarah who had been holding back. Throwing his arms around her he said, "It's all over Sarah, it's all over," as tears poured unchecked down his face to run unheeded down her neck, as she clung to him, also in tears.